Days of Summer

by

Suzie Peters

G·W·L
PUBLISHING

First Published in 2020
by GWL Publishing
an imprint of Great War Literature Publishing LLP

Produced in United Kingdom

ISBN 978-1-910603-78-9 Paperback Edition

GWL Publishing
2 Little Breach
Chichester
PO19 5TX

www.gwlpublishing.co.uk

Also by Suzie Peters:

Escaping the Past Series

Finding Matt

Finding Luke

Finding Will

Finding Todd

Wishes and Chances Series

Words and Wisdom

Lattes and Lies

Rebels and Rules

Recipes for Romance Series

Stay Here With Me

Play Games With Me

Come Home With Me

Believe in Fairy Tales Series

Believe in Us

Believe in Me

Believe in You

Standalone Novels

Never Say Sorry

Time for Hope

Never Too Late

Days of Summer

Dedication

For S.

Chapter One

Summer

I hate black.

I don't know why, but I've always hated it. Maybe it's because, with my light auburn hair, pale skin, and freckles, black always makes me look so washed out. Or perhaps it's because I just like lighter colours; they're more cheerful, more hopeful… and a lot less depressing.

Still, no matter how much I hate it, black is kind of traditional at funerals, isn't it?

I let out a long sigh and glance down at my one and only black dress, which buttons up the front, has three-quarter length sleeves, and a tie at the waist. It's not really my usual style, but I bought it for my mother's funeral, four months ago, and although the weather's much warmer today, it'll do for the few hours I have to wear it.

The same goes for my son, Roan, who's making do with dark grey shorts and a white polo shirt. Essentially – school uniform. But then, given that it's the beginning of the school holidays and the shops here are full of summer clothes and little else, what was I supposed to do?

I shake my head as we approach the church, the ancient thirteenth century building with its square clock tower, situated at one end of the triangular green which lies at the centre of the village, noting the small crowd gathered outside. Compared to a lot of the other villagers, in their dark finery, no doubt dragged from the backs of wardrobes and dusted down for the occasion, I feel rather casually dressed. But then, I'm a 'casually dressed' kind of person, and as a few of them turn and nod their heads in our direction, I'm more aware than ever that, having only lived here for two years, Roan and I are outsiders. We're fairly welcome outsiders, but that's because of Maggie, to whom we're here to say a very fond farewell. And when all is said and done, in spite of Maggie's influence, we're still outsiders.

"You've heard, he's looking for a developer to buy the house, I suppose." Mrs Penrose seems to be holding court at the moment, her shoulders back, her arms folded across her virtually non-existent chest, and a frown etched onto her brow, beneath her steel grey hair. She lives on the other side of the green, directly opposite the church, in a double-fronted, detached house, which she used to share with her husband, before his death about three years ago, and is renowned for being the worst of the village busy-bodies.

The three women surrounding her gasp, tut and shake their heads, in turn.

"I think he might have waited until after the funeral to get an estate agent in," Mrs Wilson replies, while looking over her spectacles, her ash blonde hair curled to perfection around her deceptively cherubic face. "But then he never did have much time for his mother, did he?"

That seems a little unfair to me. Typical, but unfair. And I open my mouth to say so, but Miss Hutchins, who owns the tea shop, two doors along from Mrs Wilson's village store, and who lives above the premises, gets there before me. "They put the sign up yesterday," she says. "I saw them from my bedroom window. First thing, it was." She nods her silver-grey head while she's speaking, in a rather knowing way.

"Maggie would have been so disappointed," Miss Burton laments, from beneath a rather ornate and unnecessary black hat, the last and most diminutive of the group, and they all let out a uniform sigh.

"I suppose it's only to be expected." Mrs Penrose draws herself up. "He doesn't live here. Hasn't done for years. The village means nothing to him."

The group is joined by Mr Wilson, who sidles between his wife and Miss Hutchins, much to the annoyance of the two women, it seems.

"I've reserved us a couple of seats near the front," he says, breathing heavily, which isn't that unusual for him, being as he's very overweight, his trousers being forced to hang from beneath his oversized stomach, and the buttons of his white shirt bulging in silent protest.

"Then why have you come back out?" Mrs Wilson turns to him, scowling. "Someone will take them, if you're not careful."

"I put our hymn books on them," he objects. "And anyway, it's hot in the church." He runs his finger around his collar, straining his neck at the same time. "There's no air in there."

Miss Burton rolls her eyes, and looks a little smug, perhaps thinking to herself that she's glad she never bothered to marry, choosing to remain by herself in the small house she inherited from her parents, living off the interest on the surprisingly large sum of money they left her.

"What's going on?" Mr Wilson asks, looking at each of the women in turn.

"We're just discussing Maggie's house," Mrs Penrose replies, before anyone else can.

"I can't say I blame the lad for wanting to sell." I smile to myself at Mr Wilson's response. "It's not like he's lived here for years… and the money he'd get from a developer for a plot that size…"

"That's not the point," his wife interrupts, narrowing her eyes, her lips forming into a thin line. "He should be considering the rest of the village, and not being so selfish."

"Yes… think about the impact on our way of life if they knock down Maggie's house and build several smaller ones in its place," Miss Burton joins in.

"Or a block of flats," Mrs Penrose adds.

"I don't think that's very likely," Mr Wilson says, quite reasonably. "They'd never get planning permission. Not around here."

"Well, it's not a risk we should be taking," Mrs Penrose replies, taking a step towards him.

He moves back, clearly feeling threatened. But then I don't blame him. She's a formidable woman, after all.

"Are… are you planning on saying something to him?" Miss Burton asks, a little timidly.

"I think I might," Mrs Penrose says. "I think someone has to."

"No they don't." The words have left my mouth before I'm even aware of them forming, and the five people in front of me turn as one, glaring, gazing and gaping in my direction. Roan squeezes my hand, and I squeeze his back, squaring my shoulders in readiness for an onslaught. "I'm sorry, but this is neither the time, nor the place to confront anyone."

"Young lady…" Mrs Penrose steps forward slightly, but unlike Mr Wilson, I refuse to be cowed by her and I stand my ground. "As a friend of Maggie's, I'm sure you're aware that Kit Robinson hadn't even spoken to his mother for the best part of three years, and he hadn't set foot in the village for a great deal longer than that… not until yesterday evening." She turns to the rest of her group, sneering. "Just think, his poor mother, dying the way she did, nearly two weeks ago now, and he can't even be bothered to come down here. No… He stays in London for as long as he can and just puts her house up for sale to the highest bidder. He's only interested in her money, you mark my words." She points a finger at me as she utters her final sentence, while the rest of them puff up in self-righteousness. But I'm not intimidated. Not now.

"That's a horrible thing to say, Mrs Penrose." Roan squeezes my hand again. "None of us really know Kit, and I don't think we have the right to judge him. The man's just lost his mother. And I know how that feels." They all deflate slightly, even Mrs Penrose.

"Yes… well…" she mutters.

"Please don't say anything to him. Not today," I reason with her.

"Hmm… I suppose it can wait," she muses, as though it were her idea to postpone her confrontation with the grieving stranger in our midst. "It's not like he's going to be selling the house right this minute, is it?"

"No." Miss Hutchins says, giving her friend a nudge and me a very slight smile.

4

Of all the village gossips who make up this little quartet, Miss Hutchins is probably my favourite, and I smile back at her.

The others all nod, and Mrs Wilson ushers her husband towards the church door, dusting down the back of his jacket at the same time. "We'd better see if those seats have been taken."

Miss Hutchins, Mrs Penrose and Miss Burton follow their friend into the building and I heave out a sigh of relief.

"They weren't very nice," Roan says, freeing his hand from mine and pushing his fingers back through his reddish-brown hair, messing it up.

"No, they weren't." I crouch in front of him, straightening his hair again. "But keep your voice down, can you?"

"Why?" He looks around as though checking for spies, frowning at the same time, in the cutest way imaginable.

"Because I'm in enough trouble as it is."

He doesn't have the chance to ask the reason for that, because at that precise moment, the church clock chimes three, and the vicar appears in the doorway, indicating we should all enter. A man in his early forties, Reverend James Buckley is married, and his first child – a girl, called Naomi – was born about ten days ago, which explains the dark shadows adorning his eyes, and is also why his wife, Katherine, is absent from today's congregation.

"Miss Craig," he says, as we pass him in the doorway, bowing just slightly, and I smile at him with a gentle incline of my head.

We're not regular church-goers, Roan and I – which is another source of dismay to a lot of the villagers – but Reverend Buckley is heavily involved in the school in a professional capacity. And as I'm a teacher there, we come into contact with each other on a fairly frequent basis. Not only that, but he presided over my mother's funeral too, and was very helpful, kind, and sympathetic at the time.

Roan and I make our way down the central aisle of the church, and I note the large number of mourners, which is only to be expected, being as Maggie was such a popular character in the village, and had lived here since she was eighteen. Her sudden death in a car accident has shocked us all, but no-one more than her son, Kit, I'm sure.

Finding a space in one of the pews, on the right hand side, we take a seat, and wait for the arrival of the chief mourners... and the coffin.

Ahead, I can see Mrs Penrose, her head bent towards that of Miss Burton, and I wonder if they're still discussing Maggie's house and her son's plans for it. Built of traditional Cornish stone, the house, which is called Bluebells, is my idea of heaven. I think it's got five or six bedrooms, and at least four reception rooms, including a music room – with a grand piano – and the most perfect farmhouse-style kitchen you could ever imagine. The gardens are huge and are just magnificent. There's an orchard, and wild flower beds, and in the spring, behind the garage, there's an area that is, indeed, filled with bluebells. And like the rest of the villagers, I suppose I am worried about what might happen if it's sold to a developer. I doubt they'd leave it as it is. And the thought of it being demolished and turned into square, anonymous houses doesn't inspire me at all. I know it wouldn't have inspired Maggie either. Because she loved that house. Kit probably loves it too though. He did grow up there, after all. So I can't imagine he'd want to see it destroyed, even if he did fall out with his mother.

It strikes me as odd that I've never actually met Kit Robinson. I've known of him all my life, being as Maggie and my mother were childhood friends, but I've never even set eyes on the man, other than in the odd schoolboy photograph that Maggie had on the noticeboard in her kitchen, where she and I used to sit together, which made it clear he was tall, with dark hair and rather gangly, long arms. I heard stories of him from my mum, and from Maggie in more recent months, because she used to talk about him sometimes, especially when my grief over my mother's death became a bit overwhelming and we needed to change the subject. That's how I know that their falling out was a great source of regret for her. Although she never gave me very much detail, I know it had something to do with the death of Kit's wife, and that thought alone is enough to make my heart ache for the man. He's lost so much already. How much more does he have to suffer?

My eyes fill with tears, not for the first time since Maggie's death ten days ago, and I stutter in a breath and try to control myself, although it's hard, and I know it's going to get harder, because Maggie had become like a second mother to me, and I'm not sure how I'm going to cope without her. Who's going to change the subject for me now, when it all gets too much?

"Are you all right, Mum?" Roan nudges into me and I glance down at him, despite the fact that he's a blur through my tears.

"Yes, darling. I'm just sad about Aunty Maggie, that's all."

He nods his head, as though he understands. I'm not sure he does, though. I sat him down the day after Maggie died and explained to him that she was gone, and that she wouldn't be coming back. Not surprisingly, he wanted to know where she'd gone, so I told him she'd gone to be with Granny, remembering how Maggie had helped me tell him about my mother's death, just after Easter. Maggie said then that his granny had gone to be with the angels, but that she'd always be watching him, and while I don't believe that for myself, it's what we told Roan, because when it came to it, I thought it sounded more comforting than the alternatives. And when you're six, you need to hear about death in a comforting kind of way. Well, I think you do. Because I'm twenty-nine, and I'd still quite like for someone to make me feel comforted by the whole process of losing the people who matter the most.

God… I miss my mum. Especially at times like this.

She was always the one I could turn to, whenever I was in trouble, or needed a shoulder to cry on… or both. And nothing ever seemed to faze her. Not even when I broke the news to her that I was pregnant.

I shake my head just slightly, in the hope that no-one will notice, and think back to that cold November evening, and the surprised expression on her face, when I asked her to sit down at the kitchen table and then told her she was going to be a grandmother.

I didn't tell her what had happened, or the depth of my shame. In fact, there were quite a few things I held back from her. I didn't tell her that, just six weeks into my first job, in a lovely little primary school in Looe, near to where Mum and I were living at the time, I'd gone to a party and that at the party, which was being held at the house of a friend of mine, I'd met a man. Although I suppose 'met' might be a slightly misleading turn of phrase, in that, I'd already known this man for a while. Well, 'known' might be putting it a bit strong, being as we'd never actually spoken before that night, but I'd admired him from afar for ages. Okay... so I'd crushed on him for months. He was a friend of a friend... or at least someone I'd been at uni with, who'd brought him with her that night – in a purely platonic way. They weren't an item, and never had been. His name was Russell, and he was utterly divine, in a very Brad Pitt kind of way. And I finally got to meet him at this party, and almost fell over when he started talking to me – to the exclusion of everyone else. I nearly died when he asked me back to his place afterwards. Obviously, I didn't tell Mum that I'd willingly spent the night with Russell in his very nice, very masculine flat, losing my virginity to him, and barely getting more than an hour or so's sleep. I didn't tell her that I'd thought sex was absolutely fantastic... that I hadn't realised anything in life could give me that much pleasure, or that I'd wanted more. A lot more. Because the problem was, Russell didn't feel the same way. And in the morning, after he'd made us a cup of coffee, and cracked a rather tasteless joke about it being my first time, which I felt obliged to go along with, he'd made it very clear that, yes it had been lovely, and yes, I was really pretty, and surprisingly sexy – which seemed like a backhanded compliment to me – but he wasn't interested in settling down, or getting into anything serious. I wasn't going to let him know how upset and disappointed I was, so I made a joke of it myself, and said my goodbyes, wondering how he'd been able to take my virginity quite so lightly. I moped for a while, but consoled myself that obviously Russell was not the man for me, and that I'd had fun too... and that now I knew what sex was all about, there was no harm in finding someone else to enjoy it with. Hopefully someone who was willing to take me a bit more seriously.

What I hadn't realised was that, during one of our nocturnal liaisons, between snatches of sleep, Russell had been less than careful. That only became obvious when my period failed to arrive on time. I reluctantly took a pregnancy test, and needless to say, it was positive. That hadn't been part of my plan as a young, free, single, twenty-two year old. I'd intended working for a few years, having some fun, and maybe travelling a little, before settling down and getting married... and finally having children. But there I was, sitting in the bathroom of my mother's house in Looe, with a white stick in my hand, the word 'Pregnant' emblazoned in a tiny window, and my future falling apart in front of my eyes.

I prevaricated for days about whether or not to contact Russell, but in the end, I decided that he had a right to know. And besides, it was bad enough being pregnant, without having to be pregnant and alone. So, I asked my friend from uni for his number and she gave it to me, with a slight giggle in her voice and, that night, I called him.

He listened in stony silence while I gave him my news, and then said he was sorry, but he still wasn't interested. He wasn't the marrying kind, he informed me. I told him I wasn't suggesting marriage. We didn't love each other – we didn't even know each other – so getting married seemed like a really silly idea to me. And that was when he offered to pay for an abortion, with the air of a man who'd made that particular proposal more than once before. I hung up at that point. I didn't want to be alone, but I didn't need a man like that in my life either.

So, I told my mother instead… at least some of my story, anyway. Because, I also didn't tell her that I felt cheap, and stupid and used. And really rather ashamed. As ever, my mother was simply magnificent. She didn't need to know who the father was, or the details of what had happened, she said. The point was, it had. And we had to deal with it. And we would. Together.

She made a pot of tea and we sat at the kitchen table and she told me what we'd do.

"You can carry on working," she said, pouring out the tea and passing a cup to me. "And I'll take care of the baby, when it's born, which I'm guessing will be July sometime?"

I nodded my head. "I think so, yes."

"Well, that's good."

"It is?" I was struggling to find anything 'good' about the situation at the time.

"Yes. You'll only have to take the minimum amount of time off work, and you can go back again in the September, knowing he or she is safe here with me."

"Of course…" I let my head rock back. "I'm not entitled to maternity leave, am I?" It hadn't dawned on me until then that I hadn't been working long enough to qualify.

"No. But don't worry. It'll be fine."

"What about your job though, Mum?"

Mum was a nurse, although she was working part-time by that stage, and it was easy to see that she'd lost interest in her job.

"I'll give it up," she said, shrugging her shoulders. "I could do with a change." She rested her hand on mine. "And your career matters, Summer. You've trained too hard to sacrifice it now… especially when you don't need to." She got up and reached for the tin on top of the fridge freezer, opening it and cutting us both a large slice of chocolate cake; my mother's answer to just about every problem.

Her solution may not have been perfect – neither of us believed that – and it wasn't everything I'd wanted, or everything she'd wanted for me. But it could have been worse.

Mum was with me when Roan was born, after a difficult fourteen hour labour, and she was with me every single day since then… right up until cancer claimed her nearly four months ago, and I lost my best friend in all the world.

I wish she could be here now.

Except I don't. Because Mum and Maggie were the closest of friends and it would have hurt her so much to go through this. I know, because I saw what it did to Maggie when Mum died.

I'd seen every day, in the two years that we'd lived here, how close the two of them were. After all, it was Maggie who'd instigated our moving here in the first place. The pretty little cottage on the far side of the green had come up for sale and she'd called my mother immediately and Mum had jumped at it. It had meant downsizing slightly, so that Roan had a tiny box bedroom and we didn't have a separate dining room anymore, and had to eat in the kitchen, but Mum wanted to be close to Maggie, and after everything she'd done for me, both before, during and after Roan's birth, I wasn't about to say 'no'.

Life was made a little complicated by my having to commute back and forth to Looe for a while, but then I got a job in the village school here in Millarnick and we all settled in to a really happy, easy-going routine... until Mum's cancer was diagnosed – aggressive and terminal – and life simply stopped.

I'd have been lost without Maggie. She helped me nurse Mum through her brief battle, and was there when she died, holding me in her arms as I sobbed, then arranging the funeral with me and making sure I was never alone in those first dark weeks of mourning. She cared for Roan when it all got too difficult for me, and took him out to play on the swings so I could cry in peace. I watched her sometimes too, and saw her own pain, deep in her eyes, and knew she felt the loss, just as much as I did.

We talked a lot, often until the early hours of the morning, and although my mother was nearly always the main topic of conversation between us, we did also talk about Kit, because sometimes I just needed to think about something else, other than my own feelings. And that's how I know how sad Maggie was. She wanted to hear from him, like she wanted to take her next breath, because she missed him and she missed her granddaughter too, but he had to be the one to come to her. She always said that. It had to come from him. I often asked her why. I often said to her that my mother's death proved that life's too short to hold grudges. And Maggie would always say to me that she wasn't. There was no bitterness in her actions.

"Kit knows I'm here. He knows I'm waiting." I wasn't sure how he knew, but she seemed confident of that fact. "When he's ready, he'll get in touch."

That's what she said to me, the last time I asked her about him. And she'd seemed so sure he would.

He didn't though.

And now, it's too late.

A silence settles over the congregation and then, as the sounds of Elgar's *Nimrod* start to fill the church, and my heart breaks in my chest, tears pour onto my cheeks. They're not just tears for today, but for the all-too recent memories, and as we rise to our feet, the vicar starts his slow walk up the aisle, followed by an oak coffin, adorned with a spray of wild flowers, held high on the shoulders of four black-clad men, sombre faced and staring grimly ahead. I swallow hard, trying not to sob out loud, and reach into my pocket for the tissue I put there earlier, in preparation, just as a man walks past. This must be Kit, and while he's definitely tall, and has dark hair, there's nothing gangly about him at all. He's clasping the hand of a beautiful little girl, with shoulder length brown hair, wearing a dark blue dress, who catches my eye and smiles. I smile back and, as I dab at my eyes, I let them wander up to her father's face, sucking in a breath.

Yes, he's handsome. He's startlingly handsome.

But he's also about the saddest person I think I've ever seen in my life.

Chapter Two

Kit

I hate funerals.

I've only ever attended three, but I still hate them. My father's was the first, six years ago, and that was bad enough, helping and supporting my grieving mother through what I know would have been the worst day of her life, saying a final goodbye to the man she'd loved and worshipped for thirty years. I know how awful that was for her, because three years ago, I buried my own wife, and it was the hardest thing I've ever had to do. My mother was there for me, though. Right beside me, offering words of wisdom and guidance… and studied silences too, when she knew that was what I needed.

And now I'm back here, in the village where I grew up, laying my mother to rest beside my father. The two of them are side-by-side now, together again, at last. At least, that's the fairytale I've told myself; the lie we all tell ourselves I suppose, when death becomes too real to contemplate, when it intrudes into life and we're forced to try and face it… and yet we can't. Not in all its harsh reality. And so we fill our heads with nonsense. I know I do. All the time.

I've been telling myself lies for so long now, I'm struggling to remember what the truth is. I know one thing for certain though. My mother died without me ever being able to say 'sorry' to her, and I'll never forgive myself for that.

Yesterday, at her funeral, I could feel the eyes of the villagers on me, watching my every move. Judging me. Or so it seemed to me. Some of the people who live here, who packed the church to capacity, have known me since I was born, right here, in this house. The house my mother called home. Not that you'd know it now. They looked at me as though I was a complete stranger, a man who'd let the side down. Let his mother down. But I can't blame them for that. It's true, after all. And it was entirely my fault. I argued with Mum. I blamed her for my weakness. And then, when she'd gone, with tears in her eyes – tears caused by me, and me alone – I buried myself in grief and anger, and shame and guilt.

I lost my wife. And then I lost my mother. And finally, I lost myself.

I suck in a breath, hanging on to the garden wall for support and hang my head, the familiar remorse washing over me. In a way, I wish I hadn't needed to come back here. But as well as burying my mother, and giving the village the chance to say goodbye to her too, I have to clear out her house. And more than that, I had to come, to face up to and admit my responsibilities – to myself, if not to anyone else. After all, it's too late to make any kind of atonement to the only person who matters… she's gone

Even so, I put off my return for as long as I could, following that dreadful afternoon, when the policeman knocked on my door and broke the news, in hushed and deferential tones, that my mother had been killed outright in a car accident, while driving towards Plymouth earlier that morning. I can remember falling backwards and landing on the bottom stair, the room around me blurring. And then the policeman helping me into the living room, where I sat and listened, while he tried to give me the few details he had, the details that had been given to him by the Devon and Cornwall police, and which he'd been asked to pass on to me. Not that I took any of them in. I was too stunned to pay attention to anything, other than the fact that my mother was gone, that I'd never see her again… and that I'd left it too late to mend the great chasm I'd caused between us.

I could have come down here there and then, to be close to the memories of her, if nothing else. But I didn't. I stayed at home, telling myself I was too busy to leave straight away, that I needed to finish the job I was working on at the time… to keep the client happy. I reality, I was selfishly nursing my own wounds, keeping far away from this too familiar village for as long as was possible, arranging the funeral and wake remotely via e-mails to the vicar, who was very kind and helpful, and dealt with everything for me, taking more pity on me than I deserved. I also decided to put an announcement of her death in the obituaries column of *The Times*. Not the local paper, but *The Times*. I did that on purpose, not to assuage my guilt, but because I knew that just the sheer pomposity of it would have made my mother smile. And I liked the idea of making her smile. One last time. And finally, I arranged to put her house on the market by phone, without even leaving my living room in Kew. I used a local agent down here, informing him that, under no circumstances was he to sell to a developer. He bridled at that, telling me I'd 'get a better price and a quicker sale', but I stood my ground. I may not have been able to make things right with my mother while she was alive, but I could do this for her. I could see that her beloved house remained a home. For someone, at least. Although that someone won't be me.

I glance up again, my eyes fixing on the 'For Sale' sign, and yet another pang of shame spikes at my core, because I know my mother would have wanted me to keep the house myself, and to move down here with my daughter, Poppy, to make a home in the village and raise her in the peace and harmony of this tranquil place. But, as I told her three years ago, in the midst of our falling-out, this isn't my home anymore, for the very simple reason that nowhere is 'home' without Bryony. Not even the house we shared in Kew for the brief duration of our marriage, and which Poppy and I still live in. Because nothing feels right without her, not even drawing breath. And nothing can make amends…

I stroll over to the garage, which is to one side of the house, its old wooden doors in need of some repair. The dark green paint, which I remember from my childhood, has chipped and worn, and one of the windows is broken. It's the kind of thing I'd deal with, if I were keeping the place, and I imagine a buyer will want to knock some money off the asking price. And I'll let them. Today, I'm going to just potter out here. I could go through my mother's papers, or start clearing out her clothes, or going through the kitchen cupboards. But I can't face any of that. Not yet. We're going to be here for a month, or thereabouts, so I can afford to take my time. And besides, it's a beautiful day, and I feel the need to be outside... and this is the next best thing.

"Poppy?" I call, yanking open the door, to be greeted by the smell of engine oil and wood shavings.

"Yes?" I can hear her, but I can't see her.

"Where are you?"

"I'm in the garden."

"Whereabouts?" My mother's garden is enormous, covering the best part of an acre, and I'm a little protective of my daughter. Especially now.

"I'm exploring."

"Okay... but where?"

My question is greeted by silence, and I'm about to enquire again, but then I hear quick, light footsteps on the gravel path that surrounds the house, opening up into the wide expanse of driveway at the front, and my beautiful little girl appears around the corner of the garage, gazing up at me with her mother's amber eyes. She's wearing jeans and a t-shirt, which is already mud-smeared, and her hands are filthy. "I've been finding creatures," she says, grinning broadly.

"Creatures?"

"Yes. Around the back, under that big tree, it's all kind of dark, and there are lots of creepy-crawlies."

I shake my head and feel a slight smile forming on my lips. Making me smile is something that only Poppy can achieve these days, but I'm grateful for the miracle, every time it happens.

"You've been finding creepy-crawlies?"

"Yes." She nods her head enthusiastically.

I'm not sure whether it's because she has no real female influences in her life – other than Clare, who's an old friend of Bryony's, who takes care of Poppy sometimes, and my mother-in-law, Ruth – or whether it's just Poppy's nature, but she's the least girly little girl I've ever come across. She'd far rather be raking around in the mud, or playing football than having anything to do with dolls and teddy bears.

"What are you doing in here?" she asks, looking around the garage.

"I'm not sure. I was just going to see what there is, and work out what I can get rid of."

"Can I help?"

"If you want to."

She jumps up and down, which she's prone to do when excited, although I'm not sure why she's so thrilled at the prospect of clearing out a dusty, musty old garage. "Oh… yes please."

"Okay. But take care and don't touch anything sharp, and if you come across any bottles or tins, don't open them, even if you think they're empty."

"Don't fuss, Daddy." She steps into the dark chamber. "Did all of this stuff belong to Granny?" she asks, looking up at the ancient hoes, rakes and garden forks hanging from the wall.

"I think it probably belonged to Grandad's parents," I mutter, joining her. "And possibly his parents before them."

"Do I have a grandad then?" She looks up at me.

"Yes. You have Grandad Edward."

"I know. But he was Mummy's daddy, wasn't he?" I always bridle at her use of the past tense when she's talking about Bryony, even now. And in this instance I'm not even sure it's accurate. After all, Edward is still alive. And just because Bryony died, does that mean he stopped being her father, or Ruth stopped being her mother… or I stopped being her husband?

I don't think it does – even though I have to wear the label 'widower' now – and in any case, that thought doesn't bear consideration, so I just say, "Yes," nodding my agreement with her, because I can't get into a deep philosophical argument with a five year old.

"So, do I have another grandad… your daddy?"

"Yes, but unfortunately he died before you were born."

She tilts her head to one side, which is a sure sign she's trying to work something out in her own head, and I give her time to do so. "What was he like?"

I smile. "He was an artist."

"Do you mean he was a painter?"

"Yes. He painted landscapes. The one in your bedroom, above the fireplace, is one of his."

She raises her eyebrows and her eyes widen in awe. "Really?"

"Yes, really."

"Was he famous?"

"No, not particularly. But he loved what he did."

"And Granny loved him?"

"She did. Very much."

"And they lived here?" She notices a work bench in the corner of the garage and tries to climb up on it, failing miserably. So I go over and lift her, and she settles down, seemingly desperate to listen to my family history.

"Yes. Granny's family didn't approve of her marrying Grandad."

"Why not?" Poppy frowns at me, as though it's my fault my mother's family were too narrow-minded to see that their daughter was in love, and that in reality, nothing else matters. Because it doesn't.

"I think because Grandad was quite a lot older than Granny."

She pauses and tilts her head the other way. "How much older?"

"Well, when they met, Grandad was forty and Granny was eighteen."

"And how much older is that?"

"You see if you can work it out…"

I watch her, while she counts using the fingers of both hands. She stops after a moment, and then starts again. "I'm stuck," she says eventually.

"He was twenty-two years older," I tell her, because at least she tried.

She nods her head. "Does that matter?" she asks.

"No. But Granny's parents thought it did, and they told Granny she wasn't allowed to marry Grandad."

"Oh. That's not very nice."

"No, it's not. So Granny and Grandad ran away and got married anyway."

A smile breaks out on her face. "Good." She claps her hands. "And then they lived happily ever after…"

"Well, they moved here, which was where Grandad's parents lived at the time… and a little while later, I was born."

"And then you *all* lived happily ever after…" she says gleefully.

"We were certainly very happy," I allow, remembering as I do, how gloriously in love my parents were, and how unashamed they were of showing it. They gave me a joyful childhood too, filled with adventures and freedom, and the knowledge that I was safe, and surrounded by their love for me. Which makes my argument with my mother even harder to bear…

"You mustn't be sad, Daddy." I feel Poppy's hand in mine and am aware of her standing beside me now. She must have jumped down from the bench and part of me wants to tell her off for not asking for my help. Except I can't speak, because I know my voice will break. I know I also can't reassure her – as I should – that I'm not sad. Because I am. Sadness is a permanent cloak upon my shoulders, weighed down with its constant companions; guilt and shame and regret. "Why don't you come and see the creepy crawlies with me?" Poppy says, tugging on my hand. "That'll cheer you up."

I let her pull me from the garage, leaving the doors open to allow the air to circulate, and we go around the house and down the garden, while I clear my throat and gather my thoughts, wishing that I could feel happy… that I could even remember how happiness feels.

It's been so long…

We didn't really achieve very much today. A lengthy study of creepy crawlies and the airing of the garage, coupled with clearing out a solitary cupboard in the kitchen while the dinner cooked, doesn't amount to a dent in the mountainous task that lies ahead. My mother's house is huge, built of Cornish stone and consisting of five double bedrooms, my father's studio, and three bathrooms on the top floor and four reception rooms, a kitchen and utility room, and a large conservatory downstairs. It's the perfect family house, really, filled with light that streams in through the enormous windows, and I'm sure one day it'll ring with the sounds of laughter and happiness again.

But they won't be mine.

Lying in bed, in one of the guest rooms – having settled Poppy into my childhood bedroom – I'm struggling to sleep. That's not unusual for me these days. I've managed to cope on four or five hours of broken sleep per night, for the last three years. It's something I've grown accustomed to, like pain, and grief, and misery. It's another constant.

I stare up at the ceiling, and think back over my conversation with Poppy, adding yet another regret to my long list; namely that she has no memory of her grandparents. Not on my side of the family, anyway. And that's my fault. Well, not entirely. I suppose I can't be blamed for the fact that my father died just a couple of months before Bryony found out she was pregnant. I know my mother found great solace in our announcement though, and Bryony made a point of including Mum in everything, knowing it would help with her grief. And it did. Although Mum still found it too much at times, and surprised me by taking herself off on a cruise, all by herself, over Christmas that year. I think she just couldn't face the festivities without my dad. I can't say I blame her. I discovered myself after Bryony died, that Christmas is really tough. That, and birthdays. And anniversaries. And a lot of other days in between.

Mum doted on Poppy when she was born, showering her with clothes and toys... and, most of all, love. She used to come and stay with us in Kew, and we'd visit her here occasionally, although the journey was long with a young baby, but the bond between Mum and Poppy was obvious for all to see, and it only grew stronger when Bryony became ill...

I turn over onto my side, staring out of the picture window into the darkness, the stars twinkling brightly in the night sky, and let out a long, deep sigh.

Bryony's illness came as a bolt out of the blue. At least it did to me, and although Bryony had a few more clues to go on, I don't think even she realised the seriousness of the situation… not until it was too late. And by then it was too late for both of us. For all of us.

We'd been trying for a while to have another baby, and having found it very simple to get pregnant the first time, we didn't really understand why it wasn't working out so easily the second time around. I suggested going to see the doctor, together, to find out if there was anything wrong, but Bryony said no, we should wait a little longer. She said she'd read somewhere that they wouldn't even listen to you until you'd been trying for six, or sometimes even twelve months, and at that stage, it had only been four, I think. Even so, it didn't make sense to me, because with Poppy, Bryony had fallen pregnant the first month of trying. Literally. I can remember us laughing and saying how easy it had been.

Even parenthood was a breeze. But then I think we got lucky, because Poppy was just one of those babies who seemed to fit in with our way of life, rather than the other way around. She was always smiling and gurgling and happy, and the fact that our lives, and our love, had only been enhanced by her arrival, made us both keen to add to our family. And made the disappointment that it wasn't happening so much more intense.

Three months after that first discussion, Bryony finally relented and I booked an appointment with our GP, and rearranged my schedule so I could go with her. She told me I didn't need to, but I reasoned that it could be me who was the 'problem', and not her. She raised her eyebrows and smiled at that, pointing out that I'd fathered Poppy, so my suggestion was highly improbable. And then she hugged me, and thanked me for saying it anyway. And I hugged her back, because I knew how much our situation was bothering her. Which was why I'd said it in the first place.

We held hands in the waiting room and I tried hard not to second-guess what the doctor might say. As it transpired, he smiled at us benignly and pointed out, in a friendly but slightly condescending voice, that it was perfectly possible for things to take a little longer the second time around.

"Your body's still adjusting," he said to Bryony. "You breastfed for quite a while, and although you've been trying to conceive for seven or eight months now, that really is no time at all. It just feels like it is, because you want it to happen."

He wasn't wrong there.

"So you really don't think we should be worried?" Bryony asked, sitting forward on her seat beside me.

"No. Not unless you're having any other problems?" He looked at her over the top of his glasses, frowning slightly. "You're not, are you?"

"No."

There was something about Bryony's tone that made the hairs on the back of my neck stand on end. I think the doctor sensed it too, because he held her gaze.

"Bee…" I said, turning towards her. "Is there something you're not telling us?" She shook her head, but the tears in her eyes were a bit of a giveaway. "What is it?"

Part of me wished we'd had this conversation at home, away from the doctor, so I could have sat with her on the sofa, or the bed, or the floor, and held her in my arms, and coaxed whatever it was she was hiding out of her.

"Mrs Robinson?" The doctor prompted and she turned back to him. "Would you rather talk to me alone?"

I gripped her hand tightly. I suppose that was my way of letting her know I wasn't going anywhere, although I guess, if she'd wanted me to, I'd have waited outside. They'd have had to drag me there, but I'd have gone. If she'd really wanted it.

"N—No." Her stutter made my heart stop, and I waited, my breath stilled, until she said, "I've been bleeding."

I relaxed, because to me, it seemed that she was stating the obvious, and I couldn't see what the problem was. She'd been having periods, regularly… because she wasn't pregnant. Yet.

"I see." The doctor sounded grave and I shivered, my skin prickling with fear.

"What does that mean?" I asked, but he remained focused on Bryony.

"Breakthrough bleeds?" he said quietly and she nodded.

"What does that mean?" I repeated.

Bryony turned to me and sucked in a breath. "It means I've been bleeding in between my periods."

"You have?"

She nodded.

"How often?" the doctor asked, while I tried to work out how the hell I hadn't noticed this, when our lives were bound so intimately…

"Since I stopped breastfeeding Poppy." *That was months ago*, I reasoned silently. "I—I thought it was just my hormones settling down."

The doctor nodded and started typing. "It probably was… I mean, is," he said, speaking while he typed. "But I'm going to do you an urgent referral to the hospital."

"What for?" I asked.

"Your wife will need to see a gynaecologist." He stared at me for a moment, giving me a long, hard, yet sympathetic gaze, and then he continued to type, a stillness falling over us. "Is there any history of cancer in your family?" he asked Bryony, and the still silence became chilling. He'd mentioned *the* word, and there was no taking it back. Not now.

"My… my aunt," she whispered, and I turned to face her.

"I didn't know you had an aunt."

She nodded her head. "I was only little when she died."

"Of cancer?" the doctor asked.

"Yes. Cervical cancer."

I sat back, focusing on the wall opposite, my eyes fixing on a poster about the signs of diabetes… about sudden weight loss, excessive thirst and the need to pee more frequently, and I wondered why I was only hearing about any of this now.

The doctor leant forward, his typing completed, it seemed and, with a much kinder and more compassionate voice – his condescension a thing of the past – he reassured us that it was probably nothing but that they had to check it to be sure, and that Bryony would get a telephone call from the hospital in the next day or two, and that they'd make an appointment for an urgent consultation with a gynaecologist.

"Try not to worry," he added as we got to our feet.

That was like saying 'try not to breathe'.

I drove us back to Bryony's parents' house to collect Poppy, and although most of our journey had been spent in silence, as I parked the car on their driveway, we agreed, while both staring out of the windscreen at the back of her dad's Volvo, that we wouldn't mention anything to them for the time being. After all, there might be nothing wrong, and it wasn't worth worrying them. We were doing enough of that ourselves.

The rest of that day was hard. Neither of us talked about it at all. I was busy with work and Poppy needed Bryony, and although I could have made the time and Poppy wouldn't have understood our conversation, if we'd decided to have it in front of her, I don't think either of us was ready to talk... not until later that night.

Alone in bed, lying in the darkness, I finally plucked up the courage. "Why didn't you tell me?"

I felt a slight movement, and then heard Bryony suck in a breath, letting out a sob that broke my heart, and I turned, pulling her naked body to mine and holding her close. "I was scared," she whispered against my chest, and I stroked her hair, resolving I would never let her go again... because I was scared too.

"Whatever it is... if it's anything at all, we'll fight it together," I said out loud, and she clung on to me, even tighter.

Someone phoned from the hospital the very next morning, but after that, everything became a bit of a blur. And in a way, I'm grateful for that. It means I can't remember the horror of it all... not clearly anyway. I know that we spent the next couple of weeks going for scans and examinations, biopsies and tests. I went to every single appointment with her, although I spent more time sitting in waiting rooms than anything else. Eventually though, we were called back to see the gynaecologist – a lovely man, probably around my own age – who sat down with us and held Bryony's hand as he told her that she had stage four cervical cancer, which had spread to her bowel, bladder, kidneys and liver as well. He started talking about therapies, telling us that surgery was out of the question at this stage, but that with intensive treatment, Bryony might live for an extra couple of months… maybe a little more.

"I—I don't want to," she whispered, and I turned to her in shock.

"You don't want to live?"

"Not like that, no. Not in a hospital, wired up to machines, never seeing you and Poppy." The words left her lips on a sob.

"But…"

"Don't, Kit… please," she whispered and I reached over and pulled her close, holding her in my arms – because I'd vowed not to let her go, even though it seemed I was going to have to. Permanently.

The thing was, I'd also vowed, not that long before, to love and cherish her until death parted us. I'd just never expected death to come so soon. Bryony wasn't even thirty. She was too young. Too beautiful…

I struggled to hold back my tears, contemplating a future without her, as she wept, and wept, her body heaving into mine.

The doctor told us to take a few days, to think things over and get back to him. The fact that he said we didn't have much longer than that, if Bryony were to decide to have the treatment, was ominous in itself, and we left the hospital in a daze. I wanted to carry her to the car, but I just put my arm around her instead, to try and protect her, even though it was already too late for that. And then I drove us back to her parents' place again. And this time, we told them. We told them everything, including the fact that Bryony didn't want the treatment that was being offered. She seemed even more certain then, and I knew there was no point in trying to persuade her otherwise. She'd made her decision, and as much as I wanted to argue with her, to beg her to change her mind, to keep her with me for as long as possible, I reasoned that I didn't have the right to put her through painful treatments, just to prolong the inevitable. I loved her too much for that. So, I buried my own feelings as deep as I could, and then I stood back and watched her parents break in front of my eyes, weeping and hugging their daughter between them. Bryony fell apart too. Completely. Her parents' grief was too much for her to see first hand. And I promised myself there and then, standing in their kitchen, while Poppy napped upstairs, that I wouldn't do that. I wouldn't let Bryony see me cry.

I didn't. Not once. But I cried by myself, in the shower, and in the car when I went to the supermarket, just staring into space, tears rolling down my cheeks. I cried at night too, when both my girls were asleep, and I sat sobbing in the living room downstairs, so as not to wake them.

And sometimes, I'd drive us down here to Millarnick, to Bluebells, and while Bryony rested in the living room, covered with a blanket, because she felt the cold so much, and Poppy played beside her, I'd sit with my mother in the kitchen and she'd hold me while I cried like a baby.

The thought that haunted me most – apart from how I was going to live without my beautiful wife, and the only woman I've ever loved – was the fact that we'd gone from planning our second child, to planning Bryony's funeral, in the space of what seemed like just a few short days. We did get to plan it though, unlike a lot of people. She told me what she wanted, and what she didn't want, and I suppose I should be grateful for that.

When the end came, it was mercifully quick – mercifully for Bryony, anyway, because she'd made it very clear right from the beginning that she didn't want a long, drawn-out illness, or death. I'd wanted longer, of course. I'd wanted forever. But you can't always have what you want, can you?

Instead of forever, I got to bury my wife, and stand by her graveside, knowing I'd at least given her the farewell she'd wanted… and that I'd never be happy again.

My mother had travelled up to Kew a few days before Bryony's death, and was there with me, and Bryony's parents, at the end, while Clare cared for Poppy in another part of the house. Then they all left me alone for a while, and I lay on the bed with the body of the woman who'd once been my wife, and as I held her, I cried.

It was all right though. She didn't know. She couldn't see my tears. She wasn't there anymore.

After that, I functioned on autopilot. Mum helped me organise everything, and stayed with us for a few weeks, looking after Poppy, coping for me when I couldn't, keeping me sane. Or trying to.

It was on the day that she left, just six weeks after Bryony's death, that she suggested I should perhaps consider moving back to Millarnick and raising Poppy there, starting afresh, as she'd put it. And it was then that I lost it. Horribly. The things I said to my mother that morning – although I can't remember them all now – were vile. I know they they were vile. *I* was vile. And I know why too, although I've never explained myself to anyone. I can't. Because I'm too ashamed.

I was feeling guilty, you see. That might be a normal state of affairs for me these days, but back then, before that fateful day, I just felt sad, and angry, and lonely, and fearful of a future without Bryony. The guilt I felt on that day though, was overwhelming. Because the night before, I'd slept with someone. Someone who wasn't Bryony. And the thought of what I'd done was tearing me apart.

I'd had to go to Manchester the previous day to see a new customer, and because of the timing of the meeting, I'd decided it would be easier to stay overnight afterwards. My mother had offered to extend her stay by a day to help out and, to be honest, although I wasn't keen on leaving Poppy, the idea of sleeping somewhere other than my own empty bed, was quite appealing.

As it turned out, the meeting was worth it, and I picked up a big design job from the client, which I hadn't expected. Feeling rather buoyed up, I went for a drink in the hotel bar, and that was where I met Gabrielle.

She ordered her dry white wine and then sat next to me, asking if I was from the area. I said I wasn't and that I was going home the next day, and within minutes, we'd introduced ourselves and fallen into a conversation. I hadn't really spoken to anyone of my own age for a while, not since Bryony's death, and even then she and I hadn't talked that much, because all she'd wanted to talk about was the funeral, and my future without her, which were topics I was keen to avoid, and then later on, near the end, she'd been in too much pain to say more than a few words at a time. Gabrielle told me that she was a sales representative for a software company I'd never heard of, and that she spent most of her working week travelling around the country. And that she absolutely loved it. She looked the part, in her fitted business suit and high heels, her blonde hair tied up behind her head somehow, and her make-up simply flawless. She exuded confidence and high spirits… the polar opposite of where I was. The polar opposite of where I still am.

We talked for a while, or rather she talked and I listened, and then she offered to buy me another drink. I declined and said I really ought to be going to bed.

"Can I come with you?" she asked, her voice dropping to an unmistakably seductive tone.

"S—Sorry?" I stuttered, getting to my feet and staring down at her.

She sighed and stood up herself. "I asked if I could come with you."

"To bed?" I felt stupid for asking, but I still couldn't believe what I was hearing.

"Yes." She put her hand on my arm at that point and I glanced down at the connection, noticing for the first time the gold band on her ring finger.

"You're married," I said quietly, a frown forming on my face.

"And?" She seemed genuinely nonplussed by my comment. "I'm not suggesting we elope, or even have an affair. I'm just suggesting we spend one night together."

"Oh… are you?"

"Yes. I like you, Kit."

"And how do you think your husband would feel about this?" I shook my head at her, surprised by the smile that tweaked at the corners of her lips.

"Oh, he doesn't mind. He gets quite a kick out of it actually."

"Excuse me?"

She leant closer, moving her hands up to rest on my chest, and for a moment I froze at the intimate contact. "He knows I sometimes do this kind of thing. I mean, I don't do it all the time… just when I meet someone I really like. I think that's part of the thrill for Alec… the fact that he doesn't know what I'm getting up to. But he likes me to tell him about it afterwards. That's the rule. We don't have any secrets. And, of course, he does the same thing too. So, it's perfectly okay. You don't have to worry."

I sucked in a breath, letting it out again, before moving away, her hands falling to her sides. "I'm not worried. But I'm afraid it's not my scene. Sorry."

Her face fell. "That's a shame," she murmured. "Because I think we could have had some fun together."

I didn't reply to that, mainly because I wasn't sure what to say, and instead I just turned and walked away, heading towards the lifts and marvelling at how other people lived their lives, reasoning to myself as I pressed the 'up' button and waited, that when it came down to it, as long as Gabrielle and her husband were happy, and weren't harming anyone else, then it didn't really matter if their lifestyle was a little... strange.

The doors opened and I stepped inside the small, confined space of the lift, pressing the button for the third floor. But then, as the doors were about to close again, Gabrielle suddenly appeared and slid in beside me, catching her breath. She'd obviously run from the bar and I turned to her, surprised.

"Sorry," she said, looking up at me. "I just didn't feel like sitting down here by myself."

I nodded my head, but didn't say anything.

"Are you absolutely sure you don't want to take me up on my offer?" she added, in a soft, low whisper, moving closer as she spoke, so her body was almost touching mine, and I became very aware of her breasts, barely concealed within her tight navy jacket, heaving as she breathed in and out.

I opened my mouth to reply, but as I did, she leant up on her tiptoes and let her lips rest on mine. I don't know exactly what happened inside my head at that point. I'm not sure whether it was the frustration of the previous few months, missing Bryony so much I ached, or just a vague attraction to the very sexy woman who was standing there, kissing me, and offering herself to me... but I responded. I kissed her back. And before I knew it, we were ripping at each other's clothes. She pulled my shirt from my waistband, and I began undoing the buttons of her jacket, just as the lift door opened.

"My room," she muttered, still kissing me, her tongue clashing hard with mine.

I didn't argue. I didn't care where we went, and we made our way down the corridor, rolling off the walls, our hands seeking bare skin in a frenzied, almost drunken tango.

We fell into her room and left the door to close itself as we tore every last item of clothing from each other's bodies, leaving a trail lying on the floor in our wake. She kept on her stockings and those high heeled shoes, looking every inch the porn star she seemed to think she was, as she clambered on to the bed.

Fortunately, Gabrielle had condoms in her handbag – which I suppose shouldn't have surprised me – and she rolled one onto me and then lay back. There was no foreplay, no romance, no words even. I just took her. Hard. I didn't think. I didn't want to think. I just wanted to satisfy a need. A deep seated, urgent need...

So I did.

Afterwards, within seconds of the sounds of Gabrielle's soft, breathless moans dying in my ears, my own brief sense of fulfilment abated and the feeling of guilt literally consumed me. I was suffocating. My chest, my lungs, my heart, and then my head filled with loathing – self loathing – for what I'd done, and I climbed off the bed, barely able to control myself.

"Are you okay?" Gabrielle asked, still lying prone before me.

I didn't answer her. I couldn't even bare to look at her now and lowered my head, as I made my way to the bathroom to dispose of the condom, before I returned and began searching for my underwear.

"Hey..." She sat up, then shifted to the edge of the bed, reaching out for me. "Hey... Kit."

I looked up at last and she smiled at me. "Don't," I whispered.

"Don't what? What's wrong?"

I shook my head. "What kind of man am I?" I muttered to myself and she got up then, naked and unashamed of it.

"Quite an impressive one, actually," she said softly, smiling, and she let her hand rest on my shoulder.

"Stop it." I pulled away from her and spied my boxers at the end of the bed, lying on the floor. I went over and picked them up, pulling them on, before grabbing my chinos.

"You're leaving?" She seemed surprised, but I didn't answer. "You don't have to, you know." She came closer again. "You can stay if you want. I—I don't normally do this, but I'd like it if you spent the night. We could…"

"No!" I shouted and she startled.

"There's nothing to feel bad about," she reasoned, staying quite calm, in spite of my outburst.

"If only that were true."

She frowned, confused, and I shook my head, grabbing my shirt, shoes and socks and making my way to the door, not bothering to put them on.

"Kit," she called after me and I turned back to her. "We were just two consenting adults having a good time. And I really did have a good time. So please don't be sorry."

"I'll always be sorry," I said quietly and her face fell. I even think there might have been tears in her eyes. But I couldn't cope with her sorrow as well as my own.

I felt bad for saying that to her though. It might have been true. I would always be sorry. But I still felt bad for telling her that.

It was another layer of guilt to bear.

It was the early hours of the morning, and I couldn't possibly go home. I couldn't stay at the hotel either. So I left and drove for a while until I got to a service station, where I sat in the car park and did my best not to think.

I knew there wouldn't be any consequences to what I'd done. Gabrielle couldn't contact me. She didn't even know my surname and I didn't know hers. We hadn't exchanged numbers or anything like that. As she'd said, we were just two consenting adults…

If only that could have made it all right.

I waited until dawn before I drove back home, and when I got there, I parked outside and gazed at the house… the house I'd once shared with Bryony… and the guilt threatened to submerge me, yet again. The only thing I could think about was all the different places inside our home, where I'd loved my beautiful wife so intimately, and she'd loved me in return. Images filled my head; images that I'd not allowed myself to think about for a very long time, because I'd had to nurse her, and care for her weakening body, and watch her dying, so that wanting her had become of secondary importance, even if the need had still been there, buried beneath the surface. I pictured us then though, sitting there, that morning, the two of us together, as one… and I despised myself. For a brief second, I wondered if I'd slept with Gabrielle because I resented Bryony's decision not to accept any treatment. She'd never even asked me, and while I'd gone along with it, I'd always felt slightly left out… and very hurt.

I rejected that theory within moments though, for two reasons… firstly, when Gabrielle had propositioned me, that thought had never crossed my mind… and secondly, I would have expected to feel some kind of satisfaction after the event, and I felt none. None whatsoever.

My mother greeted me warmly when I went inside, and made me coffee and then, as we sat at the kitchen table, Poppy played quietly on the floor and Mum made her suggestion.

"I've been thinking… why don't you sell this place, Kit? Not right away, obviously, but soon. You could move back to Millarnick, if you wanted… to Bluebells. At least to start with, until you find somewhere of your own. I'll help you with Poppy, so you can work. She'd love it there…"

Her voice faded, although I was vaguely aware of the odd word… "village", "childhood", "happy".

Then she laid her hand on mine. "I know how you feel, Kit, and it'll do you good to start afresh."

And that was when I lost it.

How could she know how I felt? How could she have any idea? Okay, so she'd lost her husband – my father – three years earlier. I knew that. I'd witnessed her grief. But that was the point. *She'd* grieved… faithfully. She hadn't betrayed their love. She'd honoured it. I raged at her, without revealing my shame, blaming others – fate, the world, life itself, some greater God who'd never had a place in my life – while she stared, dumbstruck, making me even more acutely aware that, not only had I failed as a husband and a lover, I was also failing as a son. Then, as Poppy started to cry, the realisation that I was failing as a father too, washed over me.

"I'll leave," my mother said, her voice so quiet I could barely hear her above my own sharp intakes of breath.

I should have stopped her, apologised to her, even explained it to her. Because my mother was the kind of person who'd have understood. She certainly wouldn't have judged me and I have no doubt she'd have tried to help me understand too.

But I didn't. I let her go.

And then I picked up Poppy from the floor and held her to my chest, her tiny, shaking body tight against my own. She put her arms around my neck and, as I cried, she patted my head. I swore silently to myself right there, that I would be different. I would put my disloyalty to Bryony behind me; I'd honour her memory from that day forward and I'd defend and protect our daughter until my dying breath.

I've managed to achieve some of that. I've honoured Bryony's memory a great deal better in the months and years since that dreadful night, and I've done my best to protect our beloved daughter. As for putting my disloyalty behind me… that hasn't been quite so easy.

The letter arrived two days later.

My mother must have written it as soon as she got home and I read it through blurred eyes. She told me she was sorry. *She was sorry?* She said she didn't want me to dismiss her idea, but that maybe I could think it through – when I felt more like thinking. She obviously thought I'd been upset by her suggestion that I should sell the house. If only she'd known…

She also said she'd wait for me to reply to her. She wasn't going to push me, or pressure me. She knew, she said, how hard it was to grieve. And she was going to give me time to do that. And when I was ready, she'd be there. Waiting.

I've picked up my pen, and my phone, on many occasions, to contact her. But every time, the memory of that night with Gabrielle has been a barrier, and I've been engulfed with too much remorse to face my mother and confess my guilt. I've put it off. Again and again.

Only now it's too late.

She's gone.

And I'll never get her back.

Chapter Three

Summer

"Look at me, Mum!"

Shielding my eyes from the sun, I study Roan, who's scooting down the slide, with his arms in the air and a huge grin on his face.

I can't help smiling myself, not just at the sight of him, grubby t-shirt and all, but also at the memory of how he was as a toddler, when, "Look at me," was all he seemed to say.

I remember my mum telling me that, as a Leo, Roan would be a born show-off, and she wasn't wrong. He is. He loves being the centre of attention, and that's fine by me, because he's the centre of my world.

I asked my mother at the time, how she'd known that Leos were prone to exhibitionism, and she smiled at me, benignly.

"Because you were exactly the same," she said.

"Cheek!"

We laughed together, and Roan joined in, even though he didn't know what we were laughing about – but just because he hated to be left out of anything. Typical Leo.

"Look on the bright side," Mum said, as we all calmed down.

"What's that?"

"If he's anything like most Leos, he'll be a happy and loving little thing."

She'd given me another smile then. One that spoke volumes of her own love, and kindness, and tolerance.

"Are you going to go again?" I call out to Roan.

"No…" He clambers to his feet. "I'm going on the monkey bars." He starts to saunter over to the far side of the play area that nestles on one side of the village green, where we've been for the last half hour, him playing and me sitting on the blanket we brought with us.

"Be careful," I warn and he waves his hand at me nonchalantly.

With one eye on him, watching carefully, ready to leap to my feet if necessary, I glance around the village which surrounds us.

The green is the hub of Millarnick, formed in the shape of a vaguely equilateral triangle, with houses along all three sides. There are a couple of smaller roads that filter off from each of the corners, one of which houses the school, and another the doctor's surgery, but as far as the main elements of village life go, this is it. The church is at one end – the farthest end from my own house – sandwiched between a row of small terraced cottages to one side, and the vicarage to the other. Taking pride of place on the right hand edge from where I'm sitting, is The Millarnick Arms, a quaint thatched pub, perfectly suited to a chocolate box village like this, while Bluebells, Maggie's old house, is in the centre on the left hand side… the biggest house in Millarnick, by a long shot. Scattered around, between these three landmarks, is an array of houses, all in different styles, and sizes, mostly in Cornish stone, although some – like mine – have been rendered and painted in pale and tasteful tones. My own house is white, with a bright red door, and a small patch of lawn at the front, divided by a narrow footpath, and a row of dwarf sunflowers growing in pots beneath the window. They're my favourite flowers, and I have some more around the back, but you can't see them from here.

The village is fairly quiet today, but that's not surprising. Although it's the beginning of the summer holidays and we're in the heart of Cornwall, we're off the beaten track, and only get a few passing tourists, who happen upon the village more by luck than judgement.

Mrs Penrose is working in her garden, weeding, I think, although it's quite hard to tell from here. She's kneeling and prodding at something in the neat flowerbeds at the front of her house, anyway, and occasionally she looks up, just to make sure she hasn't missed anything that might be worthy of her beady eyes, no doubt. Miss Hutchins is just clearing one of the three tables that she's managed to squeeze onto the small pavement area outside the tea room, while chatting to Mrs Wilson, who's leaning against the doorframe of the village store, presumably because there's no-one inside to serve at the moment. From this distance, I've got no idea what they're talking about, but judging from the way their eyes keep wandering over to Maggie's house, and then back to Mrs Penrose, I imagine it's got something to do with Kit, or the house... or both.

I didn't get a chance to talk to him yesterday. He kept himself to himself at the wake, which was held in the pub. And we didn't stay very long ourselves. I was struggling to keep it together, if I'm being honest, and I didn't think it was going to help anyone if I started crying. So, I took Roan home, asking the vicar to make my excuses to Kit.

"Slow down, Roan," I call to him, as he starts making his way across the monkey bars yet again, placing one hand in front of the other, but not really paying enough attention, in his desperation to get to the other side. "I don't want to have to scrape you up off the floor."

He chuckles. "Yes, Mum." And he does slow down. Just slightly.

Taking a deep breath, I glance across to Bluebells myself and notice Kit leaning against the wall, his head low. He looks broken, but that's not surprising, given what he's lost, and my heart goes out to him. For a moment, I wonder about going over and talking to him. But what would I say? It's always so difficult to know, in such circumstances...

What kind of excuse is that? I scold myself. Just because I feel awkward about his grief is no reason to shy away from it. The man might be crying out for someone to share his troubles with, and if I can be that person, then I ought to at least try... for Maggie's sake.

I get to my feet, but just at that moment, he turns away and strides off towards the garage, yanking open the door and standing there, with his hands on his hips. I expect there's a lot to do. Bluebells is a big place, and having to clear it out by himself is a herculean task. I could offer to help, I suppose... it would at least be a way to start the conversation.

"Roan, let's…" I start to say, just as Kit's daughter appears around the side of the garage. She and her father talk for a moment and then she jumps up and down, rather gleefully, which is actually very cute, and they make their way in through the old wooden doors. Obviously they've got something planned, and I'd only be intruding if I went over there now.

"What is it, Mum?" Roan comes over, standing beside me.

"Oh… nothing. Don't worry. You go back to playing." I ruffle up his hair and he scowls at me, and then runs to the swings, clambering up onto one. "Push me?" he calls and I smile, shaking my head.

"Okay. You can have another ten minutes. Then we're going home for some lunch."

"Can we come out again tomorrow?" he asks, pleading, as I walk around behind him.

"Of course. But only in the morning."

"Why?" He twists in the seat, clinging onto the chains that suspend it from the metal frame, while looking back at me, and I bend, putting my arms around his shoulders and hugging him tight.

"Because we've got to go shopping in the afternoon."

"Oh, Mum…" he moans, and I laugh, pulling back the swing and letting it go.

We've eaten our sandwiches and Roan's playing with his trains upstairs, which leaves me free to get on with the ironing. It's probably my least favourite task, because it gives me time to think and even though I've put some music on in the background, that doesn't stop my mind from wandering…

My thoughts are haunted still by yesterday's funeral, by the loss of my dear friend, and by my mother's recent death. And now, I also can't seem to stop thinking about Kit. Seeing him this morning, in such despair, I wanted to go and tell him that I understand, that I know how he feels. And that, if he tries to hang onto the good times, he will get through this. Sometimes it doesn't feel like it, but it's the truth. I miss my mum every single day, but I have our memories. And while that's not enough, it's something. It really is.

I remember how much Maggie helped me over the last few months, not just by being here and listening to me, or holding my hand, or hugging me, but with all the practical things too, like clearing out Mum's clothes and going through the paperwork. There was so much paperwork too. And at the time, it felt very daunting, and I feel so grateful now that I had Maggie to share that time with. My gratitude makes me even more determined to find a way to offer Kit some help, for the sake of our mothers' friendship, and their memories.

I just need to find the right time…

Today is even warmer than yesterday, but at least there's a breeze, which catches in my hair as we stroll across the green.

"I'm going on the slide first," Roan says, tugging at my hand, until I let him go.

"All right, but be careful," I call after him, noticing that there's another child – a little girl – on the swings. "And be polite."

He waves his arm, and, raising my sunglasses on top of my head so I can see better, I focus hard on the man who's standing in the shaded area behind the swings, pushing the little girl. I notice his height – his extreme height – and his dark hair and muscular build… and realise that it's Kit Robinson. And that the little girl must be his daughter.

I smile to myself and pick up my pace just a little. After all, I was looking for an opportunity to introduce myself and offer to help, and it looks like I might have found it.

Roan's already gliding down the slide, whooping with excitement, and I notice that the little girl is eyeing him enviously, and that Kit is being very careful and modest in his swinging motions behind her.

"Can you push me higher, Daddy?" she asks, turning to face him.

"No. This is high enough. And face the front." His voice is deep. Deeper than I'd expected, but it's hard to ignore the sulking black look on his daughter's face as she twists back around again. It's hard not to smile to myself either, as I remember the first few times I brought Roan here, when he was little, and how nervous I was. And how my mother convinced me that, unless he was falling from a very great height, generally speaking, he would be fine. And that he needed to learn his own boundaries. And I had to let him. And thus, with gentle words and nudges, she guided me in giving him just enough space to be himself, while making sure he was safe. We've lived by her guidance ever since… even though she's no longer here.

With one eye on Roan, I wander around behind the swings and, without getting too close to Kit, I cough, just slightly, to let him know I'm there. He turns to face me.

"Are we in your way?" he says, with that deep, sonorous, almost musical voice.

"No. I—I just wanted to say hello."

He frowns. "Why?"

That seems like an odd response to me, and for a moment, I'm flummoxed. "Um… because…"

"I don't know you, do I?" he interrupts.

"Well, no, not…"

"I didn't think so."

He shakes his head and pulls the swing to a stop, moving to the front of it and holding out his hand, which his daughter accepts with some reluctance.

"I just…" I start to say, but he silences me with a glance.

"Can I go on the slide?" the little girl asks and for a moment Kit hesitates, as though he's about to say 'no', but then he sighs and relents.

"Just for a few minutes."

She jumps for joy, which is terribly sweet, and yanks her hand free of his, running to the back of the slide.

"Wait!" he calls after her and jogs over, catching up. "Let me help you."

"I don't need your help, Dad." She bats his hands away, but he perseveres, helping her to climb the ladder to the top, where she gets her legs muddled, and hesitates, before she sits down firmly.

"Stop arguing," he says. "Or I'll take you home, right now."

The little girl lets out a sigh that's loud enough for me to hear from where I'm standing, and then she folds her arms across her chest, sulking.

"Are you going to behave like a two year-old?" Kit says, moving to the side of the slide and tilting his head at her, while Roan stands patiently at the bottom of the ladder, awaiting his next turn. "The little boy wants to have a go, so if you're going to sit there and sulk, I'll just lift you off." He reaches for her, but she leans back, trying to pull away from him, and I step forward, sensing that she might fall, out of sheer temper, and he might let her, out of sheer stubbornness.

"I'm sure she'll be all right going down by herself," I say, stepping closer. "It's perfectly safe." Kit turns towards me. "Look... I've got a blanket in my bag. Why don't we leave the kids to play, and we can go and sit down."

His mouth forms into a thin line. "I don't know you," he repeats between gritted teeth. "Why would I want to sit with you?"

Well, that was rude.

"I have absolutely no idea," I reply, turning my back and dismissing him, because I've decided already that he's not worth wasting any more time over. Maggie might have been able to see the good in him, and might have thought he'd make amends for whatever he did to her years ago, but I firmly believe she was seeing him as only a mother can... seeing only the good. And right at this moment, I'm struggling to see any good at all in Kit Robinson. Maybe those four busybodies at the church were right about him after all...

"Why don't you play on the monkey bars?" I suggest to Roan, who's looking bemused, and still waiting his turn. "We'll leave this... um... *gentleman* alone, I think."

I hold out my hand and Roan takes it, letting me lead him away.

"I wanted to go on the slide," he says.

"Shh..." I lean down slightly as we continue walking. "I know you did, but I think it's best if we keep our distance."

He frowns at me, but doesn't ask why, thank goodness, because I'm not sure I could explain it properly. Not to a six year–old.

While he plays happily, the slide forgotten within moments, I lay out my blanket a little distance away and settle down on it to watch him, glancing only occasionally at our companions, who are still struggling over by the slide, with Kit refusing to let his daughter go down by herself, and her railing against him at every turn. I can't say I blame her, especially not when she can see Roan doing all the things she most wants to, and isn't allowed.

Hidden behind my sunglasses, and occasionally the back of my hand, I struggle to hide my amusement at their bickering endeavours, concluding that their characters are, in fact, remarkably similar. They are both incredibly stubborn, very forthright, and very brooding… although I have to say that Kit wears the brood a lot better than his daughter, who just sulks, while he adopts a dark and rather impenetrable expression, which I must admit, after a while, I find rather riveting.

I'm not excusing his rudeness, which I still think was unjustified, but even as I'm thinking that, I recall the fact that he's entitled to be cross and crotchety. Well, he's sort of entitled. After all, he has just lost his mother… and it wasn't all that long ago that his wife died. I can't empathise with him over that, but I can sympathise. I can remember how it felt some days, when all I wanted to do was to cut myself off from the world and wallow in self pity, let the grief and the pain consume me, and forget that anything and anyone else existed. Even Roan sometimes, I'm afraid to admit. Maggie didn't let me, of course. She seemed to have a sixth sense for when I was at my lowest, and she'd turn up on the doorstep and make me come out of myself, force me to face the world. She was such a good friend, and I miss her terribly. And, in spite of Kit's rudeness, deep down, I know I still owe it to her not to give up on her son. Because she never gave up on me.

I get to my feet and make my way back to the slide, where Kit and his daughter are still having their stand-off, albeit now a silent one.

"Can I help?" I offer, standing beside him, while still watching Roan out of the corner of my eye.

Kit reaches out, placing a protective hand on his daughter's arm, and lets out a sigh as his gaze roams slowly down my body, before he shakes his head, and focuses back on my face. I'm not sure what that was about, and judging by the cold, confused look in his eyes, I don't think he is either.

"I doubt it," he replies, dismissively.

"I'm not trying to tell you how to raise your child," I point out. "But if you don't let her find her own way, she's never going to learn how to do things independently."

"This is you *not* telling me how to raise my child, is it?" he murmurs under his breath, although he says it loud enough for me to hear. Intentionally, I think.

"Yes, it is." I defend myself, feeling put out. Again. "I'm just trying to help, that's all."

He frowns. "Did I ask for your help?"

"Well… no."

"Precisely."

"But then, you don't seem like the asking for help type."

He lets his hand drop to his side, releasing his daughter, and turns to face me properly. "And how the hell would you know that? You don't know anything about me… For God's sake, Pop—!"

I just about hold in my giggle as his daughter whizzes past us, hurtling down the slide, and shrieking at the top of her voice.

Kit pushes me out of the way and rushes to the bottom of the slide, crouching down and lifting her to her feet.

"What on earth did you think you were doing?" he berates her.

"Going down the slide," she replies. "I enjoyed it."

He shakes his head and then gets up, turning to me. "This is what happens when I get distracted."

"Your daughter has fun, you mean?"

He narrows his eyes. "No. I take my eye off the ball."

"Well, I apologise for distracting you." I curtsey a little half-heartedly, hoping he'll see the funny side, maybe break into a smile, or relax just a little.

"This is no laughing matter," he says, proving me wrong.

"I know." I step forward and look up at him, noting his dark, anguished eyes and the strong line of his jaw. He really is very handsome. And so very, very sad. And angry, I think. "I do understand," I say quietly. "I remember what it was like when my mother died, so I do have some idea of how you feel."

He takes a half step back, almost stumbling.

"Are you all right, Daddy?" His daughter says as we both reach out towards him.

"I'm fine." He holds up his hands. "I'm absolutely fine." I'm not sure which one of us he's talking to, but he's definitely looking at me. He's glaring at me actually, and I shiver slightly under his intense gaze. "We're going home," he snaps, lifting his daughter into his arms.

"But, Dad…" Her voice fades.

"We're going home."

She stops arguing and, with a last withering glance in my direction, he strides across the green towards his mother's house.

Watching his retreating back, I feel confused. Okay, so he was still rude, and would have to rank as probably the most ungentlemanly, bad-tempered and ungracious man I've ever met. And given my experience of men, that's saying something. But, I can't forget the torment I saw in his eyes. It's too familiar… because I used to see it in the mirror all the time, and sometimes I still do.

He needs help. I know it. And I think – in his heart of hearts – he knows it too.

He just needs to admit that.

And then accept it.

Chapter Four

Kit

Poppy's spent the whole of the rest of the afternoon and evening either glaring at me, sulking at me, or tutting at me. We've eaten dinner in silence and, at bath time, she sits in the tub and plays by herself, chattering away with her toys, facing the wall and making a point of excluding me. She hasn't actually spoken to me at all. Not one word.

Not until bedtime, when she pulls the covers up herself, rather than letting me do it, and turns over, her face to the wall, and my guilty conscience gets the better of me.

"Aren't you even going to say goodnight?" I say quietly, giving her shoulder a squeeze and a slight shake.

"No."

I sit down on the edge of her bed and she shifts towards the other side. "I'm sorry, Poppy."

"What for?" She turns on me, and just for a moment, I'm reminded of Bryony and how she could sometimes snap at me just like that when I was being annoying, or inconsiderate.

"For not letting you go down the slide?" I give her my answer in the form of a question, because years of experience have taught me never to assume anything… not where women are concerned.

"I don't care about that, Daddy," she says, sitting up and folding her arms – or trying to, because she's tired and they won't cross over properly, so she just wraps them around herself instead, which is somehow even cuter.

"Then why aren't you talking to me?"

"Because you were so… so horrible to that lady. And all she was trying to do was be nice."

I suck in a breath, wondering how to explain it to her; wondering how to tell her that sometimes things aren't that simple. But in the end, I decide I can't, and I lean forward, roughing up her dark brown hair, just a little, and kissing her cheek.

"I didn't mean to be horrible." I know that sounds pathetic, but it's probably what Poppy wants to hear.

"Well, you were."

"I know. And I'm sorry." I'm aware I'm apologising to the wrong person, but Poppy seems to accept that and, with a deep sigh, she settles back on her pillows again.

"Is it because you're missing Granny?" she asks, and I stand up, leaning over and kissing her forehead.

"Something like that. Now… time for sleep."

She nods her head and turns over onto her side, and I move out onto the landing and along to my own bedroom, because I'm not in the mood for sitting downstairs by myself. I'd rather sit up here instead.

In my own room – well, the guest room – I take a seat by the window, in one of the two high, wing-backed chairs, and gaze out over the back garden, thinking about the woman we met earlier. She's kind of hard to forget. But then, she was very beautiful. Very beautiful indeed. I first saw her when she was walking across the green towards the play area, her son running in front of her. It was hard not to notice the way the sunlight caught her light copper coloured hair, the thick ringlets cascading over her shoulders, and even from that distance, I could see that her legs were lightly tanned and shapely – and very long – and were shown off to perfection in her cut-off denim shorts. Her lacy cropped top revealed a strip of toned stomach… and as for her smile…

It was hard to concentrate on Poppy, on not letting the swing go too high, or too fast, especially when the woman came up close enough for me to observe her bright green eyes and porcelain smooth skin, with just a sprinkling of freckles across her nose. And I'll admit, I was more than distracted. Until she opened her mouth, that is. And I realised she's just like all the others. Okay, so maybe she's not exactly the same, because she's really sexy, and beautiful, and has the most amazing eyes… and legs. But why did she have to keep offering to help? I'm doing okay by myself, and I don't need help.

I let out a long sigh and shake my head slightly, resting it against the back of the chair behind me. It's really infuriating that women – no matter how sexy and attractive they are – seem to automatically assume that I don't know how to take care of my daughter, and that I need their advice, or assistance – even when I haven't asked for it.

And they're nearly always young mothers, who I'm guessing are bored with their lives, or their relationships, and are looking for someone to flirt with. Because that's what they always end up doing.

Not that the woman I met today was actually flirting. But I've come across it so many times now, I've started to expect it, and I normally manage to side-step enquiries and suggestions without getting too involved. I can only put today's debacle down to the fact that I was distracted. Very distracted…

The problem first started right back at the beginning, not long after Bryony died, before the funeral even, with a couple of the women at the mother and toddler group I'd been taking Poppy to for a few months, since Bryony had become too ill to attend. They'd heard about what had happened and, for some reason, they seemed to think I needed advice on what to feed my daughter, and where was the best place to buy a certain type of organic oat bar that was all the rage at the time. I pointed out to them – very politely – that Poppy didn't actually like oats, so I didn't need to know about such things, and that we had my mother staying with us, so she was taking care of the shopping. It seemed like the best thing to say to get rid of them, and I managed to extricate myself from their company, hoping that would be the end of it. But then came the twenty-something woman at the doctor's surgery, when I took Poppy for a check-up, who was sitting there cradling a very young baby and who insisted on telling me about the poster she'd seen for the new swimming classes they'd started at the local pool, which were specifically designed for children of Poppy's age. Ruth had already offered to take Poppy to the lessons herself the previous week, but I thanked the woman – again, politely – and moved to another seat in the waiting room, wondering why people felt the need to engage in conversation with me, when I'd done nothing to encourage them. Nothing at all. And who can forget the completely random woman we met in the park, who was pushing a pram, and who started a conversation with us by asking if we'd ever thought about getting a dog... of all things. Poppy, of course, thought this was a marvellous suggestion and spent the next six weeks badgering me for a puppy. It was an argument she was never going to win. Obviously. And finally, there's Poppy's hairdresser, Marissa, who may not be a young mother – not as far as I know – but who takes every opportunity to get in on the act and who I still have issues with. I think she might have ulterior motives, being as she uses the excuse of talking about Poppy to touch me. So far, she's got as far as running her hands up my arms and letting them rest on my biceps, or my shoulders, but even that makes me feel uncomfortable, and if it wasn't for the fact that Poppy really likes her and she does such a good job of cutting Poppy's hair, I'd find someone else for the task.

Even so, I know Poppy was right.

I was horrible to the lady we met today.

And it wasn't just because she was trying to tell me how my daughter should be allowed to play – although that was annoying enough. It was because, for the first time in a very long time, I looked at a woman and saw pure and absolute beauty, and in doing so, I actually felt like a man, for once.

I didn't feel like Bryony's husband – or her late husband – or like Poppy's father. Or like my mother's errant son. I felt like a man. With all the natural responses of a man, looking at a very beautiful, very sexy woman.

And I felt really guilty about that. I mean… I shouldn't be feeling like that, should I? And not just because of my own situation, but also because the woman has a child. She's probably in a relationship of some kind. Even thinking of her in that way is wrong… on so many levels.

I wake with a start, confusion wracking my body; remorse sparring with need, shame wrestling with desire, the images of my dream still vibrant in my mind and my arousal so intense, it hurts.

I cover my face with my hands, trying to block the thoughts, although I know I won't be able to; they're too real. So real, they're almost tangible.

I groan, half in pain, half in pleasure, as the last moments of my dream come, unbidden and disjointed, to my mind… her perfect naked form beneath me, yielding, submissive, and completely mine, to do with as I please; the sunlight playing across our sweat filmed, writhing bodies; the breeze catching in her copper coloured hair and her dazzling green eyes gazing into mine as she cries out in ecstasy.

"No!"

I throw back the covers and leap out of bed, going straight into the small ensuite, and closing the door behind me. Poppy won't come in here, not with the door shut. Thank God.

"What's wrong with me?" I mutter, getting into the shower and turning on the water, then leaning back against the cold tiles, my head dropping to my chest. How could I do that? How could I have a dream like that, and it be about someone else's wife, or partner… and, more to the point, it not be about Bryony? Not that I've dreamt about Bryony since her death. Because I switched off that side of myself after Gabrielle. Or at least I thought I had. But it seems not. Not based on that dream. A dream, the like of which I've never experienced before, because even when I did used to dream about Bryony – when she was still alive, that is – it was never like that. Ever. I cover my face with my hands and try to swallow the lump in my throat, as I slide down the tiled wall to the floor.

"Why?" I whisper to myself. "Why?" Why would I imagine myself making love to someone else? Why would that love be so fierce, so strong, and consuming? And why would I picture loving them like that outside? Of all places... Well, I suppose that part does make sense really, being as that has long been a fantasy of mine, although until I met Bryony, I never felt that I knew any of my girlfriends well enough to suggest it. I knew them well enough to sleep with them, but to share my fantasies? No. As for Bryony... she listened to my idea, when I put it to her, and for a moment, I thought she might be willing to try. But then she reasoned that our garden was quite overlooked and that someone might see us. And when I suggested we could drive to somewhere quieter, and more secluded, she seemed even more reticent. So I dropped the subject. I didn't want to pressure her into feeling like she had to do something she wasn't comfortable with, and I wasn't unhappy with our sex life. So, it's a fantasy that has remained unfulfilled. Like most fantasies, I suppose.

Even so, I don't understand why I'm dreaming about it now? And why was the woman in my dream not Bryony – the only woman I've ever loved – but the lady we met by the swings yesterday? The lady I was so rude to?

I don't know the answers to any of those questions.

I just know that I feel awful.

I feel as though I've betrayed Bryony.

Again.

"Can we go to the swings again today, Daddy?" Poppy polishes off her cereal and looks up at me. She seems to have forgotten all about yesterday's argument, and even sat still while I braided her hair this morning. And that shows a great deal of patience, because I'm not very good at it. It's something the dreaded Marissa has been trying to demonstrate to me – on and off, between touching me – and I think, because I feel so uncomfortable around her, I haven't been paying attention.

"I've got some work to do, but maybe later?"

"Okay."

I smile across the table, finishing my coffee. My daughter can be very laid back, when she's not sulking.

"Can I get down?" she asks.

"Yes. What are you going to do?"

"I was going to get my colouring book."

I nod my head. "Okay. Well, I've just got a few e-mails to answer, so you can sit here with me and do some colouring, if you want."

"And then we can go to the swings?"

"If you want to. We can go for a short while before lunch. And then this afternoon, we must get on with some clearing up."

She nods her head and jumps down from the table, scurrying out of the room, while I clear away the breakfast things and load the dishwasher. By the time I've set up my laptop, Poppy's back, with a couple of colouring books tucked under her arm, and a large tin of pencils in the other, and she sets herself up at the opposite end of the table to me.

I decided to become a freelance web designer at roughly the same time that I started seeing Bryony, which I have to admit, was fairly appalling timing, because trying to build a new business and a new relationship at the same time, was utterly exhausting. But I was fed up working for other people and she was busy too, working for a large firm of solicitors in central London and didn't begrudge me the hours it took to make my new venture a success. And I did. Well, I made it enough of a success to support us and keep us quite comfortably. And that's all I ever wanted. I work from home, from a purpose-built office at the end of our garden. And it's quite fortunate that I do things that way, being as it's enabled me to come down to Cornwall for an entire month to sort out my mother's affairs, without having to answer to anybody. I don't know what I'd have done, if I'd had to try and get time off. As it is, I don't have anything really big on at the moment, so providing I can keep up with my ongoing minor projects, and answer a few e-mails each day, I should be fine. And Poppy and I should get everything done before the end of August, and have her back in Kew in time to start the new school term at the beginning of September.

I've only got three urgent messages to respond to today, one of which is quite short, so it takes me less than forty-five minutes – and one cup of coffee – to complete my work, and I shut my laptop with a sense of satisfaction that I'm actually managing to stay on top of things, despite the remoteness of being down here, hundreds of miles from my clients.

"Can we go out now?" Poppy says, putting down her red pencil and staring at me from the other end of the table.

"I suppose so." She leaps up. "Wait a second, young lady. What about putting away your things?"

She tuts, but does as she's told, putting all the pencils back in the tin – even if they're not in the right order – and closing it tight, before placing it on top of the colouring books.

"Good girl. Now, go and put your shoes on."

"They're already on." She waves her right foot in the air and I realise now why she took so long to fetch her colouring things earlier. She was getting ready in advance. I shake my head, smiling at her and, pocketing the house keys, which I've taken to storing in a bowl on the kitchen work surface, we go out through the front door, pulling it closed behind us.

"What are we having for lunch today?" Poppy asks as we start across the green, and I look down at her.

"Um… what do you want?"

"Have we got any of that cold chicken left?"

"No. You ate it all yesterday."

"Oh." She looks disappointed.

"We've got cheese… or cheese."

She frowns. "I suppose it'll have to be cheese then."

"Looks that way. And it also looks like we'll have to go shopping this afternoon. Unless we want to starve." We brought some food down with us – enough for a few days – but we really do need to stock up.

"I don't want to starve, Daddy," she says, grinning up at me.

"Somehow, that doesn't surprise me in the least. I think we'll have to drive into Looe, and go to the supermarket." The local shop is okay, but we're running low on lots of things and I'd rather buy some of them in larger sizes than they stock in the village store, just to avoid doing the shopping every other day. It'll save time in the long run.

"I thought you wanted to clear up the house," she reminds me.

"I do. But if we have an early lunch, then we can go out and still get some work done when we get back."

She sighs. "So what you're saying is, I can't play for very long." She turns and looks longingly towards the swings and I follow her line of sight, only now noticing that there's someone else already here, and being as we're only about twenty feet away, I can see very well who they are. I curse under my breath, wondering why I didn't bother to check before we started out, to see whether there was anyone else over here… not that Poppy would have taken 'no' for an answer. But I might have been able to put her off for half an hour or so. At least until the woman who filled my highly charged dream last night had gone home… *Oh God*. How the hell am I supposed to look her in the eye now?

Poppy tugs my arm. "Can I go on the monkey bars, Daddy?"

The woman's son is hanging off of the middle bar, his face a picture of concentration, although I notice she's not supervising him. She's sitting on her blanket a few feet away, and part of me wants to ask her what's wrong with her; why she doesn't keep more of an eye on her child when he's playing, especially on such a potentially dangerous piece of equipment. But I can't. I can't say a thing to her. Because all I can see when my eyes drift towards her, is her imagined naked body, bathed in dappled sunshine, pinned beneath my own. By me. And it's all I can do not to groan out loud.

What's wrong with me? She has a son. She has a family. And I have to stop this.

"No. They're a bit dangerous for you. And anyway, the little boy's playing on the monkey bars," I reason. "Why not have a go on the slide?"

She pulls her hand free and runs towards the playground, and I follow her.

"Let me do it by myself, Daddy. Please. I managed yesterday."

She's not wrong. She did 'manage'. She managed to pull the wool over my eyes, because I was distracted by the beautiful woman who's sitting over there, on the blanket… whose legs are even longer than I dreamt they were.

Stop it!

"Just let me help you the first few times," I reason with her.

"Why?"

"Because it's safer."

She scowls at me and I can feel the woman's eyes following our progress across the play area, even though I daren't look at her, just in case she takes that as a friendly gesture and decides to come over and get closer than I'd feel comfortable with now. Not that I was comfortable with her getting close to me yesterday... but after my dream, I'm not sure how I'd feel, or whether I'd be able to get that image out of my head, of her breathless, needy body, her burning eyes and swollen lips begging me for 'more'.

God. I really need to stop this.

Poppy just about manages not to sulk and, in return, when we get to the slide, I don't hold onto her while she climbs the ladder. I just stand right behind her, poised, and when she gets to the top, I only rest my hand on her back while she slides down, rather than actually hanging onto her.

"Better?" I say as she stands up at the bottom, hoping we might have found a compromise that accommodates her need for freedom and mine to protect her.

"Sort of," she allows and then quickly jumps out of the way as the little boy comes whizzing down the slide.

"Be careful, Roan," the woman calls out to him.

"Sorry," he says, to Poppy, rather than his mother, which makes me smile to myself. He does have some manners then. And perhaps his mother was watching him, after all.

"That's okay," my daughter replies, as he runs back to the ladder to climb up again. "Why is he allowed to do it all by himself?" she says to me, once he's gone.

I crouch down in front of her to explain, "Because it's up to his mummy to decide what he's allowed to do, and it's up to me to decide what you can do. You're not used to playing on slides, not big ones like this."

"I am at school."

She is? I wasn't aware of that. "Well… I'd still prefer to keep a close eye on you, until you're more used to it."

She scowls and, for a minute, I wonder if I'm taking my protective 'thing' a bit too far. If she's used to going on play equipment at school, then maybe I am overdoing it…

I'm about to tell her that I'll stand at the bottom and wait for her, if she wants to go back down the slide by herself, when my phone rings and I pull it from my back pocket.

The name 'Alan Langley' flashes up on my screen and I let out a long sigh, rubbing my hand across my stubbled chin. *Why now?*

"Sorry, Poppy. I just need to take this…" She folds her arms across her chest and huffs out a breath.

"I'll supervise, if you like?" The woman on the blanket – the woman of my dream – gets to her feet and starts to walk over, and even though the buzzing of my phone is grating on my nerves, I can't take my eyes off of her. I'm mesmerised by the way she walks, her lithe body, the tilt of her head and the slight smile on her full lips. "You take your call," she says. "I'll watch your daughter."

I come to my senses and, with a nod of my head, I press the green button on my phone.

"Alan." My voice sounds strangled, but that's because I'm distracted. Again. And I have to turn away before I lose the ability to talk. To complete the task, I wander over to the far edge of the play area, putting some necessary distance between myself and the distraction.

"Are you okay, Kit?" The voice in my ear brings me back to my senses. Kind of.

"I'm fine. How are you?"

"Not too bad. How are things going down there? How did the funeral go?"

People always ask that. They did when Bryony died too, and I'm not sure how to answer. What does one say about funerals? You can hardly say, 'It was fabulous.' Because no funeral is ever that.

I give the standard response: "As well as can be expected," and cough again as I turn back towards the woman to find she's bending down talking to Poppy. It's hard not to groan out loud as it dawns on me that my dreams weren't exaggerated at all. She really is perfect, it seems, and my body responds to her instantly, just as she stands and looks up, our eyes seeming to meet, even though we're too far away to tell, really.

Feeling embarrassed, I turn away again, focusing on my conversation, and trying to erase the thoughts of the woman's supple body, flexing to my will, images from my dream flashing into my seemingly helpless mind. *Get a grip, Kit. For God's sake.*

"I'm sure it's been really hard for you," Alan says in my ear, although I can tell from the tone of his voice that he's making conversation, dishing out the platitudes like everyone does in these circumstances. And that thought works wonders on my wandering imagination.

"How can I help?" I ask, not giving him an answer, because I know he doesn't really want one, and getting down to the point of his call instead, because then we can end it and both get on with our days.

"I wanted to talk to you about our site," he says, which doesn't surprise me in the slightest. He's been talking to me about his website for nearly three months now, and at the end of every call, he tells me he's going to send me through the information I need to start working on the re-design he keeps saying he wants. And then a few days later, I get an e-mail, explaining that something's come up, or that he's still waiting on some photography, or a price, or that he thinks it's best if he puts it off until after the next exhibition…

"Okay?" I wait.

"We've had a meeting here, yesterday afternoon," he says, "and we've decided to go for a hard re-launch of the new site at the end of October."

That's progress. "I see."

"But, I've been wondering…" He pauses. "With everything you've got going on… do you think you're going to be able to do it still?" He coughs, but before I can say anything, he adds, "I don't mean to sound mercenary, and I don't want to be unsympathetic, but I have to think about the business."

"I know, Alan. And it'll be fine. Don't worry." I do my best to sound placatory. In reality, I'm feeling a bit disappointed. He's my oldest client, the first one I picked up when I started my business, and the fact that he could think I'd let him down, regardless of the circumstances, doesn't feel great.

"I'm sorry," he says quickly. "It's just… I've got the board on my back. This re-launch is vital to the company."

"I know it is." Which is why I've often wondered why he doesn't just get on and do it. "What do you need from me?"

"At the moment, just your reassurance."

"You've got it."

I can hear his sigh of relief. "We've added a few new products to the range," he says and I can hear paper rustling in the background and what sounds like the opening and closing of a drawer and I imagine him rifling through his desk for something. "I'm still waiting for the photography to be done…" *Here we go again.* "But once that comes through, I'll send everything over to you."

"As long as I get it all by the end of the month, it'll be fine."

"It won't take that long," he says and I think to myself that I've heard that before. In reality though, I'd rather not do too much actual work while I'm here. I've only brought my laptop with me and I'd really need my big desktop screens if I'm going to be editing photographs and re-designing logos and layouts. So, even if he gets everything to me before the end of the month, I doubt I'll do much, other than go through it and make sure I know what I'm doing. Then I can really knuckle down to it when I get home… once Poppy's back at school and I can rely on Clare and Bryony's mum and dad to cover for me, if necessary.

"Well, don't worry," I say out loud. "If your launch isn't until the end of October, there's plenty of time."

"Okay," he replies, sounding a lot more comforted. "How's the weather down there?" He reverts to the usual British topic of conversation.

"Really hot, actually." I glance up at the cloudless blue sky above my head. "Probably more conducive to lying on a beach, than clearing out my mother's house, but it's got to be done."

"I remember doing my mother's place," he says wistfully. "I never knew a person could hoard so much until I went into the attic."

"Don't..." I mutter, going along with his theme, even though I'm not that worried about the attic... not as worried as I am about my mother's bedroom, anyway.

"I suggest you have a stiff drink first." I manage a light chuckle, just as I hear his mobile ring, playing the theme tune to *Alien*. "Oh God..." he mutters, sounding depressed now, "that's just what I need..."

"Who is it then?" I ask.

"My wife. That's her ringtone."

I surprise myself, laughing out loud, as the noise stops abruptly. "Aren't you going to take the call?"

"No. She'll call back. She'll be at the tennis club, or the gym, or the hairdressers, and no doubt she's rolling her eyes right now, explaining to her friends what a useless husband I am, and how I never answer her calls."

"That might be because you don't," I remind him.

"No. But then, she never seems to have anything interesting to say anymore." He sounds absolutely desolate and I'm not sure how to reply to him. "Sorry," he says quickly, alleviating me of the problem. "I shouldn't have said that."

"Don't worry about it." I feel sorry for him. I can't understand how he feels at all, being as I was always overjoyed to hear from Bryony, no matter when she called me, and I'd give anything to hear her voice, just one more time. But I do feel sorry for him nonetheless.

"I'll send these photographs and the new copy over as soon as I can," he replies, clearly embarrassed.

"That'd be great."

"And maybe when you're back in town, we can go out for a drink."

"I'll see what I can do."

I won't. I don't have time for socialising. Not even with clients — unless it's a business lunch or better still, breakfast, while Poppy's at school. I prefer meeting clients for breakfast these days... it means I've got the rest of the day to catch up, and there's no risk of me running late to pick up Poppy either. But somehow I don't think that's what Alan's got in mind. It sounds to me like he's thinking of something in the evening… something that means he can put off going home for a couple of hours… or longer.

I end the call with him and pocket my phone, letting out a deep sigh as I turn around again… and my heart stops beating.

My daughter is hanging from the monkey bars by just one hand, and with my panic rising, I call out, "Hang on, Poppy… I'm coming," and I start to run.

Chapter Five

Summer

It seemed like the least I could do, to offer to watch his daughter, while Kit took his phone call. He looked so torn. But even so, I was surprised he accepted my offer, which I suppose means the call must be important, because after the way he spoke to me yesterday, I half expected him to say 'no', and not bother with a 'thank you' afterwards.

As I wander over to his daughter, I note the dark expression on his face and wonder to myself when it was that he last had any fun. Or if he can even remember what fun is. It's odd, being as I don't know him, but although he's quite brooding and intense, there's also something about him… something fiery behind his glowering eyes, which I notice most when he's looking at me. I smile to myself, concluding that it's probably just his fierce temper, being held in check, since I don't seem to be his favourite person.

Vaguely aware of Kit beginning his conversation, I feel a small hand tugging on my own and look down at his daughter, who's gazing up at me.

"Can I go on the slide?" she says, her accent clipped and angelic, with just a very slight lisp.

"Yes."

"By myself?" she adds, her lips twisting up slightly.

I know Kit won't like that, and I bend down to her. "Do you think your daddy would be happy with that?" I ask, putting the ball in her court and hoping she'll do the right thing.

"No." She shakes her head, a sulk starting to form on her lips. I've noticed she's good at that.

"Look. Let's make a deal. I won't actually hold onto you. I'll just stand right by the slide. Okay? But you have to promise me not to be silly, and to take it slowly."

She nods her head, grinning broadly, and I stand up, turning around to face Kit, who seems to be staring directly at me. From here, I can't see his eyes clearly, but I can imagine that dark, scowling look in them, right before he turns and starts walking away, his phone clasped to his ear, seemingly deep in conversation.

"Can I go on the swings, Mum?" Roan says, coming up to me and jumping up and down.

"No." I turn to Kit's daughter. "I'm sorry, I don't know your name."

"It's Poppy."

"Oh… what a lovely name." She smiles again and I look back at Roan. "You can't go on the swings right now, because I've said to Poppy that she can go on the slide, and I have to stay here with her. I can't watch both of you at the same time, so why don't you play on the slide for a little while too?"

"Okay," he says and races towards the ladder, making me grin. He's such a happy-go-lucky little boy and I'm grateful for that. Every. Single. Day.

"Let Poppy go first," I call out to him, standing by the side of the slide.

He steps to his right, out of the way, shuffling from one foot to the other, impatiently, and lets Poppy climb the ladder ahead of him. She reaches the top and sits down carefully and I struggle not to actually reach out, sensing her uneasiness, despite her earlier bravado. Taking a look at me, she lets go of the railing and slides all the way down, and I follow her, holding out my hand when she gets to the bottom, and helping her to her feet.

"Was that fun?" I ask.

"Yes." She nods, grinning. "I'm going again."

We step aside, just as Roan comes hurtling down, whooping at the top of his voice.

"You're a hooligan. You know that, don't you?" I ruffle up his hair, and he stands.

"Yes, Mum," he yells, running back to the ladder to sneak in an extra turn before Poppy gets there.

"What's his name?" she whispers to me, still holding my hand.

"It's Roan."

She frowns. "I've never heard that name before."

"It means 'little redhead'."

She frowns, looking at Roan as he comes down the slide again, his arms aloft. "He hasn't got very red hair," she reasons and I smile.

"No. But it's red enough that I could get away with it. I liked the name, you see."

She nods and lets go of my hand, and follows my son back to the ladder.

After a few turns, Roan waits at the bottom of the slide for Poppy and, in a touching moment that makes me smile, takes her hand in his.

"Shall we go on the monkey bars now?" he says and she nods her head.

"Oh, yes... let's."

I step forward. "Hang on a second, you two. I'm not sure Poppy's dad would approve of that."

"You can come and help," Roan reasons. "Like you used to when I was little."

"Hmm... because you're so big now." I narrow my eyes at him.

"Well... I am." He squares his shoulders and I have to admit, he does look big compared to Poppy, who's at least half a head shorter than him, even though she's probably not that much younger. "Please, Mum..." he pleads, and Poppy looks up at me, smiling.

"Oh... okay then."

They both run off, hand in hand, and I shake my head, unable to prevent the smile that's formed on my own lips, or the spring in my step as I follow them. I do love seeing Roan so happy, and it's nice to see Poppy having fun too.

There's a ladder at either end of the monkey bars and Roan climbs up first. "I'll show you what to do," he says over his shoulder, while Poppy looks on from below, watching as he sits down on the top rung and reaches for the first bar, before swinging his body out. "Make sure you've got a firm grip," Roan continues, swaying back and forth. "And then reach out for the next one." He demonstrates, moving along the bars with ease, and Poppy looks up at me.

"Your turn?" I say and she nods her head, and I stand behind her while she climbs the ladder, struggling a little, until she reaches the top and clambers through the gap to sit down on the top rung, just like Roan. "Now, lean forward…" I move in front of her, as I'm talking, standing right beneath her and watching her closely as she leans out, grabbing for the first bar. She glances down at me. "You don't have to, not if you don't want to…" I say, giving her a way out.

"No. I want to." She's determined. Or is that stubborn? I'm not sure. Either way, she pushes herself off the top rung and swings, narrowly missing me as her legs flail about. "Make sure your grip is firm." I repeat Roan's instructions and she nods her head, poking her tongue out slightly in concentration, which makes me smile, as she reaches for the second bar and I brace myself, just in case.

She swings across and then looks down at me, grinning triumphantly. "I did it!" she says, her legs still swaying from side to side.

"Yes. And now you've got to do it again." I step back to give her room.

"Am I doing it right, Roan?" she calls out, looking ahead.

I don't turn around, but watch her closely and hear Roan reply, "You're doing fine. That's really cool."

I let out a half laugh at his expression, but I'm still not taking my eyes off of Poppy, even though I can surmise that he must have got to the other end, if he's able to see her. Whether he's on the ground looking up, or still hanging off the rails, I've got no idea. Either way, he sounds just fine… just 'cool', in fact.

Poppy reaches out once more, grabbing for the third bar, and lets go of the second, just as I hear a deep male voice behind me cry out, "Hang on, Poppy… I'm coming."

I don't turn, I don't flinch, even as Poppy's grip slips and, with a panicked, startled expression on her face, and a slight cry, she falls… straight into my waiting arms. Her eyes are alight with fear… for about two seconds, but as I spin her around, smiling to put her at ease, she starts to giggle, and so do I.

"What the hell are you doing?"

I feel a big hand settle roughly on my arm, pulling me to a stop, and look up into the dark, angry glare of Kit Robinson. He steps closer, and takes Poppy from me, holding her himself.

"Are you all right?" he says his voice much softer, as he gazes down at his daughter.

"I'm fine, Daddy." She struggles to release herself from his grip and eventually he puts her down on the ground, although he takes her hand in his and keeps a firm grasp on it, before he turns back to me.

"Are you completely irresponsible?" he yells, that softer tone gone from his voice now.

"No, of course not." I take a half step back, because he really is quite intimidating.

"Then what the hell did you think you were doing? You said you'd watch my daughter for me. Since when did watching someone else's child involve putting their life in danger? Since when…"

"Wait a second." I interrupt him, holding up my hand and, much to my surprise, he stops talking. "I'm not irresponsible, and I didn't endanger Poppy's life. I was standing right beneath her, the whole time, in case you didn't notice. I knew I'd be able to catch her, just like I used to catch Roan, when he was learning. And besides, I'd never do anything to hurt any child. I'm a teacher. It's my job to keep children safe."

"You're not my idea of a teacher," he says, leaning forward, his eyes still alight with anger. "You're not caring or trustworthy enough." I blink back the tears that have already started forming in my eyes.

"That's not…" I mutter.

"Forget it." He holds up his free hand now, mirroring my action, which has the same effect of silencing me. "Just be grateful we don't live here. If we did I'd be reporting you for negligence. You ought to be ashamed of yourself."

"Oh, grow up, will you?" I manage to say, raising my own voice now, around the lump in my throat.

I turn my back on him and call Roan, who quickly joins me as I walk over to our blanket, gathering it up and throwing it over my arm. Then I pick up my bag and, taking Roan's hand in mine, we head back across the green towards our house.

I don't look back. I just keep walking, my head bowed, taking deep breaths and trying very hard not to cry, and not to think, until we get home, where I let us in through the front door.

"That man was very rude," Roan says from behind me as I dump the bag and blanket down on the sofa, taking a deep breath before I turn to him.

"Yes. He was. But he was worried about Poppy, and… well, he's got a lot on his mind."

"That doesn't give him the right to call you names, or to say all those horrible things about you."

I crouch down in front of him and take both of his hands in mine. "Sometimes you have to make allowances for people, Roan. And this is one of those times. Poppy's daddy is having a bad time… and we have to be kind to him."

"Even though he wasn't kind to you?"

"Yes."

He pauses for a moment, then tips his head to one side. "Why?"

"Because sometimes, people say things they don't mean, when they're upset."

"And was he upset?"

"Yes. He was. He is." I stand up again. "Do you want some lunch?"

He nods his head. "Yes, please."

"Okay. You go and play with your trains and I'll get some sandwiches ready."

He shoots past me to the door in the corner of the back wall, pulling it open and rushing up the stairs, while I make my way through to the kitchen, at the back of the house, sitting down at the table in the centre of the room and drawing in a deep breath.

It's hard not to recall Kit's words, or the look on his face as he said them, but I meant everything I said to Roan. The man is having a really bad time. That much is obvious. He's grieving for his mother, and also for his late wife still, I think. I remember pushing people away in those first few days and even weeks after Mum died. I remember sometimes wanting to wrap Roan in cotton wool as well. And I remember how Maggie didn't let me do either of those things. I remember how she tried to get me to carry on – for his sake, if nothing else. And now I think about it, I also recall her explaining how we all need someone when things get dark, and how Kit had helped her when her husband died, staying with her for ages, until he was sure she could cope by herself, and then telephoning her every day afterwards. She smiled when she revealed that he and his wife had come down here specially to tell her that they were expecting their first child… her first grandchild… and how that had brought a light into her life she'd never imagined could exist again. She also told me how Kit had nursed his wife through her illness too, with absolute devotion, while caring for their young daughter at the same time, only accepting the barest minimum of help from anyone else. I can imagine him being like that, and I suppose that's how I know he needs help, because whatever he's doing now, those don't seem like the actions of someone who would willingly hurt another human being. They seem like the actions of someone who's kind and generous, and caring… and good. And who's run into trouble. And who I really know needs help, even if he's not willing to admit it.

Chapter Six

Kit

The moment the woman turns away, I want to call her back. I even open my mouth to do so, only then realising that I don't know her name. So I close it again and just stare at her, trying to ignore the thought that I'm fairly sure she had tears in her eyes, as she walks slowly across the green, to the small cottage on the other side, opening the red painted front door and going inside, where no doubt she'll phone her husband, who's probably at work, and she'll tell him all about the man who was so foul to her at the swings… or maybe she'll wait until he gets home tonight. And he'll hold her and comfort her. And probably offer to come over and have a word with me. She'll tell him not to, of course, because I get the feeling she's that kind of woman. But in a way, I wish he would, because then I could tell him to tell us wife to leave me alone… and to get the hell out of my dreams. Except I could never say that to him. Could I? I could never admit to fantasising about another man's wife…

I lower my head, feeling ashamed. It's not an unusual feeling for me, I'll grant. But I know I shouldn't be having these thoughts and dreams about her. And I shouldn't have said those things to her either. Or, I should at least have apologised, once I had said them, because they were inexcusable. But how would I have done that? After all, apologising would have meant explaining, and I have no idea how to explain. It's not that I *can't* explain. I can. I know why I'm like this. But explaining would mean telling her about myself. And I haven't talked about myself for years... and years. Not since Bryony died, and I betrayed her, and then blamed my mother... for everything.

How could I explain all of that to this woman, when it would mean revealing myself... the depth of my guilt, my feelings of inadequacy that I couldn't save my own wife, that I couldn't do anything to help with her pain, or the manner of her death even, because I had to let her have control of that. She'd lost everything else, after all. How could I explain my lack of self control that led to my one night stand with Gabrielle – if you can even call it that – and the consuming guilt that followed, which caused the argument with my mother; an argument I should have taken the time and trouble to resolve while I had the chance, rather than leaving it until it was too late. My God... the list of my betrayals is endless... and now I've got highly arousing fantasies about a very sexy stranger to add into the mix. A very sexy stranger who I've just yelled at, insulted, and watched walk away from me with tears in her eyes. All thanks to my guilty conscience. Again.

I let out a long sigh as Poppy yanks her hand from mine and I look down at her. She's scowling. Hard.

"What?" I frown, even though I know precisely what's wrong.

She folds her arms across her chest, pursing her lips and I wonder for a moment if she's going to give me the silent treatment, like she did yesterday. She doesn't. "Why did you say those things?" she says, and I can hear the emotion in her voice. It adds to the burden I'm already carrying. "I was having a lovely time... until you ruined it."

"I didn't ruin it." I attempt to defend myself as best I can.

"Yes, you did. The lady was really nice. She was letting me play, and I was enjoying myself with Roan. And then you came along and spoiled it all." Her voice cracks and her bottom lip trembles, and I reach out for her, but she steps away from me. "You were horrible, Daddy," she whimpers.

I was. I can't deny that, even though a part of me feels that the woman was being a bit irresponsible. After all, she must have heard me saying that I didn't want Poppy to play on the monkey bars. Except I don't think we were actually at the playground when Poppy asked me that question; we were just coming up to it… and I wasn't exactly speaking very loudly. But even so, I'm sure she must have heard. I'm almost positive. And in any case, I know she was aware that I'm very protective of Poppy. Let's face it, she practically criticised me to my face for it just yesterday. And yet, she allowed Poppy onto the monkey bars, defying me. *Defying me?* Good Lord… since when was I that dictatorial? *Since Bryony died, I suppose, and I've been too scared of losing anyone else to let go and be myself.* Whoever that is. I'm not sure I can remember anymore.

"I'm sure she'll get over it," I say, reaching for Poppy's hand. She glares at me and walks off towards Bluebells, and for once I don't tell her off, or argue with her.

Because I know she's right.

Rather than having lunch and then going into Looe, as we'd planned, I take Poppy out straight away instead, keen to escape, and we stop at a pub for lunch on the way into town, where I let her have whatever she wants from the menu, which turns out to be fish fingers and chips. I go for a crab sandwich and a coffee, although I'd rather have that stiff drink Alan was suggesting, and after we've finished, we head for the town centre.

"Why are we here?" Poppy says as I park the car. "I thought we were going to the supermarket."

"We are, but we've got a few other things to get first."

"Like what?"

I turn in my seat to face her. "Well, I thought you might like to get some new clothes."

Her smile lights up her eyes. "Can I?" she says, reminding me, as always, of her mother, who loved nothing more than to spend an entire afternoon shopping for clothes. Because while Poppy may not be a 'girly' girl, it seems there are some things every girl loves to do… and clothes shopping is one of them.

"Of course."

I get out of the car and pay for our parking ticket, before helping Poppy down, and taking her hand in mine.

"Let's go and see what we can find, shall we?"

She trots along beside me, her earlier anger forgotten, it would seem, and we make our way down Fore Street to a shop that Bryony always loved to visit whenever we came down to see my mother, and where I know they do children's clothes as well.

Sure enough, within ten minutes of entering the shop, Poppy's already loaded me up with half a dozen t-shirts and two pairs of shorts.

"I'm not sure you really need all of this," I point out to her. "I know I didn't pack that many summer tops for you, but we do have a washing machine at Granny's house, you know." The weather was pretty appalling when we left home, so I packed warmer clothes, and a couple of summer dresses, which have turned out to be completely impractical – other than the navy blue one Poppy wore for the funeral, of course.

"I know, but these t-shirts are really cool."

Cool? I chuckle to myself. Since when did my daughter ever say 'cool'? I'll admit it sounds cute, coming from her, but I've got no idea where she's picked that up from.

She comes and stands in front of me, clutching a fleecy-lined hoodie. "This is so soft, Daddy," she says, holding it out to me, even though I don't have a free hand to touch it.

"Is it?" I frown down at her, struggling not to smile.

"Can I have this too? I mean… I know it's really hot right now, but it won't be when we go home, will it?"

I marvel at the way her brain works, as though the hot weather is limited to Cornwall, and we don't ever get any in London. If only…

"I suppose so. But that's it."

She dumps the hoodie on top of the pile I'm carrying and gives me her sweetest smile as I make my way towards the cash till.

I carry the bags out and buy her an ice cream to eat on the way back to the car, before we make the short journey to the supermarket and complete the boring task of stocking up for the week. I've always hated food shopping, but I suppose it took on a new meaning for me when

Bryony was sick, and I had to try and find things she'd eat, which wasn't much. I trawled the aisles then, picking up this and that, hoping she'd at least feel tempted to try something. Often she'd put on a brave face and attempt a few mouthfuls, just to please me. But sometimes, especially near the end, she couldn't even do that.

Still, it's easier now... Poppy will eat just about anything.

And I don't really care about things like food anymore.

Back home, we unpack together and, realising it's too late to start doing any work on the house, Poppy watches some cartoons in the living room while I make us fajitas, because Poppy likes them, and then we sit at the table rolling them up and making a huge amount of mess.

After her bath, I put Poppy to bed, reading her a few chapters of her book, before she settles down on her pillows and I let out a sigh as I bend to kiss her, grateful that she's not still angry with me about what happened this morning.

She grabs my wrist as I go to stand, reaching for the light, and I halt, looking down at her.

"What's wrong?" I ask, noting the sadness in her eyes.

"If we meet the nice lady again, please will you try and be kind to her?" she says and it's hard not to feel her disappointment in me.

I lean over again and kiss her forehead. "I'll try," I whisper and she sighs deeply, snuggling down into her pillows.

As I'm closing her door, it dawns on me that I'd rather face the woman's inevitable anger while I do my best to apologise to her, than feel like such a failure in my daughter's eyes.

My own groaning wakes me and I sit bolt upright, sweat gleaming on my chest and arms, the sheets creased and dishevelled and my arousal even more painful than it was yesterday. It's barely light outside, and I flop back down onto the bed, safe in the knowledge that Poppy won't be awake yet, and certainly won't be coming into my room any time soon. Which is just as well, given my current state.

I run my hands down my face and then up again and through my hair, leaving my arms resting above my head, which is full of images...

so real they feel like memories. Except I know they're not. Because I've never made love to anyone the way I did in my dream. I've never held a woman down and taken her as hard as that, her body accommodating mine so willingly. I can see the scene, even now, as clear as the day that's about to dawn… the crisp white bedding, soft sunlight beaming across the sparsely furnished room, a white curtain billowing in the breeze, and her naked body lying across the mattress, expectant… compliant; her flaming hair fanned on the pillow, her sea-green eyes following me as I move around the room, and finally climb onto the bed and crawl up her perfect body, kissing, licking and occasionally biting, before capturing her hands in mine…

"Stop it," I mutter, clenching my fists, before I turn over and bury my head beneath the pillow.

How is it that I can dream about sex that feels so real, and so right, even though I've never experienced anything like it in my life? In my dreams, I'm forceful, commanding… almost savage. Almost. But not quite. Because there's a tenderness between the woman and me. A real, honest, bone-deep tenderness. As though, in joining our bodies so ravenously, I'm soothing something else… something that is crying out to be healed. For both of us. I hold her. I touch her. Our foreheads rest together, and we kiss, with a fire that burns so bright, it almost consumes us. And all the while, our eyes are locked. Permanently. Even as I love her, so damned hard. It's ferocious. Untamed. It's like nothing I've ever done, or felt before.

And that's what makes it so strange.

It's like I'm reinventing myself, even though I've never felt the need to in reality.

I always felt that Bryony was perfect for me. She was certainly no prude, not by any means, and she always seemed to enjoy whatever we did together. But I suppose she was quite a delicate creature, even before her illness made her a shadow of herself. And our lovemaking was a reflection of that delicacy, I think. It was always gentle and slow; patient and calm. And I was never dissatisfied with that. Or with her. She suited me, and I suited her. Always. Right from that very first time…

Not that she was my first. And neither was I hers. I have no idea how many men she'd slept with before me, although I can't imagine it was a vast number; she wasn't that kind of woman. But I never asked. I didn't need to know. As for me... I'd had a few lovers before her. Not many, but a few, starting in my second semester at university, with Stephanie, who was really pretty, but absolutely crazy, and who lasted about three months, before I couldn't handle her weird moods anymore... and ending with Penny, who was so laid back, it was ludicrous, and who I lived with on a kind of on-off basis, for a while, before I got together with Bryony. I dated quite a lot in between, but I didn't sleep with every woman I came across. Sometimes I didn't want to, and sometimes they didn't. And in any case, I think I was on a learning curve with most of them. A learning curve that led to Bryony. Because until I met her, no-one had come close to meaning anything, and neither had sex. It could be hugely satisfying, in a purely physical way, but there was always something missing as far as I was concerned. And that 'something' – of course – was love, and when I finally woke up to that, which took me a while, I realised how different everything could be. And I mean *everything*. Things that had previously been a bit mechanical, perhaps, suddenly became magical instead. Rather than looking upon sex as being all about the destination, it became about the journey, and I surprised myself by discovering that I enjoyed Bryony's pleasure almost as much as I did my own... and sometimes more.

And when she died, I knew I'd never find that again.

And I haven't. Because even though I've had sex since, it wasn't the same.

Speaking of which, there was Gabrielle too, of course. I can't forget her. No matter how much I want to. I tried to say 'no', to deny the urge, but I think the need for some kind of physical release was just too much for me. Let's face it, Bryony and I had gone from having sex pretty much all the time, trying to conceive our second child, to not having sex at all, because we'd found out she was dying... and sex suddenly didn't seem very important anymore. A few weeks after her diagnosis, once we'd got used to the idea – if you ever can get used to the idea of living with death – we started making love again. She asked me to, and although I wasn't sure, I went ahead with it. She cried afterwards, lying in my arms, and I held her, feeling torn between the joy of having her naked body against mine once more, and the heartache of her tears. We both found it tough, and I wondered if she might not want to try again. But she did. It always ended the same way... in floods of tears. Although once or twice, she cried while I was inside her, making love to her still, and she clung to me, sobbing that she didn't want it all to end. I found it hard to keep it together then, but would control myself until after she'd fallen asleep, when I'd go to the bathroom and sit on the floor, crying silently to myself. And then, as her illness worsened, and she became too sick, everything stopped. And I'm ashamed to say, I felt relieved. I felt grateful that I could just switch of that part of myself and avoid the emotional turmoil.

Obviously I didn't do a very good job of switching it off though, because I gave in at the first hurdle... to Gabrielle. But even I know she was just means to an end, a release from months and months of pent-up frustration. That's all. Unfortunately, knowing that doesn't make me feel any less guilty for what I did.

And besides, that's not the point. The point is, that whoever I've slept with, I've always been pretty much the same kind of lover. I was definitely more attentive with Bryony, and sex with her was better than with anyone else, but I was nothing like the man in my dreams. Not with her, or with any of them. And if that was secretly what I wanted, and I was ever going to be like him – a more bold and assertive kind of lover... the lover of my seemingly fertile imagination – that night with Gabrielle would have been the perfect opportunity to release him, wouldn't it? After all, it was a one-off. I could have been anyone I wanted to be, and she'd have been none the wiser. And it's not like there would have been any consequences to anything I did with her. We were never going to see each other again. We didn't have a future. We didn't even have one night.

Okay, so I took her hard. I can remember that much. But it was nothing like my dreams. There was nothing possessive or masterful about the way I was with Gabrielle. I just needed to have sex. That's all. And that's why these dreams don't make sense to me. I've had my chances to be different. I've had plenty of opportunities, not just with Gabrielle, but in the past, to try something 'different'. And I've never taken them. I was happy with what Bryony and I had together. I really was. I loved her absolutely. I loved that gentle and considered way we had with each other, all the while we could… all the while her illness would allow it. So why is it that I'm so aroused by the idea of taking control, being dominant, and having wild, passionate, frenzied and deeply, deeply, intensely loving sex, with a woman I don't know?

And why do I still want that now, even though I'm wide awake, and my eyes are filled with tears, my throat is closing over, and my heart is overflowing with self-loathing, for daring to think like that?

Especially about another man's wife…

Poppy actually helps to clear away the breakfast things today, but she's only being helpful because she wants to go and play on the swings again. I'm not so keen myself, just in case the woman and her son are there. The thought of facing her after the way I behaved yesterday doesn't inspire me, and nor does trying to look her in the eye, after my very heady and erotic dreams. Two nights in a row is starting to feel like a habit. And it's a habit I'm going to have to try and kick, if I'm going to stay sane.

"Come on, Daddy." Poppy drags me from the kitchen into the hall, her shoes already on her feet. "If we go for a play now, then we'll be able to spend the rest of the day clearing up the house."

I can't argue with her logic, although a part of me wants to tell her that playing isn't a pre-requisite of my day.

I close the door behind me, pocketing the keys, and glance up, checking to see whether the swings are vacant, or not, my heart constricting in my chest when I see the woman sitting on the ground and her son swinging from the monkey bars. I'm reminded of my horrible attitude yesterday, and instinctively, I pull back on Poppy's hand.

"Why don't we leave it until later?" I suggest.

She looks up at me, then follows the line of my gaze. "No, Daddy."

"But we don't want…"

"You need to say sorry," she interrupts, tugging on me. I don't move though. "You'd make me say sorry, if I'd been rude." I can't deny that. I would. And I can't forget the look on her face last night when she asked me to be kind to the 'nice lady', as she put it.

I shrug my shoulders, which Poppy seems to take as my agreement, and she pulls me across the green, while I try and think about how to start the inevitable conversation – because it would be beyond awkward for the woman and I to stand there and ignore each other while our children play. I suppose I'm going to have to apologise, even though I'm still not completely convinced that I was entirely in the wrong. The fault, if there was one, lay in my execution of the argument, because I had no right to say she was being irresponsible, or that she was endangering Poppy's life. I overreacted. And now I'm going to pay for that.

We get to the play area and I steel myself for the humiliation that I know will follow if, like a lot of women, she enjoys scoring points whenever men admit they got something wrong. She surprises me though, by getting up and walking straight towards us, with a big a smile on her face.

My breath catches in my throat as I allow my eyes to wander down her body, taking in her top, which has narrow straps, and is a pale lilac, darkening to a deeper shade of purple at the hem, one side of which is tucked into her frayed, pale denim shorts. God, she looks good… too good. And I avert my gaze, focusing on my daughter instead.

"Hello, Poppy," the woman says, the moment she reaches us.

"Hello." Poppy grins up at her, and squeezes my hand, giving me a not very subtle reminder that I'm supposed to be saying sorry.

"How are you today?"

Poppy doesn't reply. Instead she stares up at me, expectantly, which confuses me, until I turn to look at the woman and find she's now focused on me and not Poppy. She's asking how I am? Is this some kind of trap she's expecting me to fall into? Is she being sarcastic? It doesn't look or sound like it, but who knows…

"I'm fine," I say quietly, and then I remember my manners and add, "Thank you," as an afterthought.

"Good." Her smile broadens, and right at that moment, her son comes running up and stands directly in front of Poppy.

"Do you want to come and play on the slide?" he suggests and she nods her head, but then looks up at me again.

"Can I?" she asks.

"Okay."

"By myself?"

"I'll stand close by. All right?" I've learned my lesson about being over-protective, and besides, I don't want the woman to start interfering again. It'll only lead to another argument.

Poppy claps her hands and jumps up and down a couple of times, and then runs off after the little boy, who stands to one side and lets her climb the ladder first. The woman puts her hands in the pockets of her denim shorts and we wander over to the slide, side by side, but very much not together, being as neither of us says anything and we both look at the ground in front of us while we're walking. I know I should be the one to say something, and that the 'something' should be 'sorry', but now she's here, beside me, all I can think about is how good she looks, and how much better she looked in my dreams, because there, she was naked, beneath me, breathless... and that's really not a good place to start with an apology. Especially not an apology to a complete stranger, who's got a family of her own, and ought to have no part in my salacious fantasies... even if it seems I have no control over her being the main feature in them.

"How's it going over at the house?" she asks, as we come to a standstill beside the slide. "I imagine there's quite a lot to do, isn't there?"

I glance down at her, to find that, although she's clearly talking to me, she's concentrating on the children, keeping her eyes fixed on Poppy, as she slides down, waving her arms above her head. "There is," I reply. "Although we haven't actually done much yet. We're planning to stay until the end of the month, or thereabouts, but I think that's lulled me into a false sense of security, that I don't need to worry about actually getting started on anything." I stop speaking rather suddenly, surprised that I managed to string together that many words, considering how distracted I am by her… and not just by how sexy she looks, but also by the fact that, in spite of how rude I was to her yesterday, she's so full of smiles… as though I didn't call her negligent and irresponsible the last time we met, and she didn't tell me to grow up. Quite justifiably, of course.

She glances up at me, very briefly, before turning her attention back to her son, who's just got to the top of the ladder. "That's the problem with giving yourself time to do something," she says, her lips twisting upwards. "You keep putting it off."

"Hmm… it would have been easier if I'd decided to get everything done in a weekend. I'd have been forced to just get on with it." *And I might not have spent my time dreaming about you…* I muse. But then realise that I might not have met her either, although that thought doesn't feel quite right, considering that I shouldn't be thinking like that about her… not when she's not free…

But then, how free am I?

"I'm the same with my lesson plans," she admits, bringing me out of my confused reverie, and I'm reminded again of our argument and of the fact that she told me she's a teacher, and that I questioned her abilities, not to mention her dedication, I think. "I keep finding excuses not to do them, right up until just before the end of the holidays."

It's no good. I can't let her keep going like this, making polite conversation. I have to apologise.

"I'm… um…"

"Dad!" Poppy's shout interrupts my half-hearted attempt to say sorry and I turn to find her standing beside me.

"Yes?"

She grabs my hand for a moment. "Can you take a picture of me?"

"A picture?"

"Yes. On the slide."

"Oh… okay. If you want."

She grins and runs to the back of the slide, climbing up the ladder with confidence and I realise that, although the woman has been watching the children meticulously, I haven't. I've been watching her. And I feel even worse about all the things I said to her.

I pull my phone from my pocket and, with Poppy sitting on the top of the slide, I take a few photographs, some of her, and some with the little boy, standing behind her as well, before she shoots down the slide again, squealing with delight. At the bottom, she gets to her feet and turns.

"Come on the swings, Roan," she calls and, once he's gone down the slide, he runs after her to the other side of the play area.

The woman and I follow. "Roan?" I query, my apology forgotten for the moment. "That's an unusual name." I remember the woman calling him that yesterday… twice, I think. Once when she was telling him to take care around Poppy, and once when we were arguing. And I believe Poppy might have mentioned his name too, when she was telling me off for spoiling her fun, and being rude. But this is the first chance I've had to remark on it.

She smiles up at me, and I deliberately concentrate on the children, to avoid looking at her, because she's just too beautiful… and too unattainable, on so many levels. And while that's a good thing, it's also very disconcerting, when she's standing this close to me. "I was explaining to Poppy that it means 'little redhead'."

I tilt my head to one side, observing her son, as he climbs up onto the seat of one of the swings.

"Is his hair really what you'd call red?" I ask.

"It was much brighter when he was born," she replies, justifying her choice of name, even though she doesn't really have to.

"More like yours, you mean?" I focus on her copper coloured curls now, and she stares up into my eyes, smiling.

"No. It was always more brown than red. But I liked the name, so I gave myself poetic licence."

If find it odd that she doesn't mention her husband, or partner, having any choice in her son's name, but maybe it was something she felt strongly about. Either way, I don't suppose it's any of my business, and we each take our places behind our respective children and start to push them on the swings, although I do so with less gusto than she does, partly because I'm wary of Poppy, but mainly because I'm reminded of our earlier meeting, the first time I saw her, when I was – yet again – unforgivably rude.

"Have you tried the pub since you've been down here?" she asks out of the blue, making conversation again, I guess, although her choice of subject matter is unfortunate.

"Um… no," I mutter, keeping my eyes fixed on Poppy's back as she sways back and forth. "Other than the wake… obviously."

"Oh… God. I didn't think," she says. "I'm so sorry."

Her voice cracks on her last word and I glance at her, while still pushing Poppy, and notice she's biting her bottom lip and her cheeks are flushed. I can't see her eyes clearly enough, because she's turned her head slightly, but I'd be willing to bet there are tears gathering there, and I feel awful now. I shouldn't have mentioned the wake. I didn't have to. I could have just said 'no', and left it at that.

"I didn't really notice what it was like," I say quietly, trying to redeem myself. "I was a bit pre-occupied."

"Understandably," she replies, turning back to me, and now I can clearly see the glistening in her eyes, and I know I was right. And I feel even worse about myself.

"Is it a nice pub?" I ask.

"Yes. It is. It's changed hands recently and they've introduced a new menu. They even have live music a couple of nights a week." She's staring right at me now, and despite the fact that she's still blinking away the beginnings of her tears, her lips are twisting upwards, like she's trying not to smile. "Most of the villagers don't like that," she says, explaining her mirth and leaning towards me a little, which feels kind of conspiratorial… and breathtaking. And it enables me to catch a hint of her scent as well, which is subtle, but vaguely floral.

"But you do?" I ask.

She loses the battle with her smile, and her eyes light up, and for a moment, I'm captivated by her… until Poppy's swing hits me in the arm and I'm catapulted back to reality. The woman chuckles and nods her head at the same time. "Yes, I do," she says. "I mean… the music isn't always to my taste, but this place needs livening up."

I can't disagree with her. It's one of the reasons I left when I was eighteen, and never came back... not for more than fleeting visits, anyway. I may have had a happy childhood, but as a teenager, boredom often got the better of me.

"They have barbecues at the weekends too," she adds, when I don't respond, because I'm too busy staring at her to form any words. "We haven't actually been to one yet, but the smells are incredible." She checks her watch. "Speaking of food..." She pulls her son's swing to a fairly abrupt stop. "If you want to go to the beach this afternoon, young man, we need to go home and get our picnic ready... via the shop, because we don't have enough bread."

Roan jumps down to the ground and takes the hand she offers, looking at Poppy, who's still swinging, just gently.

"See you tomorrow?" he says.

"I'm not sure we'll be coming tomorrow," the woman says, before either Poppy or I can reply. "It's Saturday... and you know what that means..."

His shoulders fall. "Cleaning," he mutters, with a voice that makes it sound like housework is the equivalent of having your toenails forcibly removed.

"You'll see Poppy soon, I'm sure," the woman says, to pacify him and he smiles up at her, easily pleased, it seems, just by the prospect of seeing a pretty girl in the near future. And I have to admit, I'm starting to understand how he feels. "Enjoy the rest of your day," she says, looking directly at Poppy, who smiles and gives her a little wave. And then she turns to me. "And don't work too hard."

She doesn't wait for my answer, but sets off across the green in the direction of the village store, with Roan trotting by her side, and I watch them go, my eyes fixed on the way her hair bounces and swings in time with her movements, and the gentle sway of her hips.

"Did you say sorry?" Poppy's standing beside me, having climbed down from the swing, and is looking up at me eagerly.

"No," I answer without thinking.

"Daddy." She sounds exasperated, but in a very sweet, five year-old kind of way.

"I didn't get the chance. The lady didn't stop talking." Even as I'm saying that, I realise it's not true. She did stop talking, when she was listening to me. And that's the point. For the first time in years, I actually engaged in a conversation with someone. I didn't dismiss them, or make an excuse, or leave the vicinity on some pretext or other. I may not have said very much, but I did manage a few words, and none of them were rude. And that feels like an achievement. Even if I didn't say sorry.

It seems that playing by herself isn't as much fun as playing with Roan, and Poppy quickly becomes bored with the swings and slides and asks if we can go home. I'm in need of coffee, so I'm not about to refuse, and we walk together across the green to my mother's house, my mind still fixed on my conversation with the woman.

Can she really be such a happy-go-lucky kind of person? Or was she putting on an act, pretending that she hadn't really been offended by my behaviour? I know she was upset by it at the time, that much was obvious. And I was exceptionally insulting, even by my recent standards. Because before Bryony's death, I was a much kinder, much nicer, more gentle man. But since I've been alone… wracked with guilt and washed over with regrets, I don't seem to know how to behave around people. So, I wonder, was her performance today some kind of self-defence? Was she protecting herself against another onslaught? Or was it a performance at all? Was she really being as forgiving as she seemed? *God… why do other people have to be so complicated?*

Or is it *me* that's making things more complicated than they need to be? Am I seeing things that don't exist? Reading too much into reactions, and situations? The woman might just be naturally friendly, and just because she's become a feature of my dreams, and therefore my life, doesn't mean that I have the same effect on her. It would be odd if I did, considering that she's in a relationship already. No… it must be me. And that's not altogether surprising. After all, being around people isn't something I'm accustomed to any more, and I am very easily confused. I smile and shake my head, just slightly, as I recall all the times Bryony used to complicate the hell out of me so easily; how she could act like everything was fine, even though I knew it wasn't. And when I'd ask her what was wrong, she'd just say 'nothing', or 'it's fine'… over and over, sometimes for days on end. Until eventually, she'd snap, and blow up in my face about something that had happened so long ago, I'd usually forgotten all about it – and sometimes so had she. At least in any great detail. A smile twitches at my lips, at the memory of how I used to try and get around her, just to placate her… and how she'd do her best to put me off, attempting to get her point across still, because I guess it mattered to her, until eventually she'd give in… and I'd kiss her, and say sorry. I always said sorry, even though I wasn't necessarily sure what for, because I can guarantee I'd been an idiot in some capacity or other… and that and the kiss would make it all better again.

As I put the key in the lock and let us into the house, it strikes me as strange and kind of sad, that even my arguments with Bryony seem like good memories now… because we can't have them anymore.

Chapter Seven

Summer

Friday afternoon at the beach was probably a mistake. Not only was it busy, but it was really too hot, with very little breeze, and we didn't end up staying for long.

When we got back, Roan was tired though. We'd spent quite a bit of time in the sea. So he had a shower and I made us a pizza, which we ate in front of the television, before he actually asked if he could go to bed. Any parent will tell you, that doesn't happen very often, but when it does, you make the most of it. I did. And once I'd tucked him in and kissed him goodnight, I poured myself a glass of wine, switched TV channels to a more grown-up film and put my feet up on the sofa, until my eyes started to droop too, and I took myself off to bed, where I spent some time thinking over my conversation with Kit. I was quite surprised that he'd spoken to me, being as he'd been so rude the day before, but he did speak – even if it was just briefly, and only in answer to direct questions, for the best part. We may not have exchanged any life altering information, but I did come away feeling as though I'd learned a few things about him. He's shy. At least I think he is. There were certainly a couple of times when he seemed to want to say something, but then stopped himself. And he's thoughtful… and he has the most captivating eyes. They're dark brown and very intense, but they have amber flecks in them that dance – just occasionally – like when he's looking at Poppy. And I have to admit, even as I turn over and pull the covers up around myself, that my motives for wanting to help him are not entirely altruistic. Yes, I want to repay Maggie for all the times she was there for me… but I'd also like to spend more time with Kit. I'd like to get to know him better and maybe understand why he's so tortured. And, if I can, I'd like to help him not to be.

Yesterday, being Saturday, was housework day. It always is, because being a working mum, I have a busy Monday to Friday and I like to keep Sundays free to do things with Roan. And I know it's the summer holidays and I could do housework anytime, but we have a kind of routine now. And I like to stick to it.

So, after I'd stripped the beds and left Roan to clear up his room, I put on the first load of washing and set about cleaning the kitchen. It took until lunchtime to get the downstairs clean and tidy, and after lunch, I re-made the beds and vacuumed through, before starting work on the bathroom. Roan had finished tidying his room by mid-morning, but he knows better than to ask to do anything exciting on a Saturday afternoon, and spent his time watching cartoons and playing with his trains – which are his latest passion, having replaced dinosaurs in his favour about six months ago… at least for the time being.

This morning is overcast, which is almost a welcome relief, and while I know we could go to the beach again – and that it would probably be a bit quieter today – I make the suggestion to Roan that we go to the monkey sanctuary instead. I take my class there once a year, because they offer a great educational experience, and I adopted a monkey on Roan's behalf last Christmas, so he likes to pay a visit every so often. Not only that, but our tickets are valid for the whole season, so it's a free day out, which means I can afford to buy us lunch on the way.

Before we leave, though, I need to go over to the store. We've run out of milk, flour and eggs, and I'm planning on doing some baking tomorrow morning. And although I know I could pop out first thing,

I don't really want to. I'd rather just get started with cooking, knowing I've got everything to hand. And besides, I'll need the milk for a very necessary cup of tea when we get back from our outing. However, the store is only open until twelve-thirty on Sundays, so it can't wait until later on.

Roan holds my hand as we walk across the green, and doesn't ask if he can play on the swings, for once – perhaps because he's excited about our trip out, and doesn't want to hang around. Or maybe because Poppy's not there. He seems to have taken a shine to her, which is kind of sweet, and I smile to myself at the simplicity of those early childhood friendships, before hormones and external influences get in the way.

I open the door to the shop, the old-fashioned bell ringing above our heads, and I let Roan pass through ahead of me, steering him in the direction of the refrigeration units at the back of the store.

I pick up a carton of milk, which I hand to Roan to hold, being as I didn't bother getting a basket, and then lead him down the aisle, turning at the end and looking up, surprised to see Kit and Poppy, standing in front of the wine display, Kit holding a bottle of red in his hand, studying the label.

"People will talk, you know," I say, trying to make a joke, albeit not a very good one.

He turns to me, his brow furrowed, but doesn't reply, which saddens me, as he seems to have reverted to his sullen self again, despite the fact that I actually thought I'd made some headway with him on Friday morning. Still, I'm not that easily put off. Although I don't want to make a nuisance of myself and risk him getting angry with me again, so I leave him to his wine selection, with a nod of my head and a smile, and after picking up a bag of self-raising flour and half a dozen eggs, we start towards the counter.

"Can we put chocolate chips in the cakes, Mum?" Roan asks and I look down at him.

"I suppose so."

I double back to the small baking section that the store provides, and find a packet of milk chocolate chunks, which is the best we're going to get in here, and then, satisfied that we have everything we need, we go back towards the counter again, only to find that Kit and Poppy have beaten us to it and are standing patiently, waiting for Mrs Wilson to ring up their purchases, which consist of the bottle of wine, some coffee and a Sunday newspaper. I wonder for a moment, which of those items is the most essential, and hope – for Kit's sake – that it isn't the wine.

"Can we wait, Daddy?" Poppy says, as he tucks the newspaper under his arm, and picks up the wine and coffee.

"Wait for what?" He glances down at her.

"For Roan and his mummy."

There's a stilled, awkward silence, but then Kit looks up and sees Mrs Wilson awaiting his response and lets out a sigh, saying, "If you want," in a kind of resigned voice. I try not to take offence, although it's hard, hearing his detachment, and as he and Poppy move to one side, I put down our items, with Roan adding the milk he's been carrying diligently around the shop.

"Hello, dear," Mrs Wilson says, and I glance up at her, unsure whether she's talking to me or to Roan.

"Hello." I answer for both of us, because I know my son is unlikely to reply to her.

"How are you?" she says, making more conversation than she normally does, presumably because she's hoping to glean some gossip.

"We're very well, thank you." I give her a smile, accompanied by a ten pound note and she frowns, handing me my change, before she closes the till.

"It's a shame the weather's not so good," she says as I turn away.

"Oh, I don't know… I think it's quite nice to have a change," I remark and lead Roan towards the door, which Kit is already holding open. "Thank you." I look up at him as we pass through, although he doesn't make eye contact, gazing through the opening and across the green instead.

Outside, Roan joins Poppy by the noticeboard that hangs in the window of the shop. It's normally filled with postcards for people advertising second hand bikes and lawnmowers for sale. Although sometimes there is something noteworthy. And judging by the looks on the children's faces, today might be one of those days.

"Look, Daddy... there's a fair."

Kit stands behind his daughter, looking at the small poster advertising the annual summer fête that always takes place on the second to last weekend of August. The posters have been up for a couple of weeks now, and there have been regular meetings of the parish committee, every second and fourth Wednesday of the month, since the middle of May. This is the biggest event in the whole village calendar, and everyone makes an effort to do something. Even me.

"So there is," he replies, although he doesn't sound too enthusiastic. "I can't believe they're still holding it."

"Some things never change in villages," I remark and he turns to look at me.

"No. They don't."

"Can we go?" Poppy says, jumping up and down and turning to look up at him.

"I suppose," he says, shrugging his shoulders. "We're going to be here until the end of the month anyway, so..."

"Oh, you have to come." I lean down towards Poppy. "I'm in charge of face painting. So you'll have to decide what you want me to turn you into."

"A tiger," she says, without hesitating.

"A tiger?" I muse, thinking to myself that I'm going to have to get in some practice... and that I hope Roan doesn't mind being my model, because I don't have anyone else on whom I can try out my dubious skills... which leads me to wondering yet again, why I volunteered for this, rather than just offering to bake cakes, or run the tombola. "I'll see what I can do."

She claps her hands with glee and, turning away from the shop, she and Roan make their way across the green, side by side, giving her father and I no choice but to follow them.

"Are you always so cheerful?" Kit says, surprising me by speaking first, for once.

"Not all the time, no. I have my low moments, just like everyone else."

"Thank God for that. I was starting to think you were incapable of being anything other than ludicrously happy."

I turn to him, as we walk. "Is there something wrong with being happy?"

"No." He doesn't elaborate, and I'm not sure how to take his comments. They weren't made with any malice, or even criticism, but more of an inquisitiveness that he now seems to regret, judging by his silence. So I turn away again, and we continue walking a few more paces.

"Did you say you're going to be here until the end of the month?" I ask, even though I'm fairly sure he mentioned the length of his stay on Friday, when we were talking about him clearing out Maggie's house. I didn't remark on it then, because I didn't need to, but now I'm scratching around for something to say, because the silence is starting to bother me.

"Yes. Why?" He's frowning again.

"Because I was just thinking that you must have a very understanding boss, to let you take so much time off work." I wasn't thinking that at all, but one of us had to try and make conversation.

He shakes his head. "I don't have a boss."

"You don't?"

"No. I run my own web design business, which is a rather glorified way of saying I'm self employed."

"And you can afford to just take a whole month off work, can you?" I'm intrigued now. And besides, he seems to be warming to this topic, or at least participating in it, which is roughly the same thing for Kit, it seems.

His frown deepens and I wonder if I've read him wrong and he's about to tell me to mind my own business. He doesn't though. Instead, he shrugs and says, "I made sure I finished off the work I had booked in before I came down here, and I've brought my laptop with me, so I can keep up with e-mails and do anything small and basic that comes in, like the odd update, or amendment. The priority was always going to be clearing Mum's house, but if I have to work, then I can…" He stops talking, raising his head and his voice, as he calls out, "Poppy, where are you going?"

I look up and notice the children have both gravitated towards the play area, which doesn't surprise me in the slightest.

"We're just going on the swings," she calls back.

"Okay. But just the swings. Nothing else." There's a warning note to his voice and she nods her head, before she and Roan turn and run headlong onto the playground and take a swing each, rocking back and forth contentedly.

"If there's anything I can do to help…" I say, as Kit turns back towards me.

"Sorry?"

"You were saying about maybe having to work sometimes, while you're down here… and I just said, if there's anything I can do to help…"

"Such as?" There's that sarcastic, slightly unkind tone to his voice again and I wish I'd kept my mouth shut. I felt like I was making progress before, but now…

"I don't know…" I persevere, regardless. "I—I suppose I could look after Poppy for you, to give you some peace and quiet."

He lets out a sigh. "Listen, I don't mean to be rude." I think he probably does. He has done every other time. "But the thing is, I'm hardly going to leave my daughter with you when I don't know you. Obviously I get that you're a teacher, but you're also a complete stranger, so if…"

"I'm not," I interrupt.

"You're not what? You're not a teacher?" He frowns again, his eyes darkening, those amber flecks fading.

"No. I'm not a complete stranger."

"Well, I'm sorry, but I don't count a few minutes' conversation in a children's playground as sufficient knowledge of a person to leave my child in their care."

I shake my head. "No… you don't understand. What I'm trying to say is that you do know me, even if you don't realise it."

"What are you talking about?" God, he's so impatient.

"Our mothers were lifelong friends," I explain.

"They were?" His frown clears, just as quickly as it formed, even if he does still look bewildered.

"My mother was Elaine Craig." I hope he'll remember the name and I won't have to go through her entire life story before he understands who I am.

It takes a moment, but eventually he says, "You mean… you're Summer?"

"Yes." I smile at him. "I'm Summer."

"But… wow… I mean, I can't believe this." He doesn't look bewildered anymore. He looks shocked. "I've spent half my life hearing about you," he says, shaking his head very slowly from side to side. "My mother used to read me your mother's letters. All the time. Even when I was a teenager and didn't really want her to." He blushes. "Sorry. I shouldn't have said that."

"Don't worry."

"I—I feel like I've known you forever," he adds, "even though we've never met. Just out of interest, why didn't you tell me who you were before?"

He has a point. "I don't know really. I suppose I was just waiting for the right moment."

"A moment when I wasn't being unbelievably rude to you, you mean?" He looks so contrite, I can't help but take pity on him. Again.

"You mustn't worry about that. I do understand."

"Do you?"

"Yes. I do." Not that I want to go into all of that now… standing on the edge of the children's play area, without so much as a glass of wine in my hand to make it easier. "And believe it or not, in spite of appearances to the contrary, I'm actually quite a normal person and I can be trusted to look after your daughter, if it helps. I've looked after Roan on my own – other than the help Mum gave me, of course – ever since he was born."

"But… I mean… what about his father?" Kit asks, shifting his bottle of wine into the crook of his arm and balancing the jar of coffee on top, evidently getting more comfortable.

"Oh, he didn't want to know." I glance over at Roan as I'm talking. "I was just a one night stand to him... which was rather a shame, because it was my first time, and being dumped the very next morning wasn't what I'd had in mind at all... Not that I'm altogether sure what I did have in mind. But being dumped certainly wasn't it. Still, I'm not complaining. I got Roan out of it, and as one night stands go, I think it was probably pretty amazing. It was for me, anyway, even if my love life has been non-existent ever since." I stop talking, remembering where I am, and who I'm standing with, as I feel the blush rise up my cheeks, and I look up at Kit again now, to find he's staring down at me intently. "Although I've obviously never mastered the art of keeping my mouth shut."

Very slowly, his lips twitch up into a gentle smile, which is a rare and beautiful sight. "What happened to your own father?" he asks, changing the subject, which I conclude is probably a good thing. "I'm sure Mum must have mentioned him, but I can't remember..."

"If Maggie ever mentioned my dad, it probably would have been between expletives."

He chuckles, his broad shoulders shaking, and the sound pulsates through my body, which is a little strange. Nice... but strange.

"I don't recall there being too many expletives," he says eventually.

"You surprise me."

"Were your parents not happy then?" he asks, looking away for a moment to check on the children, before turning his attention back to me.

"They must have been once upon a time, I suppose. But then the beginning of their relationship was hardly the stuff of fairytales."

"Oh?"

I'm surprised he's even interested and, although I'm tempted to ask if we can open his bottle of wine and have a drink, before I start explaining my family's history, I reason that it's only ten-thirty in the morning... and we don't have any glasses. Still, we could sit down, if I'm going to tell him about myself – at least in part.

"Why don't we make use of that bench?" I suggest, nodding towards the wooden seat in the corner of the play area. "We'll still be able to see the children."

"Okay."

We make our way over and he waits until I've sat down before sitting himself, about a foot away from me, and places his shopping on the floor by his feet. I put mine beside me, on the other side to him, and focus on the children, who are swinging happily, side by side, and seem to be talking avidly.

"You were saying?" he says, beginning the conversation before I can. "Your parents' marriage didn't start well."

"I suppose it did, and it didn't. They met on holiday," I explain, turning in my seat, just slightly, so I'm facing him. "In Greece."

"So? A lot of people meet each other on holiday."

"Yes. I suppose they do. But that wasn't really the problem."

"What was?"

"The fact that, when my mother came home, she brought back more than a very nice tan and a bottle of Ouzo."

He stares at me for a moment, until I point to myself, the light dawns in his eyes, and he just says, "Oh," in a hushed whisper.

"I think she found out she was pregnant about a month after she got back, and she contacted my father in France."

"Oh yes, of course… your dad was French, wasn't he?"

"Yes."

"But then… why was your mum's name Craig? It's not the most French sounding name I've ever heard of."

I smile at him. "Neither is Summer, when you think about it."

"No, it isn't."

"And I can explain that. When I was born, my father insisted that I was called Mathilde, after his grandmother. My mother hated the name, as did I, so she, in turn, insisted my middle name should be Summer and he agreed. She called me Summer all the time, and because my father was rarely at home, it got to the point where I was so unaccustomed to hearing myself called Mathilde, that I often wouldn't answer, simply because I didn't realise I was the one being spoken to. Then, when my parents divorced, Mum went back to using her maiden name, of Craig. And I didn't want to spend the rest of my life being Mathilde Fournier, so I became Summer Craig… unofficially to start with."

"Unofficially?"

"Yes. My father wouldn't give permission for Mum to change my name by deed poll, and although he wanted nothing to do with me, he evidently had the right to prevent me being called what I wanted… at least until I was eighteen and could do it myself."

"Which you did?" he asks.

"Oh yes."

"I see."

"I'm glad about that. But we're getting ahead of ourselves."

"Yes, I suppose we are, aren't we? That's my fault."

"Not at all. I just think I should tell you about my parents' marriage before I get too far into their divorce."

"I suppose it's more conventional."

"And easier to follow. So, as I was saying, Mum found out she was pregnant, and she evidently got in touch with my father. I think they'd exchanged addresses at the end of their holiday, and even though she hadn't heard a word from him, Mum wrote and told him she was expecting, and he flew to the UK and proposed to her – which I suppose means he was a slightly more honourable human being than Roan's father."

He raises his eyebrows and I shrug my shoulders. I'm not going to apologise for thinking that about Russell, even though I know that marrying him – if he'd bothered to propose, that is – would have been a huge mistake. The fact remains, it would have been nice to be asked. It would have been nice if he'd cared.

"She accepted him," I continue, "even though his proposal came with a couple of caveats."

"Such as?"

"Such as they'd have to marry before the baby – before I – was born. His parents were insisting on that, evidently. And he also made it clear that Mum would have to move to France."

"That was quite a big ask."

"Hmm… she'd been working as a nurse for a couple of years, and she loved her job, but my father argued that she'd be giving that up anyway to be a full-time mum. That wasn't optional either. Although that was his proviso, not his parents'."

"So she gave up her career and moved to France with him?" I can tell he's surprised, even though he must know the outcome of the story, if Maggie read my mum's letters to him. He must know I was born and raised in Paris.

"She did. She always told me that she loved him – or she thought she did at the time – and didn't regard anything he was asking of her as a sacrifice. Personally, I think she was rather swept off her feet by the fact that he'd turned up on her doorstep unannounced and proposed. It was like something out of a romance novel, and I imagine it was hard to turn him down. The only thing she regretted was moving away from Maggie. Mum had been orphaned in her late teens and she used to come down to Bluebells quite a lot, before she got married, whenever she was off duty for any length of time, and she'd stay with your mum and dad."

"I do have vague memories of her being here when I was little," he says, sighing. "Mum used to laugh a lot when they were together. Dad used to just roll his eyes and give me this kind of exasperated look, and then take himself off to his studio upstairs at the back of the house, as far away from them as possible."

"I'm not surprised."

"Did she regret her decision? To marry your father and emigrate, I mean?" he asks, surprising me by his continued level of interest in my mother's story.

"At the time, no. Mum was a carefree kind of spirit and I think she saw it as an adventure. I was born in Paris, about five months after their very hasty wedding, and although my father took little interest in anything that wasn't related to his work, and his family's investments, we were quite happy there."

"What was it like growing up in Paris?" he asks, turning around properly to face me.

"The same as growing up anywhere else, I should imagine. You don't know any different when you're a child, so you accept your life for what it is. I accepted that mine was spent almost exclusively with my mother, going to markets, learning to cook and to be thankful for the beautiful things in life – because that was one of her greatest talents. If the weather was bad, she'd still find something positive, like the pattern that raindrops make on the window, or the colour of the autumn leaves as they blow down the street. If I ever felt unwell, she'd cook me my favourite foods, and she'd sit with me and tell me stories, so I didn't feel sorry for myself. She had a wonderful way of looking at the world." I feel a lump forming in my throat, and cough it away, noticing the sympathetic look on Kit's face.

"She sounds like a remarkable woman," he says.

"She was," I manage to mutter around the lump, before I get back to the safer ground of my story. "But I don't think she'd appreciated – not until the wedding, anyway – that my father's family were extremely wealthy. And I mean *extremely* wealthy. They lived in an enormous and rather grand property on the outskirts of the city... not that we went there that often, which is probably a good thing, because my only real memory of the place is how sterile it was."

"Where did you live then?" he asks.

"In a huge and very luxurious apartment not far from the Eiffel Tower. I had my own bathroom and dressing room, and the kitchen was out of this world. I suppose my most abiding memories are of that room... sitting at the table with Mum, eating wonderful soft, crumbly croissants or pains au chocolat, which our maid Sophie used to go and collect every morning from the boulangerie. And, of course, there was the sweetest, richest and creamiest hot chocolate, which my dad made when he was there, and which we drank out of really wide cups. And I remember having bread at every meal, regardless of what else we were eating... Oh, and the cheese. Oh, God... Mum used to get the most enormous slabs of oozing brie, just..." I stop talking and waving my hands around to demonstrate the size of the cheeses Mum used to bring back from the market, and look up at him. He's staring at me again, but this time with a lovely smile slowly forming on his generous lips. "What?"

"So, basically, you remember the food."

I chuckle. "Yes. It looks that way, doesn't it?"

"What went wrong?" he asks and I raise an eyebrow at him. "Well, something must have done, even if I can't for the life of me remember what. Because you and your mum moved back here. Well, not here, but to the UK, anyway."

"Yes, we did. When I was twelve, Mum discovered that Dad had a mistress. I—I don't know exactly how she found out, and she never told me, but I do remember the arguments that followed. I remember him shouting at her in French and not understanding very much of what was being said, but just being aware it wasn't good. And I remember my grandparents coming over the next morning. Dad had obviously phoned them, which I guess meant he hadn't won the argument with my mother, and was calling in the big guns. They spoke more slowly and didn't shout, which meant I could understand what they were saying, even though I wasn't supposed to be listening. They sat down in the living room, and my grandmother poured them all a cup of coffee and quietly explained that my mother couldn't possibly leave my father. She said there had never been a divorce in the family, that Mum was being silly and she just had to accept that Dad's behaviour was perfectly normal, and her demands that he should leave his mistress and devote himself to her – and to me – and that he should spend more time with us, away from his work, were completely unreasonable. I got the impression then that perhaps his mistress was someone he worked with, but I might have been wrong. I do know that my mother sat in silence throughout the whole time my grandparents were there. The 'demands' that my grandmother had spoken of must have been made to my father the night before, because she never repeated them."

"But she did leave him, didn't she?" Kit sounds confused again now.

"Yes. That same day. Almost the moment my grandparents had left. Dad had to go somewhere. I'm not sure where he went, but he left without saying goodbye, presumably thinking everything was resolved in his favour, because Mum had just sat in silence and hadn't argued at all. She clearly didn't want to hang around long enough to disillusion him, so she packed a bag, with just a few things – just what she could carry – and she called your mum…"

"Oh God, yes. I remember now." He nods his head. "There was a big fuss, wasn't there?"

"I don't know, was there?"

He smiles. "Yes, there was. I was studying for my A-Levels at the time, so I'd have been about eighteen, I guess and, frankly, not that interested in all the drama. But I do remember my mother running around the house and Dad making lots of phone calls."

"Well, it was your dad who really came to the rescue. Mum had no money of her own, you see, but your dad arranged everything. He paid for our air fares and found us a tiny flat to live in."

"Why didn't you just come and stay here?" he asks, nodding towards Bluebells and looking confused.

"Because Mum was scared Dad might come after her, and try to make us go back, and that this would be the first place he'd look. It wasn't like she had any family of her own, and Dad knew Maggie was her best friend…"

"I see."

"So your father paid the deposit and the first three months' rent on a flat in Looe, and Mum went back to nursing."

"And your dad? Did he come after her?"

"No. Although he did come back to the apartment, just before we left, which I don't think Mum expected. I think she thought he'd be gone all afternoon, but he walked back in the door while we were waiting for the taxi to arrive, and he saw our bags in the hall."

"What did he do?"

"He just glared at her. I half expected him to get angry, like he had the day before, but he just stared… and stared, like he couldn't quite believe she was daring to leave him. And then, as our taxi arrived, and Mum picked up our bags, he told her – in a very quiet and calculated voice – that she was making the biggest mistake of her life. Funnily enough, he said that in English. He rarely spoke any English, and it struck me as odd, even then. But I've sometimes wondered since, if he wanted me to understand what he was saying, so that if things went wrong for us, I'd blame her and not him."

"And he's never been in touch? Not even with you?"

"No. The divorce was handled entirely by solicitors, and to be fair, he did make a reasonable settlement on her, in the end, which she used to pay your father back, and then she put the rest into savings, which meant that she could afford to work part-time when she wanted to, and then give it up altogether, when Roan was born. My father's condition of the settlement was that she wasn't allowed to say anything about their marriage, or to ask for any further money in the future. She had no intention of contacting him at all… and no wish to discuss their time together, so she agreed quite readily. But after that, we never heard from him again, other than when he refused my mother's official request to change my name. He's remained completely silent ever since. I have no idea where he is, or if he's still alive. He was almost a stranger to me, even when I lived under the same roof as him. Now, I don't think I'd know him if he walked right up to me and introduced himself."

Kit shakes his head, frowning slightly. "You must have a fairly low opinion of men," he muses, almost to himself, as though he's trying to think something through.

"Why on earth would you say that?" I ask, and he jumps slightly, which makes me wonder if he meant to say anything aloud at all.

"Well… because of the way you've been treated, I suppose. Your dad and Roan's father have hardly shown themselves as shining examples of the male sex, have they?" His frown deepens. "And as for myself…"

"What? What about yourself?" I wonder what he's about to say.

"I… well, I think I've already said… I've been unbelievably rude to you."

"Which is hardly on the same level as my father refusing to give up his mistress in favour of my mother, or cutting me out of his life on a permanent basis… or Roan's father suggesting I get an abortion, rather than facing up to his own responsibilities."

"Roan's father suggested you should get an abortion?" That's shocked him.

"Yes. He offered to pay for it."

"That's even more reason for you to hate men, I would have thought."

"Hate men? Good Lord, no. I couldn't possibly hate men. I'm doing my best to raise one."

His face clears, and although he's not smiling, there's something about his expression which is quite arresting. And for a moment, I just stare at him.

"We... we should probably get going," he says at last, breaking that momentary spell.

"So should we."

I grab my things from the bench and he bends to pick up his own, before calling Poppy. Roan comes with her and as they approach, I look up at Kit again.

"My offer stands," I say quietly. "If you need me to look after Poppy for you, I'm more than willing to help."

He sucks in a deep breath, letting it out slowly. "Thanks for the offer, but we're fine. Really."

"Okay." I decide to leave it at that, and not push him, even though I think he's still a very long way from being fine.

Chapter Eight

Kit

That was a surprise.

No… that's not true. It was a shock. A real shock to discover that the woman I've been dreaming about is actually Summer Craig. And even now, nearly twenty-four hours later, on a breezy but sunny Monday morning, as I watch Poppy eating her cereal, I'm still struggling to get my head around the fact that the woman who's been filling my dreams every night is the same girl my mother used to tell me about when I was growing up. The daughter of her best and oldest friend. I remember that, when I was much younger, I always used to think Summer's life sounded so much more exciting than my own. After all, I was tucked away in a sleepy little village with my much older father, who spent most of his time painting, and a mother who was very youthful and occasionally embarrassing – at least she was when I was a teenager and longed for 'normal' parents… whatever 'normal' is. But I can recall my mother sitting at the kitchen table, drinking herbal tea that I used to think smelled like pond water, while reading her friend's letters out loud, and that I'd sometimes even pay attention for long enough to think how glamorous it all sounded, to grow up in Paris. I used to envy Summer that. I mean, I didn't know her, but it all seemed so exotic. A bit like Summer, really... especially when she's in my dreams, which are still continuing, even though I now know who she is.

It feels kind of weird, knowing that I've dreamt of making love to her, of taking her body, claiming her with my own in that forceful, domineering way, and yet I've known her – or known *of* her – nearly all my life. Discovering that yesterday really threw me and I struggled every so often to focus on what we were talking about. No matter how hard I tried to listen to her describing her memories of her life in Paris with her father – who, in my opinion isn't worthy of the title – every so often an image would flash across my brain, of her supple body, craving my attentions, bending to my will. It didn't help matters that she'd already explained much earlier in our conversation, that her son had been conceived during a one-night stand, which she'd revealed as having been 'pretty amazing', and – perhaps more importantly from my perspective – she'd also said that his conception had been her first, and only, sexual encounter, and that her love life had been 'non-existent' ever since. I'm almost certain that was the phrase she used, and I'll freely admit that I was overcome with relief at that moment. At least now, it seems I have one less thing to feel guilty about. I haven't been coveting another man's wife. My dreams – while still confusing – are, perhaps, not quite as sordid as they had seemed, now I've discovered that she is, in reality, unattached.

Obviously, I had to change the subject after she admitted to all of that, because the effect those thoughts were having on me was completely inappropriate for where we were – and the fact that our children were playing just a few feet away. Even so, I cannot, for the life of me, work out how someone who looks like she does, hasn't had more than one lover. Because a body as beautiful as hers should be loved... often. And hard. And that thought was what filled my mind last night, when I climbed into bed, even though I tried to ignore it. I also tried to forget that feeling of relief when I discovered that she doesn't have anyone in her life, because what does it matter? I'm fantasising about her. I'm not contemplating actually *doing* anything, am I? That would mean betraying Bryony... and while it's one thing to do that in my dreams, it's another thing altogether to consider it in real life. I've done it before, after all. I know how it makes me feel, and it's not somewhere I want to go again.

That doesn't mean I can stop the dreams though, and given my conversation with Summer, and the knowledge of who she is, I suppose it's no surprise that my dream last night was in a very domesticated setting – not a bedroom this time, but a kitchen… although it wasn't a kitchen I'm familiar with, and certainly wasn't the kitchen of my childhood, where I'm sitting now, and where my mother would sit all those years ago and read her friend's letters. In the kitchen of my dreams, the cabinets were painted pale blue, with white tiled walls and light wooden work surfaces, warm to the touch… so that when I sat Summer down on one of them, naked, with an expectant hunger in her eyes, she didn't flinch, like she would have done on cold marble or granite. The sounds of her heavy breathing crescendoed to loud moans and then full-throated screams, which died to mere whimpers, as I took her with a ceaseless need, owning her body, with such ferocity that when I woke, I could hardly breathe, and her name was a soft and husky whisper on my lips.

And that's another problem. I know her name now. She's not just a stranger anymore, a woman I can ignore for the best part, except in my elicit dreams. She's a real person. And not only that, she's someone I actually know – even if only obscurely, as a distant memory. And for that reason alone, I can't see her. I certainly can't see her today. I'm too confused by her to even contemplate looking into those deep green eyes, because even though I keep telling myself that she's just another fantasy, I know that if I spend too much time with her, it's going to get harder and harder to resist the reality… regardless of the consequences.

"What are we doing today, Daddy?" Poppy says, finishing the last of her cereal and putting the spoon down carefully in her bowl.

"I thought we could clear out the attic." I hadn't really given our day much thought at all, but it seems like a reasonable suggestion, and one which will keep us occupied and out of the way for hours… and hours.

Poppy's face falls. "The attic?"

"Yes. I'm fairly sure Granny kept lots of treasures up there."

"What sorts of treasures?" She tips her head to one side, intrigued.

"Oh, clothes, old records, letters, photographs…"

I think I had her at 'clothes', and she jumps down, taking her bowl to the sink and leaving it there, before coming back and holding out her hand to me. "Come on then," she says, and I smile to myself, getting to my feet and letting her haul me towards the stairs.

On the landing, I open the loft hatch and pull down the ladder, which I had installed after my father died, simply out of fear that my mother would try and climb up there herself, using the rickety old step ladders, and would fall and break something. This ladder is strong and sturdy and I help Poppy climb up it, switching on the loft light as soon as I can reach it.

For some people – like Alan Langley – the thought of clearing out their parents' attic might fill them with dread, but not for me. Aside from the fact that my father always kept this space immaculately clean – unlike his studio which is directly beneath us, and which was always too untidy for words – I know there are years and years of happy memories stored up here, and that Poppy and I will have fun today… and it will be a good distraction from everything else that's troubling me.

The floor is boarded, and there's some shelving around the edges of the loft space, with boxes lined up neatly, as well as two large, old-fashioned trunks, and several cases and chests stacked in piles. I don't need to necessarily go through everything, because some of the boxes are labelled, in my father's rather decorative, swirling handwriting. But others have no markings and, pulling one of the large trunks forward, I sit down on top of it, with Poppy beside me.

"We're not going to keep everything," I warn her, because I know what she can be like. "But anything that's really personal, that we think we'd like to hang on to as a nice memory of Granny, we'll put to one side to take home with us."

She nods her head, even though I'm not sure she completely understands and, dragging the first unmarked box closer, I open it and smile. It's full of vinyl records.

"What are they?" Poppy says.

"They're records." She looks up at me, puzzled. "You know how we stream music now?" I explain and she nods her head. "Well, this is how music was played when Granny was younger."

She pulls an album out of the box, holding it up and then shaking it. "There's music in here?"

I take it from her and smile. "Well, that's debatable." I flip the album over and read the track listing on the reverse. "It does contain one of the most annoying pieces of music ever recorded."

"What's that?" she asks, and I pull my phone from my pocket, going to my streaming app, and finding 'Karma Chameleon', pressing the button and letting it play.

As soon as she hears the beat, Poppy leaps to her feet and starts dancing around, and I can't help laughing at the sight of her.

"It's good, Daddy," she says. "I like it," and I let out a groan, wishing I'd never played it now, because I know I won't hear the end of it.

The track finishes and, before anything else starts playing, I turn off the app and pocket my phone again, as Poppy sits down beside me once more, a little breathless after her jigging around, and pulls out another record.

"Ahh... that's better." I take it from her. "Billy Joel..." I muse, again flipping the album over and checking the date this time. "Nineteen-eighty-three." Poppy looks up at me. "That would have been the year before Granny met Grandad," I explain. "Two years before I was born."

"How old was Granny then?" she asks.

I quickly work it out in my head, knowing that my mother was eighteen when she met and married my father, and nineteen when she had me. "Seventeen," I say out loud.

I imagine her and Elaine getting up to all sorts of mischief in Looe, where they both grew up – or trying to, anyway – and a smile crosses my lips, until my thoughts automatically turn to Elaine's daughter... to Summer, and I struggle to control my reactions as the image of her flits through my mind, although it's interrupted as I recall that other moment from yesterday's conversation, when she was telling me about how wonderful her mother was. I was so tempted to lean over, to take her in my arms, and even to kiss her, and to tell her that, in reality, she was describing herself, because I don't think I've ever met anyone who makes the world seem quite as bright as Summer does. I didn't tell her that, of course, because she was so clearly close to crying at the time, and while it wasn't my fault – for once – I didn't want to risk upsetting her.

"Are you all right, Daddy?" Poppy leans forward, looking up into my lowered face.

"I'm fine, sweetheart," I lie, replacing the record in the box.

"Can we keep them?" she asks.

"The records?"

"Yes." Her smile is infectious.

"We don't have anything to play them on," I reason.

"What do you play them on then?"

"A record player."

She nods her head, as though she knows what I'm talking about, which she can't do, because to my knowledge, she's never seen a record player in her life. "Why don't we get one?" she says, simply. "Then we can listen to Granny's music."

I want to point out that we could listen to it anyway, just by making a note of the albums, and streaming the music ourselves, but there's a connection to my mother in these old vinyl discs, that would be lost if I simply discarded them, in favour of something more modern.

"I suppose we could, if you want." She claps her hands together and grins. "But we're not getting them all out now, okay? We'll never get anything else done." I put the lid back on the box as I'm talking and, much to my surprise, Poppy doesn't argue for once, as I get up and carry it over to the loft hatch, leaving it there to take down later, before coming back to her with another one.

"What's in there?" she asks, before I've even sat down.

"I don't know. Let's have a look, shall we?" God… she's so impatient.

I sit beside her and pull the box open, to find it filled with loose papers and photographs, and before I can stop her, Poppy reaches in and grabs a handful. Luckily, she can't read very well yet, so I don't have to worry about her discovering anything personal or private about her grandmother, and I watch her discard the handwritten letters, in favour of a few photographs, which she holds up to me.

"Who's this?" she says, pointing to an image of two young women. One has short, dark hair, worn spiked on the top, and is wearing jeans and a baggy check shirt, with a narrow belt tied around her slim waist, her hand in her pocket and a rather precocious smile on her face. The other has golden red hair, styled in large curls, and has on bright blue, tight cropped trousers, and a white camisole top, and I know immediately that she's Elaine. It's obvious. She looks too much like Summer.

"That's Granny," I say, indicating the darker haired of the two women.

"And the other lady?"

"That's Summer's mother, Elaine. She was a friend of Granny's."

"Who's Summer?" Poppy looks up from the photograph and I realise she's not aware of Summer's name, just like I wasn't… until yesterday.

"Roan's mummy," I explain.

"Her name's Summer?" Poppy's eyes widen.

"Yes."

"Wow… what a cool name."

"Yes, it is," I whisper, without thinking.

"So, Summer's mummy and my granny were friends?"

"Yes. They were best friends."

She falls silent for a moment. "Do you think Summer would like to have this picture?" she suggests eventually, and I take it from her.

"I'm sure Summer has lots of photographs of her own."

I go to put the picture back in the box, but Poppy takes it away from me again. "She might not have," she says. "We can ask her, can't we?"

I'm not sure what to say to that. I can hardly tell my five year-old daughter that I'm scared of going to see her new friend's mother… my mother's friend's daughter. But in reality, I'm a grown man, and I'm absolutely terrified. And that was the whole point of hiding up here today… not that I'd admit to 'hiding', if anyone asked. But that's exactly what I'm doing. I'm avoiding seeing Summer, so I don't have to admit to my feelings for her. Even though I know I ought to, for my own peace of mind, if nothing else. Because it doesn't really matter how long I sit up here and bury myself in my mother's past, and try to pretend that I'm not really thinking about the woman who lives on the other side of the village green, with her son… who teaches in the local school, and has the sexiest body I've ever seen in my life, and a smile that could light up the world, and eyes that I'm fairly sure can see right through me… and who spends her nights in my very erotic dreams… I'm only kidding myself. Because I haven't been able to stop thinking about her since the first time I saw her.

I suppose it was okay, when I thought she was married – or at least in a relationship. Well… it wasn't okay, because I felt guilty about fantasising over another man's wife. But at the same time, there was an element of safety to my dreams. They could never be a reality, regardless of how real they felt, so there was no harm in them… other than to my sanity, I suppose. Now though… now I know she's alone – like me – regardless of what I keep telling myself to the contrary, I do keep wondering what it would be like to not be alone anymore…

And then I remember who I am.

And the guilt swarms in.

"Why don't we go over there now?" Poppy suggests, getting to her feet. "We could take the box of pictures with us and go through them together, couldn't we?"

I grab hold of her, pulling her back. "No…" I realise I've raised my voice, and make a conscious effort to lower it again. "No, sweetheart."

"Why not?"

"Because we can't just go barging into their house, uninvited. And besides, that box has some of Granny's letters in it. She might not want someone else going through it."

Poppy sits back down again, dragging the box right in front of her. "Okay then… why don't I take out all the pictures with Summer's mummy in, and then we can take them over to Summer and Roan later on?"

I can't really say 'no' to that. It's a perfectly reasonable suggestion, after all. And it's a kind gesture too.

"Okay," I reply, getting up and fetching another box, relieved to find it contains my father's accounts books, and therefore nothing that could possibly remind me of Summer... which is all well and good, except I still can't get her out of my head. And I need to. Because I can't fall for her. No matter how easy that would be. Bryony is the only woman for me, and I need to take back control of my own life, and my own body, and get over this stupid infatuation.

I start sorting through the contents of the box, trying to focus... on anything but Summer. Her smile... her eyes... her lips...

For Christ's sake... Why is this so damned hard?

We spend another couple of hours in the attic, by which time Poppy has gone through the entire box, sorting paperwork from photographs, only occasionally pointing out what she calls 'funny' pictures of her grandmother, usually where Mum's pulling a face, or wearing something outlandish. She's created two neat piles in front of her, one of letters and one of photographs, and beside her, on the trunk, is a third – much smaller – bundle of the pictures she wants to take to Summer. I've managed to find an envelope and she's put the photographs of Elaine inside and, once we've done that, we file everything else away again. I can't face going through my mother's letters right now. Like a lot of other things, it'll wait.

While Poppy's been going through the photographs, I've made fairly short work of dealing with everything else up here and have created two separate stacks of boxes by the loft access... one for dumping at the tip and the other to be taken downstairs, and eventually back to London. Maybe one day, I'll find the time – and the courage – to have a more thorough clear out.

But that day isn't today.

"I'm hungry," Poppy says from behind me, and I turn to see her standing and stretching her hands above her head.

"Well, I think we've earned lunch, don't you?"

She nods and picks up her photograph-stuffed envelope, bringing it with her and letting me hold it while I help her down the ladder, which

I push back up into the attic, closing the access door, before following Poppy downstairs.

"Ham sandwiches?" I suggest as we make our way into the kitchen.

"Yes, please."

She sits up at the table, the envelope beside her, while I prepare a couple of sandwiches and pour her a glass of milk, at the same time, making a pot of coffee for myself, and eventually bringing everything to the table.

Sitting here now with Poppy, watching her drink her milk, it's hard not to remember the times I sat here with my mother, while she read through the letters she'd received from Elaine, which were always full of news about Summer...

It's no good... no matter how hard I try, she's in my head. All the time.

I used to humour Mum sometimes, because I knew she liked having someone to read her letters to, and that Elaine was her best friend, and that she missed her company, but if I'm being honest, I did used to sometimes enjoy listening to the things that Summer was doing. Not only did her life sound so much more exciting than mine, but I was just fascinated by her... even way back then. Just the sound of her name was... well... cool, I suppose. Although I had nothing to be jealous of. Let's face it, Kit isn't exactly a traditional or boring name. And while it's normally a shortened form of Christopher, that doesn't apply in my case. I'm Kit. Just Kit. And nothing else. Unlike Summer, I don't even have a middle name. But there was something about her name... something indefinable. Enigmatic, even. I remember I used to wonder if she'd been named after the season – whether she was a true reflection of summer herself... all brightness and warmth. I had no idea then. But I know now that she is. She's like the sun's rays at dawn; full of promise and expectation.

I pick up my coffee, taking a sip. I wasn't lying when I told Summer I could still remember that day when her mum left her dad. I hadn't been fully aware of what was going on at the time. Like I said, I was busy studying for my exams, and I think that makes everything drift into a hazy blur, but I do recall Dad making lots of phone calls, some of which were in French, while he sat right here in this kitchen, at this table. Mum was really angry. Not at Dad, but at someone, although I wasn't sure who. And then I remember her crying, and Dad sitting her down on his lap and comforting her, telling her it would all be all right. I can only imagine how much worse it must have been for Elaine. And for Summer. They didn't have anyone to comfort them. Except each other, I suppose.

Summer told me yesterday that she was twelve when it happened, which I guess makes her twenty-nine now, because I'm thirty-five...

I nearly drop my cup in shock.

Twenty-nine.

Bryony was twenty-nine when she died...

My beautiful Bryony...

What am I doing?

I need to stop this. Now.

I get up, on the pretence of needing more milk for my coffee. In reality though, that's just a ruse, because what I actually need is to distract myself from thinking about Summer... and Bryony.

But mostly Summer.

As I'm going over to the fridge, my phone starts ringing, and I pull it from my back pocket, putting my cup down on the work surface at the same time, while checking the display and seeing the name 'Ian Clark'. I lean back against the countertop and suck in a breath, connecting the call to my newest and – potentially biggest – customer.

"Hello, Ian." I try to make my voice sound more cheerful than I'm feeling.

"Kit. How are you?" There's that same note of affected concern that I heard from Alan Langley. I've grown used to it now, and I've got no intention of telling him how I really feel, because he's a client and he doesn't actually care, and in any case, I never tell anyone. Not really. Not even the people who do care.

"I'm fine," I lie. Again.

"Good," he says, proving my point. "I wanted to talk to you about our online courses."

That's hardly a surprise. Ian owns a training company, based in Chiswick, and I've spent the last two months or so – on and off – building a range of online courses for him. I finished the last of them just before coming down to Cornwall, and left them with him to go over, expecting it to take a while for him to come back to me. It seems I was wrong.

"We need to make some changes," he says, when I don't reply.

"Okay."

"We've gone over everything you've done and it's not looking quite how we'd thought it would…" He pauses while I wait, wondering what's coming next. "And I'd really like to talk it all over with you, face-to-face."

"Um…" I'm not sure what to say.

"I know you're down in Cornwall at the moment, but this is important to us, Kit. We need to get it right."

"I know you do."

"I'm not asking you to come up here today… or even tomorrow. But I was wondering how you might be fixed for say… Thursday lunchtime?"

He makes it sound like he's doing me a favour, postponing the meeting for a couple of days. And I suppose, in a way, he is. This job is worth a huge amount of money – or it will be, if I ever finish it. And it's in my interests to finish it, because I won't get paid a bean until I do.

"Thursday lunchtime will be fine." What else can I say?

"That's great. Why don't we meet at the same coffee shop as last time? That one here in Chiswick? Do you remember it?"

"Yes. I can be there around twelve, if that's all right with you?"

"Twelve works well for me."

That's good, because I'm not sure I could get there any earlier. We end our call, with him expressing his gratitude, and I put my phone down on the work surface, opening the fridge, taking out the milk, and adding a splash to my coffee, before I remember that I didn't really want any extra milk in the first place. *I'm too distracted for my own good*, I muse, taking a sip.

I appreciate that clients have the right to dictate to me – it goes with the turf. But the timing of this meeting is more than inconvenient. It's a four hour drive back home, assuming there are no hold-ups – and I can't assume that, so we're going to have to leave at seven in the morning, at the very latest, just to be on the safe side. Even then, it's going to be horribly tight to get Poppy to Clare's house in Kew and get across Chiswick, to the café, before noon. Unless…

"What's wrong, Daddy?" I look up to find Poppy staring at me, her sandwich finished and her glass of milk half empty.

"Nothing. I'm just thinking."

"What about?"

I walk over and sit back down at the table. "I've got to go back home for a meeting on Thursday." Poppy's shoulders fall.

"Why?"

"Because the client wants to see me. I can't say 'no' to him, Poppy. He's paying me a lot of money."

"Well, I don't have to come, do I?"

"I can't leave you here, if that's what you're suggesting. But I was just thinking that, rather than getting up really early on Thursday morning, we could go home on Wednesday afternoon instead, and stay there overnight… and maybe get pizzas in for dinner?" There won't be any food in the house, so it feels like a good solution to me. Poppy nods her head, but with less enthusiasm that I might have expected, considering she normally jumps at the chance of pizza.

"What will I do when you go to your meeting?" she asks, sounding very melancholy about the whole thing.

"You'll go to Clare's like you normally do. You can't go to Nanny and Grandad's because they're on holiday." Bryony's parents often help out when Clare can't, but they're in Portugal until Sunday. "You'll be able to see Matthew and Natasha." I try to make the trip sound more enticing, but she doesn't look very enthralled at that prospect either, although I suppose Clare's kids are a little older, at seven and nine, respectively, and they probably don't enjoy playing with a five year-old any more than she enjoys playing with them. "It won't be for long," I add, as a final sweetener.

"And then we'll be coming back here?" she says, with renewed enthusiasm.

"Yes. We've still got a lot to do."

"I know. But I want to see Roan too."

I reach out and cover her tiny hands with mine. "I know you do." I think it's sweet that she's made friends with him so easily, and quickly banish the fleeting thought that I want to come back to see Roan's mummy... because I'm trying to stop thinking like that.

Instead, I stand again, and pick up my phone from the work surface, connecting a call to Clare. She was Bryony's best friend, the two of them having met at university long before I even came on the scene, and when Bryony died, after the funeral was over, Clare was one of the few people to actually offer practical, useful support, rather than unwanted advice about organic oat bars, or the usual platitudes of, 'Call me, if you need to talk,' which people have a tendency to say, knowing – or probably hoping – that you never will. Instead, Clare offered to look after Poppy for me, should the need ever arise. I thanked her, but dismissed the idea at the time, because to start off with, I was stupid enough to think I'd be able to cope with working full-time, running the house and caring for a very demanding two year-old. It was my mother who made me see the light. She knew it wouldn't be that easy and, before she left Kew to come back here to Bluebells, she made me sit down and face the reality of trying to do it all myself. And then she gathered everyone round... me, Bryony's parents and Clare... she cooked us a meal, and between us all, we worked out a schedule that everyone was happy with. Clare said she was pleased; she felt like she was doing her bit to help her oldest friend. My in-laws, Ruth and Edward, were relieved, because they were getting to spend a part of each day with Poppy. And I was able to get on with working, with earning a living and keeping a roof over our heads... and being the best father I could, in spite of my grief. Of course, that was all before Gabrielle... before the guilt and remorse. And the argument. But no-one else knew about that, and after Mum had gone home with my vile words ringing in her ears, no doubt, Clare, Ruth, Edward and I stuck to the schedule, and it's worked for us ever since. We've adapted it around Poppy going to nursery, and more recently, to school, so Clare does less now than she used to, only really helping out during school holidays and when Bryony's parents are away. Even so, I'd be lost without her, and while I think she probably knows that, she never mentions it.

"Hello?" Clare answers eventually, sounding busy… harassed even.

"Hi. It's Kit." I imagine she's perfectly well aware of who's calling her, but judging from he tone of her voice, I feel like it needs clarifying.

"I'm sorry," she says, for no reason. "I'm in a bit of a rush."

"I won't keep you. I just wanted to check whether you're going to be available on Thursday, around lunchtime. I know I said I wouldn't be needing you to watch Poppy for me until we got back at the end of the month, but something's come up."

"I'm really sorry, Kit, but I can't. My… um… my dad's been taken ill."

She sounds upset, like she's trying not to cry and I put all thoughts of my own problems to one side. "I'm so sorry, Clare."

"He had a stroke on Friday." she says, her voice cracking, her emotions clearly strained, even though I get the feeling she needs to talk. I remember that need, when Bryony was ill, to just tell someone – anyone, really – how my life was literally falling apart around me, and how much of a struggle it was sometimes to try and keep hold of all the pieces. "It's a bad one, and my mum's not coping at all. So she's staying with us, and I'm trying to get someone to look after the kids, while I take her to the hospital, because Tim's boss is being a complete bastard and won't give him any time off." Her husband is a marketing executive, and although the friendship was really between Bryony and Clare, whenever we got together as two couples, rather than the girls doing something by themselves, Tim and I always got along well. He's a nice guy.

"I'm really sorry to hear that, Clare. I wish there was something I could do." I can't see the point in offering to do anything practical. I'm over two hundred miles away, and saying 'let me know if I can help' would be pointless, because I can't. Not from here.

"Don't worry," she says, her voice a little stronger now. "I'm just sorry I can't help you."

"Don't give it another thought. I'll work something out." I'm not sure what yet...

"I hate to cut and run, Kit, but I really need to go," she says, sounding more anxious again.

"If you need to talk, Clare... you know where I am." I wonder, for a second whether I'm making the same platitudes I heard when Bryony died, and because I hated hearing them myself, and for the sake of their friendship, I add, "I mean it."

"I know," she says. "But I'm okay. Really. I've got Tim."

That's a bold and stark reminder – as if I needed one – that when Bryony died, after I'd argued with my mother and she'd left, I had no-one. Not really. At least, no-one who was mine. Except for Poppy. Obviously. But she was two, and I could hardly bare my soul to her.

I was alone. Truly alone.

"Take care," I say quietly.

"You too."

We end the call and I turn back to Poppy, feeling sorry for Clare, but wondering what on earth I'm going to do now.

"What happened?" she asks, looking up at me.

"Clare can't look after you on Thursday."

"Oh," she says, smiling – and I can't blame her for that. She's not aware of the circumstances and I'm not going to explain them either. She doesn't need to know. "Does that mean I'll have to stay here?"

"You can't."

"I could... if you asked Summer. I'll bet she'd let me stay with her and Roan, while you went back home."

"Absolutely not."

"Why?"

"Because we don't know them very well. It's a huge imposition."

"I'm not an impos... imposs... I'm not one of those," she says, looking affronted, even though she has no idea what the word means, and I have to smile.

"No, you're not. But I can't just ask someone I don't know if you can stay with them for a whole day."

"But you do know Summer, don't you? You said Granny and Summer's mummy were best friends. And we've got all these photographs to take over to her," she says, tapping the envelope. "So it wouldn't be an impos... one of those things." I'm wracking my brain, trying to think of a way out of Poppy's suggestion, but I'm struggling... mainly because I need someone to look after her and I don't have that many alternatives. I don't have any, actually.

Chapter Nine

Summer

"Let me open the flour and you can weigh it out," I tell Roan, who's standing beside me at the kitchen table. We've already weighed out butter and sugar, and mixed them together without making too much mess, although the eggs come next, so I know this comparative cleanliness won't last long. I don't mind that either. Roan enjoys cooking and I like helping him… although at one stage today, I thought we were never going to get started… not when the bathroom tap developed a leak and I had to dash to the DIY store to buy a new washer, and then come back and fit it. Which is why we've only just started the making the cakes we had planned for this morning, at two o'clock in the afternoon.

"How much flour do we need?" he asks, picking up the tablespoon.

"Two hundred grams."

He starts to decant flour from the open bag into the bowl, that's sitting on top of the scales, keeping a watchful eye on the digital display.

"Do you think we'll have enough to take some over to Poppy and her dad?" he asks, with the full spoon poised, mid-air.

"Probably, if that's what you want." I can't help smiling, because I think it's such a lovely gesture of his to want to share his cakes. He's always been quite good at sharing things like toys, but cake, or chocolate? They're a different matter, and it makes me wonder whether – in a very cute, adorable, six year-old way – he's got a 'thing' for Poppy… like I have for Poppy's dad.

Yes, I know he's got problems, which he needs to work out – and I'm happy to help him with that, if he'll let me. And I know he can be quite abrupt, bordering on rude, at times. But having spent almost an hour talking to him yesterday, and several hours thinking about him last night, once Roan had gone to bed, I can't deny that I like him. And I don't just like him as Maggie's son, or as Poppy's dad. I like him as a man… a troubled, but utterly gorgeous, really very sexy man, who I wouldn't mind spending a great deal more time with, preferably on our own. I'm not for one moment suggesting that he's ready to get into anything with me. He's not. But maybe if we can spend some time together, and talk some more – about him, this time, rather than me – then I might be able to help him… and who knows? Maybe there might be something in the future for us one day. Because, to be honest, there's nothing I'd like more.

"Is that enough?" Roan's voice breaks into my daydream and I turn to him.

"Yes. It says two hundred. See?" I point to the display and he nods his head rather enthusiastically, pleased with himself for getting it right, but evidently forgetting that he's still got half a spoonful of flour in his hand, which he promptly tips down my front.

"Oh… I see how it is…" I narrow my eyes at him, and reach into the flour bag, grabbing a small handful and pulling it out, before throwing it at him. "Ha! Got you!"

He giggles and goes to reach for the bag himself, just as the doorbell rings.

"Oh golly… look at the state of me." I glance down at my flour-covered bright yellow sundress and do my best to wipe the worst off as I make my way to the door and pull it open… to be faced with Kit and Poppy, who's carrying a large brown envelope and smiling broadly, unlike her father, who's frowning and looking confused.

"Hi." I greet them both, patting my hands on the sides of my already dusty dress.

"Um… hello." Kit's frown deepens and he stares at the residue of flour down my front, before his eyes move to Roan, who's standing beside me, his hair, face and t-shirt still caked with flour too. "Have we interrupted something?" Kit asks, his eyes moving back to me.

"Not really. We were just baking."

"And do you always cover yourselves in flour when you bake?"

"No. We thought we've have a flour fight."

"A flour fight?" He sounds very disapproving and the part of me that likes him most wants to tell him to lighten up… and maybe come in and join us. Because we're having fun, and it's even more obvious to me than it was before that he's forgotten how to do that.

"Yes. It wasn't intentional. Well… not entirely. We just got a bit carried away."

"I see." I'm not sure he does.

"Do you want to come in?"

"Just for a minute."

He steps into the living room, and for once, Poppy doesn't make a move to go and play with Roan, and because he's covered with flour, he doesn't ask her.

"You wouldn't have caught us in such a mess," I explain, feeling the need for some reason, "but we're a bit late starting our baking. I had to change the washer on the bathroom tap this morning, because it sprung a leak."

"You? You changed a washer?"

He sounds surprised.

"Yes. I'm quite capable, you know. I'm a twenty-first century woman. I can change plugs and lightbulbs too." I smile up at him to show I'm joking, not offended, but he doesn't smile back.

"Sorry," he says and I shake my head, because he clearly doesn't get it.

"What for?"

"For misjudging you… well, for judging you at all, really."

"You don't have to be sorry. And anyway, I don't like that word."

"Which word?"

"Sorry. I think it's one of the saddest words in the English language. And I'm not in the mood for being sad."

He stares at me for a moment, and then shakes his head, just once, just quickly – so quickly, it would have been easy to miss, if I hadn't been staring at him too.

"Well, I'm still sorry that we interrupted your baking… and your flour fight. But I've got a favour to ask of you."

"You have?" I'm surprised myself now, but I hope it doesn't show too much.

"Yes. I—I know I don't have the right to ask anything of you… especially not when I keep being so rude, but I have a problem…" *Only one?* "I've got to go back to London for a meeting on Thursday, and unfortunately I can't get out of it, and I was wondering if I could possibly leave Poppy with you for the day. She won't be any trouble…" His voice fades and a smile forms on my lips.

"I know she won't, and I don't mind in the slightest. Roan will love having her here, and I'm sure we'll have lots of fun together. Do you need me to keep her overnight on Wednesday, if…"

"No!" he barks and I actually jump. "Sorry," he says quickly, then adds, "I'm not going to stay up in town overnight, not if…" He stops talking and I wonder what he was going to say.

"It's really no bother for her to stay. She'll be perfectly safe." I try to reassure him.

"I'm going to leave early on Thursday," he says, ignoring me. "I'll drive up to Chiswick, have the meeting there and come back straight afterwards. I won't even go home."

"Really? There's no need for that, Kit. You'll be exhausted, and Poppy will be fine here with us. I promise."

"I'm not going to change my mind, no matter what you say."

It's hard to believe I'm the one doing him the favour here. But I can tell just from looking at him that it's not worth arguing over any longer, even though I do feel a little offended now, that he still doesn't seem to trust me to look after his daughter.

"Why don't you trust me?" I ask, unable to stop myself and his eyes widen, as he leans back slightly, seemingly shocked by my question. "You know who I am, Kit."

His shoulders drop slightly and he shakes his head. "It's not that. And I didn't mean to imply that I don't trust you. It's just... well..." He pauses and I wonder if he's actually going to offer an explanation, but then he takes a deep breath and says, "Since my wife... since Bryony died, I've had to rely on her parents and a friend of hers to look after Poppy for me when I'm working. But I always pick her up from them in the evenings. We used to sometimes leave her overnight with my in-laws when Bryony was alive, but I—I don't like to... not since... I'm so—" He cuts off the word and, even though I'm feeling terribly sorry for him myself, I smile and take a step closer.

"You're what?"

"I was going to say I'm sorry, but you said it makes you sad."

"Well, it does. And, in any case, you've got nothing to be sorry for. I don't think I'd like the idea of leaving Roan somewhere overnight either, especially if I was hundreds of miles away, so I do understand. Honestly. I'll tell you what, when you drop her off on Thursday morning, why don't you let me have some pyjamas, or a nightdress, or whatever she wears in bed, and I'll get her changed, and that way, if you're running late at all, she can either fall asleep here and you can just take her home, or you can put her straight to bed when you get back."

"Thank you," he says, nodding his head in agreement, and looking as though he wants to say 'sorry' again, although I don't think he will. Not now.

"What time will you need to leave on Thursday?" I ask quickly, just in case he has actually got designs on apologising for the umpteenth time, for doing absolutely nothing wrong.

"I was planning on getting away at seven."

"So you'll want to drop Poppy off just before then?"

He pulls a slightly anxious face, which just makes him look even more handsome, I suppose because he normally looks quite self assured, or angry, so this expression is rather unexpected, and a little vulnerable... and quite cute. "Is that too early?"

"No. I'll make sure I'm up. I can't guarantee Roan will be… we're both owls, not larks, but I'll do my best to drag myself out of bed."

He nods his head. "I should probably give you my number," he says. "Just in case you need to contact me… if there's an emergency or something. I don't want to forget it on Thursday morning."

"I'm sure there won't be any emergencies, but it's better to be safe than sorry."

I fetch my phone from the coffee table and he rattles off his number, while I add it to my contacts list.

"Can I have yours?" he asks, and I glance up at him. "Just in case I need to call you."

"To check up on me?" I tease, but he blushes, rather than laughing.

"No," he says quickly. "I'm sure…"

"It's okay," I interrupt, and give him my number, watching him tap it into his phone.

We stand awkwardly for a moment, and then he takes a breath. "Well, I suppose we'd better let you get back to your baking…"

"Wait a minute, Daddy. What about these?" Poppy holds up the envelope, and I suddenly become aware again that our two children are standing beside us, and have been all the while we've been talking.

"Oh, yes." He takes the envelope from her and holds it out to me.

"What's this?" I flip it open, glancing inside.

"We've been going through a few boxes in the attic this morning, and we found some photographs of our mothers, when they were younger. Poppy thought you might like to have them."

"Did she?" I look down at his daughter and give her a smile. "Thank you, Poppy."

"Aren't you going to look?" she asks, and because she's been so kind, I feel like I can't say 'no' to her, so I reach inside the envelope and pull out a couple of the photographs, seeing images of my mother as a teenager, alongside her dearest friend, their hair much too large for their faces, and their clothes so different from today's fashions. I've never seen them looking like this before… so young and carefree, and the pictures start to blur before my eyes.

"I—I'll look at them later, I think," I mumble, replacing the photographs inside the envelope, not wanting to embarrass myself by crying in front of Poppy… or Kit. "But thank you for bringing them over. It's very kind of you."

"Are you okay?" Kit steps closer… close enough that I can smell the rich, masculine, citrus scent of his body wash.

"Yes," I manage to say. "And I really am grateful. I'll look at them later. I promise."

They both nod their heads and Kit starts to move away, towards the front door, which seems like the wrong thing to do now, because their visit has ended under a cloud, when all they wanted – all Poppy wanted – was to give me something nice to remember my mother by.

"I presume the fact that you've cleared out the attic means you're making progress at the house?" I say, the words rather tumbling out of my mouth.

Kit stills and looks down at me. "Well, not really. We've done the attic, and the garage. And I've pottered about a bit, but we've still got the living rooms and – worst of all – Mum's bedroom and her writing desk to go through. I'm absolutely dreading both of those."

"Can I help?" I offer, without thinking. "I mean, I could go through your mother's clothes, if you want?"

I fully expect him to say 'no', simply because he says no to everything, but to my surprise, his eyes light up. "You wouldn't mind?" he says.

"No, of course not."

I can actually hear his sigh of relief. "I really wasn't looking forward to sorting through Mum's… um… clothing," he says, hesitating over his words, and I feel myself smiling, knowing that what he really means is he didn't want to go through his mother's underwear. He just doesn't want to say that in front of the children.

"Well, it's easier for me. She wasn't my mother." And I do remember how difficult it was when my own mum died and I had to do the same dreadful clear out, prior to moving the bedrooms around, so that Roan could have more space in the room that had been mine for a while, and I could move into my mother's old room. It was more practical that way, and I knew it made sense, but it was something I found incredibly hard to do. I also remember how Maggie was here, every single day, and how she helped me get through it.

"Are you free tomorrow afternoon?" he asks, surprising me once more with his eagerness.

"Yes. I'll have to bring Roan, obviously."

"That's fine. The children can play and, if you don't mind, I'll leave you to sort out Mum's bedroom, and I'll be free to go through all her paperwork." He pulls a face. "I've been putting it off for as long as possible, but I'd rather look through her bills and bank statements and try to work out what on earth she's managed to get up to with her money, than deal with heaven knows what in her chest of drawers." He rolls his eyes and I just about manage not to laugh, relieved that, between us, we've rescued his visit. And that I'll get to spend some time with him tomorrow. Obviously.

Chapter Ten

Kit

I don't even know how that happened.

I mean, one minute we were making arrangements for Summer to have Poppy for the day – which nearly resulted in yet another argument – and the next, I was asking her to help me go through Mum's things.

It wasn't what I'd intended at all.

I'd been trying my best to stop thinking about her. Not that my best was very good, or very successful, it would seem.

But then I hadn't expected her to cry. Or to nearly cry. Because she came close. *Really* close. And I felt bad about that, because we'd only taken the pictures over there to cheer her up, and they'd had the opposite effect. I feel bad about myself most of the time – obviously – but seeing Summer with tears in her eyes just amplified all those feelings of self-loathing that I've grown accustomed to during the last three years.

Of course, she then offered to help with clearing out Mum's things, and I suppose I said 'yes', because I felt so guilty about upsetting her…

No, that's not true. At least, it's not entirely true. I said 'yes', because I've been dreading going through my mother's personal belongings in her bedroom, and Summer was giving me a way out. And I took it.

And, naturally, I said 'yes' to make Poppy happy, because she'll get to play with Roan all afternoon too.

And I'll get to spend some more time with Summer.

That wasn't a consideration in me saying 'yes', of course. After all, we'll be in separate parts of the house, but… oh, who am I kidding? I want to spend some time with her. There's no point in trying to deny it, or fight it, any longer. I want her. Desperately.

So shoot me.

I have to admit, when we first got over there, I was kind of confused by her. She had flour on her dress and a little in her hair, and even a few smudges on her face, and Roan was virtually covered in the stuff. But there was no denying, they looked really cute. Especially Summer, who I don't think has any idea how utterly sexy and completely adorable she actually is. Even when she's not coated in flour.

Of course, seeing her like that made me want to wipe those smears away from her cheeks with my thumbs, and to straighten her hair and help her clean up her dress… all while getting up close and very personal with her.

My befuddled state of mind wasn't helped at all when she told me that she doesn't like the word 'sorry', because it makes her sad. That threw me into a quandary, because I have so much to apologise to her for, but the idea of making her sad was somehow worse than not apologising. Because she's someone who deserves to be happy. More than anyone I've ever met. Of course, being me, I had to jump down her throat, when she offered to have Poppy overnight… and my newest bout of rudeness meant I owed her an explanation – which I gave her, even though it meant talking about Bryony… albeit briefly. She was really understanding about that too. Although why that would surprise me, I don't know, being as she seems to be understanding about everything.

But that's just Summer, I think.

It's who she is.

Poppy seemed to be quite tired when we got back here, and settled herself on the enormous sofa in one of my mother's two living rooms…

the one with a television. She flicked through the channels until she came across something she wanted to watch and, once I'd got her a drink, I left her to it, fetching a roll of bin liners from the kitchen before making my way to the more formal drawing room, that was rarely used when I was a child, other than when someone came to visit, or when my father wanted somewhere quiet to sit. This room looks out over the back garden, and has french doors, leading onto the terrace, unlike the other room, where Poppy is, which has an archway that leads into the conservatory, and is much more family oriented, and where we spent much more time together.

As well as getting rid of old magazines and newspapers, which I don't doubt will be lying around, there's also a large sideboard along the wall opposite the french doors, which I really need to go through. I doubt I'll find anything much, because I know most of Mum's papers were kept in her writing desk, but while Poppy's tired, and otherwise occupied, there's no reason not to take a couple of hours, just sorting through anything else that might be in here.

I push open the door and am hit by a wall of heat, only now realising that neither Poppy nor I have been in here since we arrived… and from the way the room feels, I doubt my mother came in here very often either, so I go over to the french windows and throw them open to let in some much needed air, before turning back into the room, and surveying the scene, my heart clenching in my chest as I spy a large photograph, which has pride of place, in the centre of the sideboard, directly opposite me. It's surrounded by other framed images of my parents and myself, both together and separately, at various stages of our lives.

Like a magnet though, I'm drawn to that one photograph, and dropping the bin liners on the sofa as I pass, I make my way across the room, until I'm standing in front of the picture of myself… and Bryony. A lump forms in my throat and I pick up the frame – a rather nice marquetry one – and examine the image more closely, although I don't really need to, because I can remember the moment it was taken as though it were yesterday.

We were standing together, in the neatly arranged gardens outside the large manor house that Bryony and I had chosen for our wedding venue, beneath an arch of pink climbing roses. I was wearing a grey suit, and Bryony looked absolutely stunning, in a simple cream dress, with an embroidered bodice and flared silk skirt. This isn't one of the official photographs though. We're not looking at the camera in a studied pose. And I imagine my father must have taken this. I can remember him flitting around at the time, his camera held to his face like he was worried he might miss something if he moved it away. But he didn't miss anything here. He's captured an image so perfect… so sublime. Bryony and I are facing each other. I've got my arms around her and we're staring into each other's eyes, as though nothing else in the world exists, or matters. I can recall, even now, that it felt just like that at the time. If I remember rightly, the official photographer had just gone off to round up a couple of people he wanted to be in the next set of pictures with us, and we'd been left to our own devices. Dad must have still been there, but we were clearly oblivious to him, and were just completely focused on each other. I don't remember saying anything. I don't remember needing to. It was a brief few minutes of solitude in an otherwise busy day, when so many people made claims on our time, but I can clearly remember, at that precise moment as I held Bryony in my arms, that I felt like the luckiest man in the world. The woman who owned my heart had just vowed to be mine for life… and as far as I was concerned, it didn't get any better than that. Of course, we had no idea that the life we'd pledged to each other would be so short-lived. We just knew that we were happy. We were in love. It was our day… the beginning of everything.

The beginning of the end, I suppose.

This is the first time I've ever seen this photograph. Until now, I didn't even know Dad had captured it… not having come into this room, even on visits to the house. But seeing it here, now… coupling it together with my memories… it's all too much.

I clasp the picture frame to my chest and stumble back to the sofa, lying down along its length, and I let my head rest against the cushion behind me.

Last April would have been our eighth wedding anniversary, and although Bryony didn't quite make it to our fifth, I can still remember every single one.

For our first, my business was still getting off the ground, but I booked us a weekend away in Paris, only telling Bryony about it on the way to the airport. She thought we were just going out for dinner, and had no idea I'd packed our bags and they were hidden away in the boot of my car. She was so excited, I thought she was going to burst, and that alone made all the complicated planning and secrecy worthwhile. We had the most romantic two days, mostly spent in our hotel room, which I suppose some might argue was a waste of the airfare… except nothing was ever wasted on Bryony.

The following year, my business was much more established, and was even quite profitable by then, so I arranged for us to take a week off, and we went to Italy, spending three days in Rome and four in Florence. We planned that trip together, so it wasn't much of a surprise for Bryony, but she enjoyed it nonetheless, as did I. Because we were together.

By the time of our third anniversary, we'd had Poppy. She was two months old, and I don't think either of us was really in the mood for a romantic holiday. All we'd have done is sleep anyway. But we got Bryony's parents to babysit and went out for dinner together. We spent the evening laughing, enjoying ourselves, and looking back on our previous two anniversaries, making comparisons between those lazy, amorous holidays, and our snatched dinner. We didn't regret a second of it though. Poppy was the embodiment of our love, and we wouldn't have changed a thing about her. Either of us.

Our fourth anniversary was perfect. Again. Poppy was old enough to be left for a night – just one night – with Bryony's mum and dad. And I booked us into a very exclusive hotel in the Cotswolds. The ensuite bathroom was bigger than our bedroom at home, and that was the first – and last – time I ever made love to Bryony in a bath. It's not an occasion I'm likely to forget.

It was on that night away, lying in bed, all sleepy and satisfied, that we decided we wanted to have another baby, although, of course, our plans never came to anything in the end. Bryony made it to Poppy's second birthday, but she was very sick by then, and she was taken from me, just a few weeks later, and I spent our fifth anniversary by myself, quietly at home. I'd planned to mark the occasion by taking my beautiful wife back to the Amalfi Coast, where we'd spent our honeymoon. But that wasn't to be.

"God… I miss you," I whisper, even though there's no one to hear me.

I don't believe in an after-life. I know she isn't listening. I know she's gone, and she's never coming back. But I still miss her. Every single day.

And that's what makes my feelings for Summer so confusing. I'm not over Bryony yet. I know I'm not. So how can I be feeling the way I do for someone else?

She walks towards me, and I take in her beautiful off-white lace dress, draping along the sand behind her, the outline of her body barely disguised by the gossamer fabric, as the sun sets behind her; the plunging v-neckline doing a lot more than hinting at what lies beneath. She smiles and my heart skips a beat, as the wind catches her flaming hair, and she reaches up to adjust the garland of flowers that adorns her head, before continuing her slow progression towards me. I'm standing on the shoreline, waves lapping over my bare feet, wearing pale trousers and an open-necked shirt… waiting for my bride's arrival. Waiting for her to be mine…

She stands before me now, looking up into my eyes, and a faceless man says some words in the distance, which I can't hear – and I don't need to. And then I'm holding her in my arms, kissing her deeply and passionately, my ring on her finger, my heart in her hands.

And now… now we're in a bedroom, of sorts. It's a hut, on the beach, although there are no walls to speak of. Instead, there are posts, with diaphanous curtains held up between them, swaying to and fro, with each gentle puff of sea breeze. In the centre of the room is an enormous low bed, covered in brightly coloured throws and cushions, the setting sun radiating across its surface. Unable to wait a second longer, we've run up the beach together hand in hand, and now we're standing in this romantic space, staring into each other's eyes.

"I love you," she whispers.

"I love you more."

Her eyes are sparkling in the dimming sunlight, and she turns her back to me and, moving her hair aside, I slowly undo the buttons down her back. They're small and fiddly, but I don't mind, because with every unfastening, another inch of soft flesh is revealed and I kiss each one with tender care, until she's breathing hard and fast, desperately anticipating my touch. When my task is complete and her back is exposed, from nape to buttock, I run a fingertip down her spine and she shudders, moaning softly, before I push her dress from her shoulders, letting it fall and pool around her ankles.

She's wearing nothing but a white lace thong, which I remove before turning her around again and laying her gently on the mattress.

I quickly remove the only two items of clothing I'm wearing, and I lie between her parted legs, entering her without a word, and hearing her husky gasp at my intimate intrusion. But before she can even think about that, I start to move inside her, pushing her legs further and further apart, until her body's shaking and she's crying out my name…

The sound of the doorbell wakes me and I sit up, startled, my arousal not only painful, but also obvious.

"Daddy?" Poppy comes running in and I quickly lower the photograph I'm still clutching, to cover my discomfort. "There's someone at the door." She states the obvious and stares at me from the end of the sofa.

"I know. I'm getting there."

"Did you fall asleep?" She eyes me suspiciously as I get to my feet, still keeping the framed picture in its strategic place.

"Yes."

Poppy shakes her head and follows me out to the hall, where I open the door and actually let out a groan… because standing right in front of me is Summer… the woman who's just been occupying my very erotic, but also very romantic, dream. Roan is standing beside her, smiling at my daughter.

"Hello," Summer says, her voice whispering across my skin, and I struggle for breath, recalling the words she said to me, at least in my own head, just moments ago.

"Hi." I manage a reply and let go of the photograph with one hand, running my fingers through my hair, and making the mistake of letting my eyes stray from Summer's face. She's changed out of her yellow sundress, and is now wearing a pair of those incredibly short shorts, the hems of which are frayed, with a white vest, and on top of that, a blue-grey kimono type of thing, with a long fringe that comes down to the the middle of her toned thighs. *Is looking that good even legal?*

"We... um... we brought you some cakes," she says, rather unexpectedly and I shift my gaze up to her face again, only now realising that she's got a plastic container in her hand and she's holding it out to me.

"Cakes?" I query, although I don't take the box.

"Yes. We were making them earlier?" She must think I'm really dense to have forgotten already. But that's not surprising, being as I'm behaving like an idiot. Because I've also just realised that it's raining... not hard, but it's raining nonetheless, and I haven't had the manners to invite her and Roan into the house.

"Please... come in." I step aside.

"Is it okay to leave our umbrella there?" she says, nodding to one side, where she's obviously leant her umbrella up against the wall beside the front door.

"Yes. It'll be fine. Come in out of the rain."

They're not actually 'in' the rain, being as there's a small porch at the front of my mother's house, but it's the thought that counts, and Summer ushers Roan into the hallway, following behind, and I close the door, turning to face them.

"Do you want to come and watch TV with me?" Poppy says to Roan and he looks up at his mother, who nods her head and gives him an encouraging smile. He's surprisingly shy when he's not at home, but he and Poppy disappear into the living room, leaving Summer and I alone. I'm still holding the photograph in front of me, but the necessity seems to have passed, at least for the best part, even though she looks beautiful beyond words. I think it's probably the talk of cakes, and rain, and umbrellas... and possibly the presence of our children that's had that effect. So, I put the picture down on the seat of the monk's settle beside me, and then wish I hadn't… or at least, I wish I'd put it face down, because as Summer glances over at it, a shadow crosses her eyes.

Chapter Eleven

Summer

The smell of baking wafts into the living room, where I'm sitting on the sofa, the photographs that Kit and Poppy brought over spread out in front of me.

Roan's still upstairs playing, where I left him after we went up there to change when we'd finished making the cakes. He was far too flour coated not to at least change his top. He was literally depositing white powder everywhere. And as for myself? Roan managed to get a great blob of cake mixture on my dress, as well as the flour, so I wanted to take it off straight away and put it in the washing machine, before it marked permanently. I've changed into shorts and a vest top, and because it's clouded over, I've added a light kimono jacket as well, and have been sitting down here ever since going through the photographs.

I've surprised myself by not crying at all. I fully expected to, given my reaction when I opened the envelope earlier, but looking at the array of pictures, showing Maggie and my mum in various poses – some silly, and some much more cute – I've done nothing but smile, recalling their friendship and how happy they made each other. And they did. Friendships like that don't happen very often, and I'm glad they were able to share so much… which shows in the images before me.

"Mum?" Roan appears at the door to the stairway.

"Yes?" I look up at him.

"Are the cakes ready yet?"

I glance at the timer on the DVD player beneath the television. "In about a minute," I tell him and I gather up the photographs, putting them back in the envelope.

Roan hasn't shown much interest in them so far – probably because he's more interested in the prospect of cake – but I have no doubt he will at some point, and then I'll have to explain who these two women were, and what they meant to me... and to him. He remembers them both, naturally, but not as they look in the pictures... not young and carefree and silly, but more as two middle aged, but still fun and slightly eccentric ladies, who featured large in his life, and then were gone. Still, those reminders are for another time. Another day. For now, cake beckons.

Leaving the envelope on the table, we make our way through to the kitchen and I open the oven door, where the fairy cakes are nicely browned and ready to come out.

"They look good," Roan says, his eyes beaming.

"They do indeed."

He looks up at me. "Can we still take some over to Poppy?" he asks.

I bite my bottom lip, wondering whether I should really force our attentions onto Kit and Poppy for a second time in one day. We'll be seeing them tomorrow, after all.

"Why don't we take them tomorrow?" I suggest. "We're going there anyway."

His face falls. "I wanted to take them today," he says, "while they're warm and taste really good."

In other words, he wants to go right now.

And, thinking about it, I suppose it can't hurt. After all, it would give me the opportunity to thank them again, for letting me have those photographs... something else which I know could very well wait until tomorrow. But then, Roan's quite right... cake does taste better when it's warm.

"Oh... it's raining." I hesitate on the threshold of our house, looking up at the sky.

"Let's take an umbrella," Roan suggests, clearly determined not to be put off, and I go back inside and fetch the large umbrella from under the stairs, rejoining him at the front door, before we set off.

The village is deserted. There's no-one on the green, no-one outside the shop, and no-one in the tea room either. It may be August, but you'd never know it... not from the lack of people, or from the weather.

Getting to Bluebells, having taken the walk at a fair pace, Roan struggles with the gate, but manages it eventually, closing it again behind us, and we walk up to the front door, nestling beneath the tiny porch as I lower the umbrella and balance it up against the wall, before ringing the doorbell.

I'm fairly sure that Kit and Poppy must be at home, since his car is parked on the driveway, but we wait for quite some time before the door finally opens, and Kit stands before us, looking a little dishevelled. Utterly gorgeous – obviously – but a little dishevelled, nonetheless.

He seems surprised to see us, although that's perfectly understandable, considering he was only at our house a short while ago, and wasn't expecting us to turn up unannounced.

"Hello," I say, because on second thoughts, he seems to be actually dumbstruck, rather than just surprised.

"Hi," he replies and I notice then that he's holding a framed picture of some kind, although it's turned away from us, so I can't see what it's of. Whatever it is, he lets go of it with one hand, and pushes his fingers back through his hair, possibly attempting to straighten it, although he doesn't have much success.

"We... um... we brought you some cakes," I say, when it becomes clear he's not going to add anything to our conversation. He seems to be daydreaming, actually, like he's somewhere else entirely. I hold out the plastic container I've used to bring the cakes over, and while he looks at it, he doesn't take it from me.

"Cakes?" he replies, as though he has no idea what I'm talking about, which is odd, considering he knew we were making them. I was covered in flour when he came round, after all.

"Yes. We were making them earlier?" I remind him, and he finally seems to focus... and to notice that it's raining.

"Please... come in," he says, stepping back into the house.

"Is it okay to leave our umbrella there?" I ask, remembering that it's still propped up against the wall beside the door.

"Yes. It'll be fine. Come in out of the rain."

I nudge Roan forward and he steps inside Maggie's hallway, wiping his feet on the mat, without me having to prompt him. I follow suit and then turn to find Kit standing right behind me, having closed the door. He's still clutching that picture, but we're distracted by Poppy, who suddenly asks Roan if he wants to go and watch television with her. He looks to me for approval and I nod my head, before the two of them run off through the doorway, which I think leads to the living room.

Left alone, Kit and I stand and stare at each other for a moment until he seems to come to his senses and suddenly puts the picture down on the monk's settle beside him.

Now that I can see it, I can't help glancing at the photograph in the frame, noticing a couple – clearly a bride and groom – standing in each other's arms. The man is very obviously Kit, which must make the woman Bryony and even from here I can see how beautiful she must have been... and how in love they were.

This explains why he was looking so dishevelled when he answered the door. He must have been going through some of his mother's things and have come across this photograph. I can only imagine the effect that would have had on him... and now we've turned up and interrupted his memories... of happier times, I imagine.

"We... we really only wanted to bring the cakes over," I blurt out, putting the plastic box down on the monk's settle beside the photograph and catching a second look at the woman, her short dark hair surrounding her very beautiful face, her eyes fixed on Kit's, his arms tight around her. God... they were perfect together.

I turn and look at him again, to find him staring at me, a strange expression on his face, which I can only describe as a kind of brooding bewilderment.

"And I wanted to thank you again for letting me have those photographs of our mothers," I add, remembering the other reason for my visit. "I've just been looking at them, while the cakes were baking, but I wanted to apologise. I—I didn't mean to get upset earlier…" I let my voice fade, because I'm not sure how to explain my feelings to him… not about my mother, anyway.

"There's nothing to apologise for," he says, his voice a lot softer than I'd expected, given his appearance, not to mention the way he usually is with me. "I know how hard it can be to look at photographs."

His eyes drop to the picture beside us and the emotion on his face is heartbreaking to witness.

"Your wife was very beautiful," I whisper and he turns his attention back to me again.

"Yes," he says, letting out a sigh. "Yes, she was."

I smile up at him, but he doesn't seem capable of returning the gesture, and I decide the time has come for me to leave… for us to leave. I wouldn't go so far as to say that I regret coming over here, but I think we could have timed our visit better. I think he'd rather be alone with his memories right now… and having seen his wife, I can't say I blame him.

"We should be going," I say, stepping away from him. "Before the weather gets any worse."

He still doesn't respond and I move further down the hall, popping my head around the door to the living room, where the children went earlier, and telling Roan we're leaving. He seems disappointed, but then so am I. This wasn't how I'd expected our visit to play out.

Although I'm not sure what I'd expected.

We only came over here with cakes, after all.

Roan's been in bed for over half an hour and I'm trying to watch a really terrible film on television. I've poured myself a glass of wine to make it more tolerable, but I'm just thinking about going upstairs for a long soak in the bath instead, when my phone rings, and I pick it up, my mouth falling open when I see the name 'Kit' on the screen.

"Hello?" I answer straight away.

"Hi." His voice is deep and kind of comforting. Which is quite odd, considering I hadn't realised I needed to be comforted until just now. "I—I just called to ask if you're okay," he says after a very short pause.

"Me?" I'm shocked. Why would he do that?

"Yes. You left really suddenly earlier. I wanted to make sure I hadn't said anything to offend you... not that I actually said very much, if memory serves. But I know I'm quite good at causing offence."

I can't help smiling, even though I know he can't see me. "Of course you hadn't. I wasn't in the least offended. I got the feeling you'd been looking at the photograph of your wedding day... of your wife... and I think we arrived at a bad time. I... well, I just got the feeling you needed some time to yourself."

There's a slightly longer pause, before he says, "Thank you," very quietly.

"You don't have to thank me, Kit. We interrupted you at a difficult moment." He coughs, but doesn't say anything. "I hope you enjoyed the cakes," I add, to lighten the mood a little.

"Yes, we did," he replies. "They're really good."

"Well, Roan's more responsible for that than I am."

"Somehow I doubt that," he says, and I wonder if that's the first compliment he's paid me. I can't remember now. But either way, I'll take it.

Chapter Twelve

Kit

I hang up the phone, having just finished complimenting Summer on her cakes, and apologising again for being a bit quiet earlier. 'Quiet' would be an understatement. I was positively silent when she came over. But that was because of the dream I'd just had, which she'd interrupted at a critical moment... and because she'd seen the photograph of Bryony and me on our wedding day, and had commented on how beautiful my wife was... which was true, of course, but which only served to remind me that I'd been thinking about Bryony when I'd fallen asleep on the sofa. I'd been whispering to no-one in particular how much I missed her... and then I'd dreamt of taking Summer to bed as my bride. That had me more than confused, as well as aroused, and rather shaken.

And it showed. I know it did.

So I had to phone her and make sure she was okay.

Simply because I'd been... well, weird.

She was okay. At least she said she was. And I believed her, because I honestly don't think Summer is capable of lying, not even to make someone else feel better. She said she left because she thought I needed some time to myself... which I did. But hearing her say that was quite disconcerting. How could she have known? Even allowing for the fact that she'd seen the photograph… how could she have known that all I needed at that point was to sit by myself for a few hours – or days – to think about what the hell is going on in my head… about why my thoughts are so tied up together with these two women, why everything I do seems to weave between them, as though they're connected. Even though they've never met.

Of course, the connection between them is obvious.

It's me.

Wandering the house, with Summer's voice still ringing in my ears, unable to rest, or even contemplate going to bed, I can't deny the attraction I feel for her. It's blindingly obvious, every time she's standing in front of me, and every time I close my eyes and go to sleep. And, while I know those are only dreams, they're also a reflection of how I feel. Because I can't escape the fact that I didn't dream about sex at all – I didn't even *think* about sex at all – from the time when I walked out of that hotel room in Manchester, awash with guilt, to the moment I set eyes on Summer. And that reawakening, or whatever it is, has to mean something. I've got no idea what. But it must mean something.

At the same time though, Bryony – or the memory of Bryony, I suppose, if we're being strictly accurate – is a constant. Thoughts of her never leave my mind, and I'm not sure I want them to. Because to leave her behind would be admitting she's really gone. And while I know she's never coming back, to put our relationship in the past is a step too far for me at the moment.

I'm just not ready.

I wake with a long, slow sigh, and turn over, opening my eyes and still seeing the image of my dream, which was very different to those of the last few nights. Okay, so it was still just as arousing, but the setting had changed. Up until now, I've always dreamt of making love to Summer in the daytime. Even that honeymoon scene I dreamt up yesterday afternoon was at sunset, not at night, which might be considered more 'normal' in the circumstances. But then, I've always taken the situations of our love-making to be a reflection of Summer's personality, and then her name, once I was aware of it. However, last night, rather than us being in a kitchen, or a sunlit garden, or romantic bedroom, I pictured us at night, on a thick fur rug, in front of a blazing fire, bathed in the glow from a few candles, scattered around a darkened room. There was something established and kind of settled about the place… like it was our home. *Our* home. Not mine, or hers, but ours. And although it wasn't a room I've ever been in before, there was a familiarity to the situation, to our comfort there, which in my dream felt absolutely right… and perfect.

I could see her clearly, despite the dimness of the lighting. I could feel her body surrendering to mine, in wild abandon, hear her screams of pleasure as I bound her in my arms and made her mine. And that was what woke me this morning really… those throaty cries of rapture, and my name whispered on her breath.

I feel less flustered by my dream today, despite my state of extreme arousal. But as I turn over again in bed, just to make sure it really was a dream and that I am actually alone, the guilt still tears through me, even if it is tempered with disappointment that Summer isn't lying here beside me.

I don't think the guilt will ever leave me, probably because, regardless of the altered setting, regardless of the homeliness of it, the contented joy that seemed to surround us, I still imagined myself making love to Summer with that same fierce yearning, with which I never ever loved anyone else.

Just like the ever-present shame and remorse, that hasn't changed at all.

Poppy and I spend the morning going backwards and forwards to the tip and getting rid of the things from the attic that we don't want to take back to Kew – which is most of it, to be fair.

We get back quite late, having been held up on our last trip by someone offloading an entire trailer full of garden waste, and I prepare us a quick lunch, which we've only just finished when the doorbell rings. Poppy leaps down from the table, saving me the trouble and, while I clear away our plates, she runs to the front door and lets in Summer and Roan, bringing them through to the kitchen.

I turn around from the dishwasher, which I've just finished stacking, to find them standing in the doorway, Summer looking stunning, in a floral, kind of floaty summer dress.

"God." The word leaves my mouth involuntarily, and I snap it shut. *What's wrong with me?*

"Are you okay?" she asks, looking concerned.

"Yes. It's nothing... I mean... I'm sorry." I'm rambling, but she smiles now.

"I thought we agreed we weren't going to use that word."

"Yes, we did, didn't we?" I can't stop looking at her, at the way her hair curls in delicate ringlets around her face, those few dainty freckles across her nose, her piercing eyes... Poppy coughs, quite deliberately, and I snap out of my daydream, looking down at my daughter, who is staring at me, rather pointedly. "Um... why don't you take Roan up to your room?" I suggest and she grins, and without waiting to be told a second time, she grabs his hand and they run off towards the stairs.

"Well, that's them happy," Summer says, taking a step or two into the room. She glances down at her hands, as though embarrassed and then adds, "I wanted to apologise about yesterday. I didn't mean to intrude."

"Intrude?"

"Yes. Our timing was obviously very difficult for you... and you didn't have to phone and check up on me."

"Yes, I did." I'm not sure how to explain that, so I don't.

"Well, thank you for doing so," she says, looking shy. "And I apologise – again – if our arrival made you feel awkward in your own home... or Maggie's home..." Her voice falters and she bites her bottom lip in a way which is really very distracting.

"You have nothing to apologise for," I manage to say, although for some reason I'm struggling to control my own voice. "And anyway, I thought you didn't like the word 'sorry'."

She smiles, releasing her lip at the same time. "No... I don't. Which is why I didn't actually use it."

"No. You didn't, did you?"

"Nope." She stares at me, and it takes all my willpower not to cross the room and take her in my arms… or just take her. Right here, on the kitchen table… *Stop it, Kit, for Christ's sake.*

It was only last night I told myself I'm not ready. And I'm not. I'm really not. But this is so confusing, when my body is screaming out for her, the longing within me so consuming, I can barely hear the voice of reason in my head anymore, telling me what a stupid idea it is, and how much I'd regret it… although looking at her now, it's hard to believe I'd regret anything we ever did together. *I need to get a grip.*

"Would you like a tea, or coffee?" I ask, coming to my senses at last.

"I've just had one, thanks. And anyway, if we get started, we can use the excuse of a cup of tea to take a break."

"I think we're going to need one."

"Is it that bad?"

"Knowing Mum… yes."

We both smile at the same time and I move towards her, picking up the roll of bin liners that I rescued from the sofa yesterday afternoon, having not done anything with them in the end, and try desperately to stay focused on the job in hand, rather than how much I want to forget about clearing out my mother's bedroom, and just take Summer to bed instead.

"There are some boxes upstairs already," I explain.

"Lead the way," she says, standing back and letting me pass her, going out of the kitchen and into the hallway, and then up the stairs and around the landing, into the master bedroom.

I haven't actually been in here since we got back, but the room is familiar enough. And I guess that's why I'm not prepared for Summer's gasp when I open the door and step to one side, letting her enter ahead of me.

"Heavens," she says and I follow her in, to find her gazing around the room. "How romantic."

"Yes, I suppose it is…"

I watch as she goes further into the bedroom, across to the large four-poster that dominates the room, its white voile drapes tied at the corners.

"I'm not sure I'd go for this," she murmurs, running a hand through the delicate folds.

I join her, looking up at the enormous bed that my father had specially constructed. "I always thought it was a bit over-the-top," I comment, agreeing with her, as I put the bin liners down on the mattress. "But my parents were a very… affectionate couple." I'm not sure 'affectionate' really covers it, although it seems like a good compromise, considering I can hardly say to Summer that they couldn't keep their hands off of each other, not when the nerves in my arms are actually twitching out of sheer desperation to hold her.

She smiles up at me. "So, the opposite of my parents, then."

I remember what she told me about her father's affair. "Hmm… yes."

She puts her hands on her hips, looking around at the wardrobe that fills one wall, the large chest of drawers and the dressing table that sits in front of the window. "Where would you like me to start?" she says.

"It's up to you. I think quite a lot of the wardrobe space is empty. Mum did eventually get rid of Dad's clothes, and unless she went on a huge shopping spree, I imagine that won't be too bad. The chest of drawers was always hers, and obviously the dressing table too."

She smiles. "And what am I doing with everything?"

"I thought her clothes could go to a charity shop, except for underwear, of course… and everything else we'll just throw away."

"What about her jewellery? I'm assuming she had some?"

"Oh, God… yes. I'd forgotten about that." I glance around. "She had one of those big old-fashioned jewellery boxes with drawers at the front. But heaven knows where it is now. It used to live on the dressing table, cluttering everything up, because she always left the drawers open and strings of pearls or necklaces hanging out of it."

"Well, when I find it, I'll bring it down to you."

"Thanks."

"Where will you be?"

"In the dining room, going through Mum's writing desk." I roll my eyes. "She called it a writing desk, but really it was just somewhere she used to cram all the bills. As far as I'm aware, she never actually corresponded with anyone, except your mum, and she used to sit at the kitchen table to do that, with a glass of wine, chuckling while she wrote."

"I can just imagine Maggie doing that," Summer says wistfully. "Although I'm surprised she wasn't more meticulous with her finances. She never came across like that. I mean, she never forgot a single birthday, even when we lived in France."

"No, she was good at things like that. She had a calendar on the back of the kitchen door, with everything jotted down and she always made sure cards and presents were sent out in plenty of time. But her lack of financial organisation used to drive my dad insane… for an artist, he was meticulously tidy, at least outside of his studio, but at least once every couple of months, he'd have to go through her writing desk, and he'd find cheques she'd forgotten to cash, and household bills she hadn't paid, and he'd sit down at the dining table and sort it all out for her and then he'd kiss her on the forehead, like an errant child, and go back upstairs… and she'd take about a week to make a mess of everything again."

She chuckles. "They sound like such a loving couple."

"They were. They were polar opposites, in lots of ways, but they were so in love…" I stop talking, my voice breaking just slightly as I think about the two of them… and about myself and Bryony and how in love we were too… and about the woman standing in front of me, and how easy it would be to fall…

"Well, I suppose I'd better get started," she says, smiling at me, and I'm grateful she's not aware of the effect she's been having on me. Because day-dreaming about something that can never happen isn't honouring Bryony's memory, is it? And that's what I promised myself I'd do. Right after I completely dishonoured her by sleeping with another woman. And I can't do that again. Which means I need to stop this and get on.

"Yes," I reply, rather blandly. "I'll be downstairs. You know where to find me?"

Summer nods her head and, before I can say anything else wrong today, I leave her to get on with packing away my mother's life.

I've been at this for nearly three-quarters of an hour, and have discovered – much to my surprise – that my mother was actually a lot better at paperwork and filing than I thought she might have been. But then I suppose she'd had six years of coping by herself, since my father's death, so she had time to get herself into a routine. Her utility bills are all paid by direct debit, so I've just got to call the companies and get those transferred into my name, at least until the house is sold. I need to contact her bank as well, and luckily she doesn't seem to have had any credit cards, so there's nothing to worry about there.

I have to say that, as much as I'd dreaded this task, it hasn't been anything like as bad as I'd expected.

"Kit?" I turn at the sound of Summer's voice. She's standing in the doorway, holding my mother's jewellery box, a fairly large dark wood construction, with four drawers at the front and a lidded section on the top, just as I remember it.

"Ah… there it is." I get up and go over, taking it from her and bringing it back to the table. "Where did you find it?"

"In the bottom of the wardrobe."

I glance down at her. "Really?" I'm surprised. That seems odd, when it used to have pride of place on her dressing table. I can remember it from my childhood.

She nods her head. "Shall I go and put the kettle on?"

"Or I could."

"No, it's fine. We promised ourselves a break and you should probably take a look at that." She nods at the jewellery box. "I'll be back in a minute."

She leaves and I turn my attention to the box in front of me, lifting the lid and gazing inside at the array of rings, brooches and necklaces, laid out rather haphazardly, and I smile. This is more like my mother. I'm not sure whether she had anything of value. She certainly didn't inherit any jewels from her family, but my father may have bought her presents over the years, so I suppose I'd better get someone who knows about these things to take a more professional look, before I decide what to do with all of this.

Closing the lid, I open the top drawer, to find yet more jewellery, and even more in the drawer below. As I open the third drawer, Summer comes back in.

"Anything exciting?" she asks.

"I have no idea. I don't know very much about jewellery." I glance down at the open drawer. "Oh… this is different."

"What's that?" She moves closer, so she's right standing beside me, and I can smell that fresh, floral scent of her perfume.

"I'm not sure." I try to ignore the effect of her presence – yet again – and reach into the drawer, pulling out the bundle of letters, still in their envelopes, neatly tied with a blue ribbon.

"Now, that *is* romantic," Summer says. "They look like love letters."

"They do. And in that case, I'm going to put them right back where I found them. There's no way I'm reading through letters that my dad wrote to my mum." I turn the pile over to put it back and my breath catches, as I struggle to control my reactions, dropping the letters onto the table, like they're scalding my hand.

"What's wrong?" Summer says, looking confused.

"The handwriting," I whisper.

"What about it?"

"It's not my father's."

She picks up the envelopes, studying the writing herself. "Are you sure? It must have been years since you've seen it."

"I'm sure. My father had very artistic handwriting, all flourishes and swirls. And in any case, I was only looking at his accounts books yesterday, in the attic. I'd know his handwriting anywhere."

She looks up. "Then whose writing is it?"

"I have no idea" I take the envelopes from her again. "But I suppose there's only one way to find out."

She snatches them back. "You're going to read your mother's personal letters?" She seems shocked.

"Yes. How else will I know who they're from?"

She hesitates for a second and then passes them over to me and I untie the ribbon, letting it fall to the floor, before opening the first letter and reading:

'Maggie, my love,

I wish with all my heart that you'd change your mind.

I wish you'd take my calls, or let me come and see you, even though I know you hate me coming to the village.

I don't care about that anymore though. I just need to see you, so we can talk this through, because the thought of never seeing you again is killing me.

I understand how hard this is for you. I know how much you miss Oliver and what you had with him and I've never tried to replace him. You know that. But what we have is special too, isn't it? It's worth fighting for, my darling. At least, I think it is.

Maybe if we could be together more, it would be easier for you. You wouldn't have to live with just your memories so much of the time, because we'd be making new ones. And if that's what you want, then I'll find a way to make it work. You just have to want it, Maggie. Because I do. Just like I want you... so very much.

Write back to me, please. Tell me I at least have a chance.

Your loving,

Tony'

"Oh, my God..." I pull out a dining chair and flop down into it. "She had a lover."

Summer takes a seat beside me. "After your father died?" she whispers, uncertain, and I realise she didn't read the letter while I was, and hand it to her. "It reads that way, don't you think?"

She takes a moment, and then puts the letter down. "I'm not sure. I mean... I'm not sure they were lovers."

"You're not?"

"No." She looks back at the letter again. "He says he wants her and he wants to make it work for them, but there's nothing here that says they were actually lovers." I suppose she's right. "It's terribly sad, though, don't you think?" she adds, looking up at me again. "She's obviously broken up with him."

"Yes." I pick up the letter again and note the date at the top. "Dad had been dead for almost two years when this was written," I mutter to myself, and then leaf through the rest of the envelopes, studying the postmarks. They're in date order, with the earliest one at the bottom, which I hold up to Summer. "This is the first," I say, taking the letter out and looking at it. "It's dated six months after my father's death."

I start to read, out loud this time…

"'*Dear Maggie,*

God… that sounds very formal, doesn't it?

I know you gave me your phone number, but now I'm back home, I thought I'd write to you. I mean, I'll call as well, but there are some things I wanted to say to you that I'm not sure I want to say in a phone call, and being as we're not going to be able to see each other for a while, I thought this was the best solution.

I miss you.

There. I've said it.

I miss holding you while you sleep and waking up beside you…'"

I let my voice fade.

"So they were lovers," Summer murmurs.

"Yes. And I can't read any more of that."

She puts her hand on my arm and it feels comfortable letting her. "Is that because you don't like the idea of her having a lover?"

"No. It's because he's writing about my mother, and there are limits."

She smiles. "Do you know who he is? Do you know anyone called Tony?"

"No."

"Or Anthony?" she suggests.

I shake my head. "It sounds like he wasn't from around here though. He said 'now I'm back home', so maybe he'd come down here on holiday or something."

"And she just invited him to stay? A complete stranger? Sorry, but that doesn't sound like Maggie. Not the Maggie I knew."

"No, it doesn't." She's quite right, my mother wasn't like that.

"And anyway, in that other letter, didn't he say she hated him coming to the village?"

"Yes, he did." I pick up the envelope again, looking at the date on the postmark. "Hang on…"

"What?"

"This says January 2015."

"And? You said that was six months after your father died."

"It was."

"So?"

"She went on a cruise that Christmas... the one after Dad died."

Summer tips her head to one side. "And you think they might have met then? On board ship, as it were?"

"It makes sense. And the timing fits."

"And they had a fleeting romance, that turned into something more?" She picks up the letters, letting them fall through her fingers.

"Hmm... it looks that way."

"And you didn't notice anything? No change in her when she came back from her cruise?"

"No." I shake my head. "But then I was a bit preoccupied at the time." She raises her eyebrows inquisitively. "Bryony was pregnant. She had about two months to go, I suppose. Which meant I was panicking."

"What about?"

"Oh... everything."

She chuckles and the sound sends shivers down my spine and to give myself something to focus on, I start gathering up the letters again.

"What are you going to do with them?" she asks.

"Well, I'm going to hide them from Poppy, that's for sure. She may not be able to read them yet, not properly, but I think some of the contents might be a little... adult."

"I think they might," Summer says, smiling, and she bends down, picking up the ribbon from the floor, handing it to me. "Shall I go and finish making the tea?" she suggests. "The kettle must have boiled ages ago."

"I don't mind doing it."

She stands beside me and I look up at her. "It's fine, Kit. Really. You pack your mother's things away."

And before I can argue, she's gone.

Chapter Thirteen

Summer

It's been a very interesting day, in all kinds of ways.

Obviously, there was the discovery of Maggie's letters... or I suppose I should say Tony's letters. Not that we know who Tony was, or even where he lived, other than the postmark on the envelopes, which said 'York', and was singularly unhelpful. He hadn't put his address on the letters themselves, but then he didn't need to. Maggie knew where to write to him. Part of me expected Kit to be more outraged than he was by reading those letters, but he's full of surprises... such as inviting Roan and I to dinner at the pub... by way of saying 'thank you' for all my help today.

I pointed out that he didn't need to say 'thank you' for anything, but he was most insistent, so once he'd finished taping up the boxes of clothes for the charity shop, and made sure he'd hidden his mother's jewellery box in his car, because he felt Poppy was least likely to find it there, we walked across the green together, and because it's a beautiful evening, are sitting side by side at a table in the beer garden, watching the children play on the climbing frame, while we wait for our food to be brought out. And what's even more surprising is that Kit didn't kick up a fuss when Poppy asked if she and Roan could go and play. He just told her to be careful. He's watched her like a hawk since, but then I've watched Roan too, so I can't blame him for that.

"What are you going to do about those letters?" I ask him, taking a sip of my white wine and smiling as Roan lets Poppy climb the ladder ahead of him… ever the gentleman, at least where she's concerned.

"I've hidden them in my car." He glances at me, seemingly surprised by my question, being as he told me this earlier.

"I know. I meant, what are you going to do in the long run?"

He shrugs now, turning back to face the climbing frame. "I'm not sure I'm going to do anything. I'm certainly not going to read them."

I can't help smiling. "I don't I blame you. I'm not sure I'd want to read things like that about my mother either."

He shakes his head, smiling himself now. "It's funny, isn't it, how even now, as adults, the thought of our parents having sex is so… weird."

"I don't know," I reason, thinking through what he's just said. "I'm not sure I would have found it as weird as an adult, as I would have done as a teenager. Not that I'm aware of my mother ever having sex, now I come to think about it. As I told you before, my dad was rarely at home, and once we moved back here, I don't think she had anyone in her life. I suppose that's quite sad, when you think about it." I haven't thought about it before. Not consciously anyway. But it is sad that she spent so much of her life alone.

Kit pulls a face. "Oh, I don't know. I feel kind of jealous," he says. "My parents were the exact opposite. They couldn't leave each other alone."

I almost drop my glass. "Seriously?"

He smirks. "Let's just say they weren't exactly subtle. As a child, I didn't understand it, but as a teenager I cottoned on fairly quickly to the touching and whispering, and I thought it was gross."

"And as an adult?"

"I don't know." He pauses. "I don't think it's gross anymore… obviously. I suppose I'm torn between it being weird – like I said before – and actually quite sweet, that they were still so in love, after all that time. And they were incredibly in love, by anyone's standards."

"How did they meet?"

He looks down at me for a second. "Don't you know?"

"No. Maggie never told me."

"And your mum didn't tell you either?"

"No."

He smiles, shaking his head. "Well, I suppose it was a bit unorthodox."

"Was it?"

"Hmm…" He picks up his pint glass and takes a sip. "You know my dad was an artist?"

"Yes."

"Well, before he met Mum, he used to supplement his income sometimes by teaching art at the university in Falmouth. It's only about an hour's drive away from here, and the pay wasn't bad. Anyway, Mum was a student at the time…"

"At Falmouth?" I interrupt.

"Yes, but she was studying textiles or something… nothing to do with Dad."

"Oh. I see… sorry, carry on."

"She was studying there, in her first year, and one day she saw a poster on one of the noticeboards about the art department looking for models. They were paying a small fee, and she had some spare time so she decided 'why not?'. So, one afternoon, she turned up at the art class in question, and my dad met her at the door, invited her into the room, and told her take her clothes off."

I laugh out loud, and he chuckles.

"Mum was horrified. Here was this man, old enough to be her father, telling her to strip naked… in front of a group of ten or fifteen art students."

"What did she do?"

"She slapped him round the face, and stormed off."

"Oh dear… how embarrassing."

"Well, it would have been, except my dad obviously took a shine to her, so he told the students to get on with something else, and ran after her. Luckily, he managed to catch up with her, before she'd actually called a policeman or anything, and he apologised… and then pointed out to her that the advert had made it clear that he was looking for a life model."

I laugh even more loudly now. "Hadn't she noticed that?"

"She'd noticed, but she'd read it as 'live', not 'life'. She didn't realise what it meant. She thought it meant the model had to be alive."

"As opposed to what? Dead?"

He laughs now. "I don't know what she thought. Anyway, they sorted out their misunderstanding, and Dad invited her out for a drink… which became dinner… and then he persuaded her to let him draw her, and probably because she was a little the worse for wear, she said 'yes', and the next morning, she woke up in his bed."

"Oh, my God. Really?" He nods his head. "They told you this?"

"Yes. When I met my first girlfriend, I was intrigued by how my parents had got together – especially given the age gap between them – and I made the mistake of asking. Like I said, they never bothered to hide much. Of course, what Dad hadn't realised was that Mum's family were old money. Proper old money. And the last thing they wanted was to discover that their precious daughter had fallen in love with a penniless artist."

"So what happened?"

"They forbade her to see him ever again."

"Oh… that's shortsighted."

"And ineffective. My dad wasn't going to take 'no' for answer, especially when Mum herself was saying 'yes'. So, she dropped out of uni and they eloped."

"Seriously?"

"Yes. Mum packed a bag and snuck out of her parents' house on the outskirts of Looe, and my dad met her at the top of the drive in his rather beaten up VW Camper van, and they drove to Redruth."

I stare at him. "So they didn't run very far then?"

"No. They just wanted to be far enough away that they could hide in a large town for a few weeks, while they waited to get a licence… and then they got married. Of course, when my grandparents found out, they disinherited Mum. But she always said she didn't care. She had the only thing she ever wanted... namely my Dad."

"And they moved here?" I ask, tipping my head and nodding towards Bluebells on the other side of the green.

"Yes. The house belonged to Dad's parents at the time, but they were a bit more liberal-minded, and didn't bat an eyelid when he turned up on the doorstep with his bride... about whom they knew absolutely nothing. Of course, he was forty by then, so I suppose they'd had time to get used to his ways. And they were probably relieved he'd finally settled down... and the fact that I turned up ten months later didn't hurt."

I shake my head, smiling. "If it's not a rude question, how come there aren't more of you?"

"Do you mean, why don't I have any brothers or sisters?"

I nod my head. "If your parents were as... um... affectionate, as you say they were, I'm surprised they didn't have more children."

"They would have done," he says, lowering his voice. "Probably lots more, but Mum had a miscarriage about a year after I was born, and there were some complications... something went wrong. I don't know what happened exactly. Neither of them ever explained, beyond the fact of the miscarriage. And I never asked. I just know they couldn't have any more kids..." He stops talking and we both stare at each other for a moment, absorbing the sadness of that thought, I think. "How did we get onto this subject?" he asks eventually.

"I don't know. Oh... wait a minute. Yes, I do. I was asking you about those letters."

"Oh... yes. Which I suppose goes to prove that my mum wasn't quite as in love with my dad as I'd thought she was." He sounds a bit despondent and, dragging my eyes away from the children, I turn in my seat and look at him.

"Is that what you think?"

"She had a lover, Summer," he reasons.

"Yes. *After* your father died."

"Not that long after he died."

I sigh, because he doesn't seem to understand. "I imagine she was lonely. If she had as full and affectionate a relationship with your father as you say she did, she might have just wanted someone to make her feel loved again." He stares at me for a moment and then looks away. "And besides, you're forgetting something…"

"What's that," he murmurs, although this time he keeps his eyes fixed straight ahead.

"She broke it off with Tony. And from the sounds of things, that had a lot to do with your father and her memories of him.."

"Hmm…" he allows and we sit in silence for a moment or two.

"Are you going to try and find him?" I ask.

"Who? Tony?" He puts his glass down, turning to me once more.

"Yes."

"How? I don't know anything about him. I don't even remember the dates of the cruise."

"Do you remember where she went?" I ask.

"No. Not exactly. It was like a grand European tour or something, but I can't remember exactly where she visited. Like I said earlier, I was busy panicking about my own life at the time."

I shake my head, smiling at him. "What was there to panic about?"

"Fatherhood, responsibility, growing up."

I laugh, because I can't help it. "How old were you by then?"

"Thirty."

"And you still didn't consider yourself as grown-up?"

"No. But when Poppy was born, when I actually became a father… God, that was sobering."

"Good sobering?" I ask. "Or the kind of sobering that makes you want to go and have another drink?"

He smiles at me. "Good sobering. Most of the time. The four a.m. feeds left a lot to be desired, and I sometimes used to sit in my studio at home for hours at a time and worry about what would happen if my business failed, being as Bryony had decided not to go back to work… which I hadn't expected her to do."

He's never really spoken about his wife before, not quite like this. Not in any great detail. He's mentioned her name in passing, but that's about it… and, feeling intrigued, I sit forward.

"Did you need to worry?" I ask, to keep the conversation going.

"No. I've been lucky. My work's remained fairly consistent over the years, but at the time, when she first announced that she wanted to be a full-time mum… well, that was a moment. Bryony had always been a real career-woman, and to be honest, it had been a relief to know that, if I ever had a bad month, we had her salary to fall back on. But all of a sudden, there I was, completely responsible for two other human beings. It was scary." He stops talking for a second, but then adds, in a whispered voice, "Obviously there were much more scary things to come, but I didn't know that at the time."

"How did she die?" I ask, keeping my voice quiet. He stills and I wonder if I've overstepped the mark. "You don't have to tell me, if you don't want to…"

He shakes his head and simply says, "Cancer," before picking up his glass again, gulping down half of his beer in one go, and then adding the single word, "Cervical," as he puts his drink back on the table again. It seems as though that's all he's going to say and I sit looking at him, trying to contemplate how terrible it must have been, when he takes a breath and says, "We were trying for another baby," his voice a little strained. "We decided, not long after Poppy turned one, that we wanted to have a second child… but it wasn't working out, so we went to the doctor's and that was when I discovered that Bryony had been having breakthrough bleeds?" He forms his sentence like a question, and I nod my head. "She'd kept them to herself," he continues. "And God knows how, but I hadn't noticed."

"I imagine she hadn't wanted you to notice… she was probably scared."

He turns to me. "She was. That's what she told me, when I asked her. She said she was scared. The doctor sent her to a specialist and he ran some tests…"

"Oh." I can't think of anything else to say.

"It was advanced, and aggressive," he murmurs, staring off into the distance now. "Those were the words they used. They offered treatment, but no cure. It was just about giving her more time… and not very much more time, at that, so Bryony said 'no'."

"And how did you feel about that?"

He turns to look at me again. "It was what she wanted," he says simply.

"So you didn't feel angry, or resentful? I think I would have, in your situation."

He frowns, his eyes darkening. "I—I felt angry about the cancer. I felt angry that she was being taken from me…" He pauses, taking a deep breath. "And… and yes, I did feel angry with her. I hid it at the time, and I've hidden it ever since. I've denied it, really. But yes, I was angry. I was really bloody angry. I—I wanted her to fight it… to want to stay with us… with me. Even if it was just for a few more months."

I nod my head and reach out, putting my hand on his arm. "You do know that's okay, don't you? To be angry?"

He stares at me, his brow furrowing. "Is it? You don't think she deserved better than that?"

"No. I think you're entitled to feel however you need to feel. It can't always be about the person who's dying, Kit. Sometimes it has to be about the people who love them too."

He shakes his head, like he doesn't understand, and then looks away.

"I shouldn't have asked about her… I'm sorry," I whisper and lean into him slightly.

He turns now, gazing down at me.

"Isn't that word banned?"

I shake my head. "Not always, no."

His stare softens, but just when I think he might be about to say something, or maybe even lean in a little closer and perhaps kiss me, he stiffens and then almost lurches away from me, his face hardening. I don't know what happened in that brief moment, but whatever we've shared today – and I think we've shared quite a lot – I know it's over.

Chapter Fourteen

Kit

How on earth did that all go so wrong?

I'd kind of decided, earlier on, when we were upstairs in my mother's bedroom and I was so tempted by Summer's presence, that I was going to try and ignore my rather confusing feelings for her, and focus on honouring Bryony's memory instead. And I was doing okay with that... for about an hour. Until we found those letters... until I realised my mother had a lover... until Summer was really kind and understanding and considerate about the whole thing, and it dawned on me that, when I let her, she has a way of making me feel better. About everything.

And at the end of the day, I didn't want her to leave. I wanted to spend some more time with her, and I didn't see the point in trying to pretend otherwise. So I invited her and Roan to the pub for dinner. And we talked. I'm not going to say I didn't occasionally think about how beautiful she is, or that the way the setting sun caught in her hair, making it shine and sparkle, reminded me of that honeymoon dream, when she'd lain across the bed and I'd taken her, or that the sound of her laughter made my whole body shudder... or that I really wanted to kiss her. Very hard.

But none of that counted for anything, because all we were doing was talking.

We'd been talking for ages too, and a lot of it had been lighthearted – bordering on fun. We'd certainly laughed a few times. I think. We must have done, because I can clearly remember that shuddering sensation happening on more than one occasion. I know I'd told her about how my mother met my father – which isn't a story I share with most people, although it can be quite amusing. It made Summer laugh, anyway.

And then we got onto the subject of Bryony's death, and I told her a few details. Admittedly, it wasn't much, but she did ask, and what I told her was more than I've ever shared with anyone else who wasn't there at the time. And that actually felt surprisingly good.

What I hadn't expected was that, for the very first time, I would admit out loud that I was angry Bryony hadn't accepted the treatment. I didn't even acknowledge that at the time. I buried my own feelings back then... the disappointment, the shock, the sadness. And the anger. And I've kept them buried ever since, in a mire of guilt, consoling myself that I did okay, because I let Bryony have what she wanted. And that was what mattered. As a result of which I've avoided having to face my feelings. But when Summer asked the question, I couldn't lie. So I told her. Yes, I felt angry. I still do. I found it hard admitting that. After all, it wasn't about me, was it? It was about Bryony. So my feelings should never have come into it. But, looking back now, I did feel angry, under the surface. I still *do* feel angry. I feel *really* angry, and *really* resentful. She didn't even ask how I felt. Not once. She made her choice. She decided. For both of us. And I had to go along with it. And because she was dying, I couldn't argue. So I didn't, because I loved her. I still love her. Completely. But that doesn't mean I'm not really bloody angry with her. Saying that out loud felt good... kind of cathartic. But what surprised me even more than my own admission, or how it made me feel, was Summer's reaction. Because, rather than being shocked, or disappointed, or even confused, she told me it was okay. She touched my arm, really gently, and said it was all right to be angry, and just for a second, it was like having one of the many weights lifted from my shoulders. She'd given me permission to be angry, and suddenly, I wasn't anymore. And I felt so much better. Better than I've felt in years... right up until she apologised, and I looked at her. And I mean *really* looked at her, and I saw the depth of sorrow in her eyes, and for some reason which I still can't understand, it annoyed me.

I mean... that doesn't make sense, does it?

She'd been so kind, and so compassionate. She'd helped me to understand my own emotions, to feel better than I had done in a very long time. So why would I be annoyed by her sorrow? It was quite reasonable for her to be sad, considering I'd just told her how my wife had died. But I suppose the thing is, her sorrow was directed at me, and not Bryony. And I don't want her sympathy. I'm not sure what it is that I do want from her, other than to kiss her and make love to her – although I'm not even sure about that anymore. But I know that I don't want her pity. And seeing that in her eyes, especially given that I'd just opened up to her, like never before... well, it struck an uncomfortable note.

So, the rest of our evening passed in a sullen and stony silence, despite Summer's best attempts to keep the conversation going, especially once the waiter brought our food out and the kids joined us again.

I don't think Poppy noticed my bad mood. She certainly didn't say anything, if she did. And she didn't sulk at me when we got home either, although that might have had something to do with the fact that she was exhausted, and I ended up putting her straight to bed. She was a little bit put out that she won't be able to see Roan tomorrow, because when Roan asked the question, Summer said 'no', and reminded him they had something to do. She didn't say what the 'something' was, and I didn't ask. Of course, I wondered if the 'something' was just an excuse not to spend any more time with me, being as I'd been like a bear with a sore head for most of the evening. I wouldn't have blamed her if that was the case, although I wish it wasn't. Especially now. Because I feel really bad about the way I've behaved. Yet again.

Even if I still don't want her pity.

I managed to appease Poppy, before she went off to sleep, by reminding her that she'll be spending the whole of Thursday with her new best friend. I'd made a point of checking that with Summer, just before we parted, on the green, and she'd smiled, and said, "Yes, of course," as though she couldn't understand why I'd been in any doubt about the matter.

Which was also a bit odd, considering I know she'd noticed the change in my mood, even if she hadn't mentioned it. And yet, there she was, still smiling, and being kind, and accommodating – as ever.

I haven't slept well, which isn't at all unusual, or surprising, being as all I can think about is Summer. And thinking about Summer makes me... uncomfortable, to put it mildly. That's to say, thinking about Summer makes me aroused, and being aroused makes me uncomfortable.

Last night's dream was set on a beach, and in common with last night's fireside tryst, it was dark, just the light of the moon allowing me to see the smile playing on her lips as she lay beneath me, gazing up into my face. Of course, because it was a dream, the scene was perfect. There was a gentle breeze blowing soft across our naked bodies and waves lapped peacefully on the shore. The beach was deserted, so there was no-one to hear her feverish sighs or to see my hardened body grinding relentlessly into hers... over, and over... and over.

I get out of bed early and shower, because just the thought of that scene is too much for me, and afterwards, I go downstairs and sit at the kitchen table, and because I'm in my mother's house, sitting in this far too familiar room, I can't avoid thinking about her... and Tony.

I'm still kind of reeling from the discovery of those letters, not because she met someone else after my father died – she was only forty-nine when it happened, after all. No... I'm stunned because I didn't see it at the time. My mother, who was always very open about everything, had a romantic, physical relationship with a man for eighteen months, and I didn't have a clue.

I wonder for a minute why she didn't tell me about it. Did she think I wouldn't approve? Was she ashamed? Did she feel guilty... like me?

God, I wish I knew. I wish she was still here too, so we could talk. And share our stories, and help each other to understand.

My day today has been filled with answering e-mails, preparing for tomorrow's meeting, keeping Poppy occupied and trying really hard not to think about Summer.

I've succeeded in all but the last of those efforts, getting all of my e-mails done by ten o'clock, then spending an hour or so with Poppy in the garden, in between the rain showers, exploring the creep-crawly den again, before coming back in and getting all my preparations done for tomorrow, so I know I've got everything I need. Then after lunch, we go upstairs and pack Poppy's things ready for her day at Summer's. I suppose, it's only really then, as I'm putting Poppy's clean pyjamas into her rucksack, that I'm willing to acknowledge, quietly to myself, that Summer has been in the back of my mind all day, even when I haven't been actively thinking about her – which I have a lot of the time too.

To distract myself from where that thought might lead me, I decide to do something really out of the ordinary – and delight my daughter – and, looking up the recipe on the internet, we set to and make pizzas… from scratch. It's incredibly messy and a lot more time-consuming than I would have thought – or than the recipe would have had me believe – but it's also good fun, and although Poppy spilling flour down herself still reminds me of Summer, and I can't help thinking that this is just the kind of thing she'd do too… we have a great afternoon. And we even get to eat the end result, sitting in front of the TV, watching *Toy Story*.

When I fall into bed, perhaps a little later than I should, being as I've got a horribly early start tomorrow, I find I'm actually smiling to myself for the first time in God knows how long. And that's because, once I'd put Poppy to bed, I took a glass of wine out onto the terrace behind the conservatory, and while I sat there drinking it, I reached the conclusion – although I'm really not sure how – that, while I still feel guilty, and I'm not sure I understand what's going on, there's absolutely no point in trying to stop thinking about Summer anymore.

Because she's the only thing on my mind.

Ignoring the memories of last night's dream… dismissing the recollection of the fairy lights adorning the anonymous garden, and Summer's naked body in my arms, craving me, like I crave her, I get up at five thirty and am dressed by six o'clock. Today, I'm wearing smart jeans and a white button-down shirt, because I'm going to Chiswick and that means old tatty jeans or shorts and a t-shirt simply won't do. I go and wake Poppy, who's none too pleased to see me at this hour, which makes me smile as I recall Summer telling me that she and Roan are also owls and not larks. And I stare out of the window at the dawn sky for a few minutes, just contemplating that.

Until I remember we're on a schedule this morning, and remind Poppy to get up. Again.

Okay, so maybe giving myself permission to think about Summer all the time isn't a good idea, after all. It's distracting, to put it mildly.

Poppy gets up, moaning constantly at me, because it's too early, and if she'd stayed with Roan last night she could still be asleep.

"But you didn't stay with Roan," I point out to her. "You stayed here."

"I didn't need to though, did I?"

She has a point, even if she is putting it rather petulantly at the moment. It probably would have made everybody's life a lot easier, if I'd just gone up to town yesterday afternoon and stayed at home last night. I wonder, for a moment, if I'd have dreamt of Summer up there. But I dismiss the thought. Of course I wouldn't. My house in Kew is the home I shared with Bryony, and I can't imagine dreaming of Summer there. That would be all wrong. But… it suddenly dawns on me that perhaps that's why I've found it acceptable to think about Summer all of a sudden. Because she's not part of my 'real' life at home, where I never needed to dream, because I had the real thing… while it lasted.

The Real Thing. Oh God… Bryony. I thought I'd worked this out. I thought I was okay with it.

"Daddy?" Poppy's raised voice breaks into my thoughts. "You're in the way."

She wants to get out to the bathroom, and I'm standing in the doorway.

"Sorry." I step aside and let her pass. "I'll go and make the breakfast."

"Okay," she calls, her voice muffled, which tells me she's brushing her teeth.

Downstairs, I still can't stop thinking about Summer… and Bryony… and Summer.

Why can't I just get this straight in my head? One way or the other? Why don't I know the answers?

Perhaps because I'm not even sure what the question is…

It's ten to seven when I ring Summer's doorbell, and she opens it almost straight away, inviting us in rather than leaving us on the doorstep, and we enter into the living room, and although we've been here before, this is the first time I've really noticed the way it's furnished, which is really rather beautifully. There are two cozy-looking, cream coloured sofas piled up with cushions, facing each other either side of the open fireplace, and a long, low coffee table in between, on which there are a couple of magazines, and a paperback novel, turned onto its front, so I've got no idea what it is. The far wall is painted in a soft blue, and has two wooden doors set into it; a larger one, which is open, and which seems to lead to the staircase, and a second, smaller one, which I'm guessing opens into a cupboard underneath the stairs.

As she shuts the door behind us and comes around to stand before me, Summer stares at me for a moment, then lowers her eyes from my face to a spot just a few inches below my chin. I'm not sure what she's looking at, or why, but that's because my brain has kind of switched off. And that's got nothing to do with my confusion of earlier. I'm not even capable of thinking – clearly, or otherwise – at the moment, because I'm completely distracted by the white sundress she's wearing, and as I let my eyes roam down her body – unable to stop myself – my brain actually starts to feel like it's gradually freezing solid, and my throat closes over. The dress has narrow straps and is what might be termed a 'decent' length, finishing well below her knee, but the material itself is sheer, sheer enough that I can see the outline of her dark, hardened nipples, while the buttons at the front are straining, just slightly, revealing the swell of her rounded bare breasts.

I've noticed before that Summer has this confident way of dressing; her shorts cut very short, her tops very sexy and alluring. Although her clothes are always completely respectable... unless of course, you happen to be looking.

And I happen to be looking.

My body responds to her in an instant, and I raise Poppy's rucksack from my side to cover myself, feeling grateful now that I chose to carry it over here, rather than getting Poppy to do it, like I normally would.

"Good morning," Summer says, sounding bright and cheerful, and entirely focused on Poppy now, evidently oblivious to her own sexual magnetism, or the ease with which she's drawn me in. "Are you ready to have some fun?" She holds out her hand and Poppy takes it, and I'm completely mesmerised. For someone who claims not to like mornings, she's bubbly enough.

"I—I brought Poppy's pyjamas." I have to say something, and it only dawns on me as I'm holding out the rucksack, that I was using it to shield her eyes from my arousal. Still, it's too late now, and she takes the small pink bag from me, turning and leaning over the arm of her sofa to put it on the seat... that fine material of her dress stretching across her perfectly formed behind. It's all I can do not to groan out loud when I notice that she doesn't appear to be wearing any underwear... except... there's a band of lace, about two inches wide, hugging her hips, and another strip of fabric, leading downwards...

"Oh God." The words catch in my throat.

"Sorry?" She turns and looks at me, and it takes all my concentration not to look down... not to try and see the front of her sexy lace thong through the gossamer fabric of the dress I'd dearly love to rip from her beautiful body... if only my daughter wasn't standing between us.

"Nothing. I was just noticing the time. I need to be going."

She leans over slightly in Poppy's direction and I avert my eyes, because there's only so much a man can take. "Well, I'm sure we'll manage, won't we, Poppy?" she says.

"Where's Roan?" Poppy asks, looking up at Summer.

"He's just getting dressed. He'll be down in a minute."

Poppy nods and turns back to me. "Behave yourself, won't you?" I say, crouching down in front of her.

"Yes, Daddy." She just about stops short of rolling her eyes at me, but only just.

"She'll be fine," Summer says as I stand again. "We're going to have lots of fun. I've got all kinds of things planned for the two of them."

I nod my head, glancing down at Poppy, who's gazing at Summer with something akin to adulation written all over her face, and I struggle not to feel jealous. I can't remember the last time my daughter looked at me like that… if she ever has.

"Well, if you need me, just call. I'll keep my phone on."

"Oh, don't worry. I'm sure we'll cope."

Somehow, I don't doubt that.

"Bye, Poppy," I say and she manages to tear her gaze away from Summer long enough to look up at me and give me a smile.

"Bye, Daddy."

That's clearly all I'm getting and, with a heavy heart, I open the door and let myself out.

"We'll see you later," Summer calls after me and I turn to see my daughter clasping her hand, as I raise mine to wave.

"Bye Poppy," I call again. But she doesn't respond, and the door starts to close.

Presumably they've got better things to do.

I've been on the road for over three hours and have just joined the M3, and although my journey has been relatively easy so far, I feel as though I can finally put my foot down, now I'm on the motorway, rather than single lanes and dual carriageways.

My journey may have been straightforward, but my thoughts are the polar opposite. I can't help feeling put out that Poppy dismissed me so quickly, in favour of Summer. Roan wasn't even there, and it felt like she couldn't wait for me to leave. And yes, I know I'm being unreasonable. After all, I'm the one who's forcing Poppy to spend the day with them and not with me, while I go to my meeting. She's not making me go, is she? She's not *choosing* Summer over me. Not really. She's just making the most of the situation I've put her in. Even so, I still feel ludicrously jealous of the fact that Poppy seemed to want to be with Summer so much.

Perhaps that's because *I* want to be with Summer too. Desperately. And I know – deep down – I'd far rather be back there in Millarnick, with Poppy, and Summer and Roan, than travelling up to Chiswick. I'd far rather spend my day with them – although I've got no idea what they'll be doing – because then at least I'd get the chance to talk to Summer some more and maybe make amends for freezing her out the other night at the pub. And I wouldn't say 'no' to spending a day just staring at her in that stunningly sexy dress she was wearing. God, she looked beautiful this morning. I think she's probably the most beautiful woman I've ever seen…

What? What's wrong with me?

I grip the steering wheel and shake my head. I shouldn't be thinking like that. Bryony was beautiful. She was absolutely bewitching. I can still remember the first time I saw her, like it was yesterday. It was at an office party I'd been invited to, and she caught my eye straight away, in spite of that fact that I was actually there with someone else. And so was she. I was instantly attracted to her though… to the way her dark grey fitted suit hugged her slim figure and her short, dark hair accentuated her pale skin and high cheekbones. Her make-up was immaculate and her eyes seemed to follow me around the room, in exactly the same way that mine followed her. She was captivating. And I was caught.

And yet… there's something about Summer. Something really different. She's about the most laid back person I've ever met. Absolutely nothing seems to faze her. My rudeness and bad temper certainly haven't, not if that smile on her face this morning was anything to go by. There's something kind of natural about her too… something unaffected. Or is that uninhibited. I'm not sure. Unlike Bryony, I don't think she even wears make-up – at least not enough that you'd notice – and her hair is always long and loose and kind of wild.

A bit like her, I think. Because there's also something vaguely untamed about Summer. Her clothes could certainly never be called tailored, although they are fitted. Sometimes. And they're always sexy – without revealing too much. Okay… so they hint at just about everything, and they invite you to look. But they're never actually revealing.

There's something else about Summer, though. Something indefinable. It seems to come from inside her and although I can't put my finger on what it is, it makes me want her more than I've ever wanted anyone in my life.

Even though I know that's wrong.

Even though I know I shouldn't.

Or is it that I can't?

I wish I knew.

I manage to find a parking space down a side road and walk back to the café, arriving there at about ten to twelve, to find Ian already waiting for me.

"Good of you to come," he says, getting up from his seat and shaking my hand, as though he'd given me an option about whether or not to attend today's meeting.

"No problem." What else can I say? I'd rather not be here? That would be the truth, but it's not what he wants to hear.

He already has a cappuccino, so I get myself an Americano and rejoin him, sitting opposite him at the table he's selected near the back of the café, which is quite dark, with wood panelling and down lighters, the walls decorated with framed posters of 1930s advertisements for the London Underground.

"How was the journey?" he asks, making small talk.

"Not bad." It's the truth, but to be honest, I'd rather just get the meeting over and done with and get back to Millarnick. To Summer…

No, to Poppy.

And Summer.

"Good," he says, absentmindedly, turning and opening his briefcase, and pulling out a pristine laptop. "Now… I wanted to go through these courses with you… the ones you've created for us."

'Created' is perhaps overstating the facts, but I don't argue with him. He is the client, after all. What I've actually done is take their existing physical courses, which they normally deliver via seminars, and change them to be online and interactive instead, bringing them up to date and making them look both attractive and functional. There wasn't much 'creating' involved. But I'm not here to split hairs.

"Okay." I sit forward as he sets up his laptop, logging onto the café's wifi and pulling up a familiar-looking page on his browser.

"We're not sure you've completely understood what we wanted," he says, turning the screen to face me, as though I don't know what I'm looking at. And then he proceeds to tell me how I've 'misinterpreted' the brief by not including any modular assessments; how I haven't made the courses 'rigid' enough, and that people won't take their study programmes seriously if there's no certification at the end of it.

"You didn't want certification," I point out, when he finishes talking. "I specifically asked about that, and you said you didn't require it, because you don't offer it now."

"I don't remember that," he says vaguely. "And besides, all our competitors offer certification for their online courses, so it makes sense for us to have it too."

I know that. It's why I asked him the question in the first place… because I'd bothered to do my research, even if he hadn't. But I can hardly call the man an idiot. He's my client.

"What do you want me to do?" I ask, letting out a long sigh, because I've already got a feeling I know what's coming.

"We want you to put it right," he says, firmly. "I've had our people create the assessments and take a look at the way the courses are laid out, and we've come up with a practical solution to make them more formal and add in the certification. We just need you to re-work them."

Just? In other words – as I suspected – he wants me to add in these new elements that he's only just decided he wants, and because it's evidently my fault that I didn't put them in before, being as I'm not a mind-reader, he's not going to pay me any extra for my time. I could say 'no', but then I'm almost certain he'll refuse to pay for everything I've done to date, and considering I've been working on this project since the beginning of June, and it's worth a small fortune, I can't afford to risk that.

"You'll have to send me the *new* content…" I load my voice and the word 'new' with enough irony to let him know that I'm not that easily fooled. I know exactly what he's doing, and once this project is over with, he won't be doing it again. Not with me, anyway.

"I've brought it with me," he says, pulling a folder from his briefcase. "I thought we could go over it, while we have some lunch. That way we can avoid any further misunderstandings."

Part of me wants to tell him what he can do with his offer of lunch, but I can't afford to throw away two months' income. So I suck it up and push his laptop to one side, letting him lay out his paperwork and start telling me about all the extra work I've got to do.

By the time I get back to my car, it's nearly three o'clock and I'm so angry I'm not sure how I've managed to remain polite. Not only did I have to take the blame for something that wasn't my fault, I had to listen to him telling me how he'd got 'his people' to create the 'new' content really quickly, like they'd been doing me a favour, and then he took me through all forty-something pages of it, as though I was three years old and hadn't mastered the art of reading by myself. He even used a pen to point out words, every so often. It was beyond humiliating. And I swear to God, if this job wasn't worth so much money, I'd have walked out before our sandwiches arrived… especially as I ended up paying for them.

As it is, the only point I managed to score, was to tell him that I can't begin work on his 'changes' – as I made a point of calling them – until the beginning of September. He accepted my terms, because it was written into the original schedule, that any corrections that might be required wouldn't be done until then… mainly because I'd allowed the whole of August for him to go over the modules. It wasn't much of a point to score though, because my insistence on sticking to the schedule meant he could demand that I did too… which means I've got to have all the alterations completed by the middle of the month. That only gives me two weeks to complete a lot more work than I'd expected, once

I get back home with Poppy at the end of August, but there's nothing I can do about that. I can't do this kind of job on my laptop. I need my big screens. And they're at home… in Kew.

One thing I do know for sure is that when we get back from Cornwall, I'm going to really have to focus. Between these new changes and Alan Langley's job, I'll have my work cut out for me. Still, at least Ruth and Edward will be back from Portugal by then, and they don't mind having Poppy whenever I need them to. So, if Clare's still not available, I'll be able to call on them for assistance. Because I think I might need it…

I throw Ian's folder – which he kindly told me I could take away with me – onto the back seat, and take a deep breath, doing my best to calm down, before I take out my phone and connect a call to Summer. I'm not phoning because I want to talk to her, or to hear the sound of her voice. That's got nothing to do with the reason for my calling her. Nothing at all. It's just that I think I should probably let her know I'm on my way back.

"Hi." She takes a while to answer, although when she does she sounds as cheerful as ever.

"Hello."

"How did the meeting go?"

"Don't ask."

"Oh dear." It sounds to me like she's smiling, although I'm not sure.

"I'm just leaving to come back. I thought I'd let you know." I feel slightly smug – or is that justified – in clearly stating my reason for calling her.

"Oh… okay. What time do you think you'll get here?"

"Around eight, I imagine. Why?"

"I was just wondering if I should get Poppy ready for bed."

"It's probably best, just in case I end up running late. She's usually in bed by eight…"

"Okay. I'll make sure she's in her pyjamas by the time you're back."

"Thanks." I think about the long journey home, the hours that are going to have to pass before I see her… Poppy, I mean, obviously… and wish, even more so than earlier, that I'd stayed in Millarnick today, and not bothered coming up here. "How's she been?" I ask. "Has she been behaving?"

"She's been as good as gold. We've been having fun."

"With flour?" I ask, the words slipping out, in a kind of teasing tone, before I can stop them.

"No. I decided not to play with any flour today," she says, teasing me right back, and I can't help my lips from twitching upwards. "But we did get quite messy with paints."

"Paints?" I query.

"Yes. We did some painting earlier, in the garden. I let Poppy use one of Roan's old painting aprons to cover her clothes, so you don't have to worry about trying to wash red paint out of her top… although my picnic table has seen better days." She laughs. "And then I'm afraid I took advantage of your daughter being here and practiced my face painting skills."

"So what does she look like now?" I ask.

"She looks like herself. I had to make sure the paint washed off afterwards, so I cleaned the children up when we'd finished."

"And if it hadn't washed off?"

"Then your daughter would have been walking around with a face like a tiger for a while."

"In that case I'm glad it washed off."

She chuckles. "We've been a lot less messy this afternoon. So far, all we've done is make finger puppets."

All they've done? I sit in stunned silence, wondering why it is that I never find time to do things like that with Poppy. Making pizza with her last night was a huge achievement for me, but that was a means to an end. It was dinner, not just something we did for fun. Although I reason to myself that, obviously, I'm on my own, and I'm working a lot… but then so is Summer. She's a single parent too, and she has a full-time job. Maybe she's just better at this than I am…

"I see. And what are you doing now?" I ask, wondering if she's got them learning to play a musical instrument, or speak a foreign language, or split the atom, in the few hours before I get back.

"I was just getting ready to take the children to the beach," she says… and for some reason, something inside my head just flips. I'm not sure whether it's jealousy that she seems to be so much more fun and more organised than me, or that she's planning an outing without me being there with them, or whether it's the way that Summer has just assumed I won't mind what she does with my daughter, but I can feel the fire start to burn inside me, and there's nothing I can do to put it out…

"Excuse me?"

"I said…"

"I heard what you said, I just can't believe you said it. How dare you decide to take my daughter to the beach, without consulting me first. For your information, she can't swim… and she hasn't got any sun block."

"For heaven's sake, Kit. Let the girl live a little, will you? I'm not going to let her drown, and I've got plenty of sun block myself. I've got a child of my own, in case you've forgotten, and I'm not in the habit of letting him roast in the sunshine." She sounds a little miffed herself, but there's still that underlying good humour in her voice, which just winds me up even more. 'Live a little'? Who does she thinks she is?

"Don't try and tell me how to raise my own child. Again."

"I'm not. I've never tried to tell you anything, other than the fact that you need to loosen the reins a bit. That's all."

I open my mouth to speak, before I realise the line has gone dead. She hung up? How dare she…?

I reconnect the call and she answers straight away.

"Hi there." She sounds just as carefree as she did when I called the first time, even though we've just been arguing, and for a second I'm confused. This isn't what I expected. When Bryony and I fought, she could hold a grudge for hours – sometimes days, if the fight had been particularly bad. Summer is so damned different… and yet I loved Bryony with all my heart. So why is Summer the one who's haunting my dreams and tying me up in knots?

"Don't even think about taking my daughter to the beach," I growl down the phone, not bothering with the niceties of saying hello.

"I wasn't going to," she replies, quite calmly. "I heard you the first time, when you came over all bossy and domineering…" Christ… did she really just say the word 'domineering' to me? My head fills with images of her naked body, but I shake them away. "You don't want her to go," she says, sounding utterly reasonable. "And that's fine. She's your daughter and you call the shots. Even if I do think you're a kill-joy." There's that familiar smile in her voice… dammit.

"I'm…" The line goes dead again. "For Christ's sake."

I call her back a third time, grinding my teeth and gripping the phone so hard, it almost hurts.

She answers on the fourth ring this time, and before she can utter a syllable, I thunder, "Don't you dare hang up on me. Ever again," and then I disconnect the call, throwing my phone onto the passenger seat, and starting the engine, before I pull out of the parking space, the tyres screeching.

Chapter Fifteen

Summer

Roan may have friends in the village already, but he seems to have taken real shine to Poppy, which is why it was hard getting him to go to bed last night. He was so excited that she was coming over this morning... and that she'd be here for the whole day.

I get up early myself, even though that's not my forte, and because Roan was so late to bed, I let him have a bit of a lie-in, while I shower and dry my hair. It's been raining for the last couple of days, but today is bright and sunny, with a clear blue sky, and the forecast is for a scorching hot day, so I put on my favourite white sundress by way of celebration of the sun coming back out again. I've had this dress for years, but it's still my favourite, because it's light and the material is so soft – probably due to the fact that I've washed it more times than I care to think about.

Having woken a very reluctant Roan, I leave him to wash and get dressed, and make my way downstairs, opening the curtains in the living room and kitchen, and have just put on the coffee, when Kit arrives. I invite him in, although he seems a bit distracted, but then I suppose he's probably got a lot on his mind, what with the long day he's got ahead of him, so I don't mention it. I also don't mention the fact that he looks even more gorgeous than usual. I've become used to seeing him in jeans, or sometimes shorts, and t-shirts, usually looking a bit scruffy or messed up, because he's been doing something at Maggie's house. But today he's wearing smart dark blue jeans and a white formal shirt, with the first two buttons undone. I can see dark hairs poking through the 'v' at the top, and I'm so tempted to reach out and run my fingers through them, maybe undo a few more buttons and let my hands roam… and for a moment, all I can do is stare… and daydream… until I realise we've been standing in silence for far too long.

"Good morning." I inject plenty of good cheer into my voice, in the hope he doesn't realise I was just fixating on his chest, and how much I'd like to explore it, and I turn my attention to Poppy, who's standing beside him, grinning up at me. "Are you ready to have some fun?" I ask her, holding out my hand, which she takes, letting go of her father at the same time.

Kit extends his arm, offering me the rucksack he's been holding in front of him since he arrived. "I—I brought Poppy's pyjamas," he says, stuttering for some reason, and I take it from him, and lean over the arm of the sofa to place it on the seat. I'm just turning back around again, when I hear him utter the words, "Oh God," in a rather strangled voice.

"Sorry?" I look up at him and he focuses hard on my face.

"Nothing," he says. "I was just noticing the time. I need to be going."

I smile at him and then lean down to Poppy, to give her some reassurance, in case she's nervous about being left here with comparative strangers for an entire day. "Well, I'm sure we'll manage, won't we, Poppy?"

She looks up at me, a hint of doubt in her eyes. "Where's Roan?" she asks.

"He's just getting dressed. He'll be down in a minute."

I stand up straight again, as Poppy nods her head and turns back towards her father. "Behave yourself, won't you?" he says, crouching before her.

"Yes, Daddy." I struggle not to smile at the bored tone in her voice, and he stands up again, looking at me now.

"She'll be fine," I tell him, in the same voice I use when parents drop their children off for the first day of school and I'm never quite sure which of them is more nervous, and who needs more reassurance. "We're going to have lots of fun. I've got all kinds of things planned for the two of them."

He nods his head, although he doesn't reply, and then he looks down at Poppy again, a frown settling on his face, before he returns his gaze to me.

"Well, if you need me, just call. I'll keep my phone on."

I've got no intention of interrupting his meeting. "Oh, don't worry. I'm sure we'll cope."

He gazes at me for a second, as though he wants to say something and then seemingly changes his mind.

"Bye, Poppy," he says.

"Bye, Daddy."

He pauses for just a moment and then turns and opens the door, stepping out onto the path and starting to walk down it.

"We'll see you later," I call after him and he turns and raises his hand as though he's about to wave, just as I hear Roan hurtling down the stairs behind me, and start to shut the door. I'm almost certain I hear Kit say, 'Bye, Poppy' again, but when I open the door to check, he's already closed the garden gate and is striding across the green, in the direction of Maggie's house.

Roan and I still haven't had breakfast and, although she's already eaten, Poppy isn't averse to having a slice of toast with us, and once we've finished, I tell them that the first thing I've planned is painting… potato painting.

"We're going to paint potatoes?" Poppy stares up at me, frowning.

"No. We're going to paint *with* potatoes."

She still seems bemused by the idea and, while I'm explaining, I take them outside and between us, we set ourselves up on the picnic table that's half-way down the garden, unrolling the lining paper that we use for our art projects and taping it down so it doesn't blow away, and then we go back indoors and mix up some paints, putting each colour into a different foil tray. Once that's done, I send Roan upstairs to find his painting apron, and the old one that doesn't fit anymore, so Poppy can use it, and he brings them down, helping Poppy to put hers on, while I start cutting up a couple of potatoes and creating shaped stencils out of them.

Back outside, once everything is ready, I demonstrate to Poppy what she's supposed to do, dipping the cut-out potato into the tray of paint and then stamping it on the paper, before she takes over, and for an hour or so, they get creative, covering their fingers and hands in paint, dripping it all over the ground, and having a great time.

After they've completely filled the paper with multi-coloured shapes, and we've run out of paint, we clear up, and they go upstairs to play for a while, which gives me a chance to get rid of the potatoes and foil trays, and to clean down the picnic table… because we do need to eat off of it sometimes.

Once I've finished that, I call them down, because I've decided to take advantage of their presence to practice my face painting skills. And over the course of the next hour and a half, I manage a cat, a dog, a lion and – just for Poppy – a tiger. They're not the most skilful of renditions, and I'm working from videos I found online, but at least they do vaguely resemble the animals they're supposed to represent, and more importantly, the paint washes off, because I was dreading that it might not.

Lunch is sandwiches, which I get the kids to make themselves, choosing their fillings from a selection of things I bought in the supermarket yesterday. They get in another mess and I end up with bits of ham and cheese and the odd slice of tomato on the kitchen floor, but they seem to have enjoyed themselves and afterwards, I show Poppy how to peel an apple, all in one go, before cutting it up and letting them help themselves to slices.

"What are we doing next?" she asks.

"How about making finger puppets?" I suggest and she jumps up and down with glee. She seems to do that when she's excited and I can't help thinking how cute it is.

Getting our crafting box from behind the sofa in the living room, I find us some coloured paper and we sit down at the kitchen table, where I show them how to make small cones, just big enough to fit on their fingers, and then we draw faces on them, sticking on googly eyes. While they're doing that, I draw out some other shapes – an elephant, a lion and a panda, and let the two of them colour them in, before I cut them out, including small holes through which they can fit their fingers – two legs for the lion and panda and a trunk for the elephant.

They're walking their animals across the kitchen table, the lion and panda having a rather improbable fight with each other, and Poppy laughing loudly, when she turns to me and says, "I don't even have this much fun when I'm with Clare."

I feel a sudden pang of something quite painful deep inside my chest. "Who's Clare?" I ask, the question pouring from my lips before I can stop it. Can Kit really have another woman in his life? And why does that thought hurt so much?

"She's the lady who looks after me sometimes in the school holidays," Poppy replies, adding, "I used to go to her a lot more, but now I'm at school, I go to Nanny and Grandad's most of the time." And I remember that Kit mentioned that there was a friend of his late wife's who helps him out, slowly letting out the breath I didn't even realise I was holding.

I've never felt jealous before in my life, and I'm quite glad about that. It may only have been fleeting, but it wasn't a very pleasant experience. And it's not one I wish to repeat.

It's mid-afternoon, and we've cleared away our finger puppets, although Poppy wants to take the panda home with her, so we've left it on the window sill by the door. It's cooled off enough now for them both to play in the garden, so I've let them go out there, although I'm just wondering if we could go to the beach for a couple of hours. It shouldn't be too busy at this time of day, and it'd do them good to have a run-around – which they can't really do in my small back garden. I'm sure I can find an old pair of shorts and a t-shirt of Roan's for Poppy to wear, so it won't matter if she gets wet, and we'll just take some fruit and drinks, and the beach mats and some towels, so it won't be too much of an expedition, or too tight a squeeze in the car. Having made the decision, I reach the conclusion, just as quickly, that it's probably best to get everything ready first, before I tell the children about my plan and risk getting them over-excited. So, I go to the cupboard under the stairs, where I keep the beach mats and am just pulling them out, when my phone rings and I stand up straight, walking back to the coffee table, where I left it, and checking the screen... unable to stop the smile from forming on my face when I see the word 'Kit' on the screen.

"Hi," I answer quickly before my voicemail kicks in, and he starts to panic.

"Hello." Oh gosh. He sounds a bit deflated. I wonder what can have happened.

"How did the meeting go?" It seems like a reasonable place to start.

"Don't ask."

"Oh dear." Even though it doesn't sound like his meeting went very well, I can't help that smile on my face from growing a little, simply because he's such a grouch sometimes... but he's still a gorgeous grouch... and he's presumably coming home.

"I'm just leaving to come back," he says, confirming my thoughts. "I thought I'd let you know."

Well, that's considerate of him. Based on his past rudeness to me, it's perhaps more considerate than I might have expected. "Oh... okay. What time do you think you'll get here?"

"Around eight, I imagine. Why?"

I would have thought that was obvious, but clearly not. "I was just wondering if I should get Poppy ready for bed."

"It's probably best, just in case I end up running late. She's usually in bed by eight..."

And heaven forbid you could stretch that a little... "Okay. I'll make sure she's in her pyjamas by the time you get back."

"Thanks." He still sounds a bit down, but before I can say anything, he adds, "How's she been? Has she been behaving?" He seems to think she's some kind of monster, when in reality, she's a lovely, well-behaved child.

"She's been as good as gold," I tell him, truthfully. "We've been having fun."

"With flour?" he says, surprising me, because I never would have expected him to tease... or to flirt. And that sounds remarkably like flirting to me.

"No. I decided not to play with any flour today." I flirt back. Because I can. And because I like flirting. Especially with him. It's something he needs to do more often, I think. "But we did get messy with paints."

"Paints?"

"Yes. We did some painting earlier, in the garden. I let Poppy use one of Roan's old painting aprons to cover her clothes, so you don't have to worry about trying to wash red paint out of her top... although my picnic table has seen better days." I can't help laughing at how much paint they managed to get everywhere. "And then I'm afraid I took advantage of your daughter being here and practiced my face painting skills."

"So what does she look like now?" he asks.

"She looks like herself," I reply. "I had to make sure the paint washed off afterwards, so I cleaned the children up when we'd finished."

"And if it hadn't washed off?" he says, with more of a hint of humour in his voice than I might have expected.

"Then your daughter would have been walking around with a face like a tiger for a while."

"In that case I'm glad it washed off."

I chuckle, because I like it when he's like this. He's so much more... human. "We've been a lot less messy this afternoon. So far, we've just made finger puppets."

There's a short pause, before he says, "I see. And what are you doing now?" his voice suddenly more serious, and although I don't know why, all the flirting of a moment ago seems to have been forgotten, which is a shame.

"I was just getting ready to take the children to the beach," I explain, and am about to tell him my plans when I hear a sharp intake of breath on the other end of the phone.

"Excuse me?"

Wow… not only is he no longer flirting, he sounds angry. Very angry. What's wrong with him?

"I said…"

"I heard what you said," he interrupts in that familiar, rude tone of his. "I just can't believe you said it. How dare you decide to take my daughter to the beach, without consulting me first? For your information, she can't swim… and she hasn't got any sun block."

He's being such an idiot. Not for the first time. "For heaven's sake, Kit. Let the girl live a little, will you? I'm not going to let her drown, and I've got plenty of sun block myself. I've got a child of my own, in case you've forgotten and I'm not in the habit of letting him roast in the sunshine." Why does he have to be like this? Just when I think we're getting somewhere, he has to spoil it.

"Don't try and tell me how to raise my own child. Again."

What's he talking about? "I'm not. I've never tried to tell you anything, other than the fact that you need to loosen the reins a bit. That's all." I'm done with this conversation, and I end the call, putting my phone down on the coffee table and sitting on the sofa, trying not to take his words too personally.

I've barely caught my breath when my phone rings again and I'm not even remotely surprised to see Kit's name on my screen, for a second time.

"Hi there," I say, with my usual cheerfulness. Because, despite everything he's just said, I'm determined to still be me.

"Don't even think about taking my daughter to the beach," he snarls.

I take another deep breath, before replying, as calmly as I can, "I wasn't going to. I heard you the first time, when you came over all bossy and domineering." I wonder how he'll react to that. "You don't want her to go… and that's fine. She's your daughter and you call the shots. Even if I do think you're a kill-joy." There. I've said it. And I hang up a second time, before he can tell me I'm wrong. Because I'm not wrong. There wouldn't be any harm in taking Poppy and Roan to the beach. I won't – obviously – because he doesn't want me to, and I meant what I said. Poppy is his daughter, and that means he makes the decisions about what she can and can't do. But it really wouldn't hurt to let her have a bit more fun.

I get up, wondering what else we can do instead of going to the beach, just as my phone rings again. Surely it can't be... I glance at the screen and shake my head when I see Kit's name, before pressing the green button to connect the call.

"Don't you dare hang up on me. Ever again," he bellows, and the line goes dead.

Well... I guess that told me.

I've left the phone in the living room, because now that Kit's had the last word, I don't think he's likely to call again, and after a rummage around the garden shed, I've managed to find the paddling pool, which I've set up in the garden.

The kids are thrilled with the idea and, having changed Poppy into some of Roan's old shorts and a t-shirt, instead of the denim skirt and blouse she was wearing earlier, I've left them playing for a minute in Roan's room, while I change into shorts and a t-shirt, just picking the white one that's on top of the pile on my chest of drawers, that I haven't found time to put away yet – because while I like my dress, it's a bit impractical for playing in the garden, and I don't want to get it soaked... which I have a feeling might happen.

Once we're all ready, I smother both of the children in sun cream, even though it's now nearly four o'clock, and with the paddling pool filled, we let the fun commence...

Chapter Sixteen

Kit

I've taken the drive back to Millarnick a lot faster than the journey this morning, only stopping once for a necessary bathroom break, and even that annoyed me, because it slowed me down. I'm angry. Actually, I'm livid. How could Summer be so damned irresponsible? I mean… what's wrong with her? Okay, so she's beautiful, and incredibly together, and she's as sexy as hell – my dreams and the dress she was wearing this morning are testimony to that – but that doesn't give her the right to dictate to me what my daughter can or cannot do, or to talk to me like she did. Poppy is mine, and I know what's best for her. I know how to keep her safe and happy, and no-one – not even Summer Craig – has the right to say otherwise.

An accident on the M5 held me up for about twenty minutes, so it's just before a quarter to eight by the time I park up outside my mother's house, leaving my things in the car, locking it and walking straight over to Summer's house. I'm still struggling with my temper, but I've resolved that I won't get angry with her. I won't be rude either. After all, she has been kind enough to look after Poppy for the day, which got me out of a hole, and she didn't take the children to the beach… or at least she said she wouldn't…

I suck in a breath as I open the gate to her house, determined not to let myself down, and to pick up my daughter and be polite, just as the sound of squealing laughter reaches my ears. I may be tired, and fed up and angry still – despite my best intentions – but I have to smile, because I recognise Poppy's voice as she yells, "No, don't," with a giggle in her voice, and I wonder what on earth is going on... and when I last heard such happiness from my own daughter.

I ring the doorbell and step back, waiting... and waiting. But no-one answers, so I ring again, noticing the sunflowers beneath the window, although they don't hold my attention for long. Where is everyone? What on earth is going on here? Whatever it is, I'm adding impatience to my list of issues.

"Hello?" I startle and turn to see Summer standing at the side of the house, by a wooden gate she's obviously just opened. "I'm sorry," she adds, stepping out a little further, a slightly guarded expression on her face. "I thought I heard the doorbell, but I couldn't be sure. Have you been here long?"

I can't answer, because I'm completely dazzled by her. She's changed out of that stunning dress, which would be disappointing if it wasn't for the fact that she's now wearing a pair of her customary very short shorts, and a white vest-style top, with narrow straps... and nothing underneath. I know this, because her top is wet, for some reason, and I can see right through it. And what I can see is beyond even my wildest dreams.

"Kit?" she says, dragging my attention away from my fantasies and back to reality.

"Yes. Sorry... no I haven't been here very long."

"Good." She still looks a bit wary, but I suppose that's not surprising. I did yell at her the last time we spoke, and she's probably waiting for me to yell at her again, like I normally do. Except I'm not going to. Not this time. "Do you want to come round the back?" she asks, stepping to one side.

"Yes. Thanks."

I wander over to her, but then indicate that she should go first, partly because I don't know exactly where I'm going, but also because I want to try and prove that I can be a gentleman. That said, once I've closed the gate and turned to follow her, it takes all of my concentration not to focus on the sight of her perfect behind, encased in those incredibly tight shorts, or the sway of her hips, and the curve of her long, long legs…

It seems I'm really not very good at this gentlemanly thing. Not where Summer's concerned, anyway.

We come out of the darkened, narrow pathway, with her house to one side and a fence to the other, into a smallish, but neat back garden, and I'm surprised to see that, into this tight space, Summer has somehow managed to squeeze a shed, beside which are yet more sunflowers, growing up the back wall, as well as a picnic table, a patio by the house, on which there's a huge corner sofa, and footstool, and in the middle of all this, a patch of grass, which is almost filled with a paddling pool. And that explains all the noise and laughter, and Summer's wet top, I presume, because Roan and Poppy are currently splashing each other, both soaked to the skin, their hair dripping, and both clearly loving it.

"Daddy!" Poppy spots me and steps out of the pool, running over and throwing her arms around my hips. I notice that she's not wearing her skirt and blouse, but seems to have on some dark blue shorts and a red t-shirt that I don't recognise. She hugs me tight to her and I'm soaked too now, not that I mind in the slightest, because I've missed her, and I crouch down, giving her a proper hug, regardless of the cool water seeping through my shirt.

"You look like you're having fun."

"I've had the best day," she says, stepping back a little and grinning broadly, and I feel that same slight jealousy that haunted me earlier, that the 'best' day had absolutely nothing to do with me. "We've done painting," she continues, bubbling with excitement, "and we made finger puppets too, and Summer painted a tiger face on me… and a pussy cat. And she let us make our own sandwiches for lunch, and then she did a barbecue for dinner… and we had sausages and burgers in rolls, with ketchup, and we ate in the garden…" She finally comes up for air, pointing to the picnic table, still smiling. "We had to because we were wet, and didn't want to get changed yet."

"Well, that all sounds fabulous." She starts to shiver a little. "Are you cold?"

She nods her head.

"It's probably only because we're in the shade," Summer says and although I know she's right, I can't help feeling resentful. Again. "Why don't you go back to the pool," she says, as though I'm not there, as though I can't make a decision for my daughter. "It's in the sunshine and you'll be warmer."

I let Poppy run away, and then I stand and look down at Summer. "Can we speak privately?" I say, keeping my voice quiet.

"Of course. Shall we go inside?"

She doesn't wait for an answer, but walks past me, back down the alleyway, and into the house through a side door which leads directly into her kitchen. I halt on the threshold for a moment to catch my breath, because although the walls are painted yellow, and not tiled in white, her cupboard doors are pale blue and her work surface is made of a light wood of some kind... *just like my dream.*

She turns to face me, leaning back against the work surface beside the fridge freezer on the other side of the square room and, for a second, her eyes drop to my chest, before she quickly raises them again, and I notice a slight blush on her cheeks. "What's wrong?" she says softly.

What's wrong? Nothing much... only that you've made my daughter laugh more in one day than I have in three years. I take a step towards her, my heart pounding in my chest. *Nothing's wrong... apart from the fact that you're so beautiful, I can't even find the words to describe you, and you're so sexy, I can't think straight.* Her eyes fix on mine. *Nothing's wrong at all... except that you've got my head in a spin and my heart twisted in knots, and I want you so much, I ache.* I move closer still, so my body's almost touching hers. I can barely breathe, knowing all I'd have to do is lean in... close the gap by an inch, maybe two, and I could kiss her. I notice the hitch in her breathing, and the pink hue on her cheeks. Her eyes sparkle and her lips part just slightly, and I'm shaking, because I'm aware that, if I reached down, I could clasp her waist in my hands, and lift her onto the worktop behind her… she's so close… so close…

"Kit?" Her whispered voice echoes through my body and I startle, stepping back again, and moving away, in the vague direction of the back door, feeling the need to retreat, I think. "What's wrong?" she repeats.

"Everything," I growl, noting the alarm in her eyes, the sudden tension in her body.

"What…?" she starts to say, but I hold up my hand, stopping her.

"Why are the kids still out playing at this time of night?" It's the only thing I can think of to hide my humiliation, because I know – deep down – that I came too close to kissing her just then, and that if I had, there's nothing in this world that could have stopped me from making at least one of my dreams a reality, right here on her kitchen work surface. And that's because the look in her eyes, the way her breathing changed and the flush on her cheeks told me she wanted me in that moment, just as much as I want her.

She lowers her head, letting out a sigh, before she goes over to the window, bending forward slightly and looking out at the back garden, I guess to check on the children, and then she turns around and leans back on the sink, staring across at me, the table between us now.

"I was just about to stop them, when you got back. You said you wouldn't be home until eight…"

"Well, I'm back now," I interrupt, being completely unreasonable, because she's quite right, I am back earlier than she expected, being as I broke a few speed restrictions along the way. I'd have been back earlier still, if it hadn't been for that accident. She blinks rapidly a few times, making me wonder if she's going to cry – or if she's trying hard not to – and for a second, I think about relenting. But I can't. The memory of that look in her eyes, when my lips hovered above hers, is just too strong… and too tempting. "It's getting cold. You should have brought them in ages ago, not waited until they freeze to death…"

"Do you mind?" she interrupts me now. "I'm not an irresponsible person, so will you stop painting me as one. This isn't the first time you've done it, and I'm getting kind of fed up with it now. The children are both perfectly safe and well and happy. And I was literally just about to get them to come indoors and change their clothes, when you rang the doorbell. In fact… I'll go and do it now."

She steps around the table then tries to move past me, but I grab her arm, just above the elbow, looking down at her. She's breathing hard, her breasts sighing against me through her damp t-shirt, her eyes alight, and it's all I can do not to lay her down on the kitchen table and take her. My whole body is screaming at me to bring my dreams to life, to claim her body as my own, to slake this thirst once and for all. My brain – thank God – has other ideas and, releasing her, I step back.

"Don't bother," I mutter. "I'll go."

I turn and exit the kitchen, pausing just outside the doorway for a moment, warring with myself, the almost all-consuming need for her battling with my floundering reason… and losing. Which is just as well, because if I let anything happen between us now, I will regret it. And so will she.

"Poppy!" I call, taking a deep breath, as I go out into the garden, and she looks up, a surprised expression on her face. "We're going home."

"But…"

"No buts. Come on." I stand still on the edge of the patio, waiting and, with a whispered, 'Goodbye,' to Roan, she clambers from the pool again and drips her way over to me, sulking.

"Here are Poppy's things." I jump at the sound of Summer's voice so close behind me, and turn to see her walking up the narrow pathway towards us, holding out Poppy's rucksack, together with her skirt and blouse, both folded neatly, and what appears to be a piece of card lying on top, coloured in black and white, looking like a Panda's face and body, with two holes cut in the bottom where the legs should be. She turns to Poppy. "I've put your Panda puppet on top," she says, and although her voice is all soft and smiley, her eyes are red and slightly puffy, like she's been crying.

Is it too late? Could I find a way of staying? Could I apologise and maybe try to explain how she makes me feel, why she's got my head in such a spin?

But how? How would I do that, when I don't even understand it myself?

"Thank you," Poppy says, as I take my daughter's things, and then, because I can't think of a single thing to say, I grasp Poppy's hand in mine, and turning my back on Summer, I walk away.

I can't sleep.

I suppose that isn't surprising, really. After all, I feel terrible.

I treated Summer appallingly. Yet again.

I know why I did it this time too. I mean, obviously it had a lot to do with my stupid, juvenile, disgruntled jealously over the fact that Summer had made Poppy so happy in my absence. That should have made me happy too, because my daughter had spent the day enjoying herself and laughing, and being a five year-old, without a care in the world, for once… except I'm too stupid to know when I'm well off these days, it seems. Also, there was the minor matter of my meeting having gone so badly, and the fact that I'm going to have to spend quite a lot of time putting right something that I didn't get wrong in the first place – and the injustice of just having to suck that up, because the client is always right, even when they're completely wrong. But more than all of that, I was rude to Summer because I came so close to kissing her… and it really was close. I could feel her breath mingling with mine. I could see the darker green circle around her bright irises, widening and shining as I moved nearer to her. I could feel the heat from her body and longed to capture her and claim her, to own her completely. This possessive need is foreign to me, and while I've been aware of it before around Summer, I've never felt it so strongly as I did tonight. Obviously, I've wanted other women in the past too – lots of times… Bryony most of all – but it's never been like this. It's never felt so powerful, so unremitting… and while I realise that it's fuelled by my dreams, standing in front of Summer this evening made me realise for the first time, how tangible my desire actually is… and how little control I have over it.

And I think that scared me.

I wake at seven-thirty, which is quite late by my standards. But that's because I only got off to sleep in the early hours, having tossed and turned for ages, trying to make sense of everything. Trying to work out how I can have loved one woman so much, and yet want another to the point of losing my mind.

I gave up in the end – because I'm not sure I'll ever be able to make sense of how I feel about Summer, and because the guilt is starting to get a bit too much, and that hasn't been helped by my dream. Even in those few short hours of sleep, I still managed to cram in another one. We were outdoors again this time, which I know is all part of that unfulfilled fantasy of mine. The place we were in was a kind of woodland, which was conveniently devoid of any other people. There were no dog-walkers, no-one out on a romantic jaunt, or even a passing jogger or two. So there was no-one there to notice that we were completely naked, or to see me push Summer back against the wide tree trunk and kneel before her, parting her legs as wide as they would comfortably go and letting my tongue slide down her exposed, delicate folds. No-one witnessed the moment when she clasped her hands behind my head and I grabbed her by the wrists and held her arms by her sides, controlling her reactions to my avid attentions. No-one heard her cries of ecstasy either, or saw me stand and enter her, even before her moans had subsided to stuttering whispers.

We were completely alone.

And yet I'd never felt more at one with anyone in my life.

After yesterday and last night – and that dream – I've decided there's no point in wasting any more time trying to analyse what's going on. I don't think I'll ever work it out, so I get up instead, and take a shower, before getting dressed and going downstairs to make breakfast.

There's no sign of Poppy yet, but I hear her surface a few minutes later and then hear her footsteps on the stairs, slowly descending.

"Good morning," I say, as she comes into the kitchen, still in her pyjamas, looking like she just woke up – which is perfectly possible, considering how much fun she had yesterday. Without me.

She doesn't reply, but clambers up onto her usual chair and stares out of the window.

She must be tired. But again, that's not surprising. When we got back here yesterday evening, she was too exhausted to even speak and, after

I'd dried her off, she got herself into her pyjamas, while I was putting the damp towel in the bathroom, and by the time I came back into her bedroom, was already fast asleep.

"Toast or cereal?" I ask, but still she doesn't respond and I go over to the table, standing opposite her. "Poppy?"

She continues to stare out of the window, slightly to my left.

"Are you not talking to me?" I ask, when the silence has stretched to ludicrous proportions and she sits up straight, staring me in the face now, which I take to be a 'Yes'. A silent 'Yes'. I let out a sigh and sit down, so at least we're on the same level. "What did I do wrong?"

She still doesn't answer.

"Poppy… I can't put it right, if you don't tell me what I did wrong."

I'm reminded of the number of times I've said that before, addressing the statement to my late wife instead of our daughter. Over the years, I've been quite good at saying or doing the wrong thing – inadvertently, I hasten to add – and Bryony, in turn, was quite good at pointing out the errors of my ways. Eventually. Once she'd made me suffer in silence for a while. I accepted that from my wife, but I'm damned if I'm going to take it from a five year-old.

"Poppy!" I shout and she startles, looking scared now, and I regret raising my voice to her. "Please, sweetheart," I say, more soothingly. "Tell me what I did wrong?"

"You were horrible," she says, her bottom lip trembling.

"When was I horrible?"

"Yesterday… to Summer. You made her cry."

"How do you know…? I mean, how do you know it was me that made her cry?" There's no point in denying that she'd been crying. It was obvious.

She narrows her eyes… *just like her mother.* "Because you were talking to her, and then you came outside, and were all cross… and then when Summer came out, her eyes were red, like she'd been crying. It was your fault, Daddy."

I feel the weight of her blame on my shoulders. But what can I say? How can I explain it to her, when I don't understand it myself?

"I'm sorry," I mutter, because I know that's the right thing to say... even if I'm saying it to the wrong person. Again.

"I had such a good time yesterday," she says, tears forming in her eyes, as though she hasn't heard me. "And you spoiled it. Summer probably won't let me go and play there anymore."

"I'm sure she will."

"No, she won't," she cries and, with a scrape of her chair, she jumps down from the table and runs out of the room.

I let my head fall into my hands and sit for a moment. I'm going to have to do something... that much is clear. Not only have I upset Summer, which is bad enough, but I've upset Poppy as well.

I get to my feet and go out into the hallway, slowly climbing the stairs, turning at the top and going along the landing to Poppy's room... my room that was. The door's ajar and she's lying on the bed, sobbing.

I don't say anything, but I go in and sit down on the bed and wait. And eventually, she turns and stares at me, the look of disappointment in her eyes making my breath catch in my throat.

"I'm sorry," I manage to whisper. "I didn't mean to spoil your day."

"Did you mean to make Summer cry?"

"No. Of course not." That's true. It's very true. The very last thing I want is to make Summer cry. She may have got my head and my heart in a mess, but that's not her fault. It's mine. And I don't want to hurt her, or upset her... and I definitely don't want to make her cry. Although I seem to have become an expert at doing all three of those things at the moment.

"Then why are you so mean to her?"

Good question.

I take a deep breath. "Sometimes grown ups say things they don't mean," I reply, trying to find a reasonable explanation for my unreasonable behaviour.

"If they don't mean to say them, then shouldn't they say sorry?" Poppy asks, and I reach across the bed, pulling her towards me and onto my lap. She lets me and sits there, gazing up at me, full of expectation. Can I let her down? I've let Summer down more than enough. And I've let myself down... can I seriously let my daughter down as well?

Of course I can't.

"Yes, they should," I whisper, kissing her damp cheek, and she raises her arms around my neck, giving me a hug. I hug her back, holding her tiny body close to mine, wondering what on earth I'm going to do next. I've got no idea what I'm going to say to Summer, or how I'm going to say it, but for the sake of my daughter, and Summer… and, if I'm being completely honest, myself… I really need to find a way.

Chapter Seventeen

Summer

I haven't slept very well.

But that's not surprising really; not after the way Kit behaved yesterday evening.

Why does he keep doing this to me? Or more to the point, why do I let him?

Well, I suppose I know the answer to that last question. I let him, because I like him. A lot. I'm attracted to him, and I want to help him. Because he needs help. That much is obvious.

As for why he keeps doing this to me… I have no idea. I don't understand him at all. One minute he's perfectly 'normal', and seemingly quite friendly, and the next, he's jumping down my throat. I suppose yesterday was the perfect example of that. We were getting on just fine on the phone, until I mentioned taking the children to the beach, which he obviously didn't agree with, but rather than just saying so, he yelled at me. Repeatedly. But then when he got back here, when I half expected him to carry on his argument, he actually seemed like he was going to be okay again… for about five minutes. I wasn't sure why he asked to see me privately, but I suppose a part of me wondered if he wanted to apologise for yelling down the phone at me. He didn't need to apologise. Not really. I did understand his sentiments, even if I didn't agree with his expression of them.

Something happened when we got into the kitchen though. It was weird. Weird and acutely sexual, probably made more so by the fact that his shirt was wet from where Poppy had hugged him. The fabric had glued itself to his chest, and I could see the outline of his muscles, the way they flexed and rippled when he moved, and I have to admit, I stared… just for a second. But then I became even more distracted by the way he was looking at me, the way he stepped closer, like a predator stalking its prey. I didn't feel threatened by him though… just deeply aroused. There was something kind of raw and profoundly masculine about him, which was really rather intoxicating, and very stimulating, and I could feel a sort of charge between us, like electricity sparking. And for a moment I thought he was going to kiss me. I wanted that kiss. I wanted it so much, I could feel it.

And then he blew up in my face.

And that got to me – partly because I'd wanted his kiss so much – but also because it didn't seem to matter how much I explained the situation to him, he just wouldn't listen. He wouldn't be reasonable. And it was all I could do not to cry in front of him.

But then, even when I tried to do what he wanted – namely go and fetch the children – he stopped me, holding my arm and gazing deeply into my eyes, switching from evident anger to something else… something much more sensual, in the blink of an eye. And then just as quickly, he flipped back again, dismissing me.

That was too much, I'm afraid, and after he'd stormed out of the kitchen door, I let the tears flow, quickly grabbing some kitchen towel to wipe them away, just in case he came back again. He was being so capricious it was hard to know what he'd do next. He didn't return though, so I gathered up Poppy's things and took them out onto the patio for him, hoping he wouldn't notice how much he'd got to me.

Because that's the last thing I want him to know.

I don't want him to know that, even now, even after everything he's said and done, I'd still like for us to be friends, I'd still like to help him… and, more than anything, I still want that kiss.

*

Today has been even hotter than yesterday, which is annoying because I'm so tired and I can't seem to raise the enthusiasm to do anything.

Fortunately, Roan has been really good all day and he's upstairs now playing with his trains, while I'm sitting on the sofa with my feet up, reading a romantic novel one of my fellow teachers recommended to me before we broke up for the holidays. I'm not sure it's really my 'thing', and I'm struggling to get into it, but maybe that's because I can't suspend reality to the extent that romantic fiction seems to require. After all, if life were like a romance novel, Russell would have woken up after our night of undiluted passion, declared his undying love for me and proposed marriage, just on the basis that he couldn't live without me. He certainly wouldn't have dismissed me so flippantly and suggest I abort his child... the beautiful little boy who's playing so happily upstairs. If life were like a romance novel, my father would have been more committed to my mother, rather than to his mistress – whoever she was – he'd have spent more time with us, and made sure we were happy, rather than just focusing on himself. And if life were like a romance novel, I'd know what Kit wanted from me, because he'd be able to tell me. Because men in novels can do that... unlike men in real life.

I let out a sigh and turn the page, only then realising that I haven't been following the plot at all, for the last twenty minutes, and I have to turn back to the beginning of the chapter and start again.

I must have drifted off to sleep, because the ringing of the doorbell startles me awake and I clamber to my feet, putting my book down on the table, and straightening my sundress, before I go over and pull the door open, trying not to gasp, or to smile at the scene that greets me.

Poppy is standing right on my doorstep, almost hidden behind a huge and beautiful hand-tied bouquet of flowers, and a step or two behind her is Kit. He's holding a bottle of white wine, but it's the look on his face that really grabs my attention. I don't think I've ever seen anyone look so pained in all my life.

I open my mouth to speak, to invite them in, but before I can say a word, he holds up his hand, silencing me.

"Me first," he says, and I notice his voice seems a little deeper than usual. "I—I need to apologise to you. Not for the first time, I was appallingly rude to you yesterday, and I'm truly sorry."

Well, that was an apology, if ever I heard one, and I smile up at him, before standing back and silently inviting them in.

Poppy walks past me first, followed by Kit, and as he passes, I whisper, "Thank you," to him and he sighs, shaking his head.

"Don't thank me," he murmurs.

"Why not?"

I close the door and turn to face him.

"Because Poppy had to persuade me to come over here and say sorry to you."

Oh. That makes his apology a little less special. But at least he was honest.

"I see." I look down at his daughter, who's still holding the flowers, gazing up at her father, expectantly. "And why was that?" I turn my attention back to Kit.

"Because I'm an idiot?" he suggests.

I shake my head now, and reach out, placing my hand on his forearm, feeling his muscles flex beneath my touch. "No, you're not."

"I think we'll have to agree to disagree on that, but the point is, am I forgiven?"

"Of course you are. And it doesn't matter why you came; what matters is that you did." He tilts his head slightly, looking a bit confused, I think… but I don't want to dwell on that, or on what's gone before, and releasing my grip on his arm, I move further into the living room. "Would you like to have a cup of tea? I was just going to make one." That's not strictly true, being as I was just fast asleep, but I am thirsty and now that he's here, I'd like for him to stay.

"I'd rather have a glass of wine," he says, smiling and holding up the bottle, condensation forming on the outside of the pale green glass.

I'm surprised, but I do my best to hide it. "Well, I'm not going to say 'no'."

I glance down at Poppy. "Roan's upstairs, if you want to go and find him."

She grins and turns away, but then stops and holds up the bouquet of flowers to me. "These are for you. They're from Daddy really, not me. But he made me carry them."

I take the flowers from her, feeling myself blush, and she runs up the stairs, as I turn to Kit and he shrugs his shoulders.

"Trust a five year-old to blurt out the truth," he mumbles.

"You didn't have to buy me flowers," I whisper, walking into the kitchen.

"Yes, I did," he replies, following behind me. "I've been far too rude to you ever since we got here, for me not to at least buy you something by way of an apology." I stand at the kitchen table and look up at him as he continues, "And when we went to the florists, they had a poster up behind the counter, which revealed that flowers have meanings. I never realised that, so rather than just getting them to make up a nondescript bouquet, I chose them all myself… and all of these…" He looks down at the flowers that I'm still holding between us. "The roses, and these ones…" He points to a pale yellow blossom.

"Carnations," I offer.

"Yes, those. And the… um…" He points to a bright orange bloom this time.

"Gerberas," I say, smiling.

"Yes, those too. Well, they all mean sorry. Except the sunflowers, which I picked because you seem to like them."

He stops talking and I gaze up into his face, noticing the flush on his cheeks, before I turn and put the flowers down on the table beside me.

"That's the nicest thing anyone's ever done for me," I whisper. "But you really didn't need to apologise. Not even with beautiful flowers. I do understand, you know."

He looks a bit startled and, putting the wine down on the table too, he runs his fingers through his hair. "You do?"

"Yes. My mother only died four months ago. I can appreciate at least some of what you're going through."

His face clears, in terms of his confusion, but then his eyes darken and a sadness sweeps across his perfect features as he steps forward a little. "Four months ago? I… I knew, from what you'd said, that she'd died, but I had no idea it was so recent," he murmurs.

I move around him, going to the sink and fetching a vase, putting it in the middle of the kitchen table, and starting to arrange the flowers.

"I'm sorry, Summer." He sounds tormented.

"Don't be. That word is officially banned. Remember? I've already told you, it's a sad word… and I don't allow sad words."

He smiles and, once I've finished with the flowers, I hand him the corkscrew from the drawer underneath the draining board, while I fetch the wine glasses from the cupboard next to the fridge freezer.

"I miss your mum," I add, turning back to him, to find he hasn't moved; he hasn't even opened the wine, and is just staring at me. "Do you want to bring that outside?" I nod towards the bottle and, he seems to come out of his trance, picking it up and following me through the back door and onto the patio, where we sit down on the corner sofa and I watch him open the wine, before he pours it into the long stemmed glasses I've brought out. We clink them together, neither of us saying anything, and then he sits back, his arm along the back of the couch, looking relaxed for once, as he takes a sip of wine.

"I like this," he says eventually and I know he's avoiding talking… about anything important, that is. And for now, I'm going to let him.

"You like what?"

"This sofa. It's comfortable."

"It's far too big for my tiny patio, is what it is," I point out. "But I've always wanted something like it, and I found it in the garden centre a few weeks ago… and it was reduced, so I decided that it didn't matter if it didn't really fit. I was going to have it."

"Do you always see something you like and go for it?" he asks. "Even if it isn't entirely practical and might not work out?"

I'm not sure what that means, but I have a distinct feeling he isn't talking about patio furniture. Not anymore.

"Sometimes. Don't you?"

I've put the ball firmly back in his court. But rather than answering me, he takes another sip of wine and then leans forward. "Does the footstool join onto the sofa?" he asks.

"Yes." I stand up, putting my wine down on the floor beside the couch, and demonstrate. "You'll have to move your legs." I tell him and he raises them, while I push the footstool into place, and he puts his feet back down on it, lying out now. "It squares up the sofa and turns it into a daybed," I explain, as I clamber back over it, getting caught up in my dress in the process. It takes me a moment, kneeling there and pulling my dress out from under my knees, before I flop back down onto the sofa again. "And I need to remember that children are far better suited to crawling than adults," I remark, shaking my head.

"Oh, I don't know," he says, and I turn to see he's smiling at me.

I smile back, and pick up my wine from the ground, raising my glass to my lips and taking a sip, all the while aware that he's watching me.

"I miss her too," he says, as I lower my glass again.

Finally. He speaks. I'm not sure who he's talking about though, being as it could be his mother, or his wife.

"Who?" I ask, gazing at him over the top of my glass and twisting in my seat so I'm facing him.

"Mum," he says, even though I know that's not all of it.

"She was an amazing woman."

He smiles. "Yes, she was."

"She was a godsend to me, when Mum was diagnosed…"

"With what?" he asks. "I mean… what did she die of?"

"Liver cancer. It was advanced and they only gave her a few months to live. We were both so shocked… but your mum was there, like an absolute rock. I don't know what we'd have done without her."

"I'm glad," he murmurs, taking a deep breath; so deep, I can almost feel his pain. "I just wish I'd been able to make it up with her before she died. I wish I hadn't left it too late."

There's a crack in his voice and, even in the shade, I can see tears in his eyes. He's in agony and I can't sit two feet away and just watch him suffer, so I move closer, letting my hand rest on his leg.

"Don't regret it, Kit. There's nothing you can do about it now, and regrets won't help you heal."

"I know… but she died so suddenly. It's not like it was with Bryony, and probably like it was with you and your mother too." He sniffs and blinks rapidly, trying to be strong, to hold his emotions in check, even though he doesn't need to. Not with me. "When Bryony died," he whispers, almost to himself, "we had the chance to tell each other how we felt, to talk about the future we weren't going to have anymore. I got to listen to what she wanted for Poppy, and to her fears, and to hide my own." Oh… I wish he hadn't done that… or felt he had to. "But Mum was snatched from me, just like that," he continues, with a kind of desperation in his voice as he clicks his finger and thumb together, demonstrating his point. "I—I mean, I don't even know what she was doing, driving to Plymouth. She didn't have any friends there, as far as I know… not that I'd know where her friends were now. But, it was so fast… in the blink of an eye, before I got the chance to tell her I was sorry. I *am* sorry."

He glances up at me, and I can tell from the look on his face that he half expects me to tell him off for saying 'sorry', when I've asked him not to. That's the last thing on my mind.

"Did she hate me?" he asks instead, completely out of the blue.

"Your mother? Hate you?" I can't believe he's asking that, but he nods his head, confirming his question. "God no."

"Even though I was so utterly hateful to her, when we argued?"

I move even closer, so I'm almost lying alongside him now. "She didn't hate you, Kit. She talked about you all the time, and she loved you so much… you and Poppy."

"Really?" He looks down at me, doubt casting a shadow over his face.

"Yes. Really."

He manages a slight smile. "I'm glad you and she were friends," he says softly, looking right into my eyes.

"So am I."

"I'm glad you had her with you when your mother was dying."

"I'm glad you had her there with you when Bryony was dying too."

His brow furrows. "How did you know she was there?"

"Because she told me about it. We talked a lot."

"Oh… so you know all about our argument, I suppose. You know how badly I behaved." He leans back slightly, away from me.

"I know there was a falling out," I say softly. "I know your mother was hurt and confused." Pain clouds his face. "But that didn't stop her from loving you, Kit, or from wanting to be there for you, to help you."

He shakes his head. "She was there for me… and she helped me so much. At least I didn't have to grieve alone. I've always been grateful to her for that."

I reach out and touch his forearm again, just like earlier, in the house. Only this time, I stroke my hand up and down, very gently and his breathing seems to quicken. "You're still grieving, Kit, no matter how hard to try and hide it. And not just for your mother. The thing is… you need to let yourself."

He looks down at me, seemingly confused, although he doesn't deny the truth of what I'm saying. I don't remove my hand from his arm and he doesn't seem to mind it being there either, and for a moment, we just sit, and I let him acknowledge to himself that he's on a journey… and he's got a long way to go yet.

"Do you want to stay for dinner?" The words leave my mouth before I've even had time to think them through, or work out whether I've got enough salad for four of us. But even as I'm saying them, I realise that I don't want him to leave. I want to spend some time with him. I want him to talk some more, to open up… and I still want that kiss. He hesitates, his eyes fixed on mine, and I wonder what he's thinking. "I was just going to barbecue some chicken," I add, hoping to persuade him, "so you can take care of that, if you like, and I'll fix us a salad." Well, I will, if I can cobble together enough ingredients. "And then afterwards, maybe the kids can watch a movie, and we can talk some more…" His eyes flicker, and I have to smile as I wonder if maybe he'd rather not talk too much… if maybe he'd like to have that kiss too. God… I hope so. "Or, if you'd prefer, we can finish off this bottle of wine, open another, and just get drunk… what do you say?"

He smiles and, without any hesitation this time, nods his head.

"We'd love to stay," he murmurs, and my smile broadens.

"I suppose we ought to let the children know." I go to stand, but he pulls me back down.

"In a minute," he says, raising his glass of wine. "Let's finish this first."

And without taking our eyes from each other, we clink our glasses together.

We didn't finish the bottle, because we knew we needed to cook dinner and be vaguely responsible for a couple of young children, but we did have another half glass each, before I went inside and called up to the children, asking them to come outside.

"Yes?" Roan says, running out through the kitchen and into the garden, Poppy following close behind. They stand side-by-side, looking at Kit and I, as we sit on the end of the day bed now, rather than lounging all over it.

"Summer's invited us to stay for dinner," Kit says, before I get the chance to speak.

"Oh… can we? Please?" Poppy says, jumping up and down, in her usual excited manner.

"Yes." He says, and both children leap up, gleefully bypassing us and crawling over to the other side of the bed, nestling on the couch part, and we turn to look at them, smug smiles on their faces, their heads bent together.

"I don't know why you're looking so comfortable, Roan Craig." I narrow my eyes playfully at my son. "You've got to help Kit with the barbecue."

"Oh… okay, Mum." He shuffles to the side of the bed and jumps down again. "Shall I get the charcoal from the shed?"

"Thank you. That would be really helpful."

"Do you want to come, Poppy?" he asks, holding out his hand, and she nods and shimmies to the edge of the bed too, before letting him help her down, and they run off down the garden.

"He's really good, you know?" Kit says, looking at both of them.

"Thank you." I can feel myself blushing. "Poppy's a lovely little girl too."

"Thanks. But I can hardly claim any credit. She's been raised, effectively, by my in-laws and Bryony's best friend. I've had very little to do with it."

I frown, turning to face him and place my hand on his thigh at the same time. "Don't say that. I know how hard it is, being a single parent, and you're doing a fantastic job."

"With a lot of help."

"So? I had help too… right up until Mum died… and then your mum took over. I've only been truly on my own for the last few weeks. So you can stop putting yourself down and painting me as some kind of superwoman. We all muddle through, quite often messing things up along the way, usually collapsing with relief, just because we've made it to the end of another day, and congratulating ourselves because we actually got to five o'clock before we opened the bottle of wine. No-one's perfect, Kit."

"Not even you?" he says, his voice a little deeper than usual.

"Especially not me."

He smiles, the sweetest of smiles and lets out a long sigh, and I'd swear he leans into me a fraction, just as Roan calls out from the bottom of the garden.

"Yes?" I sit back slightly, feeling aggrieved that I might have just missed out on a kiss... again. And I look round Kit, to where Roan is peering at us through the shed door.

"The open bag of charcoal doesn't have much in it, and I can't carry the new one. It's too heavy."

"Oh… okay. Hang on a second."

I go to get up, but Kit places his hand on my arm, the warmth of his skin seeping into me. "I think you'll find that barbecuing is a man's work," he says, grinning now and getting to his feet, releasing me at the same time, unfortunately.

"It is?"

He nods, and I shield my eyes from the sun, so I can see him better, and only narrowly avoid moaning out loud at how utterly gorgeous he looks, especially now he's relaxed a little – probably because of the wine.

"Yes. You leave this to Roan and me."

"Okay. I will. And as we're into sexual stereotyping all of a sudden, perhaps you could send Poppy back down here and she could help with the salads?"

He chuckles and nods his head, and then turns to leave, but stops suddenly and looks back at me. "Do you always include Roan in everything?"

I frown at him, even though I'm smiling.

"Not absolutely everything, no. But I try to include him in as many things as possible."

He nods his head, raises his eyebrows just briefly, and then walks away.

I wonder what on earth that was about?

I'd got two chicken breasts out of the freezer already, so I cut them in half and marinate them in garlic and lemon juice, with a little of the white wine, and then dig out some burgers and sausages – which I always have in the freezer anyway - putting the whole lot in separate bowls on a tray and carrying it out to the back garden, with Poppy in tow, who's carrying the barbecue tongs.

Roan and Kit seem to have set everything up and the charcoal's heating – although it's not quite ready yet, which is just as well, because there's a lot of salad to prepare… and what I mean by that is, I've got to get creative with a few ingredients, to make a lot of salad.

"Come back inside with me," I say to Poppy, taking her hand, once we've put the tray down on the picnic table. "We've still got work to do."

She smiles at Roan and then at her father, who gives me a wink that makes my stomach flip over, because I guess I'm still thinking about that kiss we haven't had yet, and we head back to the kitchen, where I distract myself, finding I've got some new potatoes, and half a white cabbage in the salad drawer of my fridge.

"We can make potato salad and coleslaw," I announce, pulling them out.

"*Make* them?" Poppy says, wide eyed.

"Yes." I turn to her, and pulling out a saucepan to cook the potatoes, we set to work.

Chapter Eighteen

Kit

The thought of spending the evening with Summer, whether we end up sitting and talking, or sitting and getting drunk – or even just sitting – was just too good to turn down.

I know I've spent the last few days battling with myself, fighting my attraction to her, but sitting out here with her – or more to the point, *lying* out here with her – on her day bed, in her tiny garden, in the shade of her quaint little cottage, I've never felt more at ease with anyone. I've certainly never talked to anyone like I've talked to her this afternoon, with no holds barred... well, except Bryony, of course. Although it's hard not to recall the fact that she kept her suspicions about her illness from me, hid the death of her aunt, and let fear get in the way of her diagnosis... until it was too late. I wonder, for a moment, if Summer would do something like that, but as she leans forward, pulling up the skirt of her dress by a few inches and rubbing her leg, I realise she wouldn't. She's a very open person... in all kinds of ways. What you see is what you get with Summer and I smile to myself, remembering how cute she looked earlier on, when she was trying to crawl back up the daybed on her knees and her skirt got caught. She had to stop and free it, giving me a glimpse of her perfect thighs, which I've seen before –

obviously – because she wears the shortest of shorts, but seeing them like that… revealed rather tantalisingly beneath her pale blue and white striped sundress was somehow even more erotic.

It made me really glad that Poppy talked me into apologising. Of course, the manner of the apology came from me, and after Poppy had finally been persuaded to eat some breakfast and get dressed, we drove into Looe, where we found a florist, who arranged the bouquet of flowers to my specification, and then I went to the supermarket and bought the wine. I thought the flowers might be enough of a 'sorry', especially given that I'd selected each and every stem myself, but I was kind of hoping Summer might invite us to stay for a while, and the wine was a prelude to that… an offering, if you like. And she took it, even after I'd explained that the apology was Poppy's idea – because I had to tell the truth, despite putting myself on dangerous ground at that point. It probably didn't hurt that I told her about the flowers… about what they signify, and how I'd picked them out personally. I think that meant something to her. It meant something to me, I know that.

And then we sat and talked – well, she talked to start with, because I was still reeling… from the fact that she'd accepted my apology in the first place, and from how aroused I was by the sight of her in yet another tempting sundress… and from the fact that she's just such a genuine, decent, beautiful, human being.

I think it was Summer's openness and decency that made me finally decide to talk to her. She'd given me a couple of opportunities earlier on, which I'd chosen to ignore, but just seeing her like that, lying beside me, so natural and enchanting, I didn't want to hold back anymore. I wanted to talk. For the first time in years. And she seemed to want to listen. She was good at it too. She tried to make me feel better about the argument with my mother, although I didn't explain the reason behind it. I didn't feel ready for that level of disclosure… And she made some really kind – and very observant – comments too. Such as reassuring me that my mother didn't hate me; that in fact, she loved me – and Poppy – right to the end, in spite of the fact that I was so hateful to her. Summer also pointed out that, regardless of what I try to tell people, I'm still grieving for Bryony. I mean, I've always known that on the inside, but I try to hide it. And yet, she saw it straight away, and somehow made it feel okay… just like she does with everything else. It's odd, but I think if anyone other than Summer had said any of that to me, I'd have argued with them. Ruth's tried it a few times in the last year or so, and even Clare has from time to time, and I've always dismissed everything they've said. But with Summer, I didn't. That in itself is unusual, being as I've done nothing but argue with her since I first met her. But the thing is, it was like she could see right through me, so there was no point in trying to clam up or hide, or even be dismissive. She wouldn't have believed me if I'd said, 'It's been three years, and that's long enough,' or 'I don't have time for grief,' or any of the things I occasionally say to other people – including myself – when I'm lonely enough to let the weakness show on the outside.

She touched me every so often, on my leg, or my arm. It was intimate and personal, and yet it wasn't sexual. Perhaps that was because of what we were talking about… or maybe because her touch meant so much more than mere physical contact. I don't know… just like so many other things that I don't know about her.

I do know that, when we were talking about the children, she made me realise that I've been utterly stupid. Not for the first time. I've been so petty and jealous, seeing her as getting everything right and seeing my own failings at every turn, when in reality – as she explained – she's needed just as much help as I have to get to this point… only hers has been snatched away. I hadn't allowed for that, and she wasn't asking me to. She was just telling me to let up… to give myself a break.

I wanted to kiss her when she said that, and I think I would have done if Roan hadn't interrupted us. It's probably just as well that he did though, because I don't want our first kiss to be anywhere near the children… because the other thing I know is that it's not going to stop with a kiss.

Not now.

Summer's brought out a tray with some chicken breasts, burgers and sausages and, I get the feeling, because the chicken is cut up, that she's cobbling this meal together. Part of me wants to offer to go to the store and get us some extra food, but I don't want her to feel insulted. She offered this invitation and I'm assuming she thought it through, and I don't want her to think I don't have any faith in her. I do... So, Roan and I set to and start cooking.

Like his mother, he's really cheerful and happy to help. We talk quite amicably, and although he asks a fair few questions, he doesn't seem to have any ulterior motive. In fact, the things he's most interested in are my car, which is a fairly new black BMW... and Poppy. Which makes me smile. He and Summer clearly have a really close relationship. She said she includes him in as much of her life as possible, and I know I could – and should – take a leaf out of her book, when it comes to Poppy. Which was why I asked that question in the first place. I wanted to know how she keeps her son so cheerful. And now I have the answer, I'm going to try harder. I really am. Because I can see how contented they are together... and I want that for my daughter too.

As I'm turning the sausages and Roan runs back inside to see whether his mother wants him to lay the table – at his suggestion, not mine – I wonder to myself, given my knowledge of his father and his actions, whether he and Summer haven't been better off on their own.

Roan returns with some cutlery, and Poppy, who's carrying a bowl, rather carefully.

"What's that?" I ask her.

"It's coleslaw. We made it."

"You made it?"

"Yes." She beams up at me. "Summer's making potato salad too."

It's been years since I had home-made potato salad, or coleslaw... not since I left home, actually, and I leave the barbecue, taking the bowl from Poppy and putting it on the table... while mentally taking back everything I might have just been thinking about Summer. Even if she is cobbling this meal together, she's doing a damn fine job of it.

Dinner is fantastic.

Summer's potato salad is probably one of the best things I've ever eaten, and for someone who gave up caring about food quite some time ago, that's saying something. We polish off the whole lot between us, after which we all clear away together, while Summer loads the dishwasher.

"Mum?" Roan says, bringing in the last of the dishes from the table. "Can Poppy and I go up to my room and watch *The Incredibles*?"

She glances at the clock on the wall before answering, "You can, but only for half an hour. Poppy has to be in bed by eight… and so do you."

She looks over at me as she finishes talking, perhaps remembering all the horrible things I said to her yesterday, and I smile at her, reassuringly, I hope. Because I want to forget about yesterday. I want to forget all the times I've been horrible to her.

"I'm sure we can let bedtime slide, just a little bit," I say to her, although I'm really talking to everyone, I suppose.

Poppy leaps up and down and Roan just says, "Yay!" before they both run off upstairs.

"Well… they're easily pleased," I say to Summer and she smiles at me.

"Shall we open that second bottle of wine?" she suggests. "We finished the first one with dinner."

"Why not?"

She goes to her fridge and retrieves an Italian white, handing it to me. "I think the corkscrew is still outside," she murmurs.

"Hmm… so are our wine glasses. I left them by the day bed."

"I wondered what had happened to them."

"Roan was getting a little too keen with his clearing up, and I thought we might want to have another drink yet… so I rescued them."

She tips her head and smiles at me. "Well, let's make the most of a little peace and quiet, shall we?"

I'm not sure what to read into that, or whether I should read anything into it at all, so I don't say a word, and let her lead me back out into the garden, which is shrouded in shadows now.

I climb onto the day bed, kicking off my shoes first this time, so I can be more comfortable… and also because I've noticed that Summer rarely wears shoes at home. She wanders around with bare feet, which seems very liberating… and worth a try. But before I settle back, I find the corkscrew on the floor, and open the bottle, turning to find Summer right beside me, one glass in each hand, holding them out to me.

"I'm glad I don't have to drive anywhere," I remark, pouring the wine. "I don't think I've drunk this much in ages."

She smiles. "Neither have I, but that's only because I spend so much time by myself, and people would talk if I started buying wine by the crate… especially here."

I put the bottle down on the floor beside me, taking my glass from her and clinking them together. "You shouldn't be by yourself," I murmur, hoping that doesn't sound too corny or presumptuous, even if it probably is, because as much as she's a strong, independent woman, capable of changing a tap washer, or a plug, all by herself, she's also someone who should be loved… frequently.

There's a kind of change in the atmosphere between us. It's suddenly highly charged, potent. Electric. We're staring at each other, holding our glasses, although neither of us takes a drink, but then Summer leans forward and I do too, focusing on her lips, on the soft fullness of them, and I feel my heart pounding in my chest, because I know I'm about to kiss her…

We both pause. It's obvious she's waiting for me to make the next move. And yet I can't. Even though I've wanted this since the first time I saw her. Even though I've come close on at least two occasions before now. I can't kiss her…

"What's wrong?" she whispers eventually.

"There's something I need to tell you."

She frowns and I take her glass, leaning over and putting it on the ground, alongside my own. I've been thinking all evening how open and artless she is. But I'm not. Because there's something I've been holding back. And I can't hold it back any longer.

I turn around to face her, and find that she's changed position. She's sitting with her legs pulled up, her hands clasped around them, gazing at me.

"What is it?" she says, her voice still quiet.

"I haven't been completely honest with you." That's the understatement of the century.

"In what way?"

"Because I didn't tell you the truth about my argument with my mother."

She leans back, letting her legs fall to the cushion of the daybed, and turns over so she's facing me, propping herself up on one elbow. "I don't understand," she says.

"What don't you understand?"

"What it is that you think you need to tell me. I already know what happened. Your mother told me."

I suck in a breath and let it out slowly. "And what exactly did she tell you?"

"She said that a few weeks after your wife died, she suggested that you and Poppy should move back here, to the village, and that you... well, you went ballistic at her. That wasn't her word, by the way."

"No, I can't imagine it was, although it's a fairly apt description. It also isn't entirely what happened."

"It's not?"

"No, because it doesn't take into account the reason why I went ballistic. She didn't know the reason herself, which is why she couldn't tell you, but it's why I regret more than anything that I didn't make friends with her again before she died."

"So it wasn't because you didn't like her interfering then?" she asks.

"No. Is that what she thought?"

"I'm not sure. I think she knew there was something else behind it, something else that was troubling you, because whenever we'd talked about you, I used to tell her that life's too short to bear grudges, and she always used to tell me that she wasn't... that she was waiting for you to be ready to talk to her. It was like she knew you had something you had to work out first... by yourself."

"God... she was so right. As always."

"So, what was the problem?" she asks, and then blushes, which I can just about see in the dim twilight. "Unless you'd rather not say," she murmurs.

"Of course I'd rather say. I need to, even if it's not the easiest thing for me to talk about. That's the whole point of this. That's why I didn't kiss you just now… because I was about to kiss you… in case you didn't realise." She gazes up at me through her eyelashes, with the most alluring look on her face. "Don't," I whisper, barely in control of my voice.

"Don't what?"

"Don't look at me like that." She turns her head away. "Don't turn away from me either."

"Why not?"

She looks back and gazes up at me, and I sigh, shaking my head. "It's complicated."

"I'm not going anywhere…" Her voice fades.

"Good. I hope you'll remember you said that."

"Why?"

"Because before I can kiss you – and I do want to kiss you – I need to tell you what the argument was about… what my reasons were. But after I've told you, you might not want to kiss me."

She tilts her head, first left and then right, as though thinking that prospect through. "Try me," she says eventually.

"You're sure?"

"Yes."

"Okay… but remember, I warned you."

I lean over and pick up our wine again, handing her glass back to her.

"Am I going to need this?" she asks, taking it from me.

"I don't know. But I am."

I take a long sip, keeping my eyes fixed on her, even while she watches me.

"You already know," I begin, sitting back into the corner of the sofa, my legs stretched out in front of me, "that Mum came up to us in Kew not long before Bryony died."

"Yes."

"And that she stayed on afterwards and helped out with organising the funeral, and stopping me from wallowing in my own flood of self pity for more than twenty-three hours a day. There wasn't really time to wallow, even though that was all I wanted to do. Poppy was two and didn't understand what was going on. She just knew that her mummy

218

had suddenly disappeared and that her daddy couldn't stop crying. I—I hadn't let myself cry in front of Bryony when she was alive, but after her death, I couldn't seem to stop." Summer reaches out and rests her hand on my arm again, which is comforting, and allows me to take a moment, before I continue, "Bryony's parents were there too, a lot of the time. They didn't stay at the house, but they came over virtually every day. I think their grief was almost as bad as mine... sometimes worse. They'd lost their only child and they wanted to spend time with Poppy, because she was their link to Bryony. It was hard. For all of us. And Mum was the person we all turned to... all clung to, like a life raft. She and Bryony's parents hadn't spent that much time together while Bryony was alive, because of Mum living down here, but she just seemed to know what they needed, and I know Ruth and Edward were grateful to her." I think for a second. "No... it was more than that. They were beholden to her. She made them see the light, when everything seemed so dark. She kept them afloat. She kept all of us afloat. She certainly stopped me from drowning, on more than one occasion. She got me through the funeral, and then she just carried on, doing all the practical stuff that didn't seem to matter much to me anymore... cooking and shopping, and cleaning and helping with Poppy... and just being there, in the background. I knew she'd have to go home eventually, but before she did, she helped me set up a kind of rota of childcare for Poppy. Bryony had a friend called Clare, who'd offered to help out, and so we all sat down together... Clare, Mum, and Bryony's parents, who wanted to do their bit too, and Mum concocted a schedule that worked for everyone, taking into account each person's commitments, so that I could get back to work. Because I had to. The mortgage needed paying, and I had to put food on the table. I couldn't spend my whole life feeling sorry for myself, because the woman I loved was gone." I glance up at Summer, but she's just gazing at me, her face a mixture of sadness and understanding.

"Mum set a date for coming back home," I continue, after taking a quick sip of wine. "We both knew I had to start coping by myself again. Having her there was great, but it wasn't a long term solution, for either of us. And I think she thought, if I had a date to work towards, it would make it easier for me. But then I got a call from a potential new client. I'd contacted them months earlier through their London office, before Bryony was even diagnosed, and thought nothing was going to come of it, but here they were, phoning me out of the blue and asking to see me at their head office… in Manchester. It was a bit of a pain because it coincided with the day Mum had planned on leaving. But she agreed to stay on, so I could fit in the meeting and she could be there overnight with Poppy. I probably could have shipped Poppy off to Bryony's parents' for the night, but she'd only just stopped waking up in the early hours and crying for her mummy, and I didn't want to upset her routine again."

"That makes sense," Summer says softly.

"I went up to Manchester," I sigh, wishing I could just get to the end of this now, to find out how she's going to react. "The meeting was quite late in the afternoon and dragged on a bit, but it didn't matter, because I'd already booked a hotel, so I went there afterwards, feeling quite pleased with myself, because I'd picked up what turned out to be quite a lucrative job. Anyway, after dinner, I went down to the bar, because I didn't feel like sitting in my room all by myself, and decided I'd rather sit in the bar all by myself instead, and I'd just ordered a drink, when this woman came and sat beside me."

"Did you know her?"

"No. She just came and sat right next to me… and after a kind of awkward moment, we got talking over our drinks… and then I realised it was late, and I said I really should be going to bed. And she suggested coming with me." Those last few words pour out of me, like water gushing from a tap.

"To your room?"

"To my bed."

"Oh."

"I said no," I add quickly, because I did say no. At least to start with.

"I see. So what happened?"

"I got up to leave, and she put her hand on my arm, trying to change my mind, I think… and that was when I noticed her wedding ring."

Summer tips her head again, although she doesn't gasp, or even raise her eyebrows. "She was married?" she says, quietly. She's clearly not shocked. I don't think she's even surprised.

"Yes. I was a bit taken aback by that, if I'm being honest. I mean, she'd been quite blatant about what she wanted. So, I asked how her husband felt about her propositioning other men."

"And? What did she say to that?"

I shake my head, because a part of me still can't believe what happened. "She said he didn't mind… as long as she told him about it afterwards."

"Really?" Even that hasn't shocked Summer. Instead, judging from the wry smile on her face, she seems mildly amused. "Well, it takes all sorts, I suppose," she mumbles.

"Yes, it seems so. Anyway, I did a fairly poor job of hiding my amazement that people could live like that and still count themselves as being married, and I left her standing there, and headed for the lift… and that was where she joined me."

Summer sighs now, and slowly nods her head. "Ah… I see. You don't need to tell me what happened next. I get it… confined spaces and all that… your willpower was broken."

How did she know? "Yes. She kissed me and it was like… I don't know… like I forgot everything else existed in my life. We didn't actually have sex in the lift, but we only just made it to her room…" I stop talking, leaving the rest to her imagination.

"And you felt bad afterwards?" she guesses.

"Bad doesn't even begin to cover it. The guilt was overwhelming. She wanted me to stay the night, but I ran out of there, with half my clothes under my arm, and the rest on back-to-front, I think. I went back to my room to get dressed and collect my things, and was in my car, driving back down the motorway within fifteen minutes. I parked up at a service station and waited until morning before actually going home, where my mother greeted me with suggestions of a perfect life down here, so I could grieve for my beloved wife in peace, while painting me as the ideal father. And all I could think about was that just a few hours earlier I'd been in bed with a woman who I knew only as

Gabrielle, who I knew was married, and who had some kind of kinky 'show and tell' thing going on with her husband. Bryony had only been dead for six weeks. Hell, I hadn't even organised her headstone at that point… and I'd slept with another woman." I can hear the emotion rising in my own voice and I stop talking, wondering if I should leave now, before I actually break down.

I start to shift away from the corner of the sofa, towards the edge, when Summer gets to her knees, hoisting her dress, and clambers over to me.

"Stop it," she says softly, as she kneels right beside me, putting her arms around me and pulling me into her.

"Stop what?" I mumble.

"Blaming yourself."

I lean back a little, although she doesn't let go and I'm grateful for that. "I can't make it up to them now though, can I? I let them both down… Mum and Bryony, and now they're both dead and I can't even say sorry."

She pulls me back into her again. "You don't need to say 'sorry', Kit. It was a mistake. People make mistakes, especially when they're in a really bad place. And you were. You were in the worst possible place. You just wanted to feel desired again. So what? You wanted to feel like a man again, instead of a carer, a nurse, a grieving widower and a father, and all the other labels that get attached to you… and there's nothing wrong with that."

God… she really does understand. "But…"

"Stop it," she repeats. "You need to forgive yourself."

"I'm not sure I can." I look into her eyes, and see something there that looks familiar and hopeful, and I wonder if maybe I might be able to… for her, if nothing else.

"Well, you need to try. You need to start living your life again. For you. Not for Poppy, or for Bryony, or your mother. But for you."

She leans back, sitting beside me now, her body pressed against mine, and twisting around, she reaches out, touching my lips with her fingers, tracing around them intimately, our eyes locked, and I change position slightly, moving us both downwards and turning into my side, so I can hold on to her, rather than the other way around. I bend my head, moving closer, but as I'm about to kiss her, she pushes back and I stop, instantly, confused beyond words.

"Don't," she says.

"Don't what? I thought you wanted…"

"I do. I do want you to kiss me. Very much. But I don't want to be another itch."

"Another itch?" What does that mean?

"Yes. I won't be an itch that needs scratching. If you're doing this because you just want someone… anyone – like you did with Gabrielle – then don't. Not with me. I won't be that itch for you, Kit."

"You're not." I bring my hand between us, caressing her cheek with my fingertips. "You are not an itch, Summer," I say firmly. "I promise."

"It's just…" She lowers her eyes and tries to look down, but I move my hand, placing my fingers beneath her chin, raising it and holding her gaze.

"It's just what? I've told you everything… all my worst secrets. Don't hold back on me now."

"I have already explained this to you… kind of. But maybe I didn't make it clear enough. I've been here before, Kit. With Roan's father. He wasn't just a random man I picked up. Because, believe it or not, I'm not like that. He was a friend of a friend, and someone I… well, someone I'd liked for quite some time. And…" He hurt her.

"Hey…" I interrupt, because I don't need to hear the rest of her story. "I never thought you were the kind of woman who went around picking up random men… so let's get that straight, shall we?" She smiles at me. "And I'm not the kind of man who has one night stands either, despite what I've just told you. That was a one-off. I take my responsibilities seriously."

She smiles, the cheekiest of smiles. "Somehow that doesn't surprise me in the slightest."

I tilt my head, narrowing my eyes at her. "Are you trying to say I'm boring?"

"Perish the thought," she giggles.

"Okay…" I sit up a little. "Let's see what I can do to prove you wrong, shall we?"

She opens her mouth, and touches her tongue to her lips, licking them gently, and I groan, leaning in again, just as she pulls away from me.

"What now?" I frown at her, even though she's smiling and as a result, I do too, because I can't help myself.

"I think I'd better just go and check on the children… don't you?" she whispers.

"I suppose so." I can't believe I'd forgotten all about them. But I had, and as she clambers onto all fours and crawls off the day bed, giving me a perfect view of her behind, I lie back and think about what just happened between us. Because while nothing actually has happened between us – yet – I feel like we've come an awfully long way.

Telling Summer about Gabrielle was embarrassing. Embarrassing, but necessary. I think. And I do feel so much better for finally telling that story out loud. I feel better for hearing that her one night stand with Roan's father wasn't quite so haphazard as she'd led me to believe… not because I care whether she slept with the guy on five minutes', or five years' acquaintance. That's none of my business. But the way she told me that, and the way she led up to telling me that, it led me to believe that she might care about me… or about us, anyway, and I was surprised by how good that felt. And how much more I want with her…

"You're not going to believe this…" Her voice cuts into my thoughts and I glance up into the gloom to see her standing at the end of the day bed, gazing down at me, and in the pale glow coming from the kitchen window, the light reflects through her thin dress, revealing the outline of just about everything I've ever wanted to see… leaving the rest to my vivid imagination.

"Believe what?" I struggle to focus.

"They're both fast asleep."

"They are?"

"Yep. Both dead to the world, on Roan's bed. They look really cute, actually. You should come and see them." She holds out her hand, but I shake my head.

"Not yet. I've got a point to prove."

She lets her hand fall. "You have?"

"Yes." I hold out my own hand now. "I need to prove to you that I'm not boring." A smile forms on her lips and she looks from my hand to my face and back again, via my chest… at least I think it's my chest her eyes are lingering over. "Now… come here."

She doesn't even hesitate, but with her eyes fixed on mine, she kneels down on the edge of the day bed and starts to crawl. Within seconds though, her dress is caught beneath her knees again, and she reaches down to release it.

"This damn dress," she mutters and I kneel up, going to her.

"I've got a solution for that," I whisper, taking her hands in mine and freeing the fabric from her fingers.

"What's that?" she asks, looking up at me, a little breathless.

I don't reply. Instead, I take hold of her dress myself and yank it up over her head. She gasps, but not with shock, or anger. There's longing in her eyes, coupled with what looks like exhilaration, and I shift away from her, throwing her dress aside, and take in the beauty of her body, her rounded firm breasts, their dark nipples hardening before my gaze, her narrow waist, and flat stomach, leading down to a very pretty triangle of white lace, that barely covers her.

"Here." I take her hand and lead her back to the corner of the bed, sitting myself down and pulling her between my legs, her back against my chest, my arms surrounding her, in a safe, protective cocoon, her skin feather soft as I let my hands wander, not giving her time to think, or to ask, or to wonder… my fingers caressing, fondling, and occasionally pinching, just very gently, when I reach somewhere sensitive, while her breathing becomes more and more erratic with every moment. As she starts to pant, I move that lace triangle aside, and she lets out a long soft moan as I begin to stroke her intimately, her smooth folds yielding to my touch.

"Oh, God… yes." She leans back into me, twisting slightly and raising her face to mine, and I bend to kiss her, my tongue mirroring the actions of my fingers, skimming, delving, exploring, even as she lifts her hips, squirming for more, and I feel her thighs start to quiver as she pulls back from the kiss, her body trembling in a way I've never seen before, in any woman, right before she shatters wildly around the first peak of pleasure. She bucks and writhes against me, out of control, instinctively trying to clamp her legs together, while I part them further, using my free hand, holding her in place, lengthening her orgasm. She pants and sighs, on and on, surprisingly silent, yet extraordinarily intense, all at the same time.

Calming eventually, she turns to face me, breathless and sated, but still wanting more, that deep longing ever-present in her eyes, as she kneels up and removes her thong, throwing it aside. God, she looks good. Even better than in my dreams, her skin downy soft, yet heated with desire. But before I can do anything about that, she leans forward and undoes my belt, and then the buttons of my jeans, pulling down my boxers, and finally freeing my erection.

"Oh," she says, sitting back slightly and studying me, her voice a quiet whisper. For a moment, I wonder if she's disappointed, until she looks up and I see the smile on her face. "That's nice."

"Nice?" I'm not sure I've ever been called 'nice' before, not in that department, anyway.

"Well... big, if you prefer, although that does seem like a rather obvious and maybe inadequate adjective. Perhaps 'magnificent', or 'awe-inspiring', or even 'majestic' would be better?"

I shake my head, smiling at her. "Stop talking about adjectives and come here."

She grins, and crawls up my body until we're facing each other and I claim her mouth with mine, kissing her deeply.

"You're wearing too many clothes," she says, pulling back from the kiss, after a little while.

"Then take them off."

She moves away slightly and, with a little assistance, removes my jeans and boxers and then comes back up to me and pulls my t-shirt over my head, so we're both naked.

She runs her hands down my chest, then back up again to my shoulders, and settles over me, poised. I know what she's going to do but, the thing is, as much as I want her, that's not what I've got in mind.

So I grab hold of her, one hand on her back, the other on her behind, and I tip her backwards, so she's lying across the daybed, gazing up at me, wide-eyed, her legs parted in anticipation, and I move into the cradle she's made for me, leaning over her, my face an inch or two above hers. Then I take her hands, pinning them beside her head. I don't want to talk, or wait, or even breathe. I can't. I edge forward, finding her entrance, and she moans and then gasps as I penetrate her, quite forcefully, hearing the hiss of an elongated, "Yes," escape her lips. I pause, holding on deep inside her, her body adapting to mine, before I lean up again, supporting my weight on my straightened arms now, and move one hand down, resting it just above her hip. I wait for a moment and suck in a breath, noticing how large my hand looks against her tiny waist, which makes me feel… well, dominant, I suppose. But isn't that how I want to feel with her? Isn't that what my dreams have been about? Taking her and making her mine?

"This is okay, isn't it?" I murmur.

She seems to understand what I'm asking without me having to spell it out, and nods her head. "Yes. I'm on the pill."

I swallow hard, and then, without saying another word, I start to move, slowly to begin with, for my own benefit as much as hers, but then increasing in speed, taking more. She raises her legs, pulling them higher, closer to her chest – almost like she knows what I need, or maybe it's that she needs this too? Can that be? Can it be that her needs and desires match my own? Is that even possible? I don't know… I can't think straight, and I don't care. Thinking isn't important. I lean right up and hold her legs in place, my hands in the crooks of her knees, as I take her even harder, even faster, keeping her as exposed and open to me as she can be. Because she's mine.

"Oh God… Oh God…" she whimpers repeatedly, our eyes locked, while I keep pounding into her, even when she comes apart, sighing and moaning my name, her head thrashing wildly from side to side.

She calms. Or I think she does, her body still twitching beneath me, and yet I can't stop. I don't want to. Ever. She's all I've ever dreamed of. This is all I've ever wanted. And yet, I still want more.

"Again…" I murmur, my heart hammering, beads of sweat forming on my chest and back.

"I can't."

"You can. Again, Summer." I speak through gritted teeth, releasing one of her legs, although she holds it in place somehow, and I move my hand up beside her head again, leaning down to her, tempering the pace. She brings her hands up, letting them rest on my shoulders and I grind into her, slowly and deliberately, my forehead resting against hers, as I love her. Deeply. "Now…"

"I—I can't," she stutters, breathing hard and I nibble at her bottom lip with my teeth, before tracing a line of kisses along her jaw to the soft skin at the nape of her neck, sucking and biting, leaving my mark on her, before I move down slightly kissing my way to her breasts, where I lick and bite her extended nipples until she's breathless, writhing beneath me.

"Now," I growl, raising myself up again, taking her faster, and so much harder than before. The need is consuming… unrelenting. "Summer… please. Come for me…" And as though at my command, she shatters once more, her nails puncturing my skin right before she slams her palms down on the bed, her body bucking into mine and I plunge deep into her, losing myself… once and for all.

The first thing I'm really aware of is Summer's damp skin against mine, because I've collapsed onto her, totally spent.

The second thing I'm aware of is our breathing… laboured and deep, her breasts heaving into my chest.

The third thing I'm aware of is shattering, devastating guilt – worse than anything I've felt before – washing over me in endless waves.

I'm drowning in it and, no matter how hard I try, this time, I can't surface.

"No," I manage to say out loud, between anguished breaths, pain eating into me as I raise myself up, and she lowers her legs, staring at me in confusion. I shake my head, the bewildered look on her face just adding to my shame. "No…" I mutter a second time, and pull out of her, even though I'm still erect, my body wanting more of her already, even if I'm too immersed in grief and sorrow and relentless guilt, to do anything about that. She winces at my sudden, slightly harsh withdrawal, but I move away, across the bed, leaving her behind me. I can't look at her now. I can't bear to.

"Kit?" I'm aware of movement, but I don't turn around. I daren't.

"No," I repeat, a little louder, feeling like I've been here before – which I suppose I have. This is like Gabrielle all over again. It's not meant to be, but it is…

"Stop saying that." There's real pain in her voice and I clench my fists, turning to face her, acknowledging, as I do, that this is nothing like Gabrielle. Because Gabrielle didn't care about me… and looking at Summer, as she's staring at me now, I have a horrible feeling she does. My earlier optimism that she might care for me, or for us, feels so misplaced now… and for her sake, I really wish she didn't. She's sitting up, naked, in the middle of the bed, her knees bent and her arms clasped around them, very defensively. And I don't blame her, because I think we both know I'm about to hurt her. Badly. What she doesn't realise though, is that there's nothing I can do about it.

"I'm sorry," I whisper.

"Don't say that either." I can see the tears in her eyes, but I can't move. I should. I know I should. I should hold her in my arms and explain this… tell her how I feel. Except I can't do that either, because I can't remember how I feel anymore. I thought I knew. I thought I'd worked it out. Earlier on, when we were talking. Or was it yesterday that it finally made sense to me? Or even the day before? Whenever it was. I thought I'd worked out that this was what I wanted. I thought this was what I needed. I thought Summer was what I needed. It felt like she was. Before. But if that was the case, why do I feel like this now? After. Why do I hate myself, like I've never hated myself before? And why do I feel like this is the worst betrayal yet… not only of my wife, but also of the beautiful woman sitting in front of me, tears now rolling down her cheeks.

I can't be here. I can't face this.

I turn away and pick up my boxers, pulling them on, followed by my jeans and my t-shirt. I slip on my shoes and, running my fingers through my hair, I stand at the end of the bed.

"I'll go and find Poppy."

I don't look back at her, or wait for her to reply, or even offer to come with me. I go straight into the house and up the stairs, although I don't have a clue where Roan's bedroom is. It can't be that hard to find in a house this small. And it isn't. I find it first time; the two children lying together side by side, fast asleep, the TV still on quietly in the background.

The sight of them makes me feel worse, because I know how close these two are, and that my selfish, stupid, irresponsible actions can only hurt them too… in the long run. Am I talking about the selfish, stupid, irresponsible action of making love to Roan's mum, like my life depended on it? Or, the selfish, stupid, irresponsible action I'm about to take, of walking out of her house, when I know deep down, that I should stay – even though I can't – and that walking away from her now is unfair and unreasonable… and unforgivable. And that if I do it, she'll probably never let me back in again. The answer is, I have no idea which of my actions will hurt them the most. I just know that they will. I bend and gently pick up Poppy from the bed, and as I do, she mumbles softly in her sleep, but nestles into me, and I carry her carefully out of the room and down the stairs, startling at the bottom when I find Summer standing there, fully clothed, waiting for me.

I don't know why I'm surprised. I mean… did I actually think she was going to sit outside by herself and simply let me walk out of her house, after what I just did to her?

She stands before me, her hair dishevelled, her lips swollen, the bite mark on her neck clearly visible, red grazes showing on the tops of her breasts where my stubble scraped her soft skin… the picture of a woman who's been thoroughly loved… by a man who isn't brave enough to admit to own his feelings, and who certainly doesn't deserve her.

I expect her to berate me, even if she does so in whispers, because I know she'll be mindful of Poppy, sleeping in my arms. But she doesn't. Instead, she reaches out and touches my cheek, her fingers brushing gently against my skin. And just that simple gesture makes my heart stop beating in my chest.

"Please don't feel bad," she whispers.

"How can I feel anything else?" I manage to say.

"Why are you doing this? Why are you leaving?"

I can't answer that, so I don't, and we stare at each other for a few seconds, until my gaze falls to that mark on her neck again. "Did I hurt you?" I ask, worried now.

She tilts her head. "How do you mean?"

It's a fair question. After all, I must be hurting her now. "Outside. I was… a bit rough. Did I hurt you?" I need to know.

She moves a little closer, so her body is touching my arm, and I find it hard to breathe, just feeling her that near to me. "No," she whispers. "I didn't think you were rough. I thought you were… passionate. Intense." She searches for the words and finds a couple that I guess she thinks are appropriate. She's not wrong either. What we did was passionate. It was intense. And fierce. It was everything I've ever dreamed of with her. "I—I liked it," she adds, stammering. "It made me feel…"

"Don't say it," I interrupt.

"Wanted." The single word spills out of her at the same time, stabbing at my heart.

I wish she hadn't said that. She *is* wanted and I wish I could tell her that. Because wanting Summer has been the thought that's occupied my head for so long now, I can't actually remember not wanting her… even though I've only known her for such a short time. And yet, saying any of that feels so wrong, which is why I can't. Because even *thinking* it feels wrong.

"I'm sorry," I repeat softly, because I don't know what else to say to her.

She shakes her head, placing her fingertips against my mouth. "Don't say that," she murmurs. "You know that word is banned."

"Because it makes you sad?"

Her eyes glisten and I know she's fighting back tears. "Yes."

"I won't say it then. I'll just think it… all the time."

She shakes her head again. "Don't do that either, Kit. It's not right."

"Nothing's right." Certainly not this. Certainly not hurting her. Even though I can't help myself.

"Why don't you stay? You can put Poppy back upstairs. We can talk."

"I can't."

"Can't, or won't? Or don't want to?" She adds that last option as an afterthought, but I don't need to think about my answer.

"Can't."

She pauses for a second and then nods her head, stepping aside and letting me pass. I walk slowly to the door and open it, looking back to her. She's got one hand clasped around her waist – the waist I held in my much bigger hand just a few minutes ago, while I loved her so hard. Her other hand is in her hair, her fingers pushing it back behind her ear and I can tell from the glistening in her eyes and the tremble of her lips that she's barely holding it together.

Just looking at her pierces my heart and I want to say sorry again.

But what would be the point? It would only make her sad.

Chapter Nineteen

Summer

I wake late, and for a moment, the only thought in my head is Kit, and I have to smile and let my body stretch out across the bed. God... he felt good last night. He was so demanding, and strong, and masculine, and yet tender and passionate at the same time, and he made me feel so wanted – as though there wasn't a single thought in his head other than satisfying me. Whatever it took. And I did feel satisfied, right to my very core. And happy too. Happier than I've ever been.

And then I remember... and a crushing pain fills my chest, just like it did last night, when he stood up from the day bed and looked down at me, and I knew... I knew he was going to leave me.

Because no matter how satisfied or happy I was... I wasn't enough for him to forget the past.

I know that's where his problem lies... although knowing that doesn't help in the slightest.

I also know he wasn't ready. I think I might have known that even before we made love. But that doesn't help either, because the idea of stopping something that felt inevitable, and that felt so good too, was just impossible. And completely beyond me.

I turn over and look out of the window, struggling not to recall how it felt the last time this happened, although it wasn't quite the same back then. Roan's father didn't leave me. He didn't walk away straight after we'd had sex. And he wasn't wracked with guilt. He just told me – quite blandly really, over a cup of rather bitter coffee – that he didn't want anything to do with me. He was a player, plain and simple. And I was just his latest victim. Of course, I didn't know I was pregnant at the time – and at least I know I'm not pregnant now. But I do remember how hurt and used I felt. Because I'd liked him and I'd read more into it than there was. And, even though I know the circumstances are different this time, it's really hard not to feel like that now.

Except Kit isn't Russell. He didn't set out to use me. At least, I don't think he did.

I think he wanted me just as much as I wanted him.

And I did want him.

And I think there was more to it than just sex too. He showed me a side of himself that I hadn't even realised existed. There was something in his eyes, in the way he looked at me… and in the way he made love to me. He made it like everything I've ever dreamed it could be, but hadn't dared to let myself imagine. He was forceful and dominant, like he wanted to own me, to make me his. And although I know it sounds pathetic, and probably a bit out of character, I was happy to let him. I still would be.

Because I don't just like Kit. I love him.

And I want to be his.

Even if he doesn't want me anymore.

I get up and shower, too sad now to just lie in bed, although I still can't get Kit out of my thoughts. I wish he'd stayed last night. I wish he'd been willing to sit down with me and talk, so I could have found out what was going on in his head, why he'd changed from the man who seemed to want me so much he could barely breathe, to the man who couldn't wait to get away from me.

I want to understand, to help him, to see if we can find a way to work it out between us. Because I'd like that more than anything.

But even as I get out of the shower and dry my hair, I know there's nothing I can do. I can't go over there and knock on his door. I can't phone him and ask the question. I can't push him in any way. Kit needs to do this at his pace, or not at all.

He needs to come to terms with his grief, to understand his guilt over what happened when his wife died – which he's clearly struggling with, or he wouldn't have bothered to tell me about it. I think he thought I'd be shocked by that revelation, but I wasn't. As I said to him yesterday, he was in a bad place, and needed some human comfort, and having no-strings sex with a total stranger was probably the best way to go, to get that release. It's a shame he can't see that, but I'm not sure he's seeing anything very clearly at the moment. Do you ever see anything very clearly when you're wracked with grief, and pain, and guilt?

It would have been so much better for both of us though, if he'd stayed and talked. And I hope that, in the cold light of day, he'll realise that and maybe come over here and see me. It has to come from him… I know that. Just like Maggie, I know I can't force him to accept the past, or want the future. He has to work out his own path, in his own way, in his own time.

I just have to hope that, when the time comes, he wants me somewhere on that path beside him.

I put on a pair of denim shorts and a light blue vest top, and leaving my hair to dry naturally, I go downstairs and stand in the doorway to the kitchen, wishing that I'd taken the trouble to tidy up a bit before going to bed last night.

Admittedly, I wasn't really in the mood for tidying up, because I was crying at the time… uncontrollably. Kit had just walked out, with Poppy in his arms, and although I'd managed not to actually cry in front of him, the moment the door closed, I sobbed my heart out, and it was all I could do to lock the doors and turn the lights out, before making my way upstairs.

I checked on Roan, who was still fast asleep in his shorts and top, and I didn't have the heart to wake him. He'd have wanted to know why I was crying, and I'm not sure how I'd have explained that one to him. So I left him sleeping, and went into my own room, where I took off my dress and fell into bed… which reminds me…

I dart through the kitchen, grab the keys and open the back door, cursing the fact that I've got nothing on my feet, and the paving stones are cold, and damp, and hard, down the shady side alleyway, as I make my way to the patio, trying not to picture myself here... beneath Kit, captive, held, desired. Loved? *No... not that. It was never about that. Not for him.*

A lump forms in my throat, but I swallow it down and move forward, picking up the half empty bottle of wine and glasses from the ground, where he left them.

I'm surprised I'm not more hungover actually. We did get through a bottle and a half of wine last night, which is a lot more than I'm used to drinking. But my head is surprisingly clear today... other than the fog of emotions... and that seemingly ever-present doubt that's been festering since I woke this morning.

Why wasn't I enough to make him forget?

With the bottle under my arm, and the glasses in one hand, I turn to the day bed and, nestled in the corner, I find what I'm looking for... my white lace thong. I guess that's where it ended up last night, when I took it off and threw it over my shoulder. I couldn't find it in the darkness, when I dressed in such a hurry, desperate to catch Kit before he left, but I reach over now and grab it, screwing it up and putting it in my pocket, just in case Roan should appear and wonder why I'm wandering around with my underwear in my hand.

My timing is perfect, because as I turn, I hear Roan in the kitchen, and I go back inside to greet him.

"Good morning, sleepy head." I smile down at him, because however sad I might be, I won't let him see it.

"Hi, Mum." He looks down at his creased clothes. "I think I fell asleep."

"You certainly did."

"Did Poppy fall asleep with me?" he asks, and I have to smile even wider, because that's such a beautifully innocent thing to say.

"Yes, sweetheart."

"But she went home?" He sounds ever so disappointed.

"Hmm… Kit came up and got her and carried her home." *After he'd shown me how good it is to really love a man.*

He nods his head, and then tips it to one side, looking at the wine bottle and glasses I'm still carrying. "Didn't you clear up last night?" he asks.

"No. I was tired."

He sighs, and turns away. "Well, at least I don't have to get dressed today," he says, sauntering back into the living room.

"In your dreams, young man," I call after him. "You're going to shower and put some clean clothes on."

"I've already got clothes on." I can hear the smile in his voice.

"Yesterday's clothes don't count."

"They do when I'm wearing them."

I surprise myself by laughing, although I can't help wondering – not for the first time – whether he gets his quick repartee from his father. The problem is, I didn't know the man well enough to judge that. And maybe that says more about me than I'd like to admit.

I put down the glasses and bottle on the table, casting an eye over the flowers, nestling in their vase… the flowers that said 'sorry', when 'sorry' and the present seemed to matter more to Kit than the past, and then I strike the thought, because I can't afford to cry in front of Roan. I can't afford to have to explain. And instead I follow him into the living room, where he's sitting on the sofa, watching me.

"Shower," I say firmly, managing a smile at the same time.

"Okay, Mum." He chuckles, knowing that he's beaten, and he gets up again, making for the stairs. And as I sit in his place, I think to myself that even though I didn't know Russell at all, I somehow doubt Roan got his easy-going nature from him.

Roan and I have a late breakfast in the end – more of a brunch really – because by the time he's showered and dressed, with some assistance from me, and I've finished clearing up from last night, which is about as much housework as I can face today, even though it's Saturday, and I've put Kit's flowers over on the work surface by the microwave, so I won't have to look at them all the time, it's nearly eleven o'clock, and being as toast and cereal seem a bit inadequate by that stage, I cook us bacon and eggs, which I think we both need. As I'm eating, I wonder to myself if I am, indeed, a little more hungover than I'd thought, because the fried food seems to be hitting the spot more than usual. And Roan definitely appreciates it.

He finishes before me, and has gone to watch a DVD in the living room, leaving me to clear away and use the kitchen table to lay out my lesson plans. I've been putting this off for long enough now, and I need something to distract me from thinking about Kit… and wondering why he hasn't been in touch.

I mean… the answer to that question is obvious, really. He doesn't want to get in touch. If he did, he would have done. But that doesn't mean I want to face that answer. So I'll look at my lesson plans instead.

And I'll drink coffee.

Lots of coffee.

I've set up my laptop and laid out the various papers that I need from my folder. The only problem is, I've got no idea where I put my marker pens. I know I bought some when Roan and I were last in Looe, and I always find them useful for highlighting the things I need to focus on the most. It saves me the time and effort of trawling through notes. I thought I'd unpacked them into my school box, along with the rest of my stationery, when we got home, but I've got the new stapler, and the pack of sticky notes, and I bought them at the same time. So it doesn't make sense that I can't find the marker pens.

"Roan?" I call out, checking back through my plastic storage box, and coming up blank a second time.

"Yes?"

"Have you seen my new highlighter pens?" I know it's a long shot, but it's worth asking.

"No." *Thanks.*

I shake my head and, exasperated, tip the whole box out onto the table… pens, pencils, paper, spare staples, and heaven knows what else, all tumbling out.

And just at that moment, the doorbell rings.

"Damn…" I mutter under my breath, casting a quick eye over the table, and not seeing the marker pens, before I go through to the lounge and open the door, my breath hitching as I see Kit standing before me, Poppy right beside him. His eyes focus on mine for a second, and then drop to my neck, to the deep purple bite mark he left there, and I wish now that I'd covered it up. Roan hasn't mentioned it, or the very slight reddening over the tops of my breasts, which is just about visible above my t-shirt… the faded markings caused by Kit's stubble grazing over my skin. I shudder at the memory and he stares for a moment or two, and then opens his mouth, but before he can say anything, Roan comes up behind me.

"Hello, Poppy," he says, sounding pleased.

"Hi." She smiles.

"I'm watching *The Lion King*. Do you want to come and watch it with me?"

"Okay…"

He holds out his hand and she takes it, letting him lead her back into the house.

"Um… Poppy?" Kit says, sounding doubtful, but they've already gone.

"Don't worry. They're fine," I murmur, trying not to stare at him, trying not to remember what he looked like naked… because he looked so damned good; all muscle, and glistening skin… and I can't think about that at the moment.

He stands awkwardly in front of me, clearly not wanting to come in himself, even though I've stood aside to let Poppy pass.

"I—I mean we… we just came over to bring back Roan's clothes," he says, reaching out and handing me Roan's blue shorts and red t-shirt, neatly folded, and I remember Poppy was wearing them the other night, when he walked out of here in a temper… the night before he made love to me, and walked out on me again, that is. "I washed them yesterday, but they weren't dry enough to bring back… last night…" He hesitates before saying that and I look up at him, wondering if he's thinking about 'last night' in the same way I am. It's hard to tell. His expression isn't giving anything away.

"Thanks." I remember my manners at last and take Roan's clothes from him. "You can come in, you know?"

"Yes…" He hesitates, still seemingly unsure what to do, and then eventually steps forward into my living room.

The children are watching their DVD, with the sound up fairly loud.

"Come through to the kitchen," I say over my shoulder, not giving him a choice in the matter. If he's come to talk, it would be nice to at least hear what he's got to say. And if he hasn't come to talk, I'd rather we stared awkwardly at each other away from the prying eyes of our children.

I'm aware of him following me, and put the clothes down on the edge of the work surface, the table being littered with my school things, and then I turn to face him, and I see the anguish in his eyes, wondering whether it pains him that much to be near me again.

"What's wrong, Kit?" I have to ask, because seeing him like this hurts. And not really understanding why he won't just talk to me hurts even more. He didn't have a problem opening up to me before we made love and I hate the idea that things can have changed so much between us… and so badly.

"Nothing." His voice is flat and monotone. And completely insincere.

"Well, that's not true. There's clearly something wrong…" I decide to take a risk and hope it doesn't come back to bite me. "Do you regret what we did last night?"

"No." He sounds defensive now, and he still won't make eye contact with me, which I guess tells me everything I need to know.

"Could you try saying that again, but with a bit more conviction this time… because at the moment, I'm feeling a bit like that itch… remember? The one that needed scratching." My voice catches, and I pause… and he takes a half step towards me, sucking in a breath, but before he can say anything to make matters worse, I go on, "Do you know, I'm starting to wonder, if maybe I'm destined to go through life having incredible one night stands, but never being quite right for anything more… never being quite… quite good enough." Tears start to form in my eyes and although I blink a few times, there's nothing I can do to stop them brimming there. I look up at him, and he frowns for a moment, but then stares at the space between us, like he doesn't know what to do, or say. "You said you wouldn't treat me like that, Kit," I croak. "I—I mean, I get that it's difficult for you… I even get that it was probably too soon, and that you weren't ready… but why did you say one thing and then do another? And why can't you talk to me? I do understand, you know?"

"Really?" he says, finding his voice at last, and looking right at me now.

"Yes. I didn't expect to find myself pregnant at the age of twenty-two, and a single parent at twenty-three, but I guess the thing is, when things don't go quite to plan in your life, you have to make a decision… to make the most of the hand you've been dealt, and look forward, or to keep looking back, wondering what if, and beating yourself up all the time."

He steps closer, with the slow, considered movement of a cat about to pounce on its prey, just like he did the other day, his eyes locked on mine. Only this time, there's no latent desire, no heat… no longing. "To start off with," he growls, "it's a bit rich to say 'things didn't go quite to plan' in my life. My wife died, Summer. So you'll forgive me if I have a slightly different perspective to you."

"I'm sorry." I shake my head. "That's not what I meant."

"What did you mean then?" There's still a menacing tone to his voice, but I refuse to be intimidated by the man who made love to me like he did last night… by the man who let me see the love he keeps hidden so deep inside him. Even if it isn't meant for me.

"I know my circumstances are very different. I know I didn't lose my partner…"

"Damn right you didn't," he shouts and I jump, startled by the rage in his voice and the raw fury in his eyes. "You didn't have to sit and watch the woman you love die right in front of you… knowing there wasn't a damn thing you could do about it. You didn't have to tell your daughter that her mummy wasn't coming home, over and over, until the words rang hollow, because she was too young to understand that death means forever. You had *choices*, Summer. And you *chose* this life.

So why don't you sort out the mess you've made of it, and stop judging me?"

Without giving me a chance to say anything, he turns and walks away, and I hear him call Poppy's name, just seconds before the front door opens, a breeze billows through the house, and then it slams shut again.

The first tear hits my cheek before I make it to the chair, flopping down into it and holding my head in my hands, great sobs wracking through me.

"Mum?" I turn and suck in a breath, trying to control myself.

"Yes?"

Roan steps closer, uncertain what to do, I think, although I can see the worry in his eyes, because he's never seen me react like this, no matter what. Simply because I never have reacted like this, to anything, or anyone. Ever.

"Are you okay?" He comes and stands beside me, patting my arm.

"I'm fine." That's a blatant lie, and I think we both know it. I'm very far from being 'fine'.

He pauses for a long moment and then says, "I don't feel like being kind."

My brow furrows and I look into his narrowed eyes. "Sorry?"

"You said that Poppy's dad was rude because he was having a bad time… and that we had to be kind to him… But I don't feel like being kind."

I put my arm around him and hug his little body close, taking a deep breath to try and stop myself from shaking. "No, sweetheart… neither do I."

Not any more.

Chapter Twenty

Kit

I must be certifiable.

I mean, why did I think that going to see Summer today – after what happened last night – could possibly end well?

What even possessed me to go over there?

Obviously, I had to return Roan's clothes, but that could have waited, or I could have found some other way to do it. And Poppy might have been nagging at me all morning, because she wanted to go and see Roan, but I could have just said 'no'. And meant it. And put up with her sulking.

I could have found any number of reasons not to go over there.

But I didn't.

Because I'd been awake all night, and while I'd like to say that meant I wasn't thinking clearly this morning, in fact, I knew exactly what I was doing.

After taking Poppy up to her room and putting her to bed, I'd spent the night sitting in my mother's living room, because I was too scared to go to bed myself, in case I fell asleep and ended up dreaming of Summer again. Having made love to her and discovered that the reality was – is – so much better than anything I'd imagined, I knew my dreams would probably be so much more intense. So, I sat, staring out of the window, into the darkness… thinking. And feeling guilty.

I spent the first few hours feeling guilty about Bryony, which is fairly standard practice for me. It was so much worse this time, than it had been with Gabrielle. And I know why. It's because this time, it actually means something, and I knew that was true, even as I was walking down Summer's garden path, carrying Poppy back here and wishing I'd been man enough to stay and face up to what I'd done… to talk it through and explain how I feel. To tell Summer that my reactions aren't her fault. That nothing I do is a reflection on her. That I'm just so confused about everything that's happening, I can't begin to explain it… even to myself.

I kept closing my eyes, trying not to picture Summer's body, trying not to recall the things we'd done together, and how good it had all felt, but every time I did, all I could see was Bryony's face. And that didn't help. It just fuelled my guilt. She didn't look angry with me, or disappointed, or even sad. She was just staring at me, like she didn't understand what was going on either. And that made the whole thing even more confusing.

And then, at about five o'clock this morning, as the darkness was just starting to turn to light, I had a weird moment of clarity.

It wasn't that I suddenly understood everything, or even that any of it made the slightest bit more sense than it had done ten minutes earlier, or last night. It wasn't that I suddenly worked out what to say to Summer, or how to say it. It was that I knew I had to go back and see her. Not because I'd made any momentous decisions about us. I wasn't ready for that yet. But I had reached one conclusion. Making love to Summer was different to making love with anyone else – including Bryony. And while I wasn't sure how I felt about that, because there was a lot of guilt associated with that thought, I knew I had to go back to her. I suppose I wanted to make sure I hadn't hurt her… physically, or emotionally. Although I think I already knew the answer to both of those questions. Even so, I needed to be certain. But I think… I think I also needed to ask her to give me some time. I'm not sure quite how I was going to phrase that, being as my feelings were still in a complete turmoil, but I think I'd have liked to ask her to wait for me, while I tried to work out what's going on in my head... because only when I've done that can I really give her my heart.

The problem is, that even though that was my plan, it didn't work out like that.

I suppose it didn't help that, when Summer opened the door, the first thing I noticed – apart from the fact that her eyes were a bit puffy, which told me she'd been crying and confirmed that I had, indeed, hurt her – was the mark on her neck, where I'd branded her last night. She still had slight red grazes on the tops of her breasts too, and she hadn't bothered to try and hide any of it. Those marks glared at me; the physical evidence of my actions.

I wanted to say 'sorry', for leaving marks on her beautiful, soft skin – even though I didn't really regret doing it. But at that precise moment, Roan came running up and dragged Poppy off to watch *The Lion King* with him. I wasn't sure about that... it felt like Poppy had been my safety blanket up until that moment, preventing my conversation with Summer from getting too personal. And yet, I'd gone over there to have a personal conversation with her... to enquire whether the way I'd behaved had hurt her. That had to be easier out of the earshot of our children... surely?

I suppose I was nervous that Summer might be more hurt or angry – or worse still, sad – than I'd anticipated, but that she'd hold it back in front of Poppy and Roan, and yet she invited me in, seemingly quite unfazed by being alone with me.

Of course, that was when she threw me, by asking if I regretted what we'd done last night. I hadn't been expecting that. I suppose I'd been expecting to lead the conversation, to ask my own questions, the way I'd planned them out in my head. So I just answered her instinctively, and honestly, telling her that I didn't. Because I don't. I can't regret something that's made me realise who I really am. I can't regret something that felt so damn good either. That doesn't mean I necessarily understand it all, but I don't regret it. Of course, I didn't say all of that. I just said 'No', because that was the truth. Except she didn't believe me, and that was when she got upset. She was certainly fighting back her tears, and the temptation to reach out and hold her was overwhelming... except the hurt and anger pouring off of her were more than enough of a barrier to that. She sounded heartbroken. I hated hearing her say she didn't feel good enough, because that's the opposite of how things really are, and I felt terrible about what I'd done to her... especially when she said she knew I wasn't ready. Because essentially she'd hit the nail on the head. She had to have done. I'd gone over there to ask for more time, so what she'd said had to be right, didn't it? And yet hearing her say it felt all wrong, because as I stood there watching her, listening to her, I wanted her again... like nothing else mattered. Like I've never wanted anything. So I had to be ready. Surely. I was still trying to work that out, when she dropped the next bombshell, by saying that she understood. I mean, how on earth could she possibly claim to understand? I didn't understand myself. I still don't. That seemed really... I don't know... arrogant, I guess. And it only got worse when she made that comment about things not going quite 'to plan' in my life... or her life... or someone's life... whichever it was. I thought that was uncharacteristically insensitive of her, even though I think I knew that wasn't how she meant it. I think I knew that, even before I picked her up on it... even before I started yelling at her. Again.

I don't think I've ever lost it like that before... not quite that spectacularly. Not even when I fell out with Mum. I know I scared Summer then. I could see it in her eyes. And yet I couldn't stop myself. All my plans to tell her that last night had meant so much more to me than anything else ever had, and that I needed some time to get my head around that, and my past... and my life... and to ask her to wait for me while I did that... they all went out of the window. And instead, I accused her of making a mess of her life. *Her. Summer.* The woman who's about as together as anyone I've ever met. The woman who copes with everything life throws at her, and just keeps smiling, no matter what. The woman who's forgiven me, every single time I've messed up. And I have messed up, more times than anyone should ever have to allow for. Because *I'm* the one who's a mess.

We've been home for two hours and Poppy's still not talking to me.

I don't blame her. If it wasn't for the fact that I'm going insane, I wouldn't be talking to myself.

And yet I can't help it. Because all I've done since we got back here and I slammed the door shut, watching while Poppy ran upstairs to her room, is to pace the floors, occasionally sitting down, only to get up and pace again… and wonder to myself how the hell I let that get so out of hand.

Finally, exhausted and wrung out, I flop down on the sofa, the sound of *The Lion King* filtering through from upstairs and bringing a wry smile to my face. Poppy must have found her own DVD and put it on in her bedroom… and so I sit back, and close my eyes, and think about what Summer said, before I exploded at her.

She's right… just like she's always right… I do spend too much time looking back. And I do often wonder 'what if' and beat myself up over what might have been. And maybe that's why I blew up at her so savagely. *Because* she was right, and I didn't want to admit it.

I mean, let's face it… I often sit around at night, when we're at home, once Poppy's gone to bed, and I'm alone, and I contemplate how my life would have been if Bryony hadn't died. I often wonder if we'd have had that second child we were trying so hard for… and maybe even a third? Bryony was a natural when it came to motherhood, and I think she'd have liked us to have more kids. We'd have had to move house, I think, if we'd had a third child, because our home in Kew only has three bedrooms, and the third one is really a bit of an excuse. Would we have stayed in Kew? It was always handy for Bryony's work, but she'd given that up, and I couldn't honestly see her going back, not for a long while. And it might have been nice to live somewhere with a bit more space…   One thing I do know is I'd never have slept with Gabrielle. I'd probably have still gone on that business trip, but when Gabrielle had made her suggestion, I'd have vetoed it and made sure she understood. I'd never even have been tempted, because I'd never have cheated on Bryony… if she'd still been alive. But then I was a different man when Bryony was alive. I was carefree then, and happy… and I wasn't wracked with guilt. Her death changed me, and I wish I could change back... or at least grow away from the man I am now, into someone new... someone better.

I thought I had a chance of that... with Summer. After last night, I really thought I might have found a chink of light in all of that darkness. A hope for a new start. A new me. And maybe I did have a chance, right up until today, when I yelled at her and told her I thought she was a mess. She's the opposite of a mess. I don't think I've met anyone in my life who's coped as well as she has. Okay, so our circumstances are very different, but we've both ended up in the same place... we're both alone, with young children, trying to make sense of our situations. And she does that, and gets on with life, caring for her son, with a smile on her face, and she does a fantastic job of it. I, on the other hand, am just a mass of mixed up emotions. I never seem to know what I'm doing with Poppy. To begin with, I couldn't even work out how to tell her Bryony was dead... so, when Poppy cried out for her mother at night, like she did in those first few weeks, or just said 'Mummy?' inquisitively which she did for a while, until 'Daddy?' became her point of reference instead, I used to tell her that Mummy had gone away and then find something to distract her. She accepted that, because she was only two and didn't understand. And then, she stopped crying, and she stopped asking, and for a while it was like Bryony had never existed for Poppy, and I let that happen. I buried the problem of how to tell her, knowing I'd have to one day. I put it off, and I put it off... until the day finally came when she ran out of nursery school at the end of that first week, a week when I'd made a point of collecting her every day, rather than leaving it to Clare, or Bryony's mum. She had tears flooding down her cheeks, and asked me straight out, why she didn't have a mummy. I couldn't lie to her, so I told her what had happened. And that's when she asked if that meant her mummy was 'never ever' coming home again. And I said 'yes'... and then I had to say 'yes' again, when she asked the question the second time... and the third. Because when you're three years old, it's hard to get your head around the idea that someone who was once there – even if you don't remember them – is gone. Forever. It's hard when you're in your thirties, and you remember them as clear as crystal. I should know.

I've wrapped Poppy in cotton wool, when I should be letting her live and laugh… and be a five year-old, simply because I'm scared of losing her too.

I've hurt Summer, when I should be learning from her, simply because I'm too frightened to admit that I care about her… that I'm falling for her… that I've fallen… that I've fallen… *Oh. Oh God…*

What the hell have I done?

"Poppy!" I shout, getting to my feet.

I'm greeted by silence.

"Poppy. Come down here. Now!"

I wait and eventually, I hear her footsteps stomping down the stairs, and she appears in the living room doorway, glaring at me.

"Get your shoes on. We're going out."

Chapter Twenty-one

Summer

I didn't bother looking at my lesson plans, because there was no way I was going to be able to think straight. So, I packed everything away again into the plastic storage box, and left it in the corner of the kitchen, resolving to face it all another day, and then went and watched the end of *The Lion King* with Roan. It's one of his favourite Disney films, even though it's quite old now, and we often sit and watch it together, but today, I wasn't really in the mood for watching. I was thinking and trying hard not to cry, because I could tell he was worried about me.

The trying not to cry part was really hard, because I was so hurt by what Kit had said, and by the cruel way he'd said it. And by the fact that making love to me clearly hadn't meant anything to him at all, while it had meant so much to me.

I'd like to be able to laugh at the irony of my love life. But it's not funny. I mean… what's funny about reaching the age of twenty-nine and only having had sex twice? The first time was fun… it was exciting and really, really pleasurable… but I never expected to end up pregnant. And I know I've got Roan as a result, and I'm not complaining. Not for one moment. I wouldn't change a thing about him. I'm just saying, it wasn't what I'd expected. As for the second time.

Last night. Well, that was something else. That was something I'll probably never experience again, quite simply because I can't believe it will ever be that perfect again. It just doesn't happen that way twice in a lifetime. And it won't be happening between me and Kit again either… because this time, he's gone too far. I meant it when I told Roan that I don't feel like being kind anymore. I don't.

Ever since Kit first walked into my life, I've tried to be understanding and compassionate. I've tried allowing for his grief, and for his feelings, even though he's never allowed for mine. I was even willing to forgive him for walking away from me after we made love. But I can't forgive him for what happened earlier today. He scared me, and I think he knew it. And I won't let any man do that to me. Ever.

The film finishes with Simba's young cub being presented to the assembled animals and, for the first time, instead of thinking how sweet and happy it all is, I'm moved to tears. Not because of the whole 'circle of life' thing, but because Simba and Nala and their newborn cub are a family… and I don't remember how that feels. I'm not sure I've ever been part of a family. Not in the real, conventional sense. Even when my parents were married, my dad was never there, and it was always just me, and my mum. And I was okay with that. But now she's gone… and it's just me and Roan. Except, I suppose, for some unknown reason, I'd allowed myself to dream… that maybe, one day – when he'd worked out his grief and sorrow, and guilt – Kit might want to make something of a life with me. I'd let myself hope that, anyway. I'd let myself hope that making love to me – especially in the way he did – actually meant that maybe – just maybe – we might have a future together. That *we* could be a family.

Some hope.

"Do you want to go to the swings?" I ask Roan. I need to snap out of this, for his sake, if not my own. He's worried enough about me as it is.

"Okay."

"Go and get your shoes on then."

He jumps down and I switch off the television and DVD player, and run upstairs to find a scarf, because although I don't mind wandering around my own house with my tainted neck exposed, I'm not going to give the village gossips anything to tittle-tattle about.

Roan's waiting for me when I get back down and doesn't comment about the addition of my new neckwear, and takes my hand as we leave the house, making our way across to the swings.

He starts off on the slide and, because I didn't bring a blanket, I sit down on the bench, and all I can think about is the time I sat here with Kit, and we had our first real, polite conversation... the time when I told him who I am, and that our mothers were friends. I have to stop thinking about him like that though. I have to stop remembering the times when things were good between us... when I had hope...

"Look at me, Mum!" Roan shouts from the monkey bars and I look up to see him, half way across, his legs swinging wildly.

"Very good," I call out and then startle, as Poppy runs up behind me, giving me a wave over her shoulder and going straight across to him.

"Hello, Roan," I hear her say, as I sit up straight, my nerves on edge, because I know if Poppy's here, her father will be too.

"Hi." Roan looks down at her, then across at me, frowning and quickly making his way to the other end of the monkey bars, just as the tall figure of Kit comes and stands right in front of me. He's a dark shadow against the bright sun behind him, but I can still make out the concern in his face, the softness of his lips, the confusion in his eyes.

"Summer?" My name is a whispered question on his lips, but I don't reply. I lower my head, and look past him, slightly to the left, focusing on the empty swings instead.

He crouches, coming back into my line of sight again, pushing his fingers back through his hair.

"Summer, I'm sorry," he says quietly.

"Get away from her!" We both turn at the sound of Roan's raised voice, as he runs straight towards us, his eyes alight with anger.

"Roan, no." I get to my feet, and Kit does too, taking a step back to give me space.

"Mum… you don't have to talk to him." Roan stands in front of me, between Kit and myself, looking up at me, and then turning to face Kit.

I place my hands on his shoulders and lean down to him. "It's okay, Roan."

"No, it's not." He pulls free of me and takes a step towards Kit, who's staring down at him, rooted to the spot. "You made her cry," Roan says, accusingly, and I can hear the emotion in his own voice.

"I know," Kit says, calmly, although I can see he's shocked. "I'm sorry."

Roan doesn't seem to know what to say or do in the face of Kit's apology, and he turns back to me. "It's okay, sweetheart." I bend down and kiss the top of his head. "You go and play with Poppy."

He hesitates, frowning, and looks from me to Kit again.

"I'm not going to hurt your mum," Kit says. "I promise."

I want to tell him it's a bit late to be making promises like that, but saying those words in front of Roan isn't going to help, and after a few moments, my son narrows his eyes at Kit and says, "Make sure you don't," in a very cute six year-old way, and then walks off towards Poppy, who's been standing by the slide the whole time, watching us.

I stare after him for a while, making sure he's okay, and then turn back to Kit, although I don't look him in the face, focusing instead on the second button of his shirt and trying not to think about the fact that I know what his chest looks like beneath it.

"I meant what I said," he murmurs, so the children won't hear, I think. "I'm not going to hurt you."

"It's a bit late for that." I put my thoughts into words, because Roan isn't here anymore. "You've already hurt me."

"I know. And I'm sorry."

"You're good at saying sorry." I raise my face to his, ignoring the tiredness in his eyes… and the sorrow that's lurking there too. Because I can't let him get to me. Not again. "But then you're also good at hurting me. You're good at leaving me. You're good at shouting at me… at scaring me…"

"I never meant to scare you." He steps closer.

"But you meant everything else?"

"No."

"And that's the problem, Kit. You don't mean to do any of it… and yet you do it anyway. You shout, you leave, you hurt…"

"I know. I'm sorry."

"Stop saying that."

"Because it makes you sad?" he asks and I feel the tears welling in my eyes.

"No… because you don't mean it." My voice cracks and I lower my head again, just as he reaches out and places a finger beneath my chin, raising it. I put my hand on his wrist and pull it away. "Don't touch me. You gave up that right…" I can't finish my sentence, and I blink back my tears instead.

"When I left you last night?" he suggests.

"No." I look up at him again. "No. I understood why you left. It hurt that you did it, and I wished you could have stayed and talked instead, but I did understand. No… you gave up the right to touch me, when you shouted at me; when you thought it was okay to come into my home and frighten me, and call me names."

"Please… can we just…"

"No." I hold up my hand and he stops talking. "I don't know what you're going to say, Kit, and I don't care." That's not strictly true. I do care. I care very much.

"I promise I…"

"Your promises don't mean anything," I interrupt.

He frowns. "How do you know? Have I ever broken a promise to you?"

"Yes."

"When?" he asks, looking confused.

"When you told me I wasn't just another itch. You promised I wasn't."

"And I meant it. You weren't. You're not," he says.

"Well, I feel like I am. And regardless of that, you can't promise me that you won't hurt me, or you won't make me cry, or you won't shout at me, or scare me… when you've already admitted that you didn't mean to do all of that the first time. How do you know you won't do it again?"

"Because I won't."

"That's not a very reassuring answer, Kit. And it's not a good enough answer for me."

He takes a half step closer, looking down into my eyes, and I hold his gaze. "What do you need to hear?" he says.

"I don't need to hear anything." He frowns. "I know you're grieving, and I know you're in pain… and I've tried so hard to help you, to allow for your feelings and to forgive you. And I have done. Over and over. But I'm done, Kit. I can't be your emotional punchbag anymore."

He steps back now, pain and shock flickering across his face. "Is that how it feels?"

"Yes. I can't keep being punished because you feel guilty."

I blink, a single tear falling onto my cheek, but as I raise my hand to rub it away, he gets there first, wiping it with his thumb.

"Don't cry," he whispers.

"Do you want try telling me not to take my next breath instead?" He tilts his head to one side. "Can't you see? I don't want it to end like this, Kit."

"End?"

"Yes. Well, I suppose it never really got started, so 'end' may not be the best word. But what I'm trying to say is, I have to protect myself from you… because you…" My voice cracks, and I cough to clear it. "You could really break me. And I can't afford to let you."

I can't look at him anymore. It hurts too much.

"Roan!" I call and he comes running. "We're going home."

"Okay." He looks from me to Kit, but doesn't say a word, and instead he waves at Poppy, calling out a 'goodbye', before we start back towards the house.

I don't look back.

Unlike Kit, I'm not a 'looking back' kind of person.

Chapter Twenty-two

Kit

'Emotional punchbag'.

It felt bad enough to know that, in raising my voice, I'd scared her. It felt bad enough to know that I'd hurt her, and made her cry. But 'emotional punchbag'? Did I really make her feel that bad? I must have done, or she wouldn't have said it. I already know that Summer is too open and honest for any kind of deceit, so if that's how she thinks of me, that must be how it is.

She said she needed to protect herself from me too. She said I could break her. I guess that must mean she cares, because only someone you care about can hurt you. Only someone you love can break you.

But she felt punished by me… so it doesn't matter if she cares about me, or even if she loves me. It's too late. I've hurt her too much. I've gone too far… and she wants nothing more to do with me. And I don't blame her. I don't want anything more to do with me either. I'm sick of being me.

I'm sick of being the kind of man that a six year-old boy feels he has to defend his mother against. Roan was so angry with me. But he was only doing what I'd have done if someone had made my mother cry. That's one of the things about sons and their mothers… we will defend them with every ounce of our being. Until we lose our way, and forget to be a son to them, that is.

He must have seen her crying earlier today, because it can't have been last night, when I left her, broken, and trying desperately to hold it together. He was fast asleep then. I guess at least her tears today would have been easier to explain to him. She would have been able to tell him that I'd just yelled at her for no good reason, like I normally do, rather than having to try and find a way to excuse the fact that, last night, I'd loved her so damn hard… and then I walked out on her.

Dear God… what have I done?

"Daddy?" Poppy comes and stands beside me. "What's happening?"

I look down at her upturned face, seeing her confusion, feeling my own, and knowing that Summer was right to do what she's just done. She was right to walk away. Because she's worth more than a man like me.

"We're going home."

Poppy nods her head and puts her hand in mine and, together, we walk slowly across the green.

After dinner, Poppy goes to bed and I set about packing.

She didn't understand what I meant when I said we were going home, but I've decided it's best for everyone if we leave Millarnick and go back to Kew. I can't drive back there tonight though – I'm too tired. But I'll get a decent night's sleep – or the best I can manage – and we'll set off first thing in the morning.

I doubt Poppy will be happy about my decision, but I know it's the right thing to do. It'll make things easier for Summer… and I owe her that much. I owe her some peace. I owe her a lot more than that. But this is the best I can do. At least she won't have to worry about us seeing each other, and she won't have to feel scared of me either… because the thought of her feeling scared of me is terrifying. And deeply, deeply shameful.

Once I've loaded up the car and packed my own case, knowing I can do Poppy's in the morning, I go to bed, although despite my tiredness,

I still struggle to get off to sleep. I suppose that isn't surprising, really, considering everything that's happened in the last twenty-four hours... all the things I've done that I never meant to do. Which is something I'm good at. Evidently.

Did I mean to make love to Summer when I went over there yesterday afternoon? No. It wasn't planned. I just went over there to apologise, with the flowers that I'd chosen especially to say 'sorry'. And to maybe spend some time with her. I didn't intend making love to her. But I don't regret that I did. Even now.

Did I mean to leave her after I'd made love to her? No, of course not. It had felt right. It had felt bloody perfect, actually. So leaving her had been the last thing on my mind... until I did. And I regret that now, with all my heart.

Did I mean to go back there today and shout at her? Definitely not. I wanted to work things out with her. I didn't know how I was going to do that... because it seems I never know what I'm going to do. But I did want to try and work it out. And I certainly didn't want to scare her.

Except I did. I did all the things I didn't mean to do.

I turn over in bed and stare out of the window, the image of Bryony coming into my mind, and even though I don't really want to think about her at the moment, it's hard not to compare the way we met, the way we got together, with what's happening now... simply because the differences between the two situations couldn't be more marked.

I was instantly attracted to Bryony the moment I saw her, just like I was to Summer, but that's where the similarities end.

I first met Bryony at a party I'd gone to with my girlfriend, Penny, who I'd been seeing for about a year, and who had basically taken up a kind of semi-permanent residence in my flat, in that she slept there most nights... well, every weekend, and some weeknights, when she didn't have an early start, because, like Summer, I'm more of an owl than a lark. I didn't want to go to Penny's office party though, because it struck me as being a waste of time. I wouldn't know anyone there, after all, and I couldn't think of anything more boring than listening to complete strangers making small talk. But she begged and cajoled...

and Penny could be very persuasive when she wanted… and so, I gave in. Anything for a quiet life.

Penny and Bryony were both recently qualified solicitors and had become friends when they'd done their internship together, although that office party was the first time Bryony and I had ever met. I thought she was stunning, and was surprised when every time I looked at her, she seemed to have her eyes on me too, and that made me wonder if the feeling was mutual. I thought it might be nice if it was, but we were both with other people, being as she'd come to the party with her boyfriend, Stuart. And even though we met up again a few times over the next couple of months, at pubs and a couple of dinners, we didn't do anything about the attraction… until Penny came round to my place one Friday night and told me that she'd had a conversation with Bryony over lunch, and had learned that Bryony had ended her relationship with Stuart the previous weekend.

That left me in a quandary. I liked Bryony. A lot. But I was with Penny still. And I'm not the kind of man who cheats. I never have been. I'm also not the kind of man who dumps one woman, just because the grass seems greener elsewhere. But Bryony was now free and single… and very, very beautiful… and that thought was driving me insane.

It was Penny who saw the truth of the situation in the end, after the three of us had been to a concert together, and we'd dropped Bryony off at her flat, before going back to Penny's place, because it was closer than mine. I was getting undressed when she asked me outright if I wanted to be with Bryony, and I remember turning around and looking at her, sitting there in the middle of the bed with her legs crossed, still fully clothed, staring back at me.

I couldn't lie to her, so I pulled up my jeans, sat down beside her and said, "Yes."

She didn't yell, or scream, or get hysterical. She just nodded her head.

"I'd like you to leave," she said simply. "I don't want to be with a man who'd rather be with someone else."

That seemed fair enough to me, so I left.

I never kept any of my things at her flat, because I didn't stay there very often, so I could walk out in a fairly dignified manner. But Penny had a few of her belongings at my place and she called me the next day and asked if she could pick them up. I agreed. Naturally. So, she came round that evening, and she was quiet, thoughtful, but polite... and I reasoned to myself that, as break ups went, it had gone okay.

I hung on for a couple of weeks before I called Bryony, because I was trying not to appear too keen, or desperate, but when I phoned her, she told me she was about to go on holiday... to Thailand... for a month.

So I waited. And when she got back, she called me, and we arranged to go out for a drink together.

It was kind of awkward, even as first dates go. I think we were both aware that, having been with other people when we'd met, we may have caused them some pain in getting to that point, so it was hard to know what to talk about. We hadn't actually done anything wrong, other than accidentally meet someone that we preferred the idea of being with, while we were with someone else. Neither of us had cheated, or lied. I'd never said I loved Penny, and she'd never said it to me either. But Bryony did tell me that Penny wasn't talking to her anymore... so while she may have appeared quite philosophical and calm about it to my face, she clearly wasn't. And that didn't feel too good.

We managed to get through that first date though, and arranged a second... and then a third. I'm not sure how many dates later it was, but I know we'd been together for about three months, when we eventually fell into bed. We'd been working up to it, and that night, after we'd been out to dinner, it just happened. It was like we'd finally stopped feeling bad about ourselves, and stopped making excuses for the way we'd got together, and decided to let ourselves be happy. And we were.

I wasn't in love with Bryony then. I loved being with her. She was beautiful and funny and smart, but the falling in love part was a bit more restrained. It just kind of dawned on me one day, when we'd been seeing each other for around six months, and I woke up beside her one

Sunday morning, and watched her sleeping for a while, that I was where I belonged. And that I loved her. Completely.

The contrast between then and now is almost too much for my brain to comprehend. With Bryony, it was very gradual. Very definite, but very gradual. There was none of this emotional turmoil. I don't remember ever feeling like my guts were being wrenched inside out, or my heart crushed to smithereens in my chest. I don't remember ever feeling like I was losing my mind.

And that doesn't make sense to me.

Bryony was the love of my life, wasn't she?

So how can I be feeling something so utterly consuming for another woman? How do I even begin to work that out?

"What does it matter?" I whisper into the darkness.

It doesn't matter what I feel, or even whether I can understand it. Because it's too late.

Chapter Twenty-three

Summer

I've spent my morning trying to keep busy.

Luckily, I found my marker pens, in my handbag, although what they were doing in there, I don't know. But at least I've been able to get on with my lesson planning now, even if I have found it hard to concentrate, because I can't stop thinking about Kit.

He seemed so genuinely sorry yesterday. Obviously he had a lot to be sorry about, but there was something about the way he looked at me, about he way he spoke to me. He seemed like a different person... and yet he was very much the same. The same as he'd been the other night, that is, before he walked out on me. He seemed strong, thoughtful, considerate... caring. Just how I remember him. He was offering all the kinds of things I want in a man, and all the things I can't necessarily trust him to provide. Not all the time.

So, I suppose what I'm saying is he was just as capricious as ever.

So what was different? I don't know. But something was.

And I guess it's that difference that's been making me think.

I've spent the night tossing and turning, and wondering if I was right in saying what I did.

I meant every word of it when I said it, because I know he could hurt me. I know he could break me. For the simple reason that I'm in love with him, and only the people you truly love can ever really hurt you. But I also meant it when I said I didn't want it to end... whatever 'it' is. And, again, that's because I'm in love with him. And therein lies my confusion. Therein lies my quandary. Because when you're in love with someone, you make it work. You fight... you don't walk away. You don't hide, and you don't give up. You put your heart out there and hope that the other person loves you back enough not to break it.

Maybe that's what I should have said.

Maybe that's what I should have done.

Maybe I should have taken that chance with him, because even though I am fed up with being his emotional punchbag, and even though I sometimes hate the way he talks to me, I didn't give him the chance to be the man I know he can be. Yes, I know I forgave him lots of times. But did I really give *us* a chance?

No, I didn't. And now I'm feeling the weight of that regret, like a millstone around my neck. I know it's only going to get heavier too, and that the best way to avoid that is to talk to Kit... to listen to what he has to say, and to explain myself properly. And then see what happens, knowing that I really did do everything I could.

But maybe not today. I'm not feeling in a talking, or listening mood today.

It'll wait until tomorrow.

I check the clock in the corner of my laptop and see that it's nearly noon, and I'm not really getting very far.

Roan's been playing in the living room most of the morning, just coming in here for drinks when he needs them, but I think it's time I admitted defeat and made us some lunch... and a very vital cup of coffee.

Usually we have sandwiches for lunch, but because I've got a bit of time, and to make up for the last couple of days being a bit traumatic, I thought I'd make macaroni cheese today.

First, I think I'll make that coffee, though, and then I'll start the pasta cooking.

I go over to the fridge and let out a groan.

"How can that have happened?" I hold up the carton of milk and give it a shake, as though that's going to miraculously make it refill itself. It doesn't, of course, and I put it back in the door of the fridge. "Roan?"

"Yes, Mum?"

"We're going to have to go to the shop... quickly, before they shut."

"Why?"

He appears in the doorway to the living room.

"Because we're out of milk."

"Can we get some chocolate biscuits as well?" He looks up at me, pleadingly.

"I suppose."

I can't say 'no' to him. Not today. Not when he was so marvellously chivalrous yesterday, leaping to my defence like he did. It may not have been strictly necessary, but I was proud of him, nonetheless.

I grab my purse and keys and, taking his hand, we leave the house, walking across the green to the shop. I wonder for a moment if Kit might be there, like he was the other day, and whether we might bump into each other and find a way to start a conversation. After what I said yesterday, I suppose there's every chance he won't want to talk... but then he might. He looked like he wanted to talk yesterday. He sounded like he wanted to work things out, and maybe we could have done, if I hadn't shut him down.

What will I tell him, if I do see him? That's the question. I suppose I'll have to explain my change of mind, because it will seem rather strange to him that, yesterday I told him how much he'd hurt me and that I couldn't afford to let him do that to me again... and yet today, I'm willing to give it a try. I suppose I'll have to tell him the truth – just so he can make sense of that. I'll have to tell him that, as well as claiming my body, he's also claimed my heart... and that I'd like to give him the chance to prove he won't break it.

The swings are deserted today, and as we walk, I can't help looking over in the direction of Maggie's house, and I notice Kit's car isn't there. It's possible he's gone shopping in Looe, rather than at the village store, or perhaps he's gone on one of his many trips to the tip, with yet more of Maggie's things. I remember doing that when my mum died and how awful it felt to be throwing away so much of her life, even if it wasn't practical to keep everything. And I wasn't selling a house, like he is… which is a reminder, along with the 'For Sale' sign by the gate, that he won't be here forever, and that maybe I shouldn't be giving him my heart, because he'll be gone soon.

Except, if there's one thing I've learned from losing the people I love too early in life, it's to take my chances… and this feels like a chance. A real chance to be happy. And that has to be worth taking, doesn't it? Even if it is complicated.

Although, judging from Kit's absence, it doesn't look like I'll get the opportunity to take my chances today… or at least not until later on. But then, that's not necessarily a bad thing, because I'm still not sure I'm in a talking mood yet. I need to be sure about exactly what I'm going to say… because I don't think either of us can afford to get it wrong again.

Inside the shop, Mrs Wilson is talking to Miss Hutchins from the tea room. She doesn't open on Sundays, even in the summer, because she claims it's a day of rest… although she doesn't have a problem with coming shopping – clearly – being as she's bought a basket full of groceries.

I collect my milk and let Roan choose his biscuits, and we make our way over to the counter, where the two women are still gossiping, while Mrs Wilson slowly rings Miss Hutchins' items through the till.

"And he's definitely gone, has he?" Miss Hutchins says, taking a tin of tomatoes from Mrs Wilson and putting them in her canvas bag.

"Yes."

"For good?"

Mrs Wilson nods. I've got no idea who they're talking about and I glance around at the display of birthday cards to my left, because I'm not really interested in their gossip. I assume, from what they're saying that some poor woman's husband has left her, and two of Millarnick's most avid gossips are feasting on the scant information Mrs Wilson has somehow managed to glean.

"How did you find out?" Miss Hutchins asks, although I wonder why she bothers. Mrs Wilson has a radar for gossip – especially if it's bad news.

"He came in here this morning, before he left."

"And he just told you?" Miss Hutchins seems surprised. "That doesn't seem like him. He's kept himself to himself all the time he's been here."

"I know. But he had his little girl with him, and she was crying, and he told her they'd be home soon... and that he just needed to get a few things, because there would be nothing in the fridge when they got back to London."

'London'? 'His little girl'? I turn back to them, my heart pounding. *It doesn't mean anything. It might not be him...*

"It seems a shame the little girl was so upset," Miss Hutchins muses.

"Yes. I gave her a lollipop." That's uncharacteristically generous of her. "And he thanked me... which gave me the chance to ask him outright, if he was leaving." So, she had an ulterior motive in her open-handedness.

"And what did he say?"

I lean forward, trying not to appear like I'm actually eavesdropping, even though I am.

"He said, 'Yes,'."

"Just like that?"

"Yes. And then he told me that we didn't need to worry."

"We?" Miss Hutchins queries.

"The village. He told me he'd given the estate agents very firm instructions not to sell Bluebells to a developer."

Mrs Wilson is looking rather smug now, although she's also starting to blur, and I know I have to get out of here, before I break down in front of them.

"Excuse me," I say, stepping forward. "I'm really sorry to interrupt, but I've got to get home. Do you mind if I pay you for the milk and biscuits."

Mrs Wilson smiles. "Of course," she says, looking at the two items in my hand. "That's two pounds ten."

I'm foraging in my purse for the change, when Miss Hutchins takes a step closer. "Have you heard the news?" she says, as though she hasn't just heard it for herself. "Maggie Robinson's son has gone back to London."

I want to correct her and tell her he doesn't live in London. He lives in Kew. But I can't speak. So I just nod my head and hand over the money to Mrs Wilson, grateful that at least I had the exact change and can leave the two of them to continue their gossip without me.

He's gone?

He's really gone?

And he didn't even bother to tell me.

Or to say goodbye.

Roan and I walk home in silence and I fight back my tears all the way, because it seems that while I've been thinking about offering him my heart and hoping he won't break it, he's taken matters into his own hands… and decided to crush it anyway. I meant nothing to him. Nothing special, anyway.

He's no different to Roan's father.

Okay, so he didn't leave me pregnant, but he left me, nonetheless. And he left without saying goodbye.

And that hurts.

Chapter Twenty-four

Kit

We've been back home for four days now, although I'm not sure either Poppy or I have recovered from the journey yet.

She eventually stopped crying after the first hour and a half, but still wouldn't talk to me, no matter how hard I tried to explain that I had to get back home 'for work'. That wasn't true, of course, but what else was I going to tell her? That I've fallen for Roan's mummy? That I've hurt her too badly to be forgiven? That I've been a coward? It was easier to blame work than to admit any of that. So I didn't. Although if I hadn't been such an idiot, hadn't hurt Summer so much, hadn't been a coward, and had instead just fallen in love with Summer, plain and simple – if anything about love is ever plain, or simple – then I'd have told Poppy the truth. And I'd have told her gladly... because I think she'd have liked that. But if that had been the case, we'd never have been leaving in the first place, would we? We'd have been staying down at Bluebells, trying to build a future with the woman I love, and her son.

As it was, once Poppy had finished crying, and I'd given her my 'I need to work,' excuse three or four times over, and been ignored each time, we completed our journey in silence. And that was hard, because I could have done with the distraction of having someone to talk to. It might have stopped me from thinking about how much I missed Summer, even though we'd only been apart for a few hours… and it certainly would have prevented me from remembering the dream I had about her the night before… when I finally managed to fall asleep. I suppose it shouldn't have surprised me that I'd had my most erotic dream yet, being as that was the first time I'd actually slept since making love to her, but it was so real I could feel her, right there with me. Her skin… her breath… her touch… her gaze... her presence. And when I woke up with a start, to the sound of my own voice calling her name, and found I was alone, it was all I could do to keep it together. Because don't think I've ever felt so lonely in my life. And that's saying something.

I wished – I still do wish – that I'd plucked up the courage to go and say goodbye to Summer. I feel like even more of a coward for just leaving like I did. But what would I have said to her? 'I love you, but I'm doing what's best for you'? How facile does that sound?

I've always maintained that I'm an honourable man – well, fairly honourable anyway. I'm a man who doesn't shirk his responsibilities, at least. Or that's what I've always told myself. It's what I told Summer too, right before I made love to her, and in doing so, made her my responsibility. Right before I left her, and completely failed her. In every way imaginable.

I've thought about that night a lot since we've been back here, and while the guilt over Bryony is still there, lurking in the back of my mind, as ever, I have to admit that the guilt I feel over what I did to Summer is much greater. It's a constant. Along with the knowledge that making love to Summer changed me… for the better, I think, as a lover, and maybe as a man too. I was certainly more demonstrative and physical with her than I've ever been before. And even though I've got no intention of making love to anyone else, and I completely understand why she couldn't forgive me for the way I treated her, I wish I'd taken the chance to tell her what she did for me, and to thank her, for helping me to finally find my true self.

Since we got back on Sunday night, the house has felt completely empty, like we don't belong here anymore. I know Poppy feels the same, because she just wanders around, aimlessly. Lost. This may be the only home she's ever known, but she doesn't want to be here. That much is obvious. And neither do I.

I suppose the reason for that is obvious. The woman I love is hundreds of miles away, and that's where I want to be too. Even if I can't.

The other problem – if you can call it that – is that my dreams have continued, even though I'm back here, sleeping in the bed I shared with Bryony. The first night, I woke up in darkness, feeling ashamed, and aroused in equal measure. It felt wrong to be dreaming about someone else, in 'our' bed, but at the same time, I can't deny how I feel about Summer. Not any more. I'm in love with her. I want her. There's no point in trying to pretend otherwise.

I lay awake for some time, beating myself up, but then I remembered Summer's words, and decided that wasn't getting me anywhere. And eventually managed to get back to sleep... and dreamt of Summer again.

She's in my head. And my heart.

And there's nothing I can do about that.

No matter where I am.

But as a result of the last few days, and how both Poppy and I seem to have reacted to being back here, I can't help wondering if maybe the time has finally come to sell up.

I never thought I'd want to do that, but everything feels different now, and even if I can't have what I really want... because I've left that behind in Millarnick... maybe I can think about doing what Summer suggested and actually learn something from my mistakes, rather than just dwelling on them. Maybe I can finally stop living in the past, and look towards the future... not that I'm sure what I want the future to be, because the idea of a future that doesn't include Summer is kind of hard to contemplate.

In the meantime, even though I told Poppy I was coming back for work, we've actually spent the last few days getting her ready for school.

It may still be a little while until she goes back, but I knew I'd have to knuckle down to work at some point, so it seemed like a good idea to buy her uniform before my own schedules and deadlines got in the way. Or it would have done, if Poppy hadn't spent the whole time we were in the department store, asking me why we couldn't have stayed in Cornwall – because she'd obviously noticed I wasn't actually doing any of the work I'd claimed I had to come home for. She also made a point of reminding me that there's a perfectly good school in the village… the one Summer teaches at… and that, if we lived there, she could go to school with Roan every day.

I didn't have any answers for her – although I was relieved she'd broken her silence and was finally talking to me – because I wished we could have stayed in the village too. I know it's not possible. I know I went too far this time, and for us to have stayed there would have made Summer's life very difficult, possibly even miserable. I was already making her feel bad… making her feel 'punished' and like an 'emotional punchbag'… and I can't put her through any more. I love her too much.

It's just a shame, for all of us, that I left it too late to work that out.

We've managed to make it through our first week, although it's been a trial, being as the weather has turned against us. Down in Cornwall, apart from a couple of rainy days, it was basically perfect summer weather, but since we've been back, it's been much more autumnal… which isn't bad, considering it's still August.

We don't have a huge back garden, unlike at my mother's place, but with the weather being so cold and damp, Poppy's been confined to the house anyway. I've tried doing things with her… taking a leaf out of Summer's book, but I think I'm a poor substitute. And I think she's missing Roan too. A lot of her own school friends are away on holiday, and she blames me for cutting short our time in Cornwall.

I'm not surprised.

I blame me too.

I spent Friday going through Ian Clark's job, and then on Saturday, I called Clare to see whether she'd be available to have Poppy at all. She won't be. I mean, obviously she wasn't expecting me to be back from Cornwall yet anyway, and although her dad is a little better, she's still making daily visits to the hospital, and has her mum staying with her for the foreseeable future. So taking care of Poppy is out of the question. I asked how she was getting on, noticing that she seemed slightly less stressed than she was the last time we spoke and she explained that Tim's managed to get a couple of weeks off work, and once the kids go back to school, she's hoping things will calm down a bit. She was apologetic for not being able to help out with Poppy, but I completely understood… and called Ruth.

She was overjoyed to hear from me and quite surprised too, although I offered no explanation, other than 'work', for our sudden return. She was saddened to hear about Clare's dad too, because she's known Clare longer than I have, and before I could even ask the question, she said, "Of course, Poppy must come here, whenever you need," which I knew she would. They love looking after her, and we arranged that I'd drop Poppy off there this morning, which I did at nine-thirty, leaving it a little later than usual, to avoid the traffic.

I used 'work' as my excuse again, when Ruth invited me in for coffee, because I knew she'd want to ask how things had gone in Cornwall, and with Poppy there, I imagined Roan would come up… and probably Summer as well. So I beat a hasty retreat, waving goodbye as I backed out of the driveway.

Ruth means well, but I really didn't want to talk about Summer. Not yet. And certainly not in front of my daughter… the one person here who can testify to my appalling behaviour. Well, to some of it, anyway, because I dread to think how disappointed she'd be if she knew the whole story. And besides, if I'm going to keep using work as an excuse for not talking, and for being back here in the first place, I really ought to actually do some.

At least, that was what I reasoned to myself on the drive back home.

I've surprised myself.

I've only thought about Summer for some of the time today, catching myself daydreaming occasionally, staring out of the window and remembering her smile and her laugh, and how she looked in that stunning sundress… and how she felt in my arms… all of which was quite distracting, but which evidently didn't stop me working, because as the clock ticks around to five-thirty, I check the notes I made on Friday and find I've actually achieved quite a lot. More than I expected, in fact. My planning session has paid off it seems, and I'm so far ahead of schedule that, although I thought I'd need at least two weeks to get Ian's modules corrected and back to him, I think, if I can really focus, I can have them done by this Friday. And that's good, because I'm not being paid for what I'm doing now, so the less time I spend on it the better, and then I can move on to Alan's job… which *is* going to pay me. Quite well. Not that he's actually sent me in all the information I need yet. But that's Alan for you. And, in any case, I did give him until the end of the month… and we're not there yet. So I can't complain.

Of course, because I've been so busy, I haven't had lunch, and I've barely stopped for a cup of tea or coffee, and now I've finished for the day, I do feel hungry… and thirsty. But I can't really do anything about that, because if I don't go and get Poppy, we won't have any time together before she has to go to bed. So, picking up my phone from the desk, and closing up my office, I return to the sterile, empty house, that used to be my home, passing through it and straight out of the front door, and then getting into my car.

Ruth and Edward's house is in Barnes, which should be about a ten minute drive from where we live in Kew. But at five-thirty in the afternoon, it takes at least twice that length of time, so it's nearly six o'clock when I pull into their driveway.

They have a fairly spectacular home, and I can still remember the first time I came here. Bryony and I had been together for about seven months, I suppose, and although she still hadn't met my parents, she insisted on bringing me here to meet hers. That felt like quite a big step to me… because, even though I'd recently worked out that I was in love with her, I hadn't actually told her. I was still trying to decide if it was too soon, whether she felt the same… if I'd scare her off. And none of that uncertainty was helping, when she parked her car on the driveway, and I looked up at the enormous house.

"You grew up here?"

She nodded, and I gazed back at the red brick building in front of us, with its twin gables and bay windows, either side of a rather grand entrance. Okay… so it wasn't actually much bigger than Bluebells, where I'd been born, and had spent the first eighteen years of my life. But I wasn't an idiot. I knew that geography made a huge heap of difference when it came to houses, and that the property I was looking at was probably worth at least two or three times as much as my parents' place. And for the first time, I started to wonder if I knew Bryony at all. And whether she knew me.

It was a Sunday lunchtime in July, and her parents were having a barbecue, and I've never really known – not to this day – whether they invited us, or whether Bryony did that for them, but they made me very welcome right from the word 'go'. I got on well with both Ruth and Edward, and we sat in their garden, enjoying a really tasty barbecue and drinking excellent wines, all afternoon.

I was surprised by how large their garden was, and after we'd finished coffee, Bryony offered to take me on a tour, to show me around. I accepted, of course, and hand in hand, we wandered off across the lawn, both of us knowing, I think, that her parents were probably watching us.

We got to the far wall, where there was some kind of climbing plant, the variety of which remains a mystery to me, although I think Bryony may have told me. I've forgotten now, because she turned to me at that point and looked up into my eyes.

"Can I tell you something?" she said, and from the worried, fearful look on her face, I wondered if she was about to say she didn't want to see me anymore. Bringing me to her parents' house and letting us sit through lunch first, seemed like rather an elaborate way of doing that, but it dawned on me that she might have wanted them there for back-up, or something, and then might have lost her nerve, and had only just regained it. With hindsight, that really doesn't make much sense, but at the time, her whole demeanour had me really confused.

"Yes," I said, feeling nervous myself now. After all, I had just worked out that I was in love with her. I didn't relish the idea of being dumped.

She stepped closer, resting her hands on my arms, before she moved them up around my neck… and I started to relax at that point, because it didn't feel like a break-up anymore.

"I'm not sure how to put this," she murmured, biting her bottom lip. "So I'm just going to say it and hope you don't run a mile." She paused, but before I could speak, she blurted out, "I love you, Kit."

I couldn't stop the smile from forming on my lips as I leant down and, regardless of her parents, kissed her deeply.

"You… you didn't run a mile," she said, breathlessly, once we'd broken the kiss.

"No. I'm not going to either. Because I love you too."

She smiled back at me then, and we carried on walking around the garden, in a kind of trance.

"Did you bring me here specially, to tell me that?" I asked eventually, interrupting a very easy, very happy silence.

She looked up at me and smiled. "Yes. I—I was nervous about how you'd react. I thought it might be easier if I was on home turf, so to speak."

I stopped walking then and turned to her, cupping her face with my hand. "You didn't have to be nervous. I've been trying to work out how to say 'I love you' for weeks."

"You have?" She was genuinely surprised and I leant down and kissed her again.

It wasn't until later, when we were lying in bed and she was fast asleep, that I realised how anxious she'd been all day… how little she'd eaten at lunch, how she'd chattered on about nothing in particular on the drive over to Barnes, how worried she evidently must have been by my response to her loving me. And that bothered me, because it meant she'd had no idea how I'd felt about her. Obviously my actions over the previous few weeks hadn't made it apparent to her that I felt exactly the same way she did. Clearly, that was mutual. Let's face it, I'd half expected her to dump me. So she must have shielded her feelings from me too. But I resolved that night, that she would never again doubt my love for her, that I'd go out of my way to show it, so she would never need to wonder, or worry… or be nervous. Ever again. And I did. Every day.

Until the day came when I couldn't anymore.

Because she wasn't there.

I climb out of the car and am making my way slowly to the front door, when Ruth opens it, smiling. She has dark hair, like Bryony's was, and wears glasses, which she tends to look over the top of when she's not best pleased and wants to get maximum 'glare' value. She's an inch or two shorter than Bryony, and dresses a lot more informally than my late wife ever did, wearing jeans and a blouse today… something Bryony rarely, if ever, did.

Unfortunately, the fact that she's anticipated my arrival means she'll probably have seen me sitting in the car, reminiscing to myself, and I just have to hope she doesn't read too much into that, or I'll be here all night.

"Come in," she says, stepping back, and I enter the wide hallway. "Edward's taken Poppy over to the common. But they'll be back soon." I nod my head, knowing there'll be no quick escape now, and wondering if she planned this. "Do you want a cup of tea?"

It would be rude to say 'no', and I am thirsty, so I accept her offer and follow her to the end of the hallway, passing the living and dining rooms, and going into the enormous kitchen that runs along the whole of the back of the house.

She and Edward had this room re-designed a couple of years ago and it's very modern, with an island unit in the centre, at which I sit, like I usually do when I come here, while Ruth fills the kettle, switches it on and then turns, her eyes fixed on me.

"Poppy's looking well," she says as her opening gambit, and I want to tell her to just come out and say whatever it is she wants to say, rather than skirting around the issue. It'll be quicker. And we both know she'll get there eventually anyway.

"Yes."

"Cornwall must have done her good."

"Hmm…"

She fetches a couple of brightly coloured mugs from the cupboard, putting them down between us. "How did the funeral go?"

There's that question again. "As well as any funeral ever does."

"And how are you?" Finally... we're getting there.

"I'm fine."

She leans forward, tilting her head slightly. "Hmm... why don't I believe you?"

"I don't know, Ruth. Why don't you? Has Poppy been saying something?"

She shakes her head, then lowers it slightly, looking at me over the top of her glasses... and that's when I know I'm in trouble.

"No, she hasn't. But I'm not blind. You've got to stop this."

"Stop what?" I feign ignorance.

She leans back again, folding her arms. "You've got to stop beating yourself up, Kit." I'm suddenly struck by how Summer used that exact phrase to me as well, but before I can dwell, Ruth goes on, "Bryony died. It was tragic. But it wasn't your fault. And it was three years ago."

"So? You think that makes a difference? You think there's a time limit on grief?" I sit forward, feeling angry with her for being so blasé about it. She normally understands better than this. Or she seems to, anyway.

"No." She stays completely calm. "She was my daughter and I miss her every single day. I will never get used to the idea that she's not coming back; that she's never going to come walking through that door, ever again. But you need to stop living in the past."

God... Summer said that too. And without warning, I feel tears pricking at my eyes. I can't do this here... I just can't. I go to get up, but Ruth leans across, placing her hand on my arm.

"Talk to me, Kit," she says softly. "Tell me what's wrong."

I stare at her, for a moment seeing the woman I will always love reflected in the gentle eyes gazing back at me.

"I—I met someone," I whisper, and much to my surprise, she smiles.

"Well, that's good."

She lets go of me and I settle back into my chair, letting out a deep sigh. "Yes... well, it might be, if I hadn't messed it up."

She turns away, going over to the kettle, placing teabags into the teapot and adding water. "And how exactly did you mess it up?" she says, over her shoulder.

I try to think it through for a moment, to remember the course of events, the litany of ungentlemanly behaviour that's beset my relationship with Summer, right since that very first meeting. "The first time I saw her, I was really rude to her," I murmur, although I don't add that I was also very, very attracted to her as well.

Ruth turns back to me, bringing the teapot with her. "That doesn't sound like you."

"Really?" I raise my eyebrows and she smiles.

"Okay… you can be abrupt sometimes, since Bryony died… but I wouldn't have said you're ever rude."

"Well, I was to her."

"What happened?"

"Oh… she just came over to me at the children's playground and started talking to me. I thought she was just like all those other women… you know, the ones who keep trying to tell me how to do everything."

"And was she?"

"She told me I should let Poppy go down the slide by herself… so yes, she seemed that way."

"You mean, you were insisting on holding onto her?" Ruth seems surprised, bordering on incredulous. "She's five, Kit."

"I know. And don't start."

She smiles again, shaking her head at me. "I'm going to guess this lady's advice didn't go down well?"

"No. But it got worse, because the next time we met – which was at the playground again – she forgave me for being so horrible to her and she offered to watch the kids…"

"Kids?" she interrupts, picking up on that.

"Yes. She has a son… Roan."

"She's not married, is she?" She frowns at me.

"No. She's a single parent. Like me. It turned out that Roan's father didn't want to know, when Summer found out she was pregnant."

"Summer?" she says. "That's a lovely name."

"Yes, it is. It suits her."

She smiles again. "And it sounds like you must have managed to have at least one conversation with her, after you'd finished being rude, if you were able to find out about her little boy's father."

"Yes. I did. But only after I'd yelled at her, and called her negligent… oh, and incompetent. I think."

"You called her what?"

I know Ruth's question is rhetorical, and I don't need to repeat myself, which is just as well, because I'm ashamed of the things I called Summer. Even now.

"She'd offered to watch the kids," I repeat, going back to my original telling of the story, "because I had to take a call from Alan Langley. Only, when I turned round, after I'd finished speaking to him, Poppy was hanging off the monkey bars… and then she fell."

"Oh my God." Ruth's hand darts up to her mouth and she pales.

"Don't worry. She was fine. Summer caught her."

"Then I don't understand." She lowers her hand again. "Why did you yell at her?"

"Fear, I think. And guilt…"

"Oh… that. Again."

"Yes. Not that it's any excuse for my behaviour. Even when she told me that she's a school teacher, and perfectly capable of looking after a couple of children by herself, I still had to get a jibe in…" I let my voice fade,

"What kind of jibe?"

I feel myself blush. "I told her it was a good thing we didn't live in the village, because if we did, I'd have reported her to the authorities."

"For catching your daughter when she fell?"

I look up at her, feeling embarrassed, but don't reply, and she pours the tea, passing me the milk to add to mine, because she takes hers black.

"What happened next?" she asks, once she's put the teapot back over by the kettle, out of the way, and the milk back in the fridge.

"We met up again, by accident, in the local shop…"

"That must have been awkward."

"You would have thought so. But it wasn't. Summer was really friendly, even though I hadn't actually apologised for being rude to her – on either occasion – and we walked home from the shop together and, while the kids played on the swings, we actually managed to have a conversation… without me being rude to her that time. And that's when I found out about Roan's father, and that Summer was bringing up her son by herself – and doing a fantastic job of it, I have to say. And that our mothers had been friends."

"So Maggie knew Summer's mum?" she queries, clearly as surprised as I was when Summer first told me.

"Yes. They'd known each other all their lives."

"And yet, you'd never met Summer before?"

"No. I knew of her, obviously. I always have done. But she's six years younger than me, and she grew up in France for the first twelve years of her life. By the time she came to live in England, I'd left home and gone to university. Our paths just never crossed… until now."

"But she knew you?"

"Yes. Well, I suppose she knew of me, just like I did her. She knew I was Mum's son, and she knew about our argument…" I let my voice drop, recalling how I told Summer all about that… and how Ruth has no idea of the reasons behind my falling out with my mother. And she never will.

"So did you stop being rude to her? Once you'd both worked out exactly who you were?"

"No. Not really."

"Kit…" She frowns at me, over the top of her glasses, with a scolding tone to her voice.

"I know, I know. We did have one really nice evening together… at the pub." I'm not going to tell her about the letters from Tony that we'd found that afternoon, which I think brought Summer and I closer together. I feel like that's something between my mother and her lover. "Summer had been helping me clear out some of Mum's things," I explain. "So I took her and Roan out to dinner to say 'thank you'."

"And?"

"And she and I spent the evening talking."

"You? Talked?"

I narrow my eyes at her, but it's done with good humour. "A bit. Yes. I told her how my parents met, and… and I even managed to tell her a little bit about how Bryony died." I decide, in that moment, that I won't tell her that I admitted to my feelings of anger towards Bryony. Ruth is a very understanding woman, but I don't know how she'd feel about that. I kept it to myself for a very long time, and as far as my in-laws are concerned, I can go on doing just that.

Ruth raises her eyebrows. "Really?" There's no sarcasm to her voice this time. She's genuinely astonished. I guess that's understandable. She's been trying to get me to talk about Bryony for ages, without success. The fact that I talked to Summer, especially about how Bryony died, must tell Ruth how much Summer means to me, and even if she doesn't actually comment on that, her surprise is written all over her face. "So things improved between you?" she says, eventually.

"No."

"Why on earth not? I mean, what did you do wrong?"

"I love how you know it was my fault."

"You've already told me as much. You said it was you that messed up, remember?"

"Yes. I did." I lower my head. "I really messed up."

"How?" she asks.

"Summer was doing me a favour. She was looking after Poppy for me for a whole day, while I came back up here for a meeting."

"You came back up here?" She's confused by that, I think.

"Yes."

"And you didn't call in?"

"You were in Portugal still."

"Oh yes. Of course." She nods, taking a sip of tea and wincing because it's hot.

"If you'd been here, I'd have brought Poppy with me and left her with you for the day, but as it was… with Clare's dad being sick, I had to ask Summer to help me out. She said yes, of course, and Poppy stayed with her and Roan for the day. And when I called her after my meeting, to let her know I was on my way back, she said she was going to take the kids to the beach… and I lost it."

"Why?" She doesn't understand, and I'm not sure I do. Not anymore.

"Because Poppy can't swim." I give her the reasons I gave Summer. "And because I wasn't there…"

"Oh… and you think responsible school teachers, with children of their own, are in the habit of drowning other people's offspring, do you?"

"No. But my meeting had gone really badly… and I took it out on her." I don't mention my childish jealousy of Summer and how inadequate she was making me feel that day, because that'll just make me sound like even more of an idiot. And I'm doing a pretty good job of that already, even with my edited version of events.

"Well, I hope you apologised," she scolds, making me feel like an errant schoolboy.

"I did. Eventually. Not that night, though, because I was too busy making a complete fool of myself. But the next day, after Poppy had given me the silent treatment, I went round there to say sorry…"

"You mean it took Poppy's influence to get you to do the right thing?" I can almost feel her disappointment, as well as being able to see it in her eyes, and I know where my daughter gets that look from now.

"No. I mean it took Poppy's *persuasion* to get me to do the right thing. I'm not proud of myself, Ruth."

She lets her frown fade. "I take it Summer accepted?"

"Yes, as graciously as ever. And then she invited Poppy and me to stay for dinner." I leave out the fact that, when I'd got back from London the previous day, I'd been struggling with my feelings for Summer, and also trying very hard not to kiss her. She doesn't need to know that much information. No-one does. Except for me… and Summer.

"So you stayed for dinner?" she prompts, getting me back on track, and picking up her tea at the same time.

"Yes. And we spent the entire evening together… and I found out that she'd lost her mum too, not that long ago, and I—I actually managed to talk to her. Properly that time. In much more detail."

"About Bryony?" Ruth asks, her voice a cracked whisper.

"Yes. And about me… about the argument with Mum… about how I felt."

She leans forward again. "That's good, Kit. That sounds promising."

I shake my head. "It might have been, if I hadn't messed it up. And I mean *properly* messed it up. I wish I hadn't… but I did… and now it's too late." I don't want to tell her any more than that. It's too personal.

"Are you sure about that?" she asks, clearly sensing my reticence to elaborate this time.

"Yes. Absolutely. I—I behaved very badly towards her. So badly that even I knew I needed to apologise that time, but when I tried, she… well, she made it very clear she couldn't forgive me… for what I'd done, and the things I'd said. And I don't blame her." I lower my head and mumble, "I can't forgive myself."

"That's part of the problem, Kit." Ruth raises her voice and I look up again. "You can't forgive yourself for any of it." She puts her cup down and comes to sit beside me, taking a deep breath. "But you need to," she says, softening her voice again. "You really do. And you need to try and work things out with Summer, because you can't go on as you are."

I turn to face her and I know I have to be honest. "I felt so guilty, at the time… being with her. It was overwhelming."

"Because of Bryony, you mean?"

"Yes. I felt like I'd betrayed her." It would be so easy, and more honest to add, 'Again' to that statement. But I don't. Instead I watch her closely as she tucks her hair behind her ear.

"You're being silly," she whispers. "Bryony didn't want this life for you. She wanted you to be happy… to find someone else. To love again. She wasn't jealous about who you might end up with. She just didn't want you to be lonely and unhappy. She told me that a few days before she died, just before she asked me to keep an eye on you… you and

Poppy. She said she wanted you to find someone who was right for you, who'd understand you and love you… and who'd be a mother to Poppy."

My sight blurs and I look down at my lap, muttering, "I know. I know all that. We had the same conversation. More than once. I didn't want to listen, but she kept repeating the same things, and I kept dismissing them, because I couldn't accept that we weren't going to grow old together, that we wouldn't have the future we'd planned… because without her, I didn't want any of it."

"That's no way to live," she says, with feeling. "You've got Poppy to think about, and before you jump down my throat and tell me that you do think about her, I know that. I know you love her and care for her, and that you put her first in everything, but there's more to being a parent than putting a roof over her head and food on the table. And protecting her." She stares at me knowingly. "You need to set an example, Kit. You need to help her to understand that love and happiness are the most vital ingredients in life. And that without them, she'll be very much poorer. You owe her that much. And you owe it to Bryony too, above and beyond anything else. Because that was what she wanted for you. You might think you're honouring her memory by staying faithful to her…"

"I haven't," I interrupt, and then wish I hadn't.

"Yes, you have."

I look up at her again, fixing her with a gaze. "No, I haven't, Ruth."

"You have in your head… or at least you've tried to. That's why you keep beating yourself up whenever you're with someone else. That's why you're making yourself miserable, feeling guilty for finding any kind of happiness that doesn't involve Bryony." She stops talking and leans back, taking a breath, but then reaches out and clasps my hand in hers, in probably the most intimate gesture of our relationship. "It sounds like Summer was good for you," she says firmly. "It sounds like she made you feel comfortable with yourself. At least she made you feel like you could talk… which is something you haven't been able to do with any of us… not since Bryony died."

"I know. Believe it or not, I did actually manage to work that out for myself."

"And you didn't do anything about it?"

"Yes. I did. Well, I tried to. That's when I went to speak to her… after I'd messed up. And that's when she told me she couldn't forgive me. She… she said she was fed up with being punished by my guilty conscience… with being my emotional punchbag. She said she had to end it between us, because she had to protect herself from me." I look into her eyes, to find they're glistening with what look like unshed tears. "Do you have any idea what that feels like?"

She shakes her head. "No. But I know what it sounds like… it sounds like she's as much in love with you as you are with her."

I not going to bother to deny that I'm in love with Summer. It's the truth. And I'm obviously that transparent. Or maybe it's just that I've finally let my guard down…

"Well, even if you're right, she won't be now, being as I left Millarnick without saying goodbye to her… without even telling her I was leaving."

Ruth gets up and goes back around to the other side of the island unit. "That was probably a mistake," she muses, like she's trying to work something out. "But I think Summer sounds like an incredibly kind and forgiving sort of person. I think you should go back and try saying 'sorry' to her."

I remember Summer's rule about that word. "I really doubt she'd want to hear it. She was pretty adamant."

"Even if she was, wouldn't you rather try and take a chance at happiness? It doesn't come around very often, Kit, and when it does, you should grab it and cherish it."

"I know." I know that better than anyone.

"Then go back to her. Show her how much she means to you. Work things out. And when you've done that, do you think you could bring her here?"

"Here?" My surprise must show, because Ruth smiles at me, tilting her head slightly.

"Yes. Here. If Summer is going to be part of your life – and I sincerely hope that she is – then she'll be part of Poppy's life too. And Edward and I would love to meet her… and her son."

I love her optimism, that Summer will accept my apology and agree to try again. It's… encouraging. "You would?"

"Yes." She reaches over, once again taking my hand. "Stop worrying about the past, Kit. It's gone, and there's nothing you can do about it. Concentrate on the future instead. It has so much more to offer."

Lying in bed, staring at the ceiling, the street lights making shadows of the breeze-swept trees, all I can think about is Summer. That's not unusual, although my thoughts are…

Perhaps it's because I've talked about her to someone else for the first time, or maybe it's because I miss her so much… I'm not sure. But I'm thinking about her in a completely different way tonight, and instead of focusing on my dreams, and the even more potent reality of making love to Summer, my mind is filled with reminders of all the things she's done for me… even though I'm not sure she knew she was doing them at the time. I know I wasn't. First and foremost, I suppose, she gave me permission to be myself, both physically and emotionally; as Ruth put it, she made me feel comfortable with myself, and while it may not always have felt that way at the time, it must have worked, or I'd never have been able to open up to her like I did. She let me make love to her in a way I never knew I needed until I found it with her. And now I've discovered that, nothing will ever be the same again. She also helped me to see that grieving isn't a 'weakness', any more than sorrow, or anger, or loneliness. I've come to perceive my feelings like that over the last three years, but I was wrong. Summer made it feel okay to miss my wife and my mother, and to accept that I don't have to hide my emotions, and that talking about them really does help. My conversation with Ruth proved that. And because of Summer, I've come to understand that, while the life I have now may not be the one I planned, I don't have to focus on regret. I can make something else of where I've found myself. Something new.

It's taken me some time to work all of that out, but now I have, I've also come to the conclusion that what she did is about the most generous thing that anyone has ever done for me.

I've spent a whole week away from Summer, trying to convince myself that I'm doing the best thing for her, because this was what *she* wanted... but I keep asking myself, what if it wasn't? What if it isn't?

I know she said she needed to end it between us. But she also said she didn't *want* to.

Is that enough though?

Would she be willing to give me another chance?

She's given me so many already. Is it too much to ask for one more? I don't know.

But then, the thought of living without her, knowing I don't have to... that we could be together, and that I'm choosing not to, is actually worse than losing Bryony... because I had no choice in that. She was taken from me. But I'm *choosing* to let Summer go.

And that's about the stupidest thing I've ever done.

And while I may be over-protective, and impatient, and rude... I'm not stupid.

Well... I'm not any more.

Chapter Twenty-five

Summer

Kit has been gone for an entire week, and there hasn't been a word from him. Not a sound… not a peep.

I didn't expect there to be, but every time I think about his secretive departure and his continued silence, I can't help wondering why.

Why did he leave like that? He seemed to want to make things right between us at the end, so why didn't he at least come and say goodbye? Or better still, give us another chance?

I'm still hurting, I can't deny that. But the last seven days without him have given me time to think, and although I know he won't come back, my memories of our time together have mellowed. They haven't faded, but they have mellowed. Yes, I can still remember his harsh words. They were the reason for our parting, after all. But when I think about him – which I do, all the time – it's not that version of Kit that I recall. I don't think about him angry, or confused, or struck down with guilt. I think about the man who made love to me. I think about the fire in his eyes and his kisses. I think about the uncontrollable heat between us, the way he held me, consumed me… loved me…

The bite on my neck has almost disappeared, but I can still remember the pleasure of being marked by him… branded as his. And if that sounds a bit submissive, I don't care. Besides, it wasn't like that. He didn't want to control me. He wasn't looking to defeat, or crush me, in either body or mind, or spirit. He wanted to make *love* to me. Completely. To make my body his. And I was happy to let him, because he gave me so much in return. He gave me himself. It was reciprocal. Or at least it was in part. Because he gave me a glimpse of himself, of the man he could be, if I'd been willing to let him. And I know now that we could have been so much more...

If only I hadn't sent him away.

I wish he'd been as strong and forceful about staying and making me listen to him, about making me his forever, as he was about claiming my body, because as perverse as it sounds, regardless of the fact that I told him to leave... I wish to God, he'd stayed.

He may not have contacted me, but I've thought about phoning him a couple of times. I even typed out a long text message one evening, after a couple of glasses of wine, but deleted all of it, and left my phone on the table, going to sit outside instead, despite the fact that it wasn't really warm enough.

I sat on the corner sofa, trying hard not to picture us making love there, my cardigan wrapped around me against the cool wind and the memories, and repeated over and over, in my own head, 'If he'd wanted me, he'd never have left me'.

He'd certainly have come and told me he was leaving... even if only to give me the chance to beg him not to.

Which I guess means he didn't want me.

Not enough, anyway.

Not like I want him.

Over the last few days, there have been a lot more people coming to view Maggie's house. It's strange... while Kit was here, there weren't any viewings at all, I don't think. But since he's been gone, there have been six or seven. There have been three families with young children, and two couples, or maybe even three... and one man on his own, although I didn't get to see him. I just heard about him from Mrs Wilson, when Roan and I went to buy some bread.

"I don't think he'll go for it," she said. "It's far too big a place for a man on his own."

"He might not be on his own," I reasoned, a bit snappily, because it always makes me so cross that she and her gossiping friends jump to conclusions about people. "He might be married, with children… and maybe his wife was busy and couldn't come and see the house on the day of the appointment."

She frowned at me then, and I realised I was being no different to her… inventing a history for a man I'd never even seen, let alone met.

And walking home, with our loaf of bread under one arm, and Roan's hand clasped tightly in mine, I looked over at Maggie's house and contemplated what it would feel like to have someone else living there… and by 'someone else', I wasn't thinking of someone other than Maggie, I was thinking of someone other than Kit. And for the first time since he arrived, I wished he'd sold the house to a developer already. Because then I wouldn't have to be reminded of what might have been every time I look at the place.

Roan has noticed that I'm not myself and keeps asking if I'm okay. I tell him I'm fine… obviously. And I know he's missing Poppy too. So I've tried to make sure we do something fun every day, just to take our minds off how sad I think we're both feeling.

I've been practising my face painting on him a bit more, because the summer fête is only next weekend now, and he's been really good and has sat still while I've tried various designs on him… some more successful than others. One thing I know for sure after our experiments is that I'm definitely not going to attempt a butterfly. Ever again.

The rest of the village is also in full preparation for the fête, although the weather is causing some concern among the organising committee. Where it was hot and balmy, with very little breeze and just the occasional day of rain, it's now much cooler and windier… and that doesn't augur well for bunting and canvas stalls. Still, there's a general determination to remain optimistic, and the plan is for the whole village to turn out on Thursday and Friday to start getting everything ready in earnest.

In the meantime, I've also been keeping occupied with my lesson plans, and I've got them just about completed, which I think must be a record for me, in terms of preparedness. I've even had time to think about some of my favourite events of the school term, such as the nativity play, which I always get very involved with, and I've found some new art activities for Christmas too. The children always enjoy those, and although I've still got some of the more traditional ones lined up, it's going to be nice to try something different.

Despite my name, the forthcoming season, and school term are my favourites, because I love the changes that take place in nature, and the excitement that the children get out of them. I really enjoy going out on autumn nature walks with my class, and then making collages from the things we've found, like leaves and acorns and twigs. And then we usually do a poetry project for hallowe'en, and then decorate the classroom with pumpkins and fake cobwebs, and I've got a huge broomstick that I hoist up in the centre of the room, and a toy black cat who sits in the window. They all love it. There's always a big firework display on the green, at the beginning on November, on the first Saturday of the month, and everyone goes to that. They have stalls, selling hot roasted chestnuts and candy floss, and the pub landlord usually organises a barbecue, although, being as it's changed hands since last year, we'll have to wait and see what happens about that. And from then on, it's just a countdown to Christmas, with rehearsals for the nativity, and carol singing... and making Christmas cards and calendars for the children to take home for their parents. And getting caught up in the excitement of anticipation for the arrival of Father Christmas... who always comes to school on the last day of term, right at the end of assembly. Just seeing the looks on the children's faces is absolutely priceless. And well worth all the preparation we teachers have to do in wrapping up dozens of presents. Of course, the vicar gets the best job of all, dressing up as Santa Claus, and handing out the gifts to each wide-eyed child. Like I say, it's hard work, but it's worth it.

It really is the best term of the year... and I'm looking forward to it.

And hopefully, keeping busy will help me to forget.

Something needs to.

Because I'm so, so lonely.

I'm lonelier than I've ever been.

And that's really odd. After all, I've been on my own for years. Yes, I know I had my mum for most of that time, but as much as I loved her, that's not the same as being 'with' someone, in a relationship, knowing they're there for you, no matter what. I've never had that. Not ever. So how can I miss it, like I do?

How can I miss having someone to share my thoughts with, someone who'll listen when I need to talk, and who'll talk when they need to share, someone who'll know when I just need to 'be' with them, in silent understanding, for no other reason than that they're there, right where I need them to be? How can I miss having someone who'll love me, for me. Just me. With a bone-deep love that lasts a lifetime and never wavers, who'll make me feel like I'm the centre of their world?

How can I miss any of that, when I've never had it?

I mean, how do I know it even exists?

It makes no sense.

And I need it to.

I need someone I can sit down with, right now, to help me understand all of this... someone like my mum, or Maggie, who'd listen and let me cry, and offer words of comfort and advice. Although I'm not sure I could tell my whole story to Maggie... Kit's her son, after all. Even so, my loneliness is starting to become overwhelming. And I desperately need someone I can share that with, someone who'll hold me, and make me feel safe and whole again... except the only person I want to hold me now, is Kit.

With each passing day, though, I feel his loss more and more, and I feel his rejection, like a shadow, darkening my life. And that's not like me. I'm not a dark, shadowy person. I never have been. Until now.

How did I let this happen? How did I let a man do this to me?

Because I fell in love with him, I suppose...

Chapter Twenty-six

Kit

It was all well and good reaching the conclusion, in the early hours of the morning, that I wasn't going to be stupid any more, and that I desperately wanted to take a chance at happiness with Summer, but I still have a job to do. I still have obligations to meet and, as much as I'd love to put my heart first, my head can be very persuasive at times.

It makes sense to stay here until the end of the week and finish Ian's job... on so many levels. Getting paid being one of them. So, no matter how much I wanted to wake Poppy, jump in my car and head south-west – just on the off-chance that Summer might forgive me – by breakfast time the next morning, I'd taken the decision that Poppy and I would remain in Kew until next weekend... and that I wouldn't be telling my daughter about my plans, because I know what she's like, and she'd never let me hear the end of it.

I did tell Ruth though, the following morning, once Poppy had run off into the garden with Edward... and she grinned broadly and gave me a hug, and told me I was doing the right thing. That must have been hard for her, too, because she had to realise the consequences of what she was saying... and of my actions. Assuming they work out, of course.

Assuming Summer will even talk to me, let alone forgive me.

Not that I'm going to worry about that at the moment.

I'm too busy for one thing.

And I can't even contemplate what will happen to my heart if she rejects me again...

I've made really good progress this week, and by Thursday lunchtime, I'm absolutely confident I'll be finished in time to let Ian have his modules back tomorrow morning, as I'd planned. I know he's not expecting them yet, but hopefully he'll just look on this as an added bonus.

I've also had an e-mail from the estate agents this morning, updating me on the viewings that they've done at Bluebells in my absence, and while none of them have made an offer, the agents claim to be 'hopeful' about at least one of them. For myself, I'm wondering whether I should tell them to hold off on the viewings for now... at least until after the weekend. But, as far as I know, they've got nothing booked in, and I'm very well aware that my trip back to Millarnick could end disastrously, so I stay quiet for now, and just reply with a quick 'thank you'.

I'm making myself a coffee and contemplating whether I've got time for a slice of cheese on toast, when my phone rings. I'm not expecting any calls, and most people think I'm still down in Cornwall, so I check the screen, not at all surprised to find the number isn't one I recognise. I suppose I could leave it, and let it go to voicemail, but I'm self-employed, that lingering doubt that my work – and money – could dry up at any moment has never left me... and you never know what a missed call might mean.

"Hello?" I answer.

"Hello. Is that Kit Robinson?" The voice on the end sounds older... not ancient, but older.

"Yes. Can I help?" The man doesn't seem to be very forthcoming, so I give him a nudge. I don't have all day, after all.

"Yes... sorry. I didn't expect you to answer." I'm tempted to ask why he called, in that case, but I don't. "My name is Anthony Fletcher." He sounds as though he expects me to know him, but I've never heard of anyone called Anthony Fletcher. "I—I saw your mother's obituary in

The Times," he adds, when I don't respond. "And I managed to persuade the woman at the newspaper offices to give me your number. I'd like to see you… if you don't mind, that is."

I'm still in the dark. "You knew my mother?"

"Yes." Again, he seems surprised. "We were… um… friends."

There's a hint of embarrassment in his voice and, finally, the penny drops. "You're Tony?"

"Yes. How did you know?"

"We… um… we found your letters."

"Oh dear. Did you?" There's more than a hint of embarrassment now.

"Yes."

"Did you read them?" His voice has dropped to a whisper.

"Just a couple. The first one… and the last. We needed to know who they were from. I knew the handwriting wasn't my father's, you see."

There's a long pause. "Yes, of course," he says. Then he adds, "I'd still like to see you."

I'm not sure why, and I can only imagine the meeting will be fairly awkward, for both of us, but he seems adamant. "Okay… um… when?"

"I can fit in with you."

"Well, I'm going away at the weekend. But I can do tomorrow lunchtime?" I suggest, because that will leave me the rest of the afternoon to pack up and get ready to go back down to Cornwall.

"That would be fine. Where would you like to meet?"

I decide against inviting him to the house, because I think that could make things even more uncomfortable – for him, if not for me – and I suggest the café in Richmond Park instead. He's not familiar with it, but I give him directions and he says he'll find it, before we end our call.

I'm shocked to have heard from him, and also feeling a bit guilty that he's had to track me down, rather than it being the other way around. Still, there weren't any clues in his letters as to his whereabouts, so it would have been a fairly difficult – if not impossible – task.

I wake this morning, feeling just as aroused as usual. You'd think I'd be getting used to this by now, being as I've been dreaming of Summer every single night since I first spoke to her, but each of my dreams is different, and this morning, I can't help smiling at that thought. I didn't realise, until I met Summer, that I had such a vivid imagination… I'm also feeling a lot less bothered now than I was about having these dreams in my own home. I suppose, now that I've decided what it is I want, and what I'm going to do about it, there's less point in worrying. Compared to everything else, the dreams are quite trivial. They're arousing, but trivial. That said, I quite like having them now, much more than I used to. I'd even go so far as to say that I look forward to them. They remind me of Summer, and that's got to be a good thing. And they give me ideas for things I might get to try out with her, if she gives me the chance… because, like I say, it seems I've got a very vivid imagination, when it comes to her.

Once I've taken Poppy to Ruth and Edward's and have fought my way back home through the heavier than usual Friday morning traffic, I make the final adjustments to Ian's modules, and send him a message containing the link to the new content. I also explain that I had to come home early for 'family reasons', as I've chosen to call it, and tell him that this is how I've managed to get everything back to him sooner than expected. I add in a note that I'll be returning to Cornwall tomorrow, and therefore, any further 'changes' – as I make a point of phrasing them – will have to wait. I don't care if I'm being abrupt with a client. The guy needs telling. And if he doesn't like it, then I'm not sure I want to work with him. No matter how much he's paying me.

Once I've finished, I shut down my computer, tidy up my desk, load the dishwasher and head out of the door, making for Richmond Park.

The café where I've arranged to meet Tony is one of my favourite haunts for business meetings, especially early morning ones, because they have a great breakfast menu, although it's been a while since I've been here for lunch. I park in the car park exactly on time, and wander over, only now realising that I've got no idea what Tony looks like.

Most of the tables outside are taken, but they're occupied by families and couples, so I go inside and glance around, thinking for a moment that he can't be here yet, just as a man sitting at one of the tables near to the counter stands up and raises his hand in greeting.

This must be him, I presume, although how he knows me, I have no idea.

"Kit?" he says, smiling as I approach, and I realise from the way he's phrased my name that he must have made a lucky guess.

"Yes. You must be Tony." He nods and, as we shake hands, I incline my head towards the counter. "Have you ordered yet?"

"No. I was waiting for you."

"Okay... well, shall we get that out of the way, and then we can relax." I'm not sure that's the best choice of word, being as I doubt either of us feels very relaxed in the current situation. I know I don't.

He follows me to the counter, where we both order the burger, with rosemary salted chips, and I add extra bacon to mine. And while Tony orders a pot of tea, I decide on a large Americano, feeling that the caffeine might come in useful.

I carry our drinks back to our table, where we sit, and while we wait for our food, and he stirs his tea in the pot, I take him in. He's probably in his mid-fifties, with dark hair, greying at the temples, and wears rimless glasses. He's tanned, good looking, and seems pleasant enough, but one of us needs to start the conversation we came here to have. And because he asked for this meeting, I feel like that should be him.

Closing the lid on the teapot, he looks up at me.

"Your mother wasn't unfaithful to your father," he says, startling me somewhat with such a forthright opening remark.

"I—I know. You met on the cruise she took that Christmas. After he died."

He smiles, just slightly. "Yes. Although cruises aren't generally my thing."

"They weren't my mother's either."

His smile widens. "Hmm... she told me. Personally, I only went to get over a broken relationship. I was persuaded into it by my daughter, who thought it would be good for me."

"You have a daughter?" I'm surprised, although I don't know why. I don't know him.

"Yes." He pours his tea, focusing on what he's doing, rather than looking at me. "I suppose I should explain." Part of me wants to tell him that he doesn't have to. It's none of my business, after all. But the other part of me wants to know… "I'm originally from York. I grew up there, and I met my ex-wife not long after leaving university. We married quite quickly, and within six months she was pregnant. It was all rather a whirlwind… and with the exception of our daughter's birth, it was all rather a huge mistake. We were opposites, Carole and I. She was religious – fanatically so, some might say. And I'm an atheist. She was fastidiously tidy, and I can't see the harm in a little bit of mess. She was a vegan. I'm… well, not. As you probably gathered from my choice of lunch." He smiles again. "None of those things would be enough to split a marriage by themselves – or even collectively – but we just didn't get on. We argued fairly constantly, and when we weren't arguing, we had nothing to talk about, because other than Megan, we had nothing in common. So, not long after she turned eleven, I left. I'm amazed Carole and I lasted that long, actually, but I think we only managed it because I was rarely at home."

I'm reminded of Summer's father, although it doesn't sound like Tony had a mistress. He doesn't seem the type. And he does seem very keen for me to know my mother wasn't unfaithful. "I take it Megan's your daughter?" I query.

"Yes. Sorry. I should have explained that a bit better. I'm a sales director for an electronics company, and to be honest, it would have made more sense for me to move south after my divorce. I could have been nearer to our head office, and cut down on my travelling. But I stayed in York, so I could still see Megan at weekends. Then a few years later, I met Linda, and we lived together for the best part of a decade. But I think that was always doomed to failure too. We both spent too much time working, and not enough time together, and in the end we split up… and that's when Megan suggested I should take the cruise."

"And you met Mum?"

"Hmm…" He nods his head. "We were about five days into the journey and we had an overnight stay in Bordeaux. It was the first really long stop of the trip, so everyone was talking about what they were going to do, and what they wanted to see. I'd been to Bordeaux before, for a conference, but your mum hadn't, and we got talking… and ended up seeing the sights together, and things just kind of progressed from there." He blushes slightly, but doesn't say anything else for a moment, fiddling with the spoon in his saucer instead, until he looks up again. "The cruise ended after three weeks, in Venice, and when we got there, everything seemed so romantic, we decided we didn't want our holiday to end, so we found a hotel and stayed on for an extra few days. We'd have liked it to be longer, but I had to get back to work."

I remember now. Mum was supposed to be away for three weeks, but I got a text message saying she was having a good time, and not to worry, because she'd decided to lengthen her holiday. I didn't think anything of it at the time, other than how pleased I was that she was enjoying herself. But then, like I said to Summer, I was too busy thinking about myself… and impending fatherhood.

"What happened when you got back?" I ask him. But he doesn't answer straight away, because the waiter arrives with our burgers, neatly arranged on wooden boards, with wire baskets of crispy chips on the side.

We sit back for a moment and I take a bite of my burger to hopefully break the ice again, because it feels like the interruption hasn't helped. Tony copies my action, then looks up at me. "Good burgers," he says once he's finished chewing,

"I've never had a bad meal here," I remark and he nods his head. "You were telling me about what happened when you got home from the cruise?" I remind him, because I don't want us to get sidetracked.

He takes a breath, putting his burger down again. "Yes. Well… all the while we'd been in Venice, we'd talked about finding a way to make our relationship work when we got back home, even though we lived a good few hundred miles apart. I was in love with your mother even then, you see, and I was determined to find a way to keep seeing her."

I may have prompted the guy into speaking, but it's still quite unsettling, talking to a total stranger about his intimate romance with my mother, and I have to make a conscious effort not to let that show. "I'm sensing a but?"

"Yes." He frowns. "You said you read my first letter to her?"

"I did."

"And you didn't read the others?"

"No. Not except the last one." I shake my head, and he nods his.

"Then you won't have realised that, after I wrote to her, when we first got home, she wrote back and said she was having second thoughts. It seemed the magic of the ship, and Venice had worn off for your mother, and she was feeling guilty."

God... Her too?

"She broke up with you?" I ask.

"No. She just said she was having a hard time coming to terms with things now that she was back in the real world, surrounded by all the memories of your father. It was understandable. It was even predictable, I suppose. I wrote back and begged her to meet me, and she agreed. And somehow I persuaded her to give us a chance. I don't know whether it was the memories of what we'd had while we were away, or just the fact that she was still young and wanted to live her life a little, but I talked her round. I persuaded her that we shouldn't throw away our chance of happiness, because it's not something that comes along that often... and by some minor miracle, she decided to take a chance with me, and we had eighteen months fabulous months together."

"I gathered that from the letters... or from the dates on them anyway. As I said, I only read the first and the last ones. So, what happened?" I ask.

He takes another bite of his burger, then puts it down again and wipes his hands on his serviette. "I don't really know. I thought things were going okay between us. I wanted more than our occasional weekends, but I knew Maggie was still grieving for your father, and I allowed for that... always. But one day, out of the blue, I got a letter from her saying she couldn't keep seeing me."

"And you wrote back to her. I know you did. I read your letter."

He blushes slightly. "Yes, I did."

"Did she ever reply?"

"Yes. She wrote back the same day."

Thank God for that. The man clearly loved her very much. I'd hate to think my mother could have just left him hurting, for all these years.

"And?" I'm intrigued and he smiles.

"And she said she needed time. She said she'd gone into the relationship with me too soon after your father's death and although she'd tried to make it work, she was too conflicted. I—I didn't write back to her again, because I needed to hear her voice, and I think – more importantly – I needed her to hear mine. So I called her, and she listened to what I had to say, and then we arranged to meet up a few days later, and I agreed that I'd wait for her."

"Hang on… that was four years ago. Are you telling me you've been waiting for her ever since?"

He shakes his head. "No. Although it wasn't waiting for her that was the problem… it was the idea of losing her that really scared me. You see, one of the things your mum was struggling with was how little time we could spend with each other. She told me at that first meeting, when I was trying desperately to find a way to keep us together, that it all felt fine – well, she actually said 'perfect' – when we were with each other, but that she had too much time on her own to dwell on the past. There was too much distance between us. I could tell that was upsetting her more than anything, so I said I'd try and do something about it… to help her. And, after a few weeks of negotiating the sale of my house, and making some changes at work, I moved to Plymouth…"

"You did?"

"Yes. To be nearer to her. To make things easier."

"Wait a second. You… you mean you've driven up here from Plymouth to meet me?" I'm stunned.

"Yes. It was important. And I knew from Maggie that you lived near London, so I was ready for a long drive."

"But I was down in Cornwall just recently, clearing out Mum's house," I explain. "And I'm going back there tomorrow. I could have saved you the drive."

"I wouldn't have met you in Millarnick," he says firmly, shaking his head. "Maggie always said there were too many gossips there, and I wouldn't have wanted people to wonder about a stranger arriving at your mother's house."

"I can understand that. Although they'd probably just have thought you were coming to view the place."

"You're selling it?" He seems surprised.

"Well… yes." It seems easier to say that than to try and explain what I'm going to try and do. And besides, I can't make a final decision about any of that until I've talked to Summer… assuming she'll even see me, of course.

There's a convenient pause in the conversation and we both have a few more mouthfuls of our lunch, before I look up at him again. "So, you moved to Plymouth?"

"Yes. And I think it helped. I mean, your mum still needed time, but I think she appreciated that I wasn't giving up on us. I think she valued my commitment. She certainly understood what I'd given up in moving so far away from my daughter. We… we slowed everything down again. We stayed in touch every few days, because I wanted her to know I was there, but I didn't want her to feel like I was pressuring her, and we met up whenever she wanted to. It was always on her terms… at her pace. And then, after about a year, she agreed to start seeing me more regularly again."

"So, you mean, you've been together, all this time?"

"Yes. It hasn't been smooth sailing all the way, but we've been together. To start with, Maggie was still struggling with her feelings for Oliver… for your father. She loved him very much, and they'd been married since she was eighteen. It was hard for her. But in the last eight or nine months, I suppose, we've been seeing a lot more of each other. A lot more." I'm not going to ask what that means.

"But you never went to Millarnick?"

"No. We used to meet in pubs and restaurants, and neutral venues, but at Christmas, everything changed. Maybe it was the time of year… the reminder of the cruise, or maybe it was just that enough time had finally passed… I don't know. I just know everything changed, for the better. She agreed to spend Christmas Day at my place… and that turned into Boxing Day too." He blushes again, just slightly, and I take a sip of my now lukewarm coffee. "After that, she started driving over to my place more regularly. I'd cook, or we'd get a take—"

"Oh God…" I flop back in my chair, staring at him.

"What?" he says, looking concerned.

"Why didn't I see it before? She must have been driving to see you… when she was killed."

He pales. "I—I don't know," he mumbles. "I mean, we hadn't arranged anything."

"But she was killed on the A38, not far from Saltash. And as far as I'm aware, she didn't know anyone else in Plymouth." I suppose it could be argued that, until about five minutes ago, I hadn't known that Tony lived in Plymouth either, but it all makes more sense now, at least in my head.

He shrugs his shoulders, his face paling. "I was at home that Friday," he whispers, almost to himself. "I'd taken the day off, but we hadn't planned anything. I don't know why she'd have been coming to see me. She hadn't told me she was, and she knew I was going up to York on the Saturday for a few days, for my granddaughter's second birthday." He shakes his head. "Do you think she might have had something she wanted to tell me… something that couldn't be said on the phone, and couldn't wait until I got back, for some reason?"

It's my turn to shrug now, and looking at the expression in his eyes, I feel desperately sorry for him.

"I suppose I'll never know, will I? Not now…" He lets out a long sigh and I'm almost tempted to reach out to him… except I don't know him, and I think it would just embarrass both of us. "I only read about Maggie's death when I got back from York… in the newspaper." He looks me in the eye. "I thought about coming to the funeral, but decided against it. People would only have wondered who I was… and what I was doing there. To be honest, I wasn't even going to contact you to start with. I thought it was best to leave the past alone. But the other night, I was feeling rather low, and I was sitting in my study, going through your mother's letters and looking at some old photographs, and I realised she might have kept her letters from me too, and that I should probably get in touch, and explain, just in case you were wondering…"

"I wasn't," I say quickly. "I'd already worked out that you'd met her on the cruise. I just wish she'd told me about you and we'd been able to talk. I wish we'd been talking… full stop."

He nods his head. "I knew about your falling out with your mum." *Oh God… here we go.* "We were still in our tentative, 'getting to know each other again' phase at the time, but she told me about it when it happened." He looks down at his half-eaten burger. "It must have been hard for you, losing your wife like that."

"It was. But that doesn't excuse…"

He holds up his hand. "Grief does strange things to people, Kit. Maggie knew that, probably better than you realise."

I think I'm beginning to see that for myself now, and I wish more than ever that I'd spoken to her about what happened… about Gabrielle, and my crushing guilt, and the self-loathing… because I know now that she'd have understood. And maybe then she could have told me about Tony and about how she felt. And we could have helped each other to see through it all.

"I'm sorry," I murmur through the lump in my throat.

"Don't be." He smiles, surprising me. "I'm a lucky man. I had the love of a very special woman – even if it was just briefly. And I'll never forget that. Or her. Ever. Not every man gets to experience real love, but those of us who do… well, we're the luckiest men in the world." He looks me in the eye, like he knows something I don't, and then adds, "Aren't we?"

I can't help smiling back at him, although my heart still feels heavy and full of regret, because I know he's not wrong.

Chapter Twenty-seven

Summer

The weather is being surprisingly kind to us, which is a good thing, because today is the day of the fête, and everyone had been getting rather nervous that we might even have to cancel. Still, as luck would have it, the wind has dropped, the sun is shining, and although there are a few clouds in the sky, they're not threatening ones. It seems like the gods are smiling on us.

The last couple of days have been really busy, erecting stalls, putting out bunting and baking cakes… because you can never have too many cakes, it seems. All of that has had to be done between rain showers, with last minute decisions being taken as to when things could be done, or whether they'd have to wait. And that element of very slight panic in the air has been really useful in giving me very little time to feel sorry for myself. Or to feel too lonely, although I still miss Kit… deeply.

I know he's not coming back though, and while missing him seems to be a permanent state of mind at the moment, I know it will pass eventually. I just have to wait. And try to forget how perfect it almost was.

Keeping busy and focusing on something other than myself has – rather oddly – enabled me to reach a few decisions, the first and most important of which was that I had to pull myself out of the doldrums. I was in danger of forgetting who I really am and letting my feelings for Kit engulf me in sadness.

I'm still sad and I regret our parting. But I'm not going to let what happened between us change me. I can't. For Roan's sake, as well as my own. He's missing Poppy just as much as I miss Kit, but he hasn't asked whether she's coming back. I think he's worked out that it's not going to happen, without me having to explain it to him. And that's a good thing, because I know I'd cry again, if I had to put it into words... and the last thing I need is to let him see me in tears. I want him to realise that, no matter what life throws at you, it's possible to still be yourself, and to be true to yourself.

And that's what I'm going to do.

The fête has been running for over three-quarters of an hour now, and everyone's smiling and laughing, and even I'm struggling to feel down. I've painted several children's faces, including my own son, who wanted to be a tiger – in honour of Poppy, I think. I've also turned Peter Taylor into a panda, and Zoe Bridgeman – who is sitting in front of me now – has requested that I transform her into a Dalmatian. Not any old dog, mind you, but a Dalmatian. Well, I like a challenge.

Roan sat with me for the first ten minutes after I'd finished his own transformation, but boredom got the better of him and he's been flitting between the stalls ever since. I know he's perfectly safe, because there are enough people here who'll watch over him for me. Between Mrs Wilson and Miss Hutchins – who together are running the cake stall – and Miss Burton, who's in charge of the tombola, and Emily Featherstone, the mother of one of the boys in Roan's class at school, who's selling raffle tickets, there's no shortage of watchful eyes on the village green.

I can't help smiling as I paint a lolling tongue beneath Zoe's mouth, thinking to myself how much I love living here in the village. It took me a while to fit in here when Mum and I first moved from Looe, and sometimes I do find the gossips a bit annoying, but I love the fact that everyone is so protective of each other, and that Roan is safe.

I'm not saying that being here is going to be as easy with a stranger living in Kit's house, and I can't help wishing that things could be different. If only…

No. I'm not going to do 'if onlys'. Not anymore.

That's not who I am.

And besides, today is a good day. It's a day to start looking forward…

I've made it through to four o'clock… the end of the fete. And I'm absolutely exhausted, which is quite surprising, given that I've spent the entire day sitting down. I think it's the level of concentration that was needed for me not to mix up leopards with tigers, or giraffes with lions… and as for the snake that Sammy Waterford insisted on having… I thought I was never going to get that right… or even finished, for that matter. There were just so many scales…

Mrs Penrose, who is the treasurer of the committee, has already been round to collect my takings for the day, so now I'm just packing my paints into their box, and putting away the various designs I printed out for the children to choose from – although I have to say they've done a pretty good job of coming up with their own ideas without any tips from me. Roan's still running around and hopefully not making too much of a nuisance of himself, but then, I'm sure someone would come and tell me if he was. And there are a few stragglers wandering about, or chatting in small groups, while various committee members do their best to clear away and dismantle the stalls. I smile as Mr Wilson marches onto the green carrying a pair of step ladders, to start removing the bunting, almost taking the heads off a couple of small children, as he swings it this way and that, under the firm – if misguided – instructions of his wife.

"Hello." The voice behind me makes me jump and I turn to see a tall man on the other side of my stall. He's probably in his early thirties, and is very attractive, with dark blond hair that touches his collar at the back, and an athletic physique that suits the smart jeans and formal shirt he's wearing. He smiles at me, his blue eyes twinkling. "Sorry, I didn't mean to make you jump."

"That's okay."

"My name's Andrew, but my friends call me Drew."

I nod my head, wondering why I need to know his name, or what his friends call him, or more importantly, where he's going with this. "I'm Summer," I say, to be polite.

"Summer? What a beautiful name."

It's not as though I haven't heard that one before, but I say, "Thank you," anyway, and he folds his arms across his chest, making it clear he's not going anywhere. "You're not from around here, are you?" It seems best to make conversation… to be polite. Again.

"No. But I was here last week… looking at that house over there." He unfolds his arms again and points over his shoulder, in the direction of Bluebells. "I'm thinking of buying it."

I wonder for a moment if he might be the single man Mrs Wilson was telling me about, but I'm not about to ask, just in case he thinks I'm nosy… or interested in his marital status.

"And you thought you'd come back and sample the fête?" I ask instead.

"Yes." He smiles again. "I saw the posters, and thought it might be wise to get a taste of village life before I make my final decision."

"And have you?"

"Have I what?" he asks, tilting his head.

"Made your final decision?"

He chuckles. "Oh, I see. Let's just say it's looking promising." I'm not sure what to say to that, so I keep silent and smile as I finish packing up my things and close my paint box.

"Would you like me to help you carry that somewhere?" he offers.

"No, thanks. I'm fine. I only live over there." I nod in the vague direction of my cottage on the other side of the green.

"Oh. I see." He seems a bit deflated and steps to one side as I move around the table, which has, until now, been separating the two of us. "Can I make a confession?" he says suddenly and I look up at him, squinting into the sun.

"A confession? What about?"

"I've been watching you most of the afternoon… and although I don't know you, I'd really like to rectify that… maybe starting with taking you out for a drink?"

I'm stunned and for a moment, I just stare at him. "You would?" I manage to say eventually.

"Yes. Like I say, I'd like to get to know you… but we can call it part of my village reconnaissance, if you like. If I'm going to live here, I need to sample the local pub, don't I?"

I can't help the smile that's twitching at the corners of my lips. "I suppose so. Although there's nothing to stop you from going there by yourself. You do know that, don't you?"

"Yes," he replies, taking a half step closer. "Except I'd rather not."

"Why? Are you scared?"

"Yes," he says, surprising me.

"Really? Because I feel it's only fair to tell you that the villagers here are reasonably friendly. I mean, they haven't been known to actually eat a stranger in… oh… decades now."

He laughs out loud and then says, "I'm sure they haven't, but would you consider coming with me and holding my hand anyway?"

I sigh, and surprise myself by replying, "Well, if you're certain you need my protection…" I'm not sure if I'm trying to give him a way out, or if I'm flirting with him, but after the time I've had lately, it feels good to be noticed by a man, and Drew positively beams at me.

"I do," he murmurs, and takes a couple of steps away, expecting me to follow, I think.

"Hang on." I raise my voice slightly to attract his attention, and he turns back again, frowning, inquisitively. "I need to call my son."

"Your son?" He raises his eyebrows and I half expect him to retract his offer. He doesn't, but moves closer again, staring at me.

"Yes." I look around and spot Roan playing near the swings, with Neil Featherstone, whose mum is standing close by, watching them and talking to Polly Tompkins at the same time. "Roan!" I call out, loudly enough for him to hear me and he looks up. I wave my arm, motioning for him to come over and he says something to Neil, before he starts running in my direction.

Drew has remained motionless by my side and hasn't said a word, but as Roan comes to a standstill in front of us, the tiger paint still bright on his cheeks, I turn to him.

"This is my son, Roan," I announce and the two of them eye each other up.

"Hello," Drew says in a perfectly friendly voice.

"Hi," Roan replies.

There's just a moment's pause, and then Drew tilts his head towards the pub. "Shall we go then?" he says, looking from Roan to me, and I smile up at him.

"Okay."

"You can drop your box off on the way, can't you?" he suggests as we start walking.

"I can. Yes."

"Where are we going, Mum?" Roan asks.

"To the pub," I reply, looking down at him. "But we'll pop into home first to drop off my box."

"Oh… okay." He runs on ahead in the direction of our cottage, and Drew leans in to me a little.

"Do you mind me asking if there's someone lucky enough to call himself Mr Summer?" he says quietly.

I swallow down the lump in my throat. "I'm not sure that's how I'd phrase it, but no… there isn't."

He gives out an audible sigh of relief and reaches over, taking my box from me, and balancing it under one arm, before he clasps my hand in his. "Good," he says, tilting his head towards mine and looking down into my eyes. "I'm glad to hear it."

Chapter Twenty-eight

Kit

Poppy has been driving me completely insane all day.

I'd hoped to get our packing done yesterday, but I ended up spending the whole afternoon with Tony. He was a genuinely nice guy, and we've swapped phone numbers and addresses, and agreed that we'll keep in touch and try and meet up again. I think he appreciated that, and it felt like the least I could do for my mother, considering all the other ways I'd managed to upset her and let her down.

The consequence of my long afternoon with him, however, was that I didn't get anything else done with the rest of the day, so I ended up packing this morning, which threw Poppy into a tailspin of questions, about why we're going back to Cornwall, and how long we're going for. I haven't given her any answers, mainly because I don't have any – not definitive ones. Not yet. I won't have either, not until I've seen Summer and spoken to her, and asked – well, begged – for her forgiveness. I'm very aware of the fact that I might get shot down in flames – again – but I have to try. Because if I don't, I'll regret it for the rest of my life. I knew that before yesterday, but my conversation with Tony has served to confirm everything I was already thinking. I'm in love with Summer, and I can't just let her go… not when there's even the slightest chance we could have a future together.

As a result of my inability to give her a straight answer though, Poppy hasn't given me a moment's peace. Not since we left Kew, just after noon.

I'd intended getting away earlier than that, but between Poppy and the packing, it simply wasn't possible.

"Oh… look, Daddy. It's the fair," Poppy yells in my ear, as though I hadn't noticed the bunting and canvas stalls, and dozens of people milling about, even though it's already quarter past four and it looks like they're mostly clearing away for the day.

"I think it's finished, sweetheart. I'm sorry." I know she wanted to go and I feel bad now for letting her down. Although our tardiness isn't really my fault, at the end of the day.

I drive around the green, pulling up outside my mother's house and open the gate, before parking up on the driveway and letting Poppy out of the car.

She starts jigging around in front of me. "Can we go and see," she says, and although she's prone to jumping around when she's excited, I know there's more to this.

"You need the toilet first."

"No, I don't."

"Yes, you do. Come on."

I start towards the house and, accepting she has no choice, she follows, catching me up and then running on ahead of me, getting to the front door a few paces before I do.

I let her in, and then call out after her, "I'll start unpacking while you pop to the toilet, and if there's still time, we'll go and take a look at the fair."

"Okay." She's already half way up the stairs and I turn back, heading for the car and opening the boot. I'm just reaching in for the first of our bags, when something prickles up my spine and I turn around, catching sight of Roan, by the swings. I can't help smiling, because although I can't actually see her, I know that means Summer must be around somewhere too, and I start to search the green, my eyes darting between the stalls, wondering where she can be. She won't be far away, I know that. Not if Roan's there.

I actually gasp when I spot her, standing by a small white gazebo. She looks as beautiful as ever, and as sexy as she does in my dreams, and is wearing one of her long, floaty sundresses, although not the one that's practically transparent, I'm quite pleased to say, given that she's in full view of almost the entire village and is currently talking to a man I don't recognise. I've never seen him around here before, although I suppose that doesn't mean much. I wasn't here for that long myself…

She's in deep conversation with this man – who from what I can see, is tall, and annoyingly handsome, and seems to have Summer's undivided attention. And then suddenly, he laughs, and she joins in, and I feel an uncomfortable chill settling on my skin, as I step away from the car and stand by the gatepost, staring.

They talk a little more and then Summer turns and I duck behind the bush that's right inside the gate, fearful that she might have seen me. She hasn't though, because within seconds, I hear her calling Roan's name and I glance up again, to see him running towards her.

The three of them stand together for a moment, and then they turn and start walking away, in the direction of Summer's house. After a few paces, Roan starts to run ahead, and the man leans in towards Summer. I've got no idea what he says, but seconds later, he takes the box she's carrying, which I guess must contain her face paints, and puts it under his arm… and then my heart stops beating, as he takes her hand in his, and turns to her. Again, I have no idea what's being said, but there's an intimacy in his actions, and in her reception of them, that pierces my soul.

Leaving the car open, I stagger into the house and flop down onto the monk's settle in the hallway, because it's the first seat I come across.

She's with someone else? Already?

How can that be?

Because you hurt her. Because you left. Because you let her go.

I lean forward and rest my head in my hands, struggling to breathe. This can't be happening…

"Daddy!" Poppy comes running up and starts jumping around in front of me again. "Can we go?"

I look up at her. "Go?"

"Yes. To the fair…"

"No." That's the last place I want to be.

"But Daddy…"

"They're packing away," I explain, because it's true. They are. I saw Summer leaving, with her box of face paints… and another man.

"Then can we go and see Roan and Summer?"

"Not now, Poppy." I'm trying to control my voice, and my emotions, but it's a struggle.

"But Daddy…"

"Not now!" I bark and her bottom lip trembles. "I'm sorry." I reach out for her as she goes to run, and I pull her back. "I'm sorry, sweetheart." I hold her close to my chest and she lets me, patting my arm, as though she knows something's wrong. Which it is. My heart is breaking. And it's my own fault.

She pulls back in my arms and looks at me. "It's okay," she whispers.

"I'm just tired," I reply, by way of a feeble excuse, because I don't want her to worry, and I can't possibly tell her the truth.

"Can I go and play in the garden?" she asks.

"Of course." I ruffle her hair and she scowls at me, and runs out of the front door and around the side of the house, towards the back garden… and freedom. From me.

I sit back and stare at the ceiling, shaking my head. "How?" I mutter out loud. How did I get it so wrong? Summer said I could break her, if she let me. She definitely said that. It was why she wanted me to leave, so I couldn't do her any more harm. She was protecting herself from me… because she cared. I know that's what she meant. Even Ruth thought that was what she meant. I know I treated her appallingly, and I hurt her… and I can't forgive myself for doing either of those things. But to get over me so quickly… after saying something like that?

Does that mean she was lying?

No. That can't be. Summer would never lie to anyone, about anything.

She doesn't have a dishonest bone in her body.

"God…" I screw up my fists and press them into my eyes. Why did I leave? Why didn't I just stay and work things out with her? She might have told me she was done. She might have said we were over… but I should have stayed anyway. I should have gone back and told her how I felt.

I should have fought for us, instead of giving in… and losing her.

I get up eventually and unload the car, piling our cases in the hallway, before taking the cool bag into the kitchen and unloading it into the fridge, although it only contains some pizza and salad for tonight's dinner, and some milk, because I can't survive without coffee. As I'm closing the fridge door though, I can't help wondering to myself whether I should be bothering with any of this… or whether we should just drive straight back to Kew. Except, I can't. I don't belong there anymore.

It's taken me the last two weeks – and probably a lot longer, if I'm being honest – to work out that the house at Kew and the memories I shared there with Bryony are part of the problem. They're the past, and if I'm going to have any chance of a future, I need to leave them behind.

And that means that, while I still don't know exactly where I belong, I do know it's not there.

As I go outside to lock the car, I glance over at Summer's house and wonder what she's doing.

It's hard not to think about the good times we shared, because although I treated her appallingly and I hurt her, we did have some good times. We talked, a lot. She listened, like no-one has ever listened to me before. And she understood me too. She really did. And when we kissed…

I close my eyes and picture her, naked, beneath me, yielding… surrendering herself to me, and then an image flashes into my mind of her… with him.

"No!" I say out loud, my voice surprisingly loud.

She couldn't. She wouldn't give herself to someone else, would she? Not like that…

"Daddy?" Poppy comes running around the side of the house.

"Yes?"

"Is everything all right? I heard you shout."

"Everything's fine." I don't offer an explanation, but close the gate and start walking towards the house, taking her hand and bringing her with me. "Shall we find a movie we can watch together? And then I'll make us some dinner. I brought pizzas."

"Great!" She jumps up and down, as usual, but then stops when we get to the front door and looks up at me. "Can we go and see Roan and Summer tomorrow?" she asks.

I glance down at her and then across, in the direction of Summer's house. "Yes," I say quietly, letting her go indoors ahead of me. "Yes, we can."

I have no idea what kind of reception will await me, but I have to know if I'm too late. Or if I still have a chance. Even if it's only a small one.

Because right now, I'll take whatever I can get.

Chapter Twenty-nine

Summer

We choose to sit outside, mainly because it means Roan can play on the climbing frame, rather than getting bored listening to us. I wish I'd picked up a cardigan when we stopped off at home though. It's chillier now than it was a few weeks ago, when I sat here with Kit… and on that evening, when he made love to me in my back garden… on my daybed…

I've got to stop thinking about him.

"Are you warm enough?" Drew asks, as though he can read my mind, although I'm relieved he can't.

"Yes. I'm fine." I smile across the table at him, and take a sip of my white wine.

"You have an amazing son," he says, still looking at me.

"Thank you."

"How old is he?"

"He's six."

I can tell he's fishing to find out what happened to Roan's father, whether he features in our lives still… what the story is. But I'm not in the mood for sharing. Not today. And that surprises me in a way. Let's face it, I told Kit about Russell during our first real conversation – in more detail than he probably wanted to know at the time. I mean, I doubt he was expecting to hear that Roan's conception was my first and only sexual experience... until that night with Kit... until I discovered what making love is actually supposed to feel like, when love really matters.

Stop it. I need to stop it.

"What do you do for a living?" I ask, changing the subject and getting it away from Roan and myself.

"I own a construction company in Truro."

"Truro?" I'm surprised. "And you're thinking of buying a house here?"

He smiles. "Yes. I know it's a bit of a commute."

"A bit?" I smile back at him, feeling more at ease with this line of conversation.

"Okay, so it's at least an hour's drive... but I've just bought another, smaller firm in Plymouth, and it makes sense for me to be somewhere between the two."

He sounds very focused on his business – unlike Kit, who always struck me as much more focused on life than work. Okay, so I know he was worried about his work drying up when Poppy was born. He told me that much. But that was only because Bryony had decided not to go back to work herself, and he was concerned about their finances. He wasn't trying to build an empire; he only wanted to provide for them... like any good husband and father...

For heaven's sake, Summer. Give it a rest.

And give Drew a chance. He's a nice guy.

"It's a big house," I point out, although I don't look over my shoulder at Bluebells. I can't.

"Yes, I know," he says, sipping his red wine. "Especially as I live alone."

I'm assuming that was his subtle way of telling me he's got no-one in his life, but I can't react to that. I can't pretend an interest I don't feel.

"How do you like the village?" I change the subject again.

"I like it," he replies, leaning in slightly and staring straight into my eyes. "I like it a lot."

And I feel even more awkward now.

*

"We really should be getting back." Drew looks deflated, but it is nearly seven o'clock. "I'm sorry, but I have to get Roan ready for bed."

I wonder if I'd have made that excuse if I'd been sitting opposite Kit. No... I wouldn't. Of course I wouldn't. We'd have stretched the children's bedtime, given the chance. We'd have talked for hours, held hands, kissed at every opportunity, and watched our children play. In my dreams, of course. Because in my reality, Kit left. And he didn't even say goodbye.

"Are you okay?" Drew says, tilting his head to one side, and I realise I'm struggling to hold back a wave of tears that have arisen out of nowhere... well, out of my memories and daydreams, anyway.

"I'm fine." I manage a smile and get to my feet. He stands too and waits while I fetch Roan from the climbing frame, and then we all leave the pub together.

On the way back to my house, Drew doesn't hold my hand, and we walk for a while without saying a word, just watching the last of the stalls being dismantled and the litter being picked up and put into bin liners.

"It looks like it was a successful day," Drew says, nodding towards the green.

"Yes. I think it was."

Roan has run on ahead a little and Drew deliberately slows our pace. "Summer?" he says, sounding nervous, and I know what's coming, and wish I could stop him, before he continues, "Can I see you again?"

I stare down at the ground for a moment and try to think about how to answer him... how to tell him that I can't... that I'm not ready, and I don't feel like I ever will be at the moment. I obviously delay for too long though, because he suddenly stops walking altogether and pulls me back, holding onto my hand and looking down into my eyes. "I'm going to be honest with you and tell you that I haven't decided about the house yet." I wasn't expecting him to say that. "Don't get me wrong, I love the place, but it's going to need work to get it how I want it, and I'll have to look at my finances in a bit more detail before I can make that commitment. But even if I don't buy it, I'd still like to see you again.

I really do like you, Summer, and I meant what I said earlier… about getting to know you better."

Oh… that's such a lovely thing to say. And he is absolutely genuine – I can see that in his eyes – and he doesn't come with half a lifetime of baggage, unlike some other people I could mention. He wasn't fazed by Roan, and he seems like a charming, gentle man. And in other circumstances, I'd probably jump at the chance to get to know him better too. But having spent the last hour or so in his company, I know I can't. For the very simple reason that, all the while we've been together, the only thing I've thought about is Kit. And no matter how much I want to be over him, I'm not. Not yet.

And maybe I never will be.

"Is something wrong?" Drew asks, breaking into my thoughts.

"No… well, yes."

He smiles. "If you don't want to see me again, you can just say so."

"It's not that. Well, I suppose it is… kind of." I take a breath, but not a long one. "It's just that, there was someone else…"

"Roan's father?" he interrupts.

"No. He's ancient history. This was more recent."

"And more painful?" he guesses.

"Yes."

"And you're not over him?"

"No. I'm sorry."

He nods his head and takes a half step closer. "It's okay," he says. "You don't have to be sorry. I guess our timing was just out."

"Yes. It was."

It really was. Because in another time, in another place, where there were less reminders of the man I love, I honestly think I might have said 'yes' to Drew.

As it is though…

We complete the walk to my house in silence, and I let Roan inside before I turn to Drew, who smiles down at me.

"Thank you for a lovely evening," he says.

"No… thank you. And I am sorry." God, I hate that word.

He shakes his head. "I told you. You don't have to be sorry." He leans down and kisses my cheek. "Take care of yourself, Summer," he whispers in my ear, and straightens up again. "That other guy… whoever he was… I hope he knew what he was letting go of."

"Who says he let go of me? It might have been the other way around?" I'm suddenly defensive, even though I know, deep down, that Kit did let go of me… after a hefty push.

Drew frowns, and shakes his head just slightly. "Even if it was, any man who'd let go of you – who wouldn't fight for you – is nothing short of an idiot."

"He wasn't an idiot," I murmur, struggling with my tears again. "He was just a very troubled man."

"Then I hope he gets over his troubles, and comes back for you."

"Oh… he won't do that." I can't keep the catch out of my voice and he moves a little closer and cups my face with his hand.

"In that case, I'm the one who's sorry."

He kisses me on the cheek again and, without another word, he walks away. I stare after him for a while, my eyes blurred with tears and then I turn and go indoors, closing the door behind me.

Chapter Thirty

Kit

"Come back!" I wake, my body sticking to the sheet, sweat pouring off of me, and gaze around the room, dazed, before I fall back onto the pillow, rubbing my hands down my face, and letting out a long sigh.

I haven't had a dream quite like that before.

It started just like they usually do. We were in a shower, Summer and I – one of those huge walk-in ones, the water cascading over our naked bodies, and I was holding her, caressing her soft skin and kissing her deeply. I pushed her up against the tiled wall and, raising one of her legs over my bent arm, I took her... so hard, I was lifting her standing leg off the floor. She was screaming in ecstasy – so different from the silent reality of her pleasure when we made love in her garden, her hushed fulfilment being required by the presence of our sleeping children, in the upstairs bedroom. But in my dream, in that shower, she cried with longing, clinging to me, staring up into my eyes, begging me for 'more'. And I gave it to her, exactly how she wanted it... over and over.

And because it was a dream, when we were finished, when we'd got our breath back, I held her in my arms and kissed her... just like I should have done that night.

And then she turned and walked away from me.

She left.

And when I reached out for her, she ran. And she kept on running.

I followed, sprinting after her. But every time I caught up, she fled again.

And that was when I woke up, screaming for her to 'come back', desperate for her to return to me.

I stare up at the ceiling, wondering if there can be a meaning to my dream. I've never thought of giving meanings to my dreams before. They've just been about loving Summer, in the way I've always needed to love someone… and in the way she needs to be loved.

But this time?

I don't know.

Does it mean I've lost her? Forever?

I throw back the covers, almost surprised to find that I'm not aroused for once. After all, it's the first time I've woken like this in weeks… but then the thought of losing the woman you love is enough to do that to any man. And it's not a prospect I'm willing to face. Not yet.

Not until Summer tells me, to my face, that there's no chance for me. Or for us.

"Haven't you finished yet?"

I turn from the sink, where I've just poured away the last of my coffee, to find Poppy is still taking her time over eating her cereal. At least it seems that way to me.

She looks up, confused.

"Are we going out?" she asks.

"Yes. You… you wanted to go and see Roan, didn't you?"

"Now?" Her brow furrows and she looks at the time on the microwave. She can't actually tell the time yet – not properly – but I think even she knows that eight-thirteen is a bit early to be paying house calls. Not that I care. I can't wait any longer.

"Are you done?" I ask again.

"Yes." She pushes her bowl away and dumping my cup by the side of the sink, I wander over and lift her down from her chair.

"Where are your shoes?"

"Upstairs."

"Well, run and put them on."

I know I sound impatient, but that's because I am. I didn't even bother with breakfast myself, and I barely drank any of the coffee I made. I'm too eager to see Summer. I know this might end in disaster, but I have to know how she feels… one way or the the other.

"I wish we'd come back in time for the fair," Poppy says, looking up at me. We're half way across the green and she hasn't stopped talking since I closed the front door.

"Well, we were late leaving, weren't we?" I point out and she nods her head.

"Yes, but at least I can play with Roan, even if it isn't sunny." She looks up at the sky, which is rather threatening. "You don't think it's going to rain, do you?"

"I have no idea."

I love my daughter dearly, but there are times when I wish she'd pipe down. And this is one of them. I'm nervous enough as it is – especially after having seen Summer with another man yesterday afternoon – and Poppy's constant chatter isn't helping. I wonder for a moment how I'm going to react if the 'other man' opens Summer's door when we knock, and how I'm going to explain that to Poppy.

"I do hope Roan's not playing with any of his other friends," she says, sounding worried. And it suddenly dawns on me that she's as worried that she'll have been replaced in Roan's affections, in our absence, as I am about Summer.

"I shouldn't think so," I reply, trying to sound soothing. "Not at this time of day." Of course, I can't be as assured about Summer and her new 'friend'… because the early hour is an irrelevance, if he's stayed the night.

God… I hope not.

We reach Summer's house and, with bated breath, I open the garden gate and, letting Poppy go before me, we step up the garden path to her front door, where I ring the bell, hoping against hope that Summer will be the one to answer.

Seconds pass and my stomach turns somersaults, my palms dampening, and my mouth drying, as we wait, until the door opens and I see her, and I find I'm struggling to breathe, because she looks so beautiful... and it's been so long...

She's wearing stonewashed skin-tight jeans, and a long-sleeved, light grey, sheer top, and as she suddenly leans against the open door, seemingly for support, one side of her top falls from her naked shoulder, and the lacy panel in the centre shifts downwards, just a little, revealing that soft, delicate patch of skin between her breasts, which I remember wanting to kiss. If only I'd taken the time... Her hair is loose around her shoulders and she's staring at me with her mouth slightly open, until she captures her bottom lip between her teeth.

It's hard not to notice that her eyes are glistening. And while I know she was crying the last time we met, when I was trying to say sorry to her, to make it right again, I'd hoped to be able to explain myself, before she got upset with me again...

"P—Poppy was wondering if Roan would like to play." I quickly make the decision to use my daughter as an excuse to start the conversation. It feels safer that way, and in any case, I'm feeling tongue tied now I'm standing in front of the woman who's haunted my dreams for so long.

Summer stares at me for a moment, tipping her head until it gently comes into contact with the door beside her. "When did you get back?" she whispers, ignoring my statement and blinking a couple of times.

"Yesterday."

She nods her head. "And how long are you planning on staying this time?" There's a hint of something in her voice. Disdain? Suspicion? Anger? I'm not sure. But whatever it is, I can't blame her for it. I've hardly proved myself to be the most reliable of men.

"I have no idea," I tell her, with absolute honesty, because I genuinely don't know. Whatever happens in the next few minutes will decide that... and the rest of my future. And hers too, I guess.

Poppy tugs on my hand and I glance down at her, before looking back at Summer again. "Is Roan about?" I ask. "I mean, if you're busy, or you've got plans... or c—company, then he can come to our place, if… if it makes things easier for you, I mean…" I'm aware I'm stuttering and stumbling over my words, but I'm just hoping that she's not about to tell me that it would be really great if Roan could come over to Bluebells, because it would give her time to spend alone with her new boyfriend. *Please don't let her say that…*

She frowns. "Company? At this time of the morning? What on earth are you talking about?"

I smile. Uncontrollably. "Nothing," I say, shaking my head. "Just ignore me. It doesn't matter."

She sucks in a sharp breath, focusing on my eyes and then my lips, and then blinks, much more rapidly than before, clearly struggling not to cry, and I take a half step forward. She holds up her hand, stopping me, just as footsteps sound on the stairs behind her and Roan appears through the open door in the corner.

"Poppy!" he cries and she lets go of my hand and runs into the house. I wish it could be that easy for Summer and me after two weeks apart. But it can't, because we're not children. We're adults, with a lot to talk about.

We stand and watch them disappear up the stairs together, before Summer turns back and faces me. "You left," she whispers.

"Yes."

"And you didn't say goodbye."

I take a definite step closer to Summer, who wipes at her eyes with the back of her hand. "I know," I murmur softly, desperate to take her in my arms. "And I'm sorry. And don't tell me not to say 'sorry', because I am sorry. I shouldn't have left without saying goodbye. I shouldn't have left at all."

"Why are you back, Kit?" she asks, biting her bottom lip again, and looking like she wants to burst into very loud tears. I suppose she could, now that the children aren't here anymore. But she doesn't. Instead, she narrows her eyes slightly and says, "Why are you here?" and I recognise the hurt in her voice. I've heard it often enough before, after all.

"I want to talk to you," I reply, because that is where I want to start things off… with a very long conversation. What happens after that will be up to her. "I want to sit in your living room, or your kitchen, with you, while our kids play... and I want to talk. That's all."

"That's all?"

"For now... yes."

I gaze into her sparkling eyes, hoping she'll understand that I want so much more eventually, but that talking has to come first.

"Well," she sighs, "if you want to come in and talk, you'll need to be invited."

She's going to play hard to get. She's going to make me work for this. And I'm okay with that. I deserve to have to work for it, after everything I've put her through.

I place one foot on the threshold, staring down at her. "Then invite me, Summer... please."

Chapter Thirty-one

Summer

He's here.

He's actually here. Right in front of me.

I never thought he'd come back. I never thought I'd see him again. And yet, he's here, on my doorstep, staring at me and saying he wants to talk... and looking into my eyes like he wants to kiss me too, until neither of us can remember how to talk anymore.

So, why am I not leaping into his arms, throwing myself at him?

This is what I've wanted for days now... a second chance with him.

Why am I not grabbing it – and him – with both hands?

He wants me to invite him in... so why don't I?

Because this is the man who made you love him, who left you, who didn't say goodbye to you... and who could break you, if you let him... The voice in my head – the voice of reason – chimes loud and clear, just when I least want it to.

"Are you going to get angry again?" I ask him.

"No."

"Are you going to shout at me, or scare me again?" I can still remember how that felt.

His eyes darken, and I see the pain within them. "I didn't mean to scare you," he says quietly. "The very last thing I ever want to do is scare you. And I'm sorry I did. I just want to talk… and I promise, I won't do anything to hurt you." He pauses for a second. "And I know you think my words and my promises don't count for very much, but if you invite me in, Summer, I'll prove to you that they do."

I step aside, without giving it any more thought – because thinking isn't helping – and he enters, waiting while I close the door. Then, as I turn, he puts his hands on my waist and walks me backwards until I hit the wall behind me, his body pressed hard against mine.

"I'm sorry," he whispers, and I can feel his breath on my lips. "I'm sorry for all the vile and horrible things I said to you. I'm sorry I walked out on you that night, after I'd made love to you. I should have stayed, and held you, and kissed you, and told you how completely perfect you are for me… and then taken you to bed and made love to you again… and then fallen asleep with you, probably after we'd worked out exactly how we were going to explain to our kids why we were all still here in the morning. And I'm truly sorry I didn't do that. I'm sorry I made you think I had any regrets about what we'd done. I didn't. I honestly didn't. I still don't." He pauses, somehow moving even closer now, his feet either side of mine, our lips almost touching, and then he murmurs, "I'm sorry I left the village. I'm sorry I left without telling you, or saying goodbye. I'm sorry for everything. For all of it." He sucks in a breath with a slight stutter behind it, studying my face, like he's seeing me for the first time. "I've been trying to work things out in my head, Summer, for a long, long time time now, and I think I finally have."

I tilt my head to one side, but don't say a word, and he brings one of his hands up from my waist, cupping my cheek, caressing my lips with the side of his thumb and gazing deeply into my eyes, fixing me and letting me lose myself in him, all at the same time.

"I felt guilty about Bryony," he says, as though this is news.

"Because we'd made love?" I ask, my voice so quiet I can barely hear it.

"Partly. But also, before that… because of Gabrielle, and because I couldn't make her better… when she was sick. I had no control over any of it. She took that from me… well, I suppose the cancer did, really. But at the time, it felt like Bryony did too, with her decision not to take the treatments they were offering. There was nothing I could do except watch her die, knowing things should have been different."

"You do realise that she wouldn't have survived much longer, even with the treatment, don't you?" I point out, even though I think he knows that already. After all, he's the one who told me.

"Yes. But like I said to you before, I had no say in any of it. I felt... impotent... like a bystander in her death, just watching it all happen around me. And there was nothing I could say about it... not without upsetting her." He leans away just slightly and tips his head back, staring up towards the ceiling, like he's looking for answers – or at least a way of explaining himself. "Acknowledging that anger openly to you, for the first time... it wasn't easy." He pauses, then continues, "It was good for me at the time, because you gave me permission to be angry, and I took that, and felt a lot better – for about ten seconds. Until I started over-analysing everything again. But I think I was still harbouring the guilt I'd felt for such a long time over having that anger in the first place. I knew I should have been grieving for her and missing her, not feeling angry with her. It was always there though, deep down, like a constant sore, eating away at me, even if I couldn't talk about it... until I met you. I mean, can you believe, I even wondered at the time, whether that was a factor in me sleeping with Gabrielle? Whether I did it to get back at Bryony for her having taken away my choices."

"You don't think it was just about needing to have sex?" I suggest, because that sounds so much more logical. "I would have thought, if you'd wanted to score points over Bryony, you'd have done it sooner... maybe even while she was still alive."

He smiles. "I wasn't *that* angry with her. And I only considered the revenge theory for about thirty seconds... because I think I knew even then that it was about a much more basic need than that. But I hated myself for doing it... so damn much. I felt like I'd betrayed Bryony. I felt like I'd let her down... like I'd let myself down. Gabrielle was married, for God's sake. I should have known better."

"I don't think she took her vows very seriously," I bring my hands up from my sides and let them rest on his arms, touching him for the first time, and his eyes flicker and darken. "Not from what you said."

"I know. But that doesn't excuse my behaviour. And it doesn't excuse the consequences. I argued with Mum because of what I did that night, and how it all made me feel, and I shouldn't have done. It was so stupid. And I didn't get the chance to make it up with her, because I was too ashamed of my own actions. But in reality, it didn't matter. Not really. Not compared to what we both lost." He stops talking and shakes his head a couple of times, before he brings his other hand up, cupping my face and gazing into my eyes. "For ages now, Summer, I've felt so overwhelmed, so out of control… like everything is shifting around me, like I can't seem to find my way."

I move my hands further up across his shoulders and behind his neck, sensing that he needs the contact – or at least something more intimate than me resting my hands on his arms. "You need to stop worrying, Kit. You've been doing it for far too long… and you've forgotten how to live."

He smiles and bows his head, resting it against mine – forehead to forehead. "I know," he says softly. "Or at least, I do now. Thanks to you… and to Tony, I guess."

"Tony?" I lean back myself now, as far as the wall will allow, and look up at him. "As in Maggie's Tony?"

"Yes."

I'm stunned and for a moment I just stare at him. "Do you mean you read the rest of his letters and learned something else?"

He shakes his head. "No. I mean he contacted me… a couple of days ago."

"Oh my God." I can't believe it. "Do you want to sit down?" I suggest, because it seems he has a story to tell, and I think it would be better to get comfortable first. He takes a moment to decide.

"Okay," he says eventually, and steps back, releasing me.

"Sorry… I should have offered you a drink… a tea, or coffee?"

"I'd rather just sit and talk," he says, taking my hand and pulling me towards the sofa, not letting go until he's sat down in the corner. Then he parts his legs and, with his hands on my hips, he turns me around and lowers me into the cradle he's made of himself, my back to his front, his arms coming tight around my waist. This reminds me of the way we sat that night, outside, when he touched me… and although we're both fully clothed now, a part of me wonders if I should move away, or at least suggest it, so we're not quite so intimately bound up in each other, considering that we haven't resolved anything yet. The thing is though, I don't want to. I feel like this is where I belong. Clothes, or no clothes. And I think maybe I always did.

"Is this okay?" he whispers, as though he's been reading my mind, sensing my doubts.

I nod my head in reply and snuggle into him to prove the point, and he sighs deeply, tightening his grip on me.

"What happened with Tony?" I ask, after a few moments' silence. It's a comfortable silence, not an awkward one, but I still want to know how Tony came to contact Kit.

He moves us down the sofa, just slightly. "He phoned up, out of the blue, on Thursday," he says, and I feel his chest heave behind me, as he takes a breath, his chin resting on top of my head, and I can't help smiling, even though he can't see me… or maybe *because* he can't see me. I'm not sure yet. "He'd read about Mum's death in the newspaper and wanted to meet."

"And you agreed?"

"Yes. I think I was curious. And he really did seem quite keen on the idea, so we arranged to meet in Richmond Park, on Friday lunchtime. It turned out he'd been going through some of Mum's letters to him, he said, and he wanted to explain about their relationship."

"Oh…" That sounds kind of difficult, as conversations go.

"He worked out that I might have come across her letters, and he wanted to reassure me that she hadn't been unfaithful to Dad."

"But we'd already figured that out for ourselves, just from the dates," I reason.

"I know. I explained that to him, and we talked some more. He told me how they'd met, a few days into the cruise, during an excursion to Bordeaux, and how they'd just hit it off straight away. Evidently when the official holiday came to an end, they decided to stay on in Venice for a few days."

"Didn't you know that already? I mean, didn't you notice that your mother didn't come home as planned?" I ask, twisting around and looking up at him.

He shrugs. "I did. Sort of. I remembered getting a message from her, telling me she was having a good time and had decided to stay on, but I was too busy panicking about fatherhood at the time, to question her motives."

I nod my head and lean back into him, sideways on now. "So, what happened when they got back?"

"Mum got cold feet," he says in a matter of fact tone. "She was torn, between the life Tony was offering her, and her memories of the past… of my father. And she was feeling guilty."

I tilt my head back, looking up at him again. "A bit like you, then?"

He smiles and kisses my forehead. "Oh… very much like me, from the sounds of things."

"What did she do?"

"She didn't do anything. Tony persuaded her to give them a chance… basically that you only get one crack at life and when happiness comes along, you shouldn't turn your back on it. So she didn't. And according to him, they had eighteen fabulous months together… until Mum wrote to him and told him she didn't want to see him anymore. He wrote back…"

"That was the letter we read?" I query, interrupting him, and he nods his head.

"Yes. Mum's letter had come as a bolt out of the blue to Tony. He'd thought they were doing okay, so he wrote, begging her to reconsider."

"And what did Maggie do?" I sit up, turning to face him.

"She wrote back." He smiles and I heave a sigh of relief.

"Thank God. But then, why didn't he write back again?" I ask.

"Because he called her instead. He said he needed her to hear his voice… and then they met up and they talked, and he agreed to slow things down, to give her time. He said he didn't want to lose her." He stares into my eyes, and takes a breath.

"So they got back together?"

"Yes. Tony said it was a very gradual process to start with, while Mum got used to the idea of being with someone else... or learned to live with her feelings, I guess. And then, he said, at Christmas last year, things became more serious again... and after that they started seeing a lot more of each other." He raises his eyebrows, and smirks. "I didn't ask what that meant."

I smirk myself. "What was he like?"

"He was a nice guy," Kit says. "We've agreed to stay in touch."

"But he lives in York, doesn't he."

"No. He moved down here... to Plymouth, to be nearer to Mum."

I feel a chill down my spine. "P—Plymouth?"

He nods. "Yes."

"Plymouth?" I whisper the word a second time.

He pulls me close. "I worked it out too," he says softly. "She must have been driving to see him, when it happened. Tony said they hadn't arranged anything, but I can't see why else she'd have been going over there. I haven't been able to work that out, ever since the police told me where the accident happened. He got a bit upset when I mentioned it... wondering why she'd have been going there when he wasn't expecting her."

"It could have been anything," I muse, almost to myself.

"I think it was probably something good, rather than something bad," Kit says, sighing again. "If it had been something bad, I think she'd have telephoned, or written. But I didn't mention that. It would only have made it worse for Tony, really... so we didn't dwell on it for too long."

"That poor man..."

Kit shakes his head. "He didn't see it like that. And I suppose that's what I've been trying to tell you. In a way, he helped me to see my own life from a slightly different perspective. I mean... you helped most... more than anyone else. But talking to Tony, listening to him... it made me realise something."

I'm holding my breath, and I know it. "What?" I manage to say, my voice squeaking.

"That I've been moping around feeling sorry for myself, when in reality, I'm one of the luckiest men in the world."

"You are?"

"Yes." He smiles then sits up a little, pulling me even closer to him. "I've made so many mistakes with you, Summer. And you've given me so many chances… and I just need you to give me one more…"

Those are the words I've longed to hear, more than anything, and my heart skips a beat, even as my head tries to rein in my emotions, and my mouth opens… "Why did you do it?" I ask, unable to stop myself, as I lean away from him, just enough so I can see him better. "Why did you leave, Kit?"

"Which time?" he says.

"After you made love to me… after…"

"After what?" His brow furrows in confusion.

"After you claimed me like that." I lower my head, my voice a slight whisper, the words hovering between us, because I think we both know there was something different about what we did that night.

I feel his finger beneath my chin, and then he raises my face to his, his eyes locked on mine. "I let guilt get in the way of happiness," he says. "I knew I was doing it, but I couldn't stop myself. I had to be somewhere else. Anywhere else. I couldn't face what I'd done at the time. And please don't get upset by that. It was no reflection on you, or on what we'd done together. I was just too busy dwelling in the past, to think about the present, or the future"

"But you came to see me again. The very next day."

"Yes. I—I know that probably wasn't the best idea I've ever had, given that I was a bit of a wreck, but I wanted to know you were okay. I wanted to make sure I hadn't hurt you… even though I was fairly sure I had." He moves my hair aside and gently caresses the skin, on the nape of my neck, where he branded me, although the mark is long gone now. "And I think I wanted to ask you to give me some time, while I tried to work out what was going on in my head."

"You did? It didn't feel like that at the time."

"I know, but that's because I screwed everything up. In fairly spectacular style."

"Let's not talk about that," I murmur. It won't help either of us, and knowing that his intentions were so different from his execution makes all the difference. There's no need to rake over past mistakes, not as far as I'm concerned.

"Okay. But I have to just say one thing about those few moments in your kitchen." I wait, and eventually he continues, "You said you didn't feel like you were good enough, and I want to tell you – no, I *have* to tell you – that you're wrong. You're more than good enough. In fact you're too good. You're more than I deserve, anyway. And I think that's one of the things I wanted to say to you, when I finally got my head around it all, and caught up with you in the playground. As well as apologising, obviously. I don't know who I thought I was, telling you your life was a mess, when I was the one fouling up literally everything I touched, but I wanted to say sorry, and to try and explain. I didn't expect your forgiveness, not when you'd already forgiven me for so much. But I hoped you might find it in your heart to listen…"

"I'm sorry."

He shakes his head. "You have nothing to be sorry for. You didn't owe me anything."

"I could have at least been polite."

"You were."

"Well… I could have let you say your piece, if nothing else."

"Why? I'd been unforgivably rude… again. I'd hurt you. I don't think I realised how much, until then. But when Roan felt the need to protect you from me… when you said I could break you… that you felt like my emotional punchbag…" I wince and he pulls me back against him. "I felt like the worst kind of man, hearing that," he whispers against my hair.

"So you left?" I murmur, wanting to understand.

"Yes. I was ashamed, and I thought it was kinder to you. You said you wanted us to be over, and although we hadn't really given 'us' much of a chance, I thought it would be easier for you, if I wasn't here. I didn't want to go… not really. And I didn't feel great about doing it. I felt like a coward – especially for not saying goodbye to you, but I felt like I was giving you what you wanted… what you'd asked for."

"You didn't think to come and talk to me?"

"You didn't seem to want to talk, Summer," he reasons. "You told me that being with me was like a punishment. Why would you want any more of that?"

I can't deny any of what he's saying, although having my words repeated back to me is quite sobering. "I remember saying all of that," I whisper. "But you have to allow for how hurt I was. I'm…"

"Hey… don't even think about apologising. I deserved every word of it. I'm not going to say it didn't hurt to hear it, because it did. But mainly because I—I honestly thought that was it… I thought I'd blown it with you…" His voice fades

"And yet, you're back." I pull away from him again and look up at him once more. I need to see his face. I need to know what's changed.

"Yes. I was so bloody miserable without you," he says, and we both chuckle. "Ruth must have noticed…"

"Who's Ruth?" I ask.

"Bryony's mum. She looks after Poppy for me sometimes… well, all the time at the moment, because Clare's dad is still sick."

I nod my head. "I see."

"Anyway, she noticed I wasn't quite my normal miserable self… I was significantly worse than usual. And she sat me down while Poppy was at the park, with Bryony's dad – Edward – and she made me see sense. At least where Bryony was concerned… She made me understand that not living my life wasn't honouring Bryony at all. And it certainly wasn't doing Poppy any good. And that was when I saw what you'd been trying to tell me all along. You'd been trying to help me, right from the word 'go', to understand myself, and my situation; to see my grief for what it was… or what it is, to be more precise… and I hadn't even had the intelligence to appreciate any of it. In fact, for the best part, all I'd done was throw it back in your face. But after I'd spoken to Ruth, who probably knew Bryony nearly as well as I did, I finally understood the thing that mattered most. I worked out that, if I wanted a chance at happiness…" He sighs, gathering his emotions, I think. "If I want a chance at happiness with you, I have to let her go."

"No." I kneel up, turning to him as I clasp his face in my hands, staring into his eyes. "No, you don't. That was never what I meant... never what I intended. If you thought that, then you were wrong. Kit, you never have to let Bryony go. She's Poppy's mother. She's the woman you'd have grown old with, if she hadn't been taken from you. You'll always love her... and that's how it should be."

He nods his head and I notice his eyes glistening, as he mutters, "I know, but that's not the point," taking my hands from his face and holding them in his, between us.

"What is?"

"That I got it wrong. I'd put the dead ahead of the living. I'd walked away from you when I should have stayed," he says, his voice cracking slightly. I open my mouth to speak, to offer comfort, but he lets go of my hands and covers my lips with his fingers. "I'm not finished yet," he says, and lowers his head for a second, before raising it again. "I let my guilt and my fear come between us. I'd become so scared of losing Bryony – or at least my memory of her – that I was focusing too much on the past... on what I used to have, and what I lost when she died. And because of that, I lost you too."

"You never lost me," I whisper, and without taking his eyes from mine, he kneels up too, towering over me and, with a low growl, he captures my face with his hands and kisses me.

And I let him. Because I love him.

And I always will.

Chapter Thirty-two

Kit

I change the angle of my head, deepening the kiss and pulling her closer to me, our bodies fused, my arousal pressing against her. She moans into me and I groan in response, burying my fingers in her hair and holding her still. Right where I want her. For now.

I break the kiss eventually and lean back, looking down at her.

Her lips are swollen, but then I have just been biting them, and her eyes are still closed. It takes a moment before she opens them and focuses on me.

I was so nervous coming over here, I wasn't sure what I was going to say in the end, but when it came down to it, the words poured out of me and I just told her what's in my heart… almost. I told her how scared I've been, how guilty I've felt, how lost and worried and frightened… and she understood. She understood all of it. And that doesn't surprise me in the slightest, because Summer is the most understanding person I've ever met.

"Hello," I whisper, brushing her cheek with my thumb.

"Hello." She blinks, gazing into my eyes, although I'm not sure she understands. This is a fresh start. A new beginning. A first 'hello'. Or it will be, once I know exactly where I stand.

"Can I ask you something?" She nods her head. "Who was that man I saw you with yesterday afternoon?"

Surprise flashes across her eyes and she leans back, pulling away from me. "You saw me... I mean us?" she mutters, sitting back down on the sofa, her legs curled up underneath her.

"Yes." I'm filled with fear now, despite that kiss, which she returned with a fire that matched my own, and despite her words... 'you never lost me'. If I never lost her, then what does 'us' mean, in the context of her and another man? What's going on here? I sit down myself, in the corner of the couch again, and wait, watching her, a little distance away, playing with the hem of her top, rolling it between her fingers. "Summer... talk to me. Please?" I say eventually, unable to wait any longer.

She glances up. "His name was Drew," she says, sighing. "He came to see your house... Maggie's house, I mean."

"When? Yesterday?" I'm surprised. I wasn't aware of any viewings yesterday.

"No. He came some time last week, I think."

"Oh. I see... And?"

"And he decided he wanted to get a taste of village life, before making a decision. So he came back yesterday, for the fête."

"A taste of village life?" I repeat. "Did that tasting involve you?" God, I sound so jealous. I *am* so jealous. But I'm reminded that I haven't tasted her myself yet, and just the idea of another man being so intimate with her... She opens her mouth to reply, but I hold up my hand, stopping her. "Sorry. I shouldn't have said that. I left you and I hurt you, and I have absolutely no right..."

She leans over as I'm talking, moving nearer to me, her hand coming to rest on my leg. "Yes, you do," she whispers. "You have every right. And no, it didn't involve me. He... he asked me to go for a drink with him, and I said yes. He was a nice man, and we spent a couple of hours together, with Roan, at the pub... that's all."

"Hey..." I sit up, shifting closer to her now, taking her hand from my leg and clasping it in my own. "You don't have to explain."

"Yes, I do. I want you to know that... nothing happened."

I nod my head, trying not to let her hear the sigh of relief escaping my lips. "Are you going to see him again?" I ask.

"He asked, but I said 'no'."

"Why?" I ask, smiling, because I can't help myself. She blushes and looks down at our hands. "Why, Summer? Why did you turn him down?"

She looks up at me again. "Because I wasn't ready to see anyone else yet."

"Why?"

Her brow creases. "Because," she says, shrugging.

"Because of what?" I release her hands and move my own to her waist, leaving them there for a moment.

"Are you trying to make this difficult for me?"

"No. I just want to know."

She scowls at me. "Okay," she says, a bit grumpily. "It was because I wanted you back."

I lift her, pulling her up onto me and moving us both down at the same time, so we're lying along the length of the sofa, with her on top of me.

"You sent me away," I remind her.

"I know."

"You rejected me. You said you had to protect yourself from me." She blushes and lowers her eyes. "And yet you wanted me back?"

"Well, not at the time we were arguing, I didn't. I wasn't sure what I wanted at that moment. I…"

"Did it really feel like you were my emotional punchbag?" I ask her, interrupting her flow.

"Can you stop reminding me of all the horrible things I said to you?" She closes her eyes, biting her lip at the same time.

I pull it free with my thumb and kiss her gently. "They weren't horrible. I just want to know if it was true… if it really felt like that."

"Not always," she whispers, her eyes open again now. "Sometimes you could be lovely… sometimes you could be everything I ever wanted, or dreamed of. But that last time, here, in my kitchen…" She nods towards the rear of her house, to the room where I shouted at her and scared her. "That side of you isn't a man I want to see again."

"You won't. And I'm sorry. I'm truly, truly sorry I ever made you feel like that. I promise, I won't ever do that to you again. I won't ever hurt you… and I'll never make you cry. Not ever."

I turn us over, firstly to our sides and then again, so Summer is on her back, with me on top of her now, keeping my weight on my elbows, grateful that she has a wide sofa and neither of us ended up on the floor, thanks to that manoeuvre. She gazes up at me, with that longing look in her eyes, the neckline of one side of her top now halfway down her arm, revealing the rise of her breast.

"I promise I won't leave you, ever again," I whisper, dipping my head and tracing a line of kisses over that soft skin. She gasps, her body shuddering to my touch.

"Ever?" she rasps, and as I lean back up, I notice her frown, directed at me. *This doesn't look good.* "Why do you keep saying that? What does it even mean?" She sits up, nearly head-butting me in the process, and I kneel between her legs as she pulls her top up onto her shoulder once more, covering herself and glaring into my eyes. "You can't make promises like that, Kit."

"Yes, I can."

"You can't. You don't even live here. Not permanently. You live hundreds of miles away. In Kew. You're selling Maggie's house. And that means talking about the future, about never leaving me… well, it's not true, and it's not fair." Her voice cracks on the last word and she pulls her legs up, twisting around and sitting up on the sofa again, turning her face away from me.

I stand, needing more control of the situation, and pull her to her feet and into my arms, noticing the tears in her eyes. "Don't cry." I shake my head at her. "I promised I wouldn't make you cry. Don't make me break my promise."

"Then stop talking about forever like that. We don't have forever. I know how this will play out…"

"Do you?"

"Yes." She sounds cross now.

"Okay. Care to enlighten me?"

She leans back. "It's simple… you'll…" She falls silent.

"What's wrong?"

"I can't enlighten you," she says, her brow furrowing.

"Why not?"

"Because I don't even know how long you're staying here for, and neither do you."

"Yes I do."

She tilts her head to one side. "But earlier, you said…"

"I know what I said earlier. I know I said I had no idea how long I'd be here for… but I do now."

"I don't understand you, Kit."

"Good." I smile at her, before leaning down and kissing her again, just briefly.

"Why is that 'good'?"

"Because if you understood, it would spoil the surprise, and that would ruin everything."

She narrows her eyes, although her lips are twitching upwards at the corners now. "Who are you?" she says, shaking her head. "And what have you done with Kit Robinson?"

I chuckle. "I'm still me."

"Really? The Kit Robinson I knew was never this mysterious… never this much fun." She smiles fully and I grab her waist, pulling her close and holding onto her.

"Well, if you'll let me explain what I've got in mind, and you find it's to your liking, then maybe later on, when the kids have gone to bed, you'll allow me to show you exactly how much fun I can be… and that I really am still Kit Robinson. Exactly as you remember me."

"Exactly?" she teases.

"Yes… exactly." And I grind my hips into her to prove the point. She sucks in a breath and her body quivers in my arms, and I have to smile, just thinking about all the things I want to do with her… to her. All the things I *can* do. Now I'm back.

"So… are you going to explain?" she says, breaking into my thoughts.

"Explain what?"

She sighs. "What we were talking about... the future... the surprise."

"Oh... that. Sorry, I was distracted."

The corners of her lips tweak upwards again. "By anything in particular?"

"Yes. You."

"If I'm that much of a distraction," she says, stepping away slightly, "would you like me to leave?"

"No. Never." I pull her back and she giggles in my arms, and I savour that sound, kissing her again, more deeply this time, until she's breathless and her eyes betray her longing – which only matches my own. "You can't leave. Apart from the fact that this is your house, I need you to come with me."

I take her hand in mine and lead her towards the front door.

"Um... where are we going?"

"You'll see."

She yanks her hand from mine. "No, I won't."

"What's wrong, Summer?"

She looks up at me. "Two things... Firstly, we can't go out and leave our children here... and the Kit Robinson I know would never have forgotten that."

I close my eyes. "Okay." I open them again, smiling down at her. "I'll admit that was a bit out of character. I'll give you that."

She shakes her head. "A *bit* out of character? What happened to Mr Over-Protective Father?"

"I'll explain in a minute... for now, let's just say he's distracted. Again."

"If you insist."

"What's the other reason I'm not allowed to drag you out of your own house?"

She pauses for a moment and then moves closer, standing on her tiptoes and placing her lips by my ear. "I'm not wearing a bra."

I chuckle. "Believe it or not, I had noticed."

"And my top is kind of... flimsy and a bit transparent."

"Yep... noticed that too."

She narrows her eyes, although she's trying not to smile. "Well, I might dress like this around the house, when no-one can see me, but when I go out, I do at least put on a show of modesty."

"You call those short shorts of yours modest?"

"They cover everything that needs to be covered." She defends herself.

"And your sexy tops?"

"Again, my tops are decent. They're not too revealing."

"If you say so."

"I do. I like being comfortable..."

"Hey... I'm not complaining. I like you being comfortable too."

She shakes her head and slaps me gently on the chest. "The point is, that if we're going out somewhere, then I need to change my top and put a bra on... not necessarily in that order."

"Okay..." I tilt my head one way and then the other, as though I'm giving the matter serious thought, which I'm not. "As long as we can agree that, once we're alone again and safely away from prying eyes, you'll take them both off."

"No," she says smartly.

"No?"

She shakes her head. "But we can agree that, once we're alone again, and safely away from all eyes other than yours, then *you'll* take them off."

"Oh... I like your idea so much better." I move her hair aside and lean down, kissing her neck, right on the spot where I branded her, although the mark has disappeared now. And then I stand up straight again, looking into her eyes. "I'm glad you don't generally parade yourself in public."

"You are?"

"Yes. Because, as much as I love your body – and I really, really do love your body – I don't want anyone else to see it. Not like I do. You're mine, Summer." I feel really possessive of her right now... in a good way. I don't want to own her... well, except I kind of do. It's like I want to hold her, and keep her safe. Always. Which I guess, given my plans, is exactly what I intend doing. "You're completely mine. And later on, I'm going to take off your top, and your bra and everything else you're wearing, and I'll prove that to you… over, and over… and over."

"Oh G—God…" she stutters, letting me hold her. "Promise?" she says eventually, looking up into my eyes.

"I promise." I kiss her forehead, unable to stop myself from smiling at her reaction, and then I take a half step back, before I forget about everything else and end up taking her… right here… right now. "I guess you'd better go and change… and maybe bring the kids back down with you? And then I can try and explain my plan – insofar as it is a plan – to all of you."

She sucks in a breath, her shoulders rising and falling, her eyes locked on mine for a moment and I'm touched by the fact that she seems reluctant to go.

"I'll be right here," I say, in the hope that she's reassured by the fact that I'm not about to leave again, even though I've promised I won't.

"Okay. I won't be long." She leans up and kisses me quickly on my cheek, and then turns and darts through the door and up the stairs.

I take advantage of her absence to try and calm down. Being back with Summer again, holding her and kissing her… and knowing that I have it within my power to make her mine, and that she doesn't seem averse to that idea… is all very arousing. But I need to stay focused. At least for the next few minutes. Because I have a lot of explaining to do.

I just hope she likes my plan as much as I do.

Within a few minutes, I hear footsteps on the stairs and I turn to see Summer appear in the door of the back wall, wearing the same stonewashed jeans, but with a different top. This one is dark red, with white flowers around the shoulders, and while it has a fairly plunging neckline, it's by no means transparent, although personally, I still think it looks just as sexy. But maybe that's because I know what lies beneath…

"We're here," she says, as she steps into the room, and I finally drag my eyes from her and see that she's being followed by Roan and Poppy, who are both looking confused – especially my daughter, who comes over and stands in front of me.

"What's happening, Daddy?"

"We're going for a walk," I reply, taking her hand.

"Where to?"

I crouch down and tweak her nose. "You'll see."

And with that, I stand again and open Summer's front door, leading the way outside. She follows, holding Roan by the hand, although she pauses to close the door again, before we go down her garden path, and then make our way out onto the green.

"So where *are* we going?" Summer asks, as I start to walk.

"Bluebells." I nod towards my mother's house and she glances in the same direction, then turns back to me.

"Any particular reason?"

"Yes. And I'll explain it when we get there."

Poppy tugs on my hand and I look down at her. "Are we going home again?" she asks, looking woeful.

"Yes."

Her bottom lip starts to tremble, and I stop walking and crouch again. "Don't cry." I brush my fingers through her hair, pushing it away from her face a little. She must think I mean we're going back to Kew, poor baby. "Daddy's got a plan, okay?"

"What kind of plan?" She sounds devastated.

"Can you just wait until we get back to Granny's house? Then I promise I'll tell you everything."

She pauses and then nods her head, and standing up again, I take Summer's hand in my free one, and the four of us set off across the green.

"You're being very mysterious," Summer says quietly and I turn and look down at her.

"I know. Fun, isn't it?"

She tilts her head. "I don't know. This new version of you…" she lets her voice fade and I wonder what she was about to say.

"What about him?" I ask.

"He's different."

"Good different?"

She hesitates and I feel her eyes scrutinising my face. "I think so," she whispers, as I lean in closer to her.

"I'm not entirely new…" I whisper, so the children won't hear. "And, as I've already promised, I'll be reminding you of that later."

She moans, loudly enough for me to catch the sound, and I give her hand a light squeeze, just before I break the connection between us and let go of Poppy's hand as well, so I can open the gate to Bluebells.

"Why are we here?" Roan says, looking up at me.

I stand just inside the entrance to the driveway, facing Summer, the children between us, and I look into her eyes, hoping to God I've judged this right.

"I—I've realised," I say, stuttering over my words, as my nerves threaten to get the better of me and I cough to clear my throat. "I've realised, thanks to you, Summer, that life's too short not to live it as fully and completely as you can. And I know that, for the last three years, I haven't been living at all, let alone fully and completely. And I've decided… that has to change. From now on, I'm going to take my chances. I'm going to let myself be happy."

Summer smiles up at me, although her eyes betray her confusion.

"What are you talking about, Daddy?" Poppy says and I avert my gaze to her for a moment.

"I've reached a decision," I say firmly.

"Right…" She sounds doubtful, but for the purposes of what I'm about to say, I need to look at Summer again. So I do.

"I've decided I'm going to sell up."

Summer frowns, her brow furrowing and her eyes darkening slightly. "I know," she says, like she thinks I've taken leave of my senses. "We all know." She nods towards the 'for sale' sign by the gatepost. "We can see the sign, Kit."

I smile at her and hold up my hand, stopping her from questioning my sanity any further, and then go over to the gate and, hoping I won't make a fool out of myself, I bend down, clasping the signpost with two hands, and yank it from the ground. Fortunately, it comes out quite easily, and I throw it to one side, looking back at the three of them, who are staring at me, their faces a mixture of confusion, shock and mild amusement… that latter reaction probably caused by the fact that my behaviour is so completely out of character.

"What are you doing?" Summer says.

"I'm proving a point." I walk back to her.

"Which is?"

I move directly in front of her now, gazing into her eyes, the children standing together, holding each other's hands, right beside us. "When I say I'm selling up, I'm not talking about this house, Summer. I'm talking about my house in Kew. Poppy and I are going to move here… starting right now. Today… this minute."

Tears fill Summer's eyes. "You're going to m—move here?" she whispers, raising her hands and resting them on my chest.

"Yes."

"To stay?"

"Yes."

"Forever?"

"Forever."

"Daddy! Daddy!" Poppy's voice breaks into our trancelike moment, and I look down at her smiling face.

"Yes, sweetheart?"

"Does this mean we're not going home after all?"

I crouch down in front of Poppy, although I take Summer's hand in the process and keep hold of it. "It means we *are* home, Poppy. This is our new home."

"You mean… we're going to stay here?"

"Yes."

"And can I go to school in the village?"

"Yes," Summer says, crouching beside me.

"With me!" Roan crows triumphantly and he and Poppy start to jump around.

"Well, you won't be in the same class," Summer says, trying to calm them down.

"I know," Roan says, stopping and facing her. "But it'll still be fun to have my best friend at school with me."

Oh… that's cute.

"I suppose I'll have to speak to the headmaster about getting Poppy in at such short notice," I point out, adding a note of practicality to the celebrations.

"Or you could try talking to the head*mistress*," Summer says, smiling.

"Okay… that too."

"And I shouldn't worry. There are plenty of spaces in Poppy's year group. It won't be a problem."

I heave a sigh of relief, as both the children start to jump around again, and Summer and I stand up, still holding hands, just as the kids take off and, at Poppy's behest, run towards the garden at the back of the house, leaving us in peace for a moment… which might be a good thing.

"What are you going to do about your work?" Summer asks, turning to face me.

"I'll work from here." I glance over at the house. "I'm going to convert my dad's studio into an office."

"Your clients are all in London though, aren't they?"

"Yes, but I can travel up there, when I have to, and I'll do my best to find some local clients down here to make life easier in the long run. And besides, money won't be too much of a problem. I may not have actually put my house on the market yet, but I did have a quick look at the kind of price it might fetch, and it's… well, it's eye-watering. I've got a bit of a mortgage to pay off, but I'll be left with a very healthy bank balance at the end of it."

"You've really thought this all out, haven't you?" she says, shaking her head, in disbelief, I think.

"No. Not entirely." I move closer to her, putting my arms around her waist now and clasping my hands together behind her back. "There's one part of my grand plan that's still completely unresolved."

"What's that?"

"Us."

She leans back, although she can't pull away because I've got a firm hold on her. Even so, her face is a picture of fear. "What do you mean 'us'?"

"Exactly what I say."

"But I—I don't understand." She sounds like she's going to cry now and I hold onto her for dear life, refusing to let go, no matter what. "How can we be completely unresolved? I thought we were fine… I thought you said that later on, you wanted…"

"I know," I cut her off. "And I do. I do want to take your clothes off, and take you to bed… and remind you of how good we can be together. I want all of that." I close my eyes and suck in a breath… calming my nerves… or trying to. "But the thing is, Summer… I want more."

"More?" she whispers. "What does that mean?"

I cup her face with one hand, locking her eyes with mine and doing my best to fix her. "It means that, while I was away, while I was working and trying very hard not to think about you every single minute of the day, I realised that I've spent the last three years in a very dark place."

"I know," she says softly, touching my cheek with her fingertips.

"And I also realised that you are my light. You're my sun." She gasps. "You make everything shine, Summer." I brush my thumb across her slightly parted lips. "You were right earlier when you said I still love Bryony. I do. Not just because she's Poppy's mother, or because we should have grown old together, but because my heart belonged to her, and a part of it always will. And I think one of the most incredible things about you, is that you're not jealous of that love…"

"Of course I'm not," she interrupts. "That's how it should be. You don't have to choose between us, Kit."

I smile at her. "I know. Or at least I do now. I thought I did though. I thought I couldn't move on until I'd put Bryony, and what we had together, behind me. And I never thought I'd be able to do that. It took me a while to work out that – with you at least – I don't have to." I pause for a second, and then whisper the most important words I'll ever say, "The thing is though… as much as I love Bryony… I'm *in love* with you. Completely and utterly. Body, mind and soul. And that's different to

351

the way I feel about Bryony, because it's about now. It's about the future. *Our* future."

"You're in love… with me?" She seems unsure, like she doesn't quite believe me.

"Yes. I realise that might seem a bit difficult to comprehend, given the way I've behaved towards you, but it's the truth. I was just too caught up in the past to see what was happening right in front of my eyes. And that's the thing…"

"What is?" She still sounds kind of stunned, and I'm not sure how to interpret that.

"I know I've made mistakes with you. I didn't appreciate you, or what you do for me. But I will. I promise. Always. I didn't tell you how I feel. And I should have done. I want to now. Every single day. I didn't hold onto you. But now I don't ever want to let you go again. Not as long as I live." I step closer, resting my forehead against hers. "Life's short, Summer. I know that better than just about anyone. And I don't want to waste a single second of it." I take a breath. "I—I know you have a house of your own, and it would be easy for me to move down here, and for us to spend some time together, in the evenings and at weekends, getting to know each other a bit better… taking it slow. But that's not what I want. I don't want us to be separated, not even for a moment, not even by a patch of grass. I don't want to go to sleep without you, or wake up and find you're not right there beside me."

Her eyes are glistening, brimming with tears and I wonder if I've gone too far…

"What are you asking of me, Kit?" she says at last.

"I'm not asking you to sell your house," I reply quickly, because I'm not. That's her decision. "I'm not even asking you to move in with me… well, I suppose I am. But you don't have to straight away. Not if you're not ready. I—I know I treated you really badly, and I get that it might take you some time to fully…"

"It won't," she says, interrupting me and I frown down at her, feeling a bit confused.

"It won't what?"

"Take me any time." She sighs, shaking her head. "I'm in love with you too," she whispers. "I have been for ages."

I lean down and kiss her, tasting the hope and brightness within her… and then a saltiness as her tears tumble to our joined lips.

"Hey… you're not supposed to cry. You made me break my promise." I wipe her cheeks with my thumbs.

"You were never going to be able to keep that promise," she whispers, her voice thick with emotion. "But it's okay. These are happy tears."

"I'm glad to hear it." I kiss her swollen lips again.

"So," she says, once we eventually part, "shall we go and tell the kids?"

"Tell them what?" I'm fairly sure I'm holding my breath…

"That Roan and I are moving in here."

I let out that breath and lift her off the ground, into my arms, spinning her around and around. "You'll move in?"

"Of course I'll move in. I love you. Where else would I want to be? You're right. Life is short, and I don't want to be apart from you either."

"You don't want to give it a few days?" I ask, giving her a chance to change her mind. "You don't want to let things settle down a bit?"

"No." She shakes her head, and I lower her to the ground again.

"Positive?"

"Positive."

I suck in a breath, and because I can't help myself, because I'm so happy, I have to tease her. "So, you know you were trying to enlighten me earlier… about our future? About how things would pan out between us?" She nods her head. "Do you want to try running that by me again, now you know the plan?"

She smiles and leans into me. "Well… you and Poppy are staying," she says, a little tentatively. "And Roan and I are moving in with you… and I guess that means we'll all…"

"We'll all what?"

She blushes and looks up at me. "I was going to say 'We'll all live happily ever after', but life's not a fairy tale, is it?"

"Yes it is. From now on, that's exactly what life's going to be. A fairy tale. One with the happiest of endings. We're together, Summer, and I don't see how our future can be anything but happy."

She stands on tiptoes and kisses me. "I do love you," she says on a breath.

"I love you more," I whisper back, and for a moment we just gaze at each other.

"Do you think we ought to go and tell the children?" she suggests eventually.

"Probably."

"I don't think they'll mind somehow," she adds, smiling and looking a bit shy, for the first time, as I take her hand and lead her towards the back of the house.

"No. Neither do I."

"And once we've spoken to them, maybe we can go indoors and have a coffee?" she says. "And we can think about moving some of our things over here… and I'll make us all some lunch, if you like?"

I stop walking and turn to her. "I should probably point out that I don't actually have any food in the house. I took just about everything back to Kew with me, because I didn't think I'd be coming down here again, and I only brought enough food for last night and this morning… in case you said you didn't want to see me, and we ended up leaving straight away."

She shakes her head, although she's smiling. "I was never going to say that, but being as we all need to eat, we'll have lunch at my place, and then later on, we'll go shopping, shall we?"

"Sounds horrendous…"

"Which part?"

"The shopping… the rest of it sounds absolutely perfect." She rolls her eyes and goes to turn away, but I pull her back. "Hey… thank you."

"What for?" She looks confused.

"For giving me a second chance… and a third chance… and a fourth chance…" I hold her close to me, her body tight along the length of mine. "I promise, this is the last chance I'll ever need."

"I know," she says, leaning back slightly and looking up at me. "But we don't need to talk about that anymore. Now we need to put the past behind us, and get on with being happy."

She's right. And so I take her hand and lead my Summer… my sun… into the back garden, where Poppy and Roan are playing, underneath the big oak tree, and for a moment, we stand and watch them… the two of us, and the two of them. And then, hand in hand, we take a step forward, into our future. Together.

Epilogue

Summer

"Can you *please* stand still!"

I'm trying to fix tinsel to the Angel Gabriel's halo, and it won't stick... not helped by the fact that Neil Featherstone – who, for some reason that escapes me, was given the part of the Angel Gabriel – is jigging about, from one foot to the other.

"Do you want the toilet, Neil?" I ask, for the third time.

"No, Miss."

"Then stand still, while I try and get this straight, will you?"

He does as he's told, for once, and with the addition of a few extra strips of sticky tape, I manage to finally get the last bit of tinsel to hold firm, and standing up straight, I look around the backstage area. I think we're finally ready, which is just as well, because the nativity play is due to start in just under ten minutes.

Poppy is playing Mary, and Roan is Joseph, and I'm hugely relieved that I had no part in the casting of any of the parts, because I know I'd have been accused of favouritism. As it is, while Kit has been giving a hand with the set design, all I've had to do is rehearse, and rehearse... and rehearse some more. Oh... and answer some amusing and occasionally embarrassing questions. Jason Monmouth started it off at our first proper dress rehearsal, a couple of weeks ago. He's playing one of the shepherds, and as he was standing admiring the baby Jesus – or pretending to – he piped up with the question, "Where did Jesus actually come from?"

Miss Pettifer, who teaches year two and who's playing the piano and helping with costumes, choked on her coffee at that point, and Mrs Morris, the year six teacher, who's essentially in charge of the whole production – and who was, therefore, responsible for the casting – only made matters worse by going bright red and stuttering. I stepped in, deciding that the best bet was to stick to the Biblical version of events… that Jesus was the son of God… at which point Roan stuck his chest out and started telling everyone that he must, therefore, be God. Everyone found that highly amusing… although nowhere near as much as Kit did, when I told him about it while we prepared our evening meal that night.

Roan and I have been living with him and Poppy at Bluebells since the day they came back to Millarnick, in August. We told the children of our plans in the back garden, and although Roan was a bit confused to start with, and perhaps a little reticent about the whole idea too, because he knew Kit had hurt me, and didn't really understand what was going on, I took him to one side and told him I loved Kit – not more than I loved him, but that I loved Kit nonetheless – and I wanted us all to be together. And because he's Roan, he accepted what I said and went back to Poppy, and before I knew it, they were soon running around and whooping with excitement. We managed to finally calm them down and took them indoors, and then Roan got all excited again, when he discovered that his new bedroom was going to be right next door to Poppy's. Because heaven forbid they should be separated for more than ten seconds, it seems…

After lunch, we spent a couple of hours moving at least some of our possessions into Bluebells, much to the amazement of the rest of the villagers, some of whom stood on the edge of the green, watching us, their heads bent together, clearly trying to work out what was going on. We didn't enlighten them. And then, once we'd been shopping and filled the fridge and store cupboards, I made us a roast chicken dinner, with all the trimmings, because it was a Sunday, after all. After that, the kids fell into bed, exhausted… and finally, Kit made good on his promise to relieve me of my clothing and remind me that he hadn't really changed as much as it seemed… over, and over… and over.

Waking up next to him the following morning was a revelation. We'd fallen asleep with Kit lying on his back, his arm tight around me and my head on his chest, listening to his heartbeat slowly return to normal after our exertions. When I woke, however, we were entwined in each other, face-to-face, his arms and one of his legs enfolding me, like he didn't want to let me go. He came to a few minutes after me, and smiled the most beautiful of smiles.

"Good morning," I whispered, as he leant in closer and kissed me.

"Hmm… good morning."

His voice was husky, full of sleep, and very sexy.

"Is it always like this?" I asked, settling into his arms, enjoying the warm comfort of him.

"What?"

"Waking up with someone…" I looked up into his eyes and saw the shadow crossing them, wishing I'd kept quiet, instead of asking what had seemed like such an innocent question. *So much for 'happily ever after'*…

"Don't you know?" he replied, surprising me a little, being as I'd expected either silence, or possibly an eruption of anger, due to my own insensitivity.

"No. How would I know?"

He frowned. "You've spent the night with someone before, haven't you? Roan's father?"

"Yes… but…"

"Well, you know what it feels like to wake up next to someone." He seemed to be dismissing my question, almost like the abrupt version of Kit, turning onto his back at the same time. But because he evidently wasn't that man anymore, he kept hold of me still, pulling me with him, and I rested my head on his chest, just like I had the night before.

"No, I don't. Russell made a point of getting up before I was even awake," I explained.

He twisted slightly, looking down at me. "Roan's father's name was Russell, was it?"

"Yes."

"And he got out of bed without even waiting for you to wake up?"

"Yes."

"Idiot," he whispered under his breath, then he nodded his head and breathed deeply for a few seconds. *In, out… in, out…* "In that case, I'll answer your question…" He sighed. "No, waking up with someone isn't always like this…" His voice faded to a whisper, although the depth of emotion in his words was impossible to miss and I released myself from his grip and climbed on top of him, straddling him to start with, and then lying down along the length of him, tucking my legs inside his and letting him wrap me up again.

"I'm sorry," I whispered, and he pulled me further up his body, so our faces were at the same level, our lips almost touching.

"Don't be. There are bound to be things we say or do that remind me of Bryony, or of when we were together. It can't be helped." He managed a smile. "Waking up with her was never like this," he explained, although he didn't need to. "Bryony liked being hugged, but she'd always move back to her side of the bed when it was time to go to sleep." He shook his head, his smile widening. "She used to get really hot at night…"

"And did she like…" I started to ask, and then stopped myself.

"Did she like what?"

I sucked in a breath. "Did she like doing the things we do?"

He hesitated. "Not in the same way, no," he said eventually. He closed his eyes then, just for a moment, and let out the longest sigh. "Making love with Bryony was very different. She was kind of fragile, even before she was sick. I guess I treated her with a certain amount of delicacy."

"And I'm not fragile?" I asked, wondering how he saw me.

"In a way, yes." He ran his fingertips down the side of my face. "I know I could break you… I came too close to doing so, not to know that… so yes, you're fragile. But in bed, you're very different. In bed, you… you burn, Summer."

"In a good way?" I wasn't sure what he meant by that, and it seemed important to know.

He smiled. "Oh God, yes." He paused and then said, "I used to dream about you… all the time. I still do."

"Really?"

He nodded. "Yes. Every night, from the very first moment I met you. And back then, my dreams were very… disturbing."

"Oh. That doesn't sound so good."

His smile returned and he ran his hand down my back, letting it settle on my behind. "They were also very arousing," he added, and I couldn't help smiling at that. "I used to dream of taking you so hard, of claiming your body, controlling you."

"And what's wrong with that?" I asked him, and then my voice dropped as I whispered, "I—I like that about you…"

"I know you do," he replied. "And there's nothing wrong with it. Except, I'd never done anything like that in my life, before I met you. So dreaming of you in that way confused the hell out of me. I wanted you so much, it was all I could think about, but I couldn't work out why my dreams… my thoughts… of making love to you were so different to anything that had gone before – even with Bryony – until…"

"Until what?"

"Until we actually made love, that night in your back garden, and I realised that I'd found the real me… or rather, you had."

"The real you?" I queried, because it sounded so… well, *un*real.

"Yes." He nodded his head and sighed again. "I'm not saying I was unhappy with Bryony. I wasn't. And if she hadn't been taken from me, then I'd still be with her, I'd still be in love with her, and her alone, and nothing would have changed that. But she *was* taken from me… and meeting you was a revelation. You allowed me be me, Summer."

I cupped his cheek in my hand. "No… that's not the case at all. It had nothing to do with me *allowing* you to do anything. It was about you letting yourself be happy and free enough to understand who you really are."

"And I'd never have done any of that without you."

"Yes, you would. And besides, life's a journey, Kit. It's all about finding out new things about each other and about ourselves, every single day. It's about having new adventures and making new discoveries."

Without saying a word, he rolled me over onto my back, raising himself above me and gazing into my eyes.

"You're not part of my journey, Summer. You're my destination," he said, his voice low and throaty.

"I hope so." He nodded his head, in silent confirmation. "But that doesn't mean you have to forget the path you took to get here."

He leant down onto his elbows, his face just above mine.

"I won't," he said softly. "I can't. I can't ever forget her…"

"I don't want you to."

"God… you're so good for me," he groaned and then kissed me, long and hard, and took a little while demonstrating, yet again, that he hadn't changed in the slightest.

And he really hasn't. He's still the man I fell in love with, anyway… he's just less troubled. At least most of the time. Every so often, I'll catch him staring off into the distance, and sometimes I'll leave him alone with his thoughts and memories, if I think that's what he needs; and other times, I'll go and sit with him, and hold his hand, and let him talk, if he wants to. He knows I'm here, if he needs me, and he knows I'll gladly listen to anything he wants to tell me. Sometimes, he marvels, that I don't 'mind' about Bryony, telling me that he's fairly sure he would if things were the other way around. But as I keep reminding him, how can I possibly mind? Bryony was Poppy's mother. And, more importantly, she helped make Kit the man he is… the man I love. And for that alone, I welcome her presence in our lives.

We don't look back that often, and we don't dwell in the past either. We spend a lot of time smiling and laughing. And it's been good to see Kit so happy at last.

He even managed to stay happy during those first few weeks, when Roan was being a bit difficult. 'A bit' might be an understatement, actually, but having appeared to accept our decision to live together, he went all protective on me again, literally the very next day. He took to ignoring Kit, unless he absolutely had to talk to him, and seemed to be waiting for him to slip up. Kit and I talked about it a lot, and although I wondered if I should speak to Roan, Kit vetoed the idea and said we should just let him come to terms with the situation in his own time… And he did. And it didn't even take that long, either. Not really. He just needed to see us together, to realise and understand that there's no way Kit will ever hurt me again. And once he'd come to terms with that, the rest was simple… and really rather joyous. The breakthrough, if you can call it that, came one afternoon, after school, when we were at the playground, a few weeks after we moved in to Bluebells, and while Poppy was on one of the swings, with me pushing her, Roan yelled out, "Hey, Kit… look at me!" as he raced down the slide. I froze and so did Kit, and I wanted to cry, because my son had finally chosen to include the man I love in his own small pleasures. I know Kit was affected by it too, because once Roan had reached the bottom of the slide and turned to run back for another go, Kit turned around and bowed his head, and I knew he was finding that moment quite hard. It was only a simple gesture, made in childish innocence, but it meant the world to both of us.

Kit's first job after we'd moved in, was to convert his father's studio into an office, which didn't take much doing in the end, and then, after the first couple of weeks of sleeping in the guest room, we decided to remodel the master bedroom, making it even more romantic, I think, taking out the built-in wardrobes, painting the walls a slightly off-white, dotting them with local paintings, and fitting sheer white curtains at the large picture window. Kit stripped the floor and varnished it, and then bought an enormous bed, which has pride of place in the centre of the room, and that's become our own special bubble now, a space where we can both be ourselves. He also insisted that we have an en-suite shower room installed. The bedroom is big enough to accommodate it, and I have to admit, I'd grown used to having our own bathroom in the guest bedroom. It certainly made the mornings quicker. What I hadn't anticipated was the size of the shower that Kit had insisted on… and

I didn't appreciate why, until it was completed and he suggested we should 'christen it' together.

He had my leg raised up, bent over his arm, and was poised, about to enter me, when he stopped and whispered, "I dreamt this once."

I looked up at him. "What? Doing this, in a shower?"

"Yes."

I smiled. "Is that why you had this built?" I asked, glancing around the white tiled room. "So you could make your dreams come true?"

His face darkened then and he let my leg fall, clasping my cheeks between his hands. "I don't ever want that dream to come true," he whispered.

"Why not?" There was a look on his face that had me confused, and slightly concerned.

"Because in my dream, after I'd made love to you, you left me. You ran away. And no matter how hard I tried to catch up with you, you kept on going."

I raised my own hands now, putting them on either side of his neck. "I never have left you though, have I?"

"No. But I had that dream on the night Poppy and I got back here… the night I saw you with that guy…"

"Drew, you mean?"

"Yeah. I—I thought I'd lost you."

I could hear the emotion in his voice. "I told you then, and I'll tell you again now, you never lost me." I stood up on tiptoes and kissed him. "And you never will."

He smiled then and turned me around, so I was facing the tiled wall, parting my feet with his, own, his hands on my hips, pulling me back towards him and then bending me over at the waist. He leant over me. "*This* is nothing like my dream," he whispered, nudging his arousal against my entrance.

I sighed deeply at the welcome intrusion. "It feels like a dream come true to me..."

We haven't done much work on the rest of the house. We haven't really had the time yet. We've, been far too busy being happy. The smaller spare room is piled full of odds and ends from Kit's house in Kew, and from my cottage across the other side of the green... things we both wanted to keep close to us, but haven't yet found a home for. And the guest bedroom, which we shared so briefly, is now free for whenever Ruth and Edward come to visit... which they do. A lot.

Roan and I first met them in October, during the half term, when Kit took us up to their home in Barnes to meet them. He spoke to me about it at length before we went, and told me that he didn't want us to stay at his house in Kew. He used the excuse of it being 'under offer', but I knew he felt awkward about the fact that it had been his and Bryony's home, and I think he was concerned about how I might react to that. I wouldn't have minded being there with him, but I wanted him to feel comfortable with the situation, and I knew he didn't. So, we stayed at Ruth and Edward's, and they were absolutely lovely, making us feel at home straight away, like Roan and I had always been part of their family.

During that trip, Poppy also insisted on going to her hairdresser, who's based in Kew, not far from Kit's house. I'd tried reasoning with her – as had Kit – that there are perfectly good hairdressers in Looe, but she was adamant she wanted to go to 'Marissa', and in the end, I didn't see the harm and booked the appointment for her, once Kit had reluctantly given me the name of the salon. I questioned his continued reticence, but all he would say was that he couldn't see why she couldn't get her hair cut locally. I was inclined to agree, but it didn't seem like a big deal to me, being as we were going to be up there anyway.

The night before we were due to travel up to London, Kit and I were lying in bed, and I could sense he was really uneasy about something. Assuming it was our meeting with Ruth and Edward, I started talking to him about that, telling him not to worry, and that everything would be fine.

"It's not that," he said eventually, turning to face me and pulling me closer to him.

"Then what is it? What's worrying you?"

"It's Marissa."

"Who's Marissa?"

"Poppy's hairdresser?" he reminded me.

"Oh. What about her?"

"She's... um..."

"She's um what?" I didn't know why he couldn't just say what was wrong. "Is she no good at cutting Poppy's hair, because if that's the case..."

"No, she's really good with Poppy's hair," he interrupted, letting out a long sigh.

"Then what is it?" Even as I said the words, a thought dawned on me. "Is she someone I should know about, preferably before I actually come face-to-face with her? I mean, did something happen between you?"

"God, no." His answer was surprisingly quick, but then he added, "The only woman I've been with since Bryony, is Gabrielle... and you know all about that."

"Then I don't understand..."

"I think she *wanted* something to happen," he said, quietening down a little, and talking in a whisper again, although the children were fast asleep in their bedrooms on the other side of the house. "She... she used to flirt with me. A lot."

I tried not to laugh, because he didn't seem to be finding the situation very amusing. "Can I take it you didn't feel the same way?"

"No. I didn't."

I nodded my head. "So, are you saying you'd rather not go tomorrow? Because I hate to break this to you, but that would be really cowardly... and also, I don't know where this hairdressing salon is, so I can hardly take Poppy by myself."

"I'm not saying that at all," he whispered, kissing me gently. "I—I suppose I just thought I should warn you, being as I assumed we'd all be going. I didn't think you'd want me to leave you with Edward and Ruth when you'd only just met them, so I guessed you'd come with us to the hairdressers, but I have no idea how Marissa will react to me..." His voice faded and I reached up, cupping his face with my hand.

"I'm sure I'll cope."

"I don't doubt that... not for one minute."

As it turned out, Marissa didn't flirt with him, although she did look rather crestfallen by my presence, especially when Poppy introduced me as her 'daddy's girlfriend', which made Kit and I smile. She styled Poppy's hair beautifully, but when Kit was paying her, she asked him whether Poppy would be coming back again and he said he didn't think it was likely, explaining that they were living in Cornwall now... with me and Roan. Marissa smiled – or attempted to – and told him she was pleased. I'm not sure she meant that, but it was nice of her to say it. And I felt sorry for her. She clearly liked Kit a lot... and I couldn't blame her for that.

On the way back to Edward and Ruth's, Kit seemed relieved and explained quietly to me while the children were talking in the back of the car, that Marissa used to be 'all over' him, and how uncomfortable that had made him.

"I don't know why. She's very beautiful."

"Is she?"

"Yes. Hadn't you noticed?"

He shook his head. "I was fairly dead to everything back then, Summer. I didn't notice very much at all. Not until I met you. You lit up my world."

My breath caught in my throat and I put my hand on his leg, watching as he covered it with his own. "That's a lovely thing to say, Kit."

"It's true. You did light up my world. But then, you also messed with my head, and had me tied up in knots, so..."

"Well... we can't all be perfect," I teased.

"Yes, you can. You are. You're perfect for me." He gave my hand a squeeze, then turned and winked at me, before putting his hand back on the steering wheel and driving us back to Ruth and Edward's.

We had a lovely weekend with them, and they've been to visit us twice since. They're a very special couple. Ruth looks like Bryony. I know that, because we have pictures of her around the house, which Kit brought back with him from Kew. Edward, on the other hand, has completely different colouring. His hair is blond, without a trace of grey, and he obviously enjoys being outside a lot, as he seems to have a year-round tan. They're staying with us now, actually, because they wanted to see Poppy in the nativity play, although they made a point of saying they were here to see Roan too, which was lovely of them. They've kind of adopted him as an honorary grandson, and I love them for that… and for the love they show Kit, and Poppy… and me, for that matter. They're kind and generous people, and it's easy to see how Kit could have loved their daughter as much as he did… as much as he does.

Kit's had to go up to London a few times since we moved in with him. The first time was quite soon after we'd made our life-changing decisions, because he had to put his house on the market, and collect some more of their clothes, and bring back his computers, so he could work, being as, in between everything else, he had a fairly big project to undertake for a client called Alan Langley. He also needed to see Bryony's parents. He had to tell them about us, about what was going on; he felt he owed them that much at least, considering everything they'd done for him and Poppy, and especially considering that our decision was going to mean him moving their granddaughter several hundred miles away. In typical Ruth and Edward style, they took his news with great grace. Not that I think Kit expected anything different.

He's been back since to see clients, and to finish packing up his house, and on those occasions, he's had to stay up there – not in Kew, but with Ruth and Edward. A young couple put in an offer for his house within two weeks of it going on the market, for the eye-watering price Kit had expected, and the sale completed in the middle of November. He's got a very nice nest egg in the bank now… although he insists on referring to it as 'our' nest egg, whenever the subject comes up, and while I don't agree with that description, I do like the fact that he no longer has to worry about his work drying up. He just gets on with it… and with loving me. Which he does. Very often. And in his very own way.

As for my own house, we've spent ages trying to decide what to do about it. Kit joked at the beginning, when he first came back, that I should maybe keep it as a bolt-hole for when I needed to escape from him. But I vetoed that idea straight away, dragging him into the kitchen while the children were watching a DVD, over a large bowl of popcorn, and telling him in no uncertain terms, that I never want to escape him. I never did – not even when I pushed him away. He apologised for making a joke in such poor taste and we sat at the table and talked through my options more seriously. We didn't reach any conclusions before it was time to start making dinner though… and we still haven't, even now. The problem is, while I don't need the house anymore, it was my mother's home too, and I'm struggling to come to terms with the idea of selling it. It's like a last link with her… and I'm not ready to break it yet. Kit understands that, and doesn't pressure me to make a decision. Because he understands grief better than anyone I know.

The applause rings out and I stand in the wings, smiling and clapping the children, feeling just a little bit proud, and stealing a glance at the front row, where I know Kit is sitting with Ruth and Edward. They're all grinning and cheering, their eyes focused on Poppy and Roan, who are standing, centre stage, taking a bow. Roan in particular is milking the applause of the very appreciative and probably slightly partisan audience. But that doesn't surprise me in the slightest. He is, after all, a Leo, and a show-off. In the nicest possible way.

I'm reminded of all the times my mum used to watch him, with a smile on her face, and although my eyes cloud over with tears, I have to smile too, because I'm also remembering how Kit has helped me to come to terms with so many of those 'firsts'. Like our first bonfire night without her, when he convinced me to carry on with Mum's tradition of making a hot, warming soup for us to come home to… and our Christmas preparations at home, when he's occasionally noticed a sadness in me, and has held me tight and told me it's okay. He's never pretended that it gets any easier, but he's never made me feel bad for sometimes missing her so much it hurts either.

We'll be going back home soon, once I've made sure that all the children have been collected by their parents, and have cleared up behind the scenes a bit. And then we'll sit down together at the big table in Maggie's kitchen… well, our kitchen now… and we'll eat the stew that Ruth prepared earlier. And then Kit says he's got a surprise in store for me. I have no idea what it is, but I can't wait. Because so far, his surprises have never been disappointing… and neither has he.

And I know he never will be.

Kit

Every so often, I wonder if I should feel guilty. But I can't. I don't. I lived with guilt for so long, it became a normal part of my existence, but now it's a part of my past. It's history. I've shaken off the mantle of sadness now. Yes, I still have moments when I think about Bryony. I even have moments when I occasionally wonder 'what if', or I find myself in a kind of trance, my mind wandering back to a different time and place. And sometimes I'll just snap out of it of my own accord, and other times, Summer will come and find me, and she'll sit with me and let me talk, because she somehow knows that the grief is still there, and that it probably will be for a while to come… or maybe forever. Who knows?

The point is, I don't beat myself up over any of it. Not these days. Because grief and guilt and sadness don't dominate my life anymore. Summer does. She makes me so happy. She makes me complete. She understands me and she lets me be myself, and I suppose that's what loving someone is all about really. Loving them enough to let them be themselves. And I love her so much too, because of all of that, and more. Just looking at her is all I could ever ask for, and it would be more than enough for me. But as it is, I get to wake up beside her, and hold her while she sleeps, and make love to her, whenever she wants. And it seems she wants to quite a lot, which is good, because even four months after I came back here and she let me talk to her, and agreed to give me another chance, and told me that she loved me... which I have to admit I hadn't expected... even after we told the kids about our plans and we all went shopping together, and Summer cooked us dinner, while I watched her, in a bit of a daze, and then we hurriedly put the children to bed, before I carried her upstairs and made love to her... taking her even harder than I did the first time, pouring my love and my need into her... even now, all these months later, I still can't believe my luck. And I still can't get enough of her.

She still haunts my dreams. Every. Single. Night.

Only now I get to make them come true.

The nativity play finished a couple of hours ago, and at Summer's insistence, Ruth, Edward and I brought the kids home, while Summer stayed behind to finish clearing up. I offered to help her, but she said she wouldn't be long, and I think she sensed the kids might be happier if I was with them... well, Roan might, anyway. He gets on really well with Ruth and Edward and they love him to bits, but it's early days, and he's still finding his feet with them. He's used to being by himself, with Summer, so he can take his time to let strangers in. It's understandable.

After that wondrous weekend when I came back here, and Summer let me back into her life, I knew I'd have to go and tell Ruth and Edward of my plans, so I drove to Barnes the following Friday, after a slightly crazy, very busy, and utterly satisfying week with Summer. I needed to see the estate agent about putting my house on the market, and I had to pick up my desktop computer and large screens, so I could actually keep earning a living. And Poppy needed her school things and some extra clothes. But visiting Ruth and Edward was the main reason for my visit. They weren't surprised when I told them my plans, although I know they were disappointed that we'd be living so far away. They hid it well, but I could see in their eyes how much they were going to miss Poppy... and me, I think, and they made a point of telling me to bring Summer and Roan for a visit as soon as possible.

What with school and work and getting to know each other, and falling a little bit more in love every day, it was the October half term before I drove us all up to Barnes for our first visit. We went for the weekend, driving up after school on the Friday afternoon, and staying until the Sunday lunchtime… and it went amazingly well.

I think Summer was nervous about that first meeting and obviously, we could have stayed at my house in Kew, rather than with Ruth and Edward, because although the agent found a buyer really quickly, the sale hadn't completed by then. But I didn't want Summer to feel even more on edge, by having to sleep in the bed I'd shared with Bryony. She's been so understanding about everything else, there was no way I was going to ask that of her. And besides, I knew everyone would be fine together and staying with Ruth and Edward meant they could spend more of the weekend with Poppy, and that they had plenty of time to get to know Summer and Roan, even if Poppy did insist on a visit to the hairdressers on the Saturday afternoon, which took a chunk out of our visit.

That went better than expected too, simply because Summer was with me. Obviously her presence curtailed Marissa's flirting, but Summer just makes me feel better anyway. Every moment of the day.

The next morning, while Edward was showing Summer round the garden, Ruth and I had a chat in the kitchen, looking out of the window at them, and she told me I'd done the right thing. Not that I needed telling.

"She's so good for you," she whispered, even though we were alone in the house, being as Poppy and Roan were outside too, exploring in the garden somewhere.

"I know. I tell her that quite often, actually. And I do appreciate how lucky I am."

"You are. And don't forget it." She gave me a knowing look then, because she understood better than anyone how close I'd come to losing it all. "She's really good with Poppy too," she added.

"She is."

"And how do you get on with Roan?" she asked.

"We're okay. It was scratchy to start with. He knew I'd hurt Summer, and he was being protective of her."

She smiled. "I like that," she said wistfully, and then looked up at me. "You have a lovely family, Kit. Take care of them." I heard the crack in her voice, and put my arm around her, giving her a hug, because I knew how hard that had been for her to say.

Roan and I had been scratchy to start with. I had hurt his mum and in his eyes, I had a long way to go to redeem myself. He took a few weeks before he was prepared to start really including me in things, and to start with, he wouldn't refer to me by my name, or even talk to me very much, or ask me direct questions, getting Summer to ask them for him instead. That was hard... for both of us. But we kept talking, and waiting, and eventually it happened, and the moment he yelled out to me at the playground, because he wanted me to watch him... *me*, not Summer... that was something very special indeed, and it brought a lump to my throat, and tears to Summer's eyes, because she'd felt his reserve just as much as I had.

That was the first major breakthrough for us, and since then, Roan has turned to me more often, for explanations, or help with spellings and sums, or just when he wants to talk, or ask the random questions he's prone to do. And I like that.

I especially liked it, about two or three weeks ago, after the first dress rehearsal of the nativity play, when Summer came home with Roan and Poppy and told me about how one of the other boys had asked where baby Jesus came from. I laughed out loud while she went through her story, explaining how a couple of other teachers had fumbled their way around things, and she'd finally told the boy that Jesus was the son of God... at which point Roan, who's been chosen to play Joseph, evidently started crowing about being God. The story had me in fits of laughter, especially when Roan came into the room and chose that moment to pull out a kitchen chair and climb up on to it, holding out his arms and telling us all that we had to do what he said, because he was God. Summer dragged him off the chair and reminded him that actually, he was Joseph... or in reality, he was Roan, and he needed to go and wash his hands before dinner. Which he duly did.

When he returned, he was more serious, and over dinner, he suddenly put down his knife and fork, and asked, "Was God really the baby Jesus's daddy?"

I looked at Summer and decided this was best left to her. Not being religious and not being a teacher, I felt out of my depth. She sucked in a breath and said, "Yes," although she pulled a face at the same time, as though she felt awkward giving that answer.

"Then what's Joseph got to do with anything?" he asked, frowning. "If he isn't the baby's dad, why does he even need to be there?"

Although he seemed to be referring to the play, and his role in it, I wondered if, in reality, this was something to do with his real dad, and the fact that he'd never been there… and whether my presence was making him think more about that, or perhaps if something had been said to him at school, in the past, about him not having a father, or whether, like Poppy, he'd just noticed at some point that his home life was different to most of his friends. Either way, I looked at Summer and saw her biting her bottom lip, clearly a little unsure how to respond to him.

"Sometimes real daddies don't stay with their children," I replied, stepping into the breach. "For all kinds of reasons. Real mummies too." I glanced at Summer and she gave me an encouraging smile. "Sometimes they choose to leave, and sometimes things happen to take them away from their children." Roan nodded his head, as though he understood what I was saying. "But then sometimes, those children are really lucky and another mummy or daddy comes along…"

"But they're not the *real* mummy or daddy?" he said, seemingly still confused.

"No… but being a real mummy or daddy isn't just about…" I wasn't sure how to phrase the next bit, so I went with, "… being there at the beginning, when the baby is born," deciding he could relate to that, or at least equate it to his role in the play, if nothing else. "It's about being there every single day. Good and bad. No matter what. Because that's what mums and dads do."

He stared at me then, and I wondered what he was going to say next.

Except he didn't say anything. He just pursed his lips for a moment, nodded his head, and then got on with eating his sausages and mash.

Summer and I shrugged at each other, and finished our meals too.

Roan can be like that sometimes. I worked that out pretty quickly. He's a thinker. And you just have to go with it.

"I really like it that you've got pictures of Bryony on show," Ruth says, nodding towards the photographs on the sideboard and taking a sip of her tea as we wait for Summer to come back. Poppy and Roan are both upstairs, still in their nativity outfits, because they seemed to want to stay in them, and I couldn't see the harm, and when they asked, I said they didn't have to change, not until Summer got home, anyway, when one or other of us would probably get them ready for bed.

"That was Summer's idea, not mine," I confess and she turns to look at me, her surprise obvious.

"It was?"

"Yes. When I was about to go up to Kew to finish packing up the house, I wasn't sure what to do with all the photographs I had of Bryony, and I prevaricated for ages. I didn't want to ask Summer if it was okay to bring them, and yet I didn't feel like I could throw them away."

"So what did you do?" Edward asks.

"I didn't do anything. Summer did. She guessed something was wrong... and then she even managed to work out what it was."

"How?" I can see the confusion in Ruth's eyes.

"Because I told her I was having trouble deciding what to bring, and what to dispose of. That was as much as I could bring myself to say."

"And she worked it out from that?"

"Yes. And she sat me down and told me that she wanted me to bring back all the photographs and keepsakes I had of Bryony. She was insistent about it. She wanted to have Bryony's presence in our home... in our lives." I can remember her saying it. I can remember the look in her eyes at the time... it was a look of pure love.

"She *wanted* it? You mean for Poppy's sake?"

"Not just for Poppy's sake... for mine too. Summer doesn't want me to feel as though I have to consign Bryony to history. She knows I'll always love her, and she wants her in our present."

They both stare at me for a moment, and then Ruth whispers, "How remarkable…"

I smile across at her. "Yes I know. But then Summer is quite a remarkable person."

I pick up my own tea and am just about to take a sip when the front door opens, a chilly draft wafting through the house.

"I'm home!" Summer calls out, and I put my tea back down again, getting up and going out into the hall to greet her. She smiles up at me as she takes off her coat, and I lean down and give her a kiss. A long, slow, sensual kiss.

"You look tired," I whisper, releasing her.

"I'm exhausted."

I hope she's not too exhausted, because I've got plans for tonight… big plans.

"Too exhausted?" I ask, leaning into her.

"No." She smiles up at me. "I haven't forgotten your surprise. I'm intrigued by it, but I haven't forgotten it."

"Good." I kiss her again, and then take her hand, leading her back into the formal living room, which we actually use quite a lot now, where Ruth and Edward smile up at her, with even more enthusiasm than usual. And I suppose that isn't that surprising, given our earlier conversation.

"The play was marvellous," Ruth says from her seat in the chair by the window.

"I love doing them," Summer replies, sitting down at one end of the sofa. I join her, keeping hold of her hand, because I rarely let her go, unless I absolutely have to. "But they're nerve wracking."

"Nerve wracking?" Edward queries.

"Oh yes… you never know what children of that age are going to do." Summer smiles. "At my old school, we had squabbles breaking out amongst the shepherds, and then the Angel Gabriel punched Joseph right in the middle of *Away in a Manger*, because he liked the little girl who was playing Mary, and Joseph had been holding her hand for the previous twenty minutes. It didn't help that the boy playing Joseph then picked up the doll we were using as the baby Jesus and threw it at the Angel Gabriel, knocking his halo off, and causing a general furore."

Ruth's giggling quietly to herself. "Good heavens. How on earth do you cope?"

"I love it," Summer says, smiling. "I love the excitement of Christmas for the children and doing the nativity play is just a part of it. It's hard work, but worth it in the end. And they can be terribly funny… in hindsight."

She looks up at me and smiles, and I wonder if she's remembering Roans's exploits from the dress rehearsal, just as Roan and Poppy come running into the room. As I suspected, they're still dressed as Mary and Joseph, even down to their headdresses.

"Haven't you changed yet?" Summer says, glancing at them, and then back at me again.

"Dad said we didn't have to," Roan replies and we all fall completely silent, turning to him. He looks at each of us in turn. "What?" he says, becoming self conscious, and I'm aware of Summer stifling a sob beside me, and as much as I long to hold her, there's only one place I need to be right now. So, I give her hand a squeeze and get up, going straight to Roan and lifting him into my arms, hugging him tight.

He pulls away slightly, gazing over at his mother, who has tears falling down her cheeks.

"Come here," I say to her, and she stands and almost stumbles across the living room, joining us.

"What's wrong?" Roan says, eyeing me suspiciously. "Did you make Mum cry again?"

I smile at him. "No. Actually, buddy… you did."

He gasps. "I—I…didn't do anything." He's dumbfounded.

"It's okay," I say quickly. "Don't worry. Your mum's fine. She's crying happy tears. I promise."

"She is?"

He seems a bit confused, but I can understand that. I get confused myself sometimes, and I've had a lot more experience of women and tears than he has.

Summer is completely speechless and just stands beside us, trying very hard to control her emotions.

"Daddy?" I look down and realise Poppy's standing there, looking at the three of us, slightly left out of this moment, and I crouch down next to her, keeping hold of Roan and balancing him on my knee.

"What's wrong, sweetheart?"

"Are you Roan's daddy too now?" she asks, her eyes wide.

"If that's what Roan wants."

Summer and I both turn to Roan, and she kneels, so we've formed a kind of circle, all of us gazing at her son.

"Well?" she asks, looking at him. "Is that what you want?"

"Yes," he says simply, and I feel my heart swell in my chest.

"And does that mean Summer's my mummy?" Poppy's voice stills the room to a silence even greater than Roan's did.

Summer actually sobs loudly this time, and everything becomes a blur for me.

I didn't see that coming. God knows why. But I didn't.

I can't speak, and it seems neither can Summer, and the silence stretches, until I become aware of a shadow behind me, blocking the light from the hallway.

"Do you want Summer to be your mummy?" Ruth says gently, and I try to swallow down the lump in my throat, holding my breath at the same time.

"My real mummy died, didn't she?" Poppy sounds bemused... questioning.

"Yes," Ruth replies, her voice cracking.

I manage to blink away the tears that are forming in my eyes and focus on my daughter, noting that Summer is closer to her now.

"Poppy," she says softly, taking her tiny hands. "It's okay... if you'd rather just keep calling me Summer, I really don't mind."

Poppy gazes up at her and then looks straight at me. "Would it be okay, Daddy?" she says, her bottom lip trembling.

"Would what be okay?" I ask, finding my voice at last.

"If Summer was my new mummy?"

Oh God... I take a deep breath.

"It would be perfect," Ruth says from behind me, filling the gap that I can't, and I feel her hand on my shoulder, and reach up, placing my own over hers. "Your mummy would have loved this, Poppy. This was exactly what she wanted for you. And for your daddy."

And with that, Poppy flings herself at Summer, who catches my daughter and holds onto her.

Dinner this evening has been very emotional.

Edward and Ruth have been incredible. Utterly incredible.

That whole scene in the living room must have been hugely difficult for them, but they held it together far better than either Summer or I did, and then went and finished preparing the dinner, leaving the four of us to sit on the couch, side by side. And while Summer and I held hands, her head resting on my shoulder, the children decided that, if I'm their daddy and Summer's their mummy, then that makes them brother and sister… and while that doesn't stop them from being friends, they both seemed to like the idea of being a family much more.

Once we've finished eating, Summer and I having steered the conversation away from 'mummies and daddies' too much, for Ruth and Edward's sake if nothing else, Summer takes the children upstairs to get them ready for bed, and I turn to Ruth.

"Are you okay with this… with what happened?"

She smiles. "Of course. I told you, before you came back here, that you needed to find someone to make you happy, and to make Poppy happy. And you've done that. Perfectly. I meant what I said. This is exactly what Bryony would have wanted."

She's right. I know she is, and I feel the relief wash over me. "In which case… as the grandparents to our two children, how would you feel about babysitting?"

"When?" Ruth asks.

"Now. Tonight." She raises her eyebrows and I smile at her. "I've got a surprise planned for Summer. I planned it before any of this happened, and… well, in order for me to carry it out, I need to take her somewhere."

Ruth grins. "And when will you be back?"

"If all goes well, in the morning…?" I phrase my answer as a question, because I know I'm asking a lot.

"And if all doesn't go well?" Edward asks.

"Probably about ten minutes after we leave." They both laugh. "I —I have something I need to ask Summer," I explain. "And we need some time to ourselves for me to do that."

Ruth's grin widens, and I think she understands. "Oh… in that case, we'd be delighted to babysit."

I get up and go around the table to her. "Thank you," I whisper, giving her a hug. "And wish me luck."

She looks up at me. "Why do you need luck? You already have all the love you need… and that's all that matters."

"It's absolutely freezing out here." Summer looks up at me as we set off across the green. I've got my arm around her and I tighten my grip to keep her warm. The ground is a bit wet underfoot, but we've both got on thick soled shoes and jeans, and heavy coats, and Summer's wearing a scarf, pulled up around her neck as well. "Where are we going?" she asks.

"It's a surprise."

"Oh yes. Of course it it." She smiles and I lean into her. "Mind you, I'm not sure I've got the energy for any more surprises… not after the evening we've had."

I hope she's up to just one more surprise, because this has taken me quite a while to plan. Even so, I have to agree with her. "It has been kind of emotional, hasn't it?"

"It was hard enough when Roan called you 'Dad', but when Summer asked if I'd be her new mummy… I thought my heart was going to burst."

"I know. I felt the same."

She looks up at me, leaning back slightly, even though my arm is still around her. "You are okay with it all, aren't you?"

"I'm more than okay with it."

"And Bryony? Do you think she'd have been okay too?"

I stop walking for a second and pull her close to me. "Yes. Ruth was right. This was exactly what Bryony wanted. She told me so often enough, before she died, and while I didn't necessarily want to hear it at the time, I know that what we've got now is just what she wished for us. It couldn't get any better..." *Except for what I'm about to do... I hope that will make it just that tiny bit more perfect.*

"I won't ever let Poppy forget her," Summer whispers.

"I know."

"And I know she's still in here." She places her hand on my chest, right over my heart.

"She is. But she's a memory, Summer. Nothing more. She's a very happy, very lovely memory. You're my here and now. You're my future." I stop talking, before I blow the whole plan, and we start walking again.

"Are we going to my house?" Summer asks, once our direction becomes clear.

"Yes."

She looks up at me again, frowning this time. "Why?"

"Wait and see. You're worse than the children."

She giggles and I open the garden gate and let her in, allowing her to lead the way up the garden path, before I unlock the front door and we pass inside.

"It's warm in here," she says, unwinding her scarf from around her neck.

"I know. I came over earlier and turned the heating up."

"Why?"

I shake my head. "So many questions..."

She narrows her eyes at me, but I don't say a word and flick on the lights instead. "Are we stopping?" she asks, still clutching her scarf in her hands.

"Yes."

"Oh... in that case..." She kicks off her shoes and unzips her coat, hooking it up. I copy her, and then take her hand.

"I wanted to bring you over here because I've had an idea."

"Okay."

"I—I know you've been struggling over what to do with this place." I look around the living room. "And I wondered how you'd feel about renting it out."

She frowns. "We talked about that," she says, confused. "I said…"

"I know," I interrupt her. "I know we talked about finding a long-term tenant, but I'm talking about something else. I'm talking about turning it into a holiday let."

"Oh… I hadn't thought about that."

I move closer to her, cupping her face with my hand. "I've been giving it some thought, and I was wondering if we could maybe let it out, but make sure to keep at least one weekend free every month."

Her brow furrows. "Why?"

I smile down at her, moving closer, so our bodies are melded together. "Because we can arrange to get Ruth and Edward to come down…"

"And stay here? Why? They're perfectly happy staying with us, aren't they?"

I shake my head, then rest it against hers. "Yes. But that's not what I was suggesting. I was thinking that we could get them to come down, and they could babysit for us… and we could come over here and spend a night together… all by ourselves. Just the two of us. We've never been able to do that, Summer, and I think it would be…" I sigh into her. "Magical."

She gazes up at me. "I like that idea," she whispers and leans up, kissing me. I return the kiss, deepening it and pushing her back against the wall, holding her there.

"I'm glad to hear it," I murmur eventually, "because I've told Ruth we won't be back until the morning."

A blush creeps up her cheeks. "You have?"

"Yes."

"Oh." She breathes the word out on a sigh. "So we've got the whole night, all to ourselves?"

"Yes. And I want to take you so damn hard right now." She bites her bottom lip, her eyes widening, and her momentary shyness forgotten, it seems, and I step away from her, because as much as I want to take her – and I do – making love in her living room isn't part of my plan. I hold out my hand to her. "Come with me?"

She smiles up at me and pushes herself off the wall, then takes my hand and lets me lead her to the stairs, where I flick off the lights again, and she follows me up to the landing and into her bedroom.

I'd already closed the curtains in here, when I came over earlier, so I go in ahead of her and turn on the bedside lamp, and I wait as she takes in the sight before her, letting out a soft gasp, when she sees the what I've done.

The bed is made up with crisp white bedding, on top of which I've scattered red rose petals, and lying in the centre of it all, is a tiny black box.

"Kit?" she says, looking at me, and I walk slowly back to her, taking her hands in mine and pulling her into the room and across to the bed, where I lean over and pick up the box, opening it and turning it around for her to see the white gold solitaire diamond ring, nestling against the deep blue velvet cushion. I take it out, holding it between my thumb and forefinger, letting the box drop to the floor and looking into her eyes, which are glistening with unshed tears.

I take a breath myself, because I know I have to tell her how I feel, and I know it won't be easy.

"You saved me, Summer." She tilts her head and opens her mouth, but I place my fingers over her lips to silence her. "You. Saved. Me. I was lost. I was desperate. And you saved me. You gave me so many chances, when I didn't deserve even one. And I will never, ever, be able to repay you for what you've done for me."

She grabs my wrist and pulls my hand away from her mouth. "There's nothing to repay, Kit," she says softly, blinking back her tears.

"Yes, there is. You've made me a better father, and a better man than I could ever have been without you. And I love you more and more, with every passing day. I need you to be mine… always. So… please, please… say you'll marry me?" My voice is starting to break up and Summer moves closer, her fingertips caressing my cheek as she looks up into my eyes.

"You don't owe me anything," she whispers, her own voice betraying her heightened emotions. "Whatever I did – if I did anything – I did because I love you. And nothing would make me happier than to be yours… always."

"Is that a 'yes'?" I ask when she stops talking.

"Yes." She nods, smiling, even as a tear hits her cheek, and I lean down and kiss it away, before I take her left hand and place the ring on her finger. It fits, thank God, and she stares down at it for a moment, before returning her gaze to my face.

"If I believed in a life hereafter, I could just imagine our mothers raising a glass, and laughing their heads off right about now…" I mutter, moving closer to her.

She nods, smiling. "And Bryony?" she says, tilting her head.

"Oh… she'd be sitting there with them, saying something like, 'I told him he'd be happy again, and he didn't believe me,'." I brush my lips against hers. "And I didn't. Not until I met you."

I turn her around and lower her to the bed, crawling up over her body and raising myself above her as the rose petals billow and scatter around us.

I lean down, my lips barely an inch from hers. "You made me want a future again, Summer. And I want it with you."

"And our children," she adds, smiling.

"Hmm… all of them."

"*All* of them? Wait a second, Kit. What on earth…?"

I chuckle and silence her with a kiss, and make her mine.

Always.

Printed in Great Britain
by Amazon